Praise for *Curves Envy* by Scarlett Avery

This series deserves a five star rating for hotness alone! The author is spot on when describing the insecurity felt by most plus size ladies. Max leads Candy to find and embrace her wild side. I started with book 1 as a freebie and before I even finished it, I had to have the rest! These books are a fast easy read that will have you laughing and crying and looking for the ice and turning up the A/C! This is the second series I have read from this author and am heading directly for the third one! The A/C is cranked and the fan blowing!

— *Fredriika*

This was one good series. If you have not read it, you should start now. You will not regret it. I really enjoyed it - best love story and a little mystery. I don't want to give it away, but you will love it.

— *Margie Moran*

I just love this book because it shows that curvy girls can find that special someone just like Candy did.

— *Anna Betancourth*

Wow! Scarlett Avery delivers another scorching hot romance. This by far one of the best authors I have ever had the fortune to read.

— *Robin Shines*

Oh my GAWD! This book was fast-paced; I couldn't put it down till I finished it! It has twists that I wasn't expecting! It's hot, humorous, sexy, mysterious, exciting! And did I mention hot? This whole series was AWESOME!!! Read it and you won't be disappointed! I couldn't put it down! Enjoy ladies!!!

— *Debra Sugimoto*

Worth every star! A hot and steamy read with a little mystery thrown in to the mix! I freaking love how Scarlet Avery is able to make curvy girls sexy too! This is just another example of her mind-blowing ability to me into the wonderful world of mystery, hot sex, heartbreak and love that is Max and Candy's life. I love this series and am sad to see it end but I look forward to the next project in Miss Avery's arsenal!

— *Ali Crawley*

A journey of sadness, a lot of hot sex and ultimately love. I'm glad that Max and Candy were able to get their happily ever after. I really like this author's style writing.

— *Laura*

CURVES ENVY

Complete (Part 1-4)

Scarlett Avery

Scarlett Avery / Absolutely Naughty Publishing

Edited by RJ Locksley

Proofread by Chrissy Becker and Ali Skrzypiec

Curves Envy / Scarlett Avery
ISBN 978-1-987943-05-4

Foreword

I can't thank you enough for purchasing this sizzling read.

I'm absolutely passionate about what I do. Once I start writing, I just can't stop.

It's taking me a whole lifetime to get to the point where I'm able to live out my dream every single day.

The captivating stories and the enigmatic characters live with me throughout the writing process. I think you'll quickly notice how much care and attention I put into each one of my romance novels.

Another thing you'll discover about me is how much I love my readers!

To thank you for buying this romance novel, I'd love for you to lose yourself in even more sultriness, sexiness and seduction!

When you sign-up today, I'll send you an exclusive *Secret Chapter* for this romance.

Sign-up TODAY!
www.RomanceBooksRock.com

Alphas Love Curves

Chapter One

What time is it?

I slowly open my eyes and turn my head to find out when I need to get up.

Shit. It's eleven? How could I have slept so late?

"I guess we had a little too much fun." I look at Leonardo DiCaprio, my beautiful white Turkish Angora cat, with eyes half open. "Damn, my head hurts. Mama needs an Advil or two, Leo."

After another disastrous break-up with yet another loser of a boyfriend, my support group came to my rescue. It's interesting how Vince Guardino—the boyfriend I kicked to the curb yesterday—forgot to tell me that he was married and his wife was expecting their first child. I only found out when his baby mamma showed up at my door pissed off as hell. *Asshole.*

I'd be lost without my best friends—Devin Sinclair, Amelia (Lia) Carrington, aka my BFF since high school, and Alexis (Lexi) MacPherson, the brainiac of the group who holds a Master's in finance from Simon Business School and a MBA from the Wharton School of the University of Pennsylvania.

Since Brian, Devin's new partner, was working at Mirage—this new chic uptown club—we headed there after dinner and partied our faces off until the wee hours of the morning to the best deep soul music.

"Come on, up!" I coax myself.

I fling the sheets off the bed and look down at my naked body. I'm still not used to taking stock of my lumps and curves. At my heaviest, I used to avoid mirrors altogether, but as I trimmed down to a healthier weight, I felt more confident glancing at my body. As much as I despise Vince for his action, the four weeks we spent together were a real boost to my ego. He praised me constantly on my round thighs, my big breasts, my soft stomach and even the cellulite on my behind. It might all have been a lie, but for a short moment in time, I allowed myself to believe him and I was willing to feel good about myself.

"Leo, let's go find a cure for this hangover and I'll feed you," I say to my cat as I squat to cuddle him in my arms.

I barely have time to reach my kitchen before my phone rings.

Shit, where's my handbag? I look frantically around my apartment in search of my hidden phone. I wobbled back to my place at four-thirty in the morning too drunk and too tired to bother putting anything away. As a result, my place is a mess.

"Oh, there you are."

My handbag is plunked on top of my stove like a teakettle and I run to it to find out who's calling. It's Amelia. "Hey, Lia."

"Are you still alive?"

"Barely. I have a ridiculous headache," I say, opening a cabinet in search of painkillers. "What about you?"

"I've been up for a few hours and I've already swallowed two extra-strength Advils and a gallon of water. We partied too hard last night."

"Last night? Are you kidding me? You're the one who came to the intervention with booze super early in the afternoon," I laugh.

Before heading to Mirage, Devin, Lia and Lexi showed up at my place arms weighed down with food and booze to get the party started.

"Yeah, but I believe it's my duty as a supportive friend to bring the alcohol. Anyways, I wanted to call to make sure you were okay after Vince. I know we talked it out yesterday and God knows you had enough alcohol to never remember his name again, but I wanted to check up on you. Sometimes the morning after can be brutal once the flood of memories come crashing down like a Malibu wave."

Amelia is the best friend any woman can ever hope for. Without her I would never have survived losing my parents at nineteen.

Amelia was the first friendly face I laid eyes on when I started my first day in a new high school. Although she met me as an average-size teenager, Lia always remained a faithful friend as my weight ballooned while I was desperately trying to cope with my emotions. I was in mourning, I was in pain and I was angry at life. Who wouldn't be when they lost both parents the same day? I took out all this pent-up energy on myself and turned to food as my solace. As a result, I put on one hundred and fifty pounds in two years. It's not as if I was ever skinny. I can't say I ever knew what a thigh gap looked like on me, but the death of my parents sent me into a self-destructive spiral and Lia was there to catch me. She never judged me as I was packing on the pounds.

"You're the best for asking. I'm doing better today and it's not because of the alcohol," I joke.

"Thank God you didn't have time to develop a drinking problem." I can hear the irony in her voice.

"I guess I'm lucky. Seriously, I woke this morning grateful for the four weeks with Vince."

"How can you find anything positive about the fake pilot other than a few fuck sessions?"

"He was a caring lover, I'll give the weasel that much. Vince helped me like my body. It might all have been a lie, but his words were uplifting, Lia."

"So you're okay?"

"How can I not be? I have you, Devin and Lexi in my life. When the shit hits the fan, my friends come running."

"Funny. You've come a long way since the death of your grandma."

"Yeah. I made a promise to her."

Eighteen months ago, my whole world spiraled again when my adoring grandmother passed away. She was only in her early sixties. She was a healthy woman, but she too was mourning. I'm sure she died of a broken heart from losing her only child—my father.

I would have normally gone on a food binge to deal with my loss like before, but my grandmother made me swear on her deathbed to take better care of myself. She said the battle wasn't over. She had fought for justice after my parents died, but she didn't have the deep pockets necessary to fight the big corporation who owned the crane that dropped a deadly load that smashed my parents' car to pieces. It was a long and ugly battle, and my grandmother had to give up her fight when her money ran dry. She had nothing left on the day of her death other than the New York apartment my grandfather had bought decades ago. It's the only thing she left me in her will.

"I miss my mom, dad and grandmother so much, Lia. Without you guys as friends, I'd be an orphan alone in New York City."

"Oh, please. You know I'll always be here for you. Devin and Lexi are like our siblings. You'll never be alone. And Candy, please don't let your loneliness cause you to date another asshole. If you need a little something-something, text me and I'll buy you a new vibrator."

I burst out laughing at my friend's joke.

"Listen, it's such a beautiful day, it should be a crime to stay indoors today. Do you want to go catch a late breakfast at Vanilla Beans and we can hang out?"

"God, yes. Let's do it. Once I get rid of this nasty headache, my body will be in dire need of some caffeine and solid food."

"I hear you, girl. No one should be forced to be sociable before a latte. Why don't we meet there? We can have a leisurely brunch and then go for a long walk or window-shopping. I refuse to stay cooped up today. How long will it take you to get ready?"

"Great idea. I'm in pretty rough shape after last night, so give me a couple of hours to get ready and to get there."

"See you at one-thirty?"

"Perfect."

I hang up the phone and look around at the sorry state of my apartment. Normally, I'd be obsessed about tidying up before leaving to meet Lia, but honestly, for some reason, I don't have a care in the world. I feed Leo and hit the shower. *It's not as if any lovers are going to come around for a while.*

Chapter Two

I arrive at Vanilla Beans at one-thirty to find Lia already seated at a table for two at the back of the cozy eatery. The place is packed with hungry New Yorkers in search of a delectable Sunday meal.

A few years ago, I would never have dared to set foot here. Cozy is my code word for tiny. The tables are nearly touching each other and I'm very cautious not to bump into anyone as I make my way through the restaurant to join my friend. A few years ago when I was at my heaviest, this journey would have been mortifying and I would have insisted on ordering our food to go or I would have selected a place with more maneuvering room.

As I arrive at our table and wiggle out of my spring coat, I catch the gaze of a ruggedly handsome man sitting in the far left corner of the room. I immediately lower my gaze and then furtively look up from under my lashes. He's still looking my way.

Is he smiling at me? Down, girl. A little over twenty-four hours ago you were dealing with Vince's drama.

My cheeks burn at the sight of him, but I quickly brush it off. *I'm sure he's only looking my way because a slim hot chick is following me.* I smile widely when Lia jumps to her feet to hug me. "I'm so happy we're doing this. I think I'm going to enjoy our day out."

"I've been here for fifteen minutes and there's this electrifying energy in the air… and quite a few drool-worthy guys today," she says with a mischievous smile. "The sun is beaming, spring has finally sprung, the city is buzzing with excitement and something good is going to happen today—I can feel it."

"I hope you're right. I wasn't going to chastise myself for Vince's sins by staying locked up at home and reliving yesterday's events," I say.

"And you shouldn't. Enough about the fake pilot and his baby momma. I'm starved and I'm ready to order. Hurry and select what you want to eat before the waiter comes around." Lia is pointing impatiently at the menu in front of me.

As I lower my eyes to figure out if I want eggs or pancakes, I catch the sexy stranger staring at me again. I slightly turn my head to locate the table of models he must be looking at, but we're surrounded by ordinary people—a couple and their infant child, a bunch of Asian tourists, a group of three elderly ladies and a gay couple holding hands. *Maybe the wind caught my hair and I look like a mess.*

"Is my hair okay?" I ask Lia, running insecure fingers through my mane.

"Yes. I love the new color your chichi Fifth Avenue hairdresser selected for you. Your green eyes pop like crazy."

"Thanks." *So my hair is not all over the place.* "I'm happy Devin forced me to dye my hair. I needed the change."

For my twenty-fourth birthday, Devin paid for a total transformation with one of the top stylists in the city. Jean-Pierre Pastorale took one look at me and declared the color and shape of my eyes begged him to transform me in one of my two idols—Adele or Christina Hendricks. Since I've always secretly wanted to be a blonde, I selected the British songstress' sleek contemporary look and my French stylist chopped off my mousy brown hair that fell limply to the middle of my back. I don't know if blondes have more fun, but they sure as hell get a lot more attention.

"It's weird…"

"Huh? Something on the menu?"

"No. Don't turn around, but the guy over there wearing the blue sweater has been staring at me since I arrived."

Why is it when you ask someone not to do something they do? Lia turns and the stranger smiles when he notices both of us looking his way. *Shit.*

"I asked you not to look," I say, frowning.

"Whoa." She turns around and widen her eyes like a kid who's just seen the Easter Bunny.

"God, now he knows we're checking him out."

"How else was I going to see what he looks like? It's not as if I have eyes in the back of my head." She smiles. "Do you know Mr. Hottie?"

"No. I've never seen him in my life. I thought he was looking at a hot chick behind me, but it seems like all the sexy women are sitting near the windows way over there."

"Maybe you met him at a fashion event and you've forgotten. You have a memorable face with your big green eyes and he's simply trying to remember where the two of you met."

"I don't think so, but it doesn't matter," I say, trying to dismiss the whole thing.

I'm about to take another peek in the direction of the stranger when our waiter rushes our way to take our orders.

"Hello, ladies. My name is Richard and I'm sorry to keep you waiting. Have you decided yet?"

"I'll have the blueberry pancakes and a large latte. Have you decided, Candy?"

I smile at the waiter, concealing my discomfort. "I'll have the huevos rancheros and I'll also have a latte, but could you please make mine with a double shot of espresso?"

"Great choices, ladies. No problem on the espresso. I'll be right back with water."

"Oh, could I have a freshly pressed orange juice to start?"

"Great idea, Candy. I'll also have the same, please."

"Two fresh OJs coming." The waiter smiles warmly at us before rushing to the cash register to punch in our order.

"Thank you." Lia and I chime in at the same time as he walks away from our table.

* * *

Lia and I wolf down our breakfast all the while engaged in an animated discussion about her chances of landing a transfer to Prime News' UK office for a three-month work exchange program. She's competing with eight other candidates who applied for one of the most coveted positions in her department, but Lia is such a star at her job, I'm pretty certain she'll be selected. I'll be honest, I'm dying to see London and it wouldn't take me long after she's landed to hop on a plane and go visit her.

"I've been meaning to tell you this since you arrived, you look radiant for someone who partied so hard last night."

"It's the magic of great makeup. It's another perk of working in the fashion industry. You learn how to fool people. You should have seen me this morning. I scared Leonardo DiCaprio," I laugh.

"Your cat gets scared by his own shadow."

"Good point," I laugh.

"I love the dress on you. Is it another one of your sample sale finds?"

"Yup," I say, sitting a little straighter in my chair and lifting my breasts higher. "I hesitated to buy a dress with a print, but all the plus-size designers are creating bolder collections so I jumped on the bandwagon."

As a plus-size editor at *Sassy* magazine, I not only have the privilege of scooping the latest and trendiest fashion accessories for big girls, but I also am able to hit sample sales before the general public. *Sassy* magazine is a publication for skinny girls, but a few years ago the management made a bold move by deciding to tap into a growing market. Since the average American is not a size two, *Sassy* saw the writing on the wall and stepped forward to capitalize on the needs of curvy women. At the time, I had just lost my grandmother and I had started on my weight loss journey, which I documented on my personal blog. My former boss discovered my blog by chance and when the time came to appoint a new editor to the job, she picked me. I was thrilled and terrified to become so public about my weight issues, but the last eighteen months have been the most satisfying of my life. One of the biggest perks of this job is having my ear to the ground when it comes to better options for plus-size women.

"It's fun and the little pinkish-red lips printed all over are so flirty. Not to mention this dress accentuates your massive boobs so well. I wish I had your features," she says, tracing a circle in the air around her breasts. "I'm only a B cup, but then again it could have been worse, since Lexi is even smaller than I am."

"Leave Alexis alone. She's the same size as you and you know it," I gently scold her with a smile on my face. "Lia, you have so much going for you. You're smart, stunning and you have the best hair—ever. I only have big eyes and big boobs."

"You're crazy, Candy. I don't know why you refuse to see your beauty. How can you be so supportive of all of your readers and put yourself down at the same time?"

Lia is right. I love being the advocate for plus-size women at *Sassy* magazine and I'm the first to uplift my blog readers when they send me emails about their own weight loss journey or when they've dealt with bullying like I have so many times in my life, but I fail when it comes to being kind to myself.

"In any case, you look beautiful and I love the fuchsia bolero sweater on you. The color brings out the pink lips on the dress."

"Thanks. I do feel somewhat pretty in this dress." What I love the most about the design of this round-scooped dress is the cute flirty print. When I saw it hanging on a rack at a sample sale at a designer's showroom, I couldn't resist.

"I feel like I made no effort in my understated outfit compared to yours." Lia looks down at her head-to-toe black outfit. "I was going to select a colorful dress and shimmy my ass into some shapewear, but then I remembered it was Sunday and I thought fuck the girdle."

We both laugh.

"I don't think anyone calls it a girdle anymore, Lia."

"Well, my mom and grandmother say the name might have changed to something sexier, but it's still not the most comfortable thing to wear and it itches like crazy—especially in the winter when my skin is so dry."

"I won't argue with you. Yeah, I gave those up a long time ago."

"What are you wearing under your dress? I need something to hold it all in," she says, sucking in her stomach at the same time she sucks in her cheeks and bulges her eyes out.

We lose it laughing and call attention to ourselves in this small eatery. From the corner of my eye, I notice the drop-dead-gorgeous guy is still looking our way and I place a finger on my lips to try to contain another burst of laughter.

"Shhh, everyone is looking at us. I think we're disturbing the hot guy who's been eyeing me."

Lia leans in to take a quick peek and we both laugh again.

"So what if he's ogling at you. Your dress calls for attention and your Adele-blonde hair is so sultry."

"Thanks," I say, smoothing my hair. "I like the cut, color and style a lot. I was afraid to go there, but you know Devin, he pushed me out of my comfort zone by reminding me it's my duty to look as polished as the women I praise in the magazine or on my blog."

"You've got to love Dev, but you haven't answered me yet. What are you wearing under your dress if you've given up wearing girdles?"

"You know shapewear and I don't mix."

"Are you saying you're not wearing any support right now?"

"Not exactly. Thank God for Sexy Curves lingerie. They create fashionable collections for big girls. I can still get some support and I no longer feel like an encased sausage under my clothing."

"God, I need to get me some Sexy Curves to stop all this jiggling." She shakes her upper body like a cha-cha dancer when she says that.

Lia's words make us lose it. I slap my hand over my mouth to try to contain my hysteria while Lia throws her head back, unashamedly laughing her ass off as if no one else is watching us.

"Jesus." Lia folds over, holding her stomach.

We laugh to the point of tears and the entire restaurant starts laughing with us, not knowing why the two of us can't contain ourselves.

"Oh, God. I needed the laugh after yesterday," I barely get out through my chuckles. "Come on, let's get out of here. We've already created quite a scene." I grab my coat and the handbag I dropped at my feet.

"You're right," she says. "If we don't leave now, they'll throw us out."

When I lift my eyes, the seat at the back of the restaurant is now empty. *Hmmm, Mr. McSexy left while Lia and I were laughing our asses off.* We make our way to the cash register to pay. Vanilla Beans is one of those rare eateries in New York where you pay at the cash register. It's an original quirk that characterizes the tiny breakfast joint. Amelia and I are standing in line waiting our turn and we're still giggling like schoolgirls reliving my story.

Suddenly a voice behind me speaks. "Most New Yorkers take themselves way too seriously to have as much fun as you ladies are having."

When I turn around, my heart stops. The sexy stranger who has been gazing at me since I arrived is standing right behind me. He hasn't left after all.

He's so close, I realize now how imposing he is. Since I'm so short, anyone over five-ten is impressive to me, but this guy must easily be six-two. He's extraordinarily handsome and if I had to take a stab at his age, I'd say he's in his thirties. I'm so mesmerized, I'm staring at the beautiful hunk unable to answer him.

Shit. Say something. "Uh, I hope we weren't too loud," I fumble. I'm swooning like an imbecile. The stranger is yummy.

"Not at all. I quite enjoyed watching you." He flashes me a panty-melting smile and I hold on to the counter in front of me to steady myself. His hazel eyes—startling against his tanned face—trap my gaze, holding it frozen, and it's as if no one else exists. *Good Lord. I'm sure the ground beneath my feet has dropped a foot.*

"I hope we didn't make spectacles out of ourselves." Lia jumps in to fuel the conversation. I'm too tongue-tied to even manage to string two sentences together. I'm completely hypnotized by his drop-dead gorgeous looks. He laughs at her comment and runs his right hand through his brown hair. God, those blond streaks are so sexy on him. I usually love my men with very dark hair, but yeah, he could very easily convince me to change my ways.

"We were being silly," Lia offers.

I don't know why, but Lia's comment warms my cheeks and I lower my eyes, embarrassed by the situation. Although I'm fixated on the stranger's stylish black suede laced shoes, I can feel his gaze on me. I try to look away, but it's impossible for me to peel my eyes away from the defined thigh muscles pressing against his dark-wash jeans.

"Silly is good," the stranger says. "Two beautiful women enjoying a lazy Sunday morning while your boyfriends are doing their own thing. Nothing wrong with that."

Did he just say that?

I quickly lift my head, my eyes widening. The stranger's lips slightly curl into a smile. My legs go limp. *Damn.*

"Don't worry about it, she's *very, very, very,* single."

Seriously, Lia? She's supposed to be my best friend.

The stranger hasn't looked up at Lia once since the beginning of this conversation even though I've been standing there like a complete idiot while she's been chatting him up... or should I say washing my dirty laundry in public.

The clerk behind the counter speaks, but I'm so lost in this guy, I can't make out the words. When his eyes release from mine, I almost fall backward into Amelia's arms. He smiles warmly. "Please allow me." The stranger places his hand over mine and his touch nearly burns my skin. "It's my treat. New Yorkers are renowned for being snobs and too caught up in themselves to remember to have any fun."

The stranger pulls out a stack of money from his pocket, peels off a one-hundred-dollar bill and instructs the clerk to keep the change. *Wow. He's quite generous.*

"Ladies, enjoy the rest of your day."

Before I even have time to open my mouth, the debonair hottie has already turned on his heel and he's headed for the door. I turn to look at Lia and she's as taken aback as I am.

I run after him. "Wait. You can't pay for our meal and run away. How am I supposed to thank you?" I speak without thinking and once I realize the boldness of my question, I immediately regret every word. Pedestrians are staring at me.

He turns around, tucks his hands in his pockets and tilts his head to the side. "You just did. Your radiant smile will remain with me for the rest of the day." He walks backwards for a few steps before speaking again. "By the way, I come here every Sunday at the same time." He flashes me another panty-melting smile before turning his back to me and casually walking away.

"What the hell?" I mutter aloud.

"Damn. He's so fine. He couldn't keep his eyes off of you." Lia is standing next to me and we're both watching as the charming man who rocked my world with his words turns the corner and disappears.

"Yeah. He was sizzling hot, but he's gone. I don't know his name or anything else about him."

"He said he came here every week at the same time. Maybe we should plan on doing the same," she says, shrugging her shoulders and smiling at me.

For a brief moment I allow myself to believe a tall piece of eye-candy could be taken with me, but images of yesterday morning's drama flash in front of my eyes and I shake my head. "I'm sure this is another one of those guys who likes flirting with any woman who looks his way. I bet you, like Vince, he has a pregnant wife and babies waiting for him at home."

"Sweetie, don't let Vince ruin it for you. Not all men are scum."

"It's true, but I seem to attract my fair share of them."

"I think you're being unnecessarily hard on yourself."

"Come on. Let's not fool ourselves here. It's highly unlikely a dashing guy like him would ever be interested in me when there are so many insanely gorgeous thin women living in Manhattan."

Chapter Three

I've been consumed all week by the sexy stranger Lia and I met over brunch. I've tried my best to shake him off, but it's been impossible to erase his seductive smile. Lia tends to get the attention from men when we hang out, but this suave hunk seemed to have his eyes glued on me and I'm not used to being the one guys look at.

Whatever. It's not like I'll ever see him again. There's no way I'm setting foot at Vanilla Beans on a Sunday hoping to meet him again just to get my hopes crushed when I see him walk in with a beautiful model.

The week is packed with the humdrum of working for a prominent fashion magazine. Luckily, my new boss is out of town and like the rest of my colleagues, I decide to work from home. I get so much more done when I work remotely.

"Meow." My cat's call wakes me up from my reverie and I push back the memories of my parents who were taken from me too soon.

"I can't believe it's already three o'clock," I say, turning to my cat, when I notice the time on the upper right corner of my MacBook Air computer. "In a few hours I'm going to meet your aunt Trish for drinks. Too bad cats aren't welcomed." I caress my fluffy white cat.

A few years ago, my cousin Trish moved to LA with an up-and-coming actor she was enamored with on the pretext she was pursuing her own dreams. She left the Big Apple a few months after her mom, my aunt Caroline, moved to Augusta, Maine to run away from the painful reminder of losing her baby sister—my own mother. Unfortunately, Trish's relationship was short-lived when her actor boyfriend decided to dump her to date the daughter of one of the biggest producers in Hollywood. My cousin was understandably crushed, but she decided to remain in la-la land. We've talked on the phone and texted here and there, but Trish hasn't set foot in New York since my grandmother died eighteen months ago. I'm a bit apprehensive at seeing her again, but she's family.

Get back to work, Candy. I try to focus on the article I'm writing in the hopes of finishing it before I start getting ready, but my phone rings. I glance down on my desk to the left of my computer and see Devin's number flashing. "Hey, Dev. How are you?"

"First let me ask before I get you in trouble, can you talk?"

"Yeah, I'm working from home since my bitchy boss is out of town."

"Good to know. Now I can lay it on you. You casually ask me how am I? I should be asking you that question. Better yet, I should disown you as my friend for keeping such a big secret from me."

Oh, no, what have I done now? Why is he so worked up? "Don't be such a drama queen. We haven't spoken since Saturday night because you were working all week with the ladies of *The Chat* in Fort Lauderdale where they were shooting their spring special show. There's no way in the world I could have done anything to upset you this much," I joke.

"Listen, I got off the phone with Lia a few seconds ago and I had to wait until Thursday to find out you seduced a hot guy at brunch last Sunday. When were you going to tell me?"

"Dev, there's not much to talk about. The last time I randomly met a handsome stranger, aka Vince, he turned out to be a cheat. I'm sure this guy was having fun and I'll never see him again."

"Lia said he has brunch every Sunday at Vanilla Beans. Why don't we all go this weekend to try to catch him?"

"Give it a rest, Dev. Lia has been pestering me all week about this, but I don't want to get my hopes up just to see them crashing in front of my eyes when I realize Mr. Handsome is not so great. Let's face it, my dating record sucks."

I won't lie. I've tossed and turned in my bed every night this week reliving every moment of my magical Sunday afternoon, but when I wake up, I'm painfully aware of the fact hot men don't go for big girls—not in New York City anyways.

"Candy, you're so full of shit sometimes."

Tell me how you really feel about me, Devin. "If you called to give me a pep talk or to scold me, don't."

He sighs heavily on the other end of the phone before he goes silent. I know he's still there. He's most likely preparing his rebuttal.

"I've always thought you were selling yourself short. You made a courageous promise to your dying grandmother and you've lost a shitload of weight in the past year. Your eyes are to die for. You look like an American version of Adele. You're the sweetest person I know and you're sharp like a whip. Why can't you believe there's a guy out there who would die to find those qualities in a woman even if she's not built like a supermodel?"

"It's been my experience that hot guys want hot skinny women. I'm average-looking at best and I'm overweight."

"You win. I'm not going to argue with you or else I'll get upset. I love you so much and I wish you'd see what I see when I look at you, but we've gone down this road so many times."

I can hear the exasperation in his voice and I appreciate what he's trying to do, but I've had a love-hate relationship with my body for the past five years and it's not about to change. Nevertheless, his reaction makes me feel guilty.

"I know you care about me and I love you for being such a good friend. Yes, I kept my promise to my grandmother and I'm now a healthier person, but I'm still a big girl by society's standards. We're not living in the fifties where being plump was the norm. Our new stick-figure standards of beauty influence how men see me and for the most part, it's as someone who's undesirable."

"You kept saying Vince worshipped your body."

"At this point, everything surrounding Vince is laced with lies and deception. I have no doubt he was feeding me his crap in order to make it easier for me to spread my legs open. His wife is a skinny bitch with a swollen belly, but all of a sudden he's into big girls?"

The thought of how Vince played me for a fool makes me see red. There's a part of me desperate to believe he meant what he said and sometimes I still do, but there's also a part of me that feels nauseated by his actions.

"How's work?" Devin abruptly changes the subject. I'm annoyed and relieved at the same time. I'm sure this will boil over quickly and just like me, he'll quickly forget all about the dashing man who flirted with me on a perfect Sunday afternoon.

"It's good. Although it's been a pain since my former boss Christine decided to work from home and Jennifer Lau was appointed to the new position of editor-in-chief, I still enjoy what I do and I consider myself to be extremely lucky."

"Good. I'm happy your bitchy boss isn't making your life as much of a living hell as she did when she first started six months ago."

"Thankfully she's found new victims to harass."

I have a super-cool job at *Sassy* magazine. I love my co-workers and I love being the voice of plus-size women. I get to work with incredible designers, bloggers, photographers and artists all determined to help prove big is indeed beautiful. I still can't believe Christine discovered my blog *Voluptuous* by chance and used my daily banter about my weight as leverage when it came time to appoint a new editor for the plus-size online portal and monthly section in the magazine. It never occurred to me it would take off like it has. I've always wanted to work on my blog full-time, but a part of me lacks the confidence to believe I can stand on my own two feet.

"Yeah, but I think the bigwigs at your company must have asked her to back off after your article on Melissa McCarthy exploded on the Internet."

"You're right. I can still see the look of disbelief on Jennifer's face when I told her we had received over seven hundred and sixty-eight thousand views within twenty-four hours of me posting the article. Our Facebook page went crazy and all this buzz caught the attention of her superiors."

One of the biggest highlights so far in my career has been to predict publically the Hollywood big girl would launch her own fashion line. I forecasted this turn of event in our industry well before it was popular to even put Melissa McCarthy and fashion in the same sentence. When I saw her performance in *Bridesmaids*, I knew she'd be a huge success despite her size and let's face it, she's so gorgeous. I don't kid myself. Men don't turn their heads when I walk alongside my co-worker from the skinny side of the magazine, but my editing career has taken off like a rocket.

"You should be proud of your achievement. What a scoop."

I can't help but beam at his compliment.

"Yeah, Jennifer has no other choice now but to be nicer to me and to give me a little respect. She can no longer treat me like shit like she's done since the first day she laid her eyes on me."

"If you're working from home today, why don't you finish early and let's grab a drink."

"Are you trying to call it truce?"

"I hate when we disagree about your weight, so yeah, I'd love to hang out so I know we're okay. We can keep on talking about small things for another hour or we can see each other and hug the hell out of each other so I know we're still good friends."

"Dev, we'll always be okay. I love you like a brother even when we don't see eye to eye. Although I'd love to hang out with you tonight, I can't. Trish is on her way from LA and she'll be landing anytime now. We're meeting for drinks later tonight."

"Trish? I forgot she was coming today. Wow, you've not seen your detestable cousin since your grandmother died."

"I know. It's going to be interesting to see her reaction to my weight loss."

"Yeah, she might not be as annoyed to be around you as she used to when you were coping with the loss of your parents." Devin spits those words with disdain. He doesn't like Trish because she's always had this insidious way of putting me down. She's the queen of backhanded compliments and going to a restaurant with her when I was at my heaviest was torture because of the side glances she'd shoot my way every time I'd poke my fork in my plate. Even when I ordered salad—which I hate with a passion.

"Let's hope so. Trish and my aunt are my only last two living relatives. My cousin might not be the most compassionate person on the planet, but she's still related to me by blood."

"Whatever. In my world, she's a royal bitch. We're more family to you than she's ever been. She hasn't bothered to come back to visit in eighteen months. Not to mention when she lived in New York, she always went after your boyfriends like a piranha."

"Don't remind me, Dev. I know exactly what my cousin is capable of."

"As long as you know, you won't be so shocked when she backstabs you again. Is she staying with you?"

"No, she insisted on getting a room. She said she was coming to the city to party and didn't want to get in my way. As if I don't know how to party." Secretly, I know she doesn't want to be around me more than she has to. She's always been very embarrassed about my weight.

"Thank God. I much prefer you spend as little time with Trish as possible. In any case, where are you going to meet her?"

"You know how much of a wannabe diva she is. She's selected an outrageously posh place. We're meeting at the Brinkley Lounge inside the Bymark Hotel located on 57th Street."

"Hello! I know exactly where it's located. Since they've made a few recent changes, it's become the coolest place right now. What are you going to wear?"

I can hear the excitement in Devin's voice and I know he's found a new focus, which has temporarily allowed him to forget all about my cousin.

"I wasn't going to make much of an effort. It's not as if I have to impress Trish. I don't know. I was thinking jeans and a sweater. Maybe heels or high boots. I've not decided yet. I have plenty of time, I'm meeting her at seven-thirty." I honestly didn't plan on spending too much time getting ready to meet my cousin.

"Honey, who gives a flying fuck about Trish? You're meeting her at a place swimming with loads of hot guys. You do realize some of the most eligible men in New York hang out there. Trust me, Brian has played there a few times for private functions and I've gone to support him and to soak in the vibe. You cannot walk in wearing jeans and a sweater. You need to walk in there styling."

"Devin, I don't care about men. Remember, I'm the one who was unwittingly sleeping with a married man." I roll my eyes, still upset at myself for allowing Vince into my life.

"Exactly. You've washed Vince out of your hair and it's now time to find a real man. If you're not willing to go back to Vanilla Beans to discover the identity of your mystery admirer, this is the second-best option for you."

I can't help but laugh at his enthusiasm.

"Listen, Candy. I'm not saying to run to Saks and buy a brand-new outfit. I know what you look like when you're trying to hide behind unflattering clothes and I also know how vampy you can look when you channel the vixen in you. For tonight, be the vamp."

"Devin, you're crazy."

"Do it for me. Find a killer dress, put on those heels you bought a few months ago and shimmy your body into the sexiest lingerie you own. If nothing else, Trish will die of envy when she sees the new you."

My cousin is family, but her attitude towards me has been quite hurtful. I've never wanted to rock the boat, so I've always swallowed my emotions instead of being honest about how she's treated me in the past. Secretly, I'd love to see her speechless and open mouthed when she sees the new me.

"Vamp it is."

"That's my girl. Now, remember, I want you to send me a selfie before you leave so I can give you the thumbs up. I have to go. I love you. Knock 'em dead tonight, sweetie."

"I love you too, Dev."

I hang up the phone and look at my cat sprawled luxuriously across my desk.

"Leo, what have I agreed to?"

Chapter Four

I've just stepped out of the cab in front of the Bymark Hotel when I realize Trish hasn't texted me to confirm she's arrived.

After I hung up with Devin, I ran to my bedroom to plan my reveal. I was so preoccupied with matching the right dress with the right shoes and the right accessories, I lost track of time. I should also confess I spent nearly an hour on my makeup and my hair. I took Devin's words so much to heart, I completely ignored the fact I haven't heard from my cousin since she called me before leaving LA early this morning.

Hmmm, I hope everything is okay. Knowing Trish, she probably got caught up in one of the eligible men Devin was talking about and forgot to text me to let me know she was waiting for me.

When I arrive inside the lobby of the hotel, I make a quick beeline to drop off my coat before hopping into an elevator and heading to the fourteenth floor. I normally prefer to hang out in more casual places with my friends, but Trish believes in order to be seen as the successful Hollywood actress she thinks she is, it's imperative to select the best venues.

Wow, this lobby is so luxurious. The recent renovations have truly done this place justice. Bymark hired a very well-known French designer to transform the unremarkable hotel into a premier spot. Pierre-Henry de Papassan was all over the news for months. The media couldn't get enough of the eccentric designer and by the time the epic renovations were completed, you couldn't get a table at their restaurant or lounge for months. The waiting list was insane. I've never had any interest in coming here, but Lia's obsession with the story was amusing and she'd gladly provide an update to whoever was willing to listen.

I'm sure the cocktails are going to cost an arm and a leg. I'm also sure when the time comes to pay, Trish will have a convenient excuse to stick me with the bill.

As I get out of the elevator, I decide to text Trish as I make my way to the bar, but a text from Devin pops up on my screen. I read his message with a big smile on my face.

Bad girl, you didn't send me a selfie.

Shit, I forgot. I followed your advice and spent an insane amount of time in front of the mirror. I think I look good.

I'm sure you look smashing, honey, but I still want to see with my own two eyes.

You're impossible. I can run to the bathroom before meeting Trish and take a—

"Oh!" I bump into someone. "Shit. My phone!"

"I'm terribly sorry. Are you okay?" the stranger I bumped into asks as we both bend down to fetch my phone. As he reaches to grab my iPhone, he drops his. We're both scrambling to pick up our iPhones in the middle of the fourteenth floor of a posh hotel. How embarrassing.

"Can you believe this?" The stranger finally grabs both phones and we stand up.

During this whole exchange I've not been able to bring myself to look at him. I feel like a complete idiot for texting while walking. I quickly grab the phone the stranger hands me and when I look up to thank him, my jaw drops.

No way.

There's so much chaos in my head right now it takes me a few seconds to realize his eyes are fixed on my chest. When I follow his gaze, I realize in horror my turquoise-blue see-through bra is fully exposed.

"Crap." In all of the kerfuffle, my wrap dress has opened to reveal the Sexy Curves lingerie I selected as a pop of color to the black wrap dress I had slipped on to impress Trish. I knew I should have worn a pin. *What was I thinking? I should know better than to let my big breasts loose like this.* When you sport a pair of double Ds, I've learned the hard way the importance of containing these babies because sometimes it's like they have a life of their own. "Oh, God." It's bad enough that I'm standing in the middle of a luxurious hotel half naked, but the sexy stud smiling at me is none other than my secret admirer from last Sunday at Vanilla Beans.

"I think you might want to cover up or else you'll attract a lot of unwanted attention," he chuckles, still fixated on my boobs.

I'm mortified and babble something inaudible before covering my exposed chest with both hands and running to the bathroom.

I only allow myself to breathe once I close the door behind me. *Way to go, Candy.* I walk to the large mirror to assess the damage.

"Good Lord," I let out when I notice how exposed I am. I knew the bra left little to the imagination, but I never expected a complete stranger to be able to peer at my areolas. *Breathe. It's not as if it's the first time he's ever seen breasts.*

I try to regain my composure before fixing my dress and covering up. Once I look decent again, I grab the phone I had dropped on the counter to text back Devin and share this humiliating story. *This is weird. It's not accepting my fingerprint. What the hell?* I fumble with my phone for a few minutes before realizing the obvious—we swapped phones. *Shit.* I quickly glance at my reflection in the mirror to make sure I no longer have any body parts hanging out of my dress and grab my handbag to catch the stranger before he leaves the hotel. I swing open the door to the bathroom ready to sprint in my turquoise high heels, but his voice stops me in my tracks.

"You realized it's not your phone?"

I turn around to face the stranger I've now met twice in the same week.

"Yeah. It's not taking my fingerprint. I'm so very sorry for not being more careful. I shouldn't walk and text."

"Don't worry about it. Here's your phone," he says, handing me my device. He takes a step towards me and instinctively I'm compelled to take one back, but it's as if my legs are made of lead. I'm drawn by his energy and I'm unable to move. "While you were in the bathroom a call came in. It might be important. Or better yet, it might even be your date for the evening confirming he's arrived," he adds flirtatiously.

Something about the way he says that immediately causes my cheeks to flame up and I lower my gaze in the hopes he doesn't notice how much of an effect he has on me.

"Thanks. It's most likely my cousin. We're meeting at the bar over there." I point in the direction of the lounge.

God, did you have to give him all these details? You don't even know his name, for crying out loud.

"Your cousin? He's a very lucky man to be seen with you."

"Oh. I… Well, no…" Fuck, have I lost my powers of speech? "My cousin is a woman."

"I bet she doesn't look half as good as you do," he says, leaning into me. "I'm also pretty sure she's not wearing the same kind of outrageously sexy lingerie you've hidden under your dress."

The last sentence sends an electric charge traveling at the speed of light from my nipples to my clit. His gaze is fixed on mine and I'm so overwhelmed I can't find my words. *Jesus.*

"Gosh, you're going to make me blush."

"I have no doubt you look adorable with rosy cheeks."

"Oh." *What a smooth talker.*

"Since we've bumped into each other twice in the same week, perhaps I should introduce myself. My name is Maximiliano. It's a pleasure to meet you." He takes a long step back to extend his hand because a few seconds ago he was so dangerously close to me the only body part threatening to touch me was his cock.

"Maximiliano? I finally know your name and I can properly thank you for paying for brunch now," I say with relief. "My name is Candice."

"Candice, you forget your dazzling smile was the only thanks I needed."

"Okay, I officially don't know how to answer that," I say, nervously pushing my hair behind my ears.

"If you insist on thanking me still, why don't we both head to the lounge and let me buy you a drink while you wait for your cousin to arrive."

"She might already be there."

"If she is, I'll buy both of you a drink."

I hope to God Trish is delayed. "Sure. Why not?"

We walk side by side and I'm very aware of this gorgeous man strutting alongside me. Although I'm wearing a pair of four-inch heels, I'm still so short next to his imposing figure.

"Do you come here often, Candice?" He looks down at me before flashing me the same disarming smile he revealed before walking away last Sunday.

"No. It's my first time. My cousin prefers these types of cool places. I'm more low-key."

"You could have fooled me with the way you look tonight. You fit right in."

Holy hell. It's either dangerously hot in this hotel or I've hit menopause twenty-five years before my time. "Thank you for the compliment," I say, lowering my eyes before catching a quick glimpse at his stylish shoes.

"Here we go." He gestures for me to pass in front of him as we enter the lounge.

We barely have time to enter the bar when a voice calls his name. "Mr. Keller, it's a pleasure to see you again. Would you like your usual table?" An elegant man in an impeccable pinstripe blue suit approaches Maximiliano with a hand already extended.

"Andrew, it's always a pleasure to see you again. Perhaps you might seat us at the front. My friend Candice here is expecting her cousin and I'd love for her to join me for a drink as she waits. Candice, I'd like to introduce you to Andrew. He's the manager extraordinaire here."

"Mr. Keller, you flatter me. Candice, thank you for joining us tonight." Andrew extends his hands and gives me one of those politician handshakes, grabbing my extended hand in both of his.

"It's a pleasure meeting you as well, Andrew."

"Mr. Keller, if you can give me a few minutes, I'll ask Miguel to clean out the table on the corner over there. It's private enough, but offers a great view of the entrance. Candice will immediately know when her cousin arrives."

"Andrew, I like the way you think." Maximiliano is shaking hands with Andrew again and patting him on the shoulder.

I quickly scan the room to spot my cousin, but a wave of excitement washes over me when I don't notice the tall leggy blonde. *Yes.* I won't lie, I'm dying to know more about my mystery admirer who I've serendipitously met again and having my cousin around would be a major buzzkill. Not to mention she'd throw herself at him.

"I hope you don't mind my forwardness, but when a woman flashes me, I'm compelled to know more about her," Maximiliano says, curling up his lips in a half smile.

"I didn't flash you. It was a wardrobe malfunction."

"Sure. If you say so." He grins. "Don't get me wrong. I'm not complaining. You're a beautiful woman and I'm lucky you accepted my invitation."

"Thank you." I blush. Men usually compliment me on my eyes and lips. They'll use words like 'beautiful eyes' or 'your lips are luscious.' I've been called pretty, cute and even charming. I've dated men who were callous enough to suggest I could be pretty if I wasn't plus-size, but I usually dump their asses when they say hurtful things like that. No one has ever just called me beautiful like Maximiliano did.

"Not to mention, you have a lot to offer." He lowers his eyes and fixates his gaze on my cleavage. He's so shamelessly bold and I known I should be offended by his insinuations since we only officially met a few minutes ago, but I can't help repress a smile.

"You now know my dirty little secret. I love to flash strangers in posh New York hotels. I should go to rehab, but it's an addiction I never satisfy no matter how many times I expose myself to men."

We both smile.

"You have a great sense of humor." He holds my gaze a second too long and I turn my head to break the intense connection between us.

Down, girl. He's a stranger flirting. He most likely has a harem waiting for him at home.

Andrew comes back at the exact same moment my phone rings. I look at the number flashing and I swallow hard. *Damn. There goes my chance to get to know him.*

"I'm sorry, Maximiliano. It's my cousin. I'm going to step out for a few seconds to find out when she'll arrive and I'll be right back."

"I'll be over there and I'll wait for you." He winks.

"I shouldn't be long."

God. Is this a dream or did I actually bump into this insanely hot guy who insists on having a drink with me after I flashed him? I guess it can't be a dream since Trish has arrived.

I grab Trish's call before exiting the lounge with a lump in my throat.

"Hey, Trish. Have you arrived in Manhattan yet? I'm already at the Brinkley Lounge inside the Bymark Hotel, but I don't see you anywhere. Am I at the right place?"

"Hey, Candy. Yeah, it's the right location, but I'm stuck in Nashville. There's this rainstorm raging.

We ended up circling the airport trapped in the plane for at least an hour before we were able to land. The city is a mess and it took forever for me to recharge my phone before calling you."

"Oh, no. Are you okay?"

"It was a little scary for a minute, but I'm safe and everyone on the plane is also safe, but it seems like I might be stuck here for a few days. What a bummer. I wanted to be able to see you before I headed to Maine to see my mom."

I know Trish is family and I'm so happy she's safe and sound, but I'm also elated at the fact she won't get in the way. "It would have been great to connect before you head to visit Aunt Caroline. We'll have to connect when you come back."

"Yeah. I should be back soon. Fingers crossed I land this part in this national commercial shooting in New York. I'll keep you posted. I wanted to let you know I wouldn't make it tonight so you don't worry."

"Thanks for calling. I'm happy you're okay."

"Are you going to go home since you must be hanging out alone?"

Thanks, Trish, for assuming things you know nothing about. "You know what? I got all dressed up and I'm wearing a pair of ridiculous heels killing my feet, but since I'm here, I might pop into the bar for a quick drink."

"Alone?"

The insinuation cuts me. "Yeah. Why not? I might meet someone."

"Candy, I don't want you to get hurt. The Brinkley Lounge is a place where... how can I say this?" She pauses and I can hear the wheels in her head turning trying to find a hurtful comment. "It's a spot in New York where gorgeous models, famous celebrities and high-powered executives hang out. I'm not saying you're not a cute girl. You have the most beautiful green eyes I've ever seen, but..."

"But what, Trish?"

"I would hate to know I wasn't there to prevent others from making disparaging remarks about your size."

Fuck you, bitch.

Devin was right. Trish is a real backstabber and if it weren't for blood ties, I would have dropped her like yesterday's trash a long time ago. She has no idea I've lost ninety pounds, because I've never shared my weight loss journey or the URL to my blog with her. I couldn't stand her judging me. Heck, she doesn't even know what I do for a living. She's so caught up in herself she couldn't be bothered to find out if anything had changed in my life.

"Thanks for your concerns, Trish. I'm going to hang up now because while I was waiting for you to arrive, I connected with an eligible bachelor who happens to be sizzling hot and who, unlike you, has no issues with the way I look."

Bye bye.

I clutch my phone, enraged by her comments. How can she always find the right words to irk me so much? Even though I'm at a much healthier weight, I'm sure Trish would find a way of putting me down. *Thank God for a rainstorm.*

I shake Trish's words off when I remember my sexy admirer is waiting for me. I'm so giddy I could click my heels like Dorothy in the *Wizard of Oz*.

She's not coming, I chant in my head before turning around. *Oh, let me text Devin so he doesn't get too worried.*

Sorry about cutting our conversation short. I literally bumped into my secret admirer while I was making my way to meet Trish.

I'm so excited when he responds immediately.

What are you talking about?

I have to run, but essentially, Trish is stuck in Nashville in a rainstorm and I'm about to go have a drink with the guy who paid for brunch last Sunday. You know, the one Lia was telling you about before you called me earlier.

Shut up. I need to know more.

Kiss. Got to go.

I turn off my phone knowing full well Devin must be going out of his mind right now. I have no doubt by the time I sit next to Maximiliano he'll have texted Lia and Lexi with the news.

I walk back with a spring in my step and I can't wait to have my drink with Maximiliano. He immediately gets up like a gentleman when he sees me enter the lounge. *Is this really happening?* I take a step forward, but stop and lift my eyes towards the ceiling speakers the minute I recognize the smooth song playing. The room is immediately engulfed in a sultry mood thanks to Canadian singer Feist. Her sexy rendition of the Bee Gees' classic *Inside and Out* is a great vibe for this upscale venue. The only reason I know this song is because it's one of Lexi's favorites.

As I approach our table, I notice a silver bucket cradling a bottle of champagne in a mountain of ice cubes. Before I even have time to speak, he rebuffs any objections I might have.

"I took the liberty of ordering champagne and a few appetizers. I hope you like the selection."

I look down at the spread—tiny open-face sandwiches, cheese and mini pizza squares.

"It looks delicious." I'm impressed by the attention.

"Why not make a splash, since it's going to be the three of us? And let's not forget this is sort of a celebration."

Huh? "What are we celebrating?"

"What are the odds of bumping into the same woman in two different locations in a massive city like New York?"

"Good point. I agree, champagne is an excellent choice, but I'm afraid my cousin is stuck in Tennessee and she won't join us."

"Lucky me. I get to spend more time with you." He extends his hand to help me to my seat and I hesitate. The last time he touched me, I nearly melted and I can't imagine my body will react any differently today. *Mother of God.* The second he wraps his hand around mine I go weak in the knees and he has to hold me a little closer to catch me.

"Are you okay?"

"These heels are a bit too high," I lie.

"Those heels perfectly match your bra," he whispers in my ear.

Lord.

"I particularly love how they show off your bright pink toenail polish. Very sexy," he continues before looking down at my feet.

I'm so turned on by his proximity and his words, I can barely breathe. "Thank you," I babble. I'd love to come up with some witty repartee, but honestly this guy leaves me tongue-tied.

"Shall we sit?"

I carefully slide onto the soft cognac-colored leather sofa. When I stretch my legs I notice the cozy fireplace to my right. Past his shoulder I hear some commotion to my left and realize there's more to this lounge. Although it's only mid-April, I can't help but marvel at the brave souls crammed on the patio.

"If you prefer, we can sit on the patio. It offers a magical view of New York, but since you were waiting for your cousin, Andrew thought this might be a better spot for us."

"No. Thank you, Maximiliano. This is perfect. It's still a bit chilly at night and since I'm always cold, I'd rather be close to the fireplace."

"Before we leave, we should go up to the private VIP members' den on the forty-first floor so you can take in New York from atop. You'll never be able to look at the Big Apple the same way ever again."

He says that as if he already knows we'll be leaving together later tonight.

"I agree. I never get tired of seeing the city at my feet."

He hands me a champagne flute and holds his glass in the air. Since meeting him four days ago this is the first time I'm able to admire the different shades of browns and greens speckled in his seductive and inviting eyes. *He's gorgeous.*

"Here's to unexpected encounters."

"Here's to mysterious strangers," I cheer, holding his gaze.

"I hope by the end of this evening I'll no longer be a stranger."

I take a sip of my champagne. "I already know your name, so I'd say we're off to a good start. It's more than I knew last Sunday when we met."

"Good point."

I want to pinch myself to make sure I'm still awake. The Brinkley Lounge is packed with the typical Manhattan mix—fifty percent successful hot men, fifty percent stunning leggy women… and little ol' me. I mean there are dozens of tall, slim and sexy women in this bar, but here I am sitting with the handsome Maximiliano. He might only be indulging me because I flashed my bra at him earlier, but I really don't care. Being here with him is the kind of fairy tale that never happens to a person who looks like I do.

"And I guess I also know a lot more about you as well. I know your name and I also know you match your lingerie with your shoes," he says with a cocky smile.

We both laugh.

"I was planning on having a drink alone to ease the burden of a long and stressful week, but I must confess, your company is exactly what I needed," he declares, handing me the platter of tiny open-face sandwiches.

"Thank you." *I can't believe he said that.* "I'm happy I'm able to stick around and enjoy the lounge since my cousin can't make it and I most likely would have retreated home had I not met you."

"It would have been such a shame to rob these men of your presence."

"You said you had a long and grueling week. What do you do?" I reroute the conversation before I combust. This guy is too dangerously hot for my own good.

"It's such a typical New York question to want to know about a person's profession before getting to know them. I'd rather know more about you than your job," he says, sliding closer to me.

I bite my lower lip. His reprimand weighs on me and makes me feel like a child.

"I'm sorry. You're right, it was a silly question." I gulp my champagne to calm my nerves.

"I didn't say your question was silly. I said it was typical of the go-go mentality we suffer from as New Yorkers. For instance, I'd rather you tell me about your travels than your workload."

"My travels?" I ask, surprised, as I lean down towards the table to grab a piece of French brie.

"Yes. What was the last place you visited?"

Gosh, eighteen months ago, I wouldn't have been able to answer his question because I was too heavy to comfortably fit in an airplane seat. Since becoming healthier, I've been able to travel with more confidence without fearing the sneers and stares of unkind souls.

I lift my eyebrow before answering. My last trip was such an eye-opener. "Three months ago, I was assigned to a story at work and I had to spend a week in Cuba and another one in Jamaica."

Oh, no. Wrong answer. That's related to work.

"Hmmm, I'm quite curious to find out what story you were covering even if it's related to work." He smiles before sipping more of his champagne.

"I had to cover a growing trend amongst single women of all ages. It started a few years ago, but it caught on fire after the release of the *Eat, Pray, Love* book. I'm sure you've never read it because it's a chick book."

"I can't say I read too many of those."

We both laugh.

"How is the book related to your travels? Now you've piqued my curiosity and since I doubt I'll ever read the book, I'd love to understand the connection."

"Basically, more and more women in North America and Europe travel to poorer countries in search of companionship, sex and even love. My colleague, Josie, covered the growing trend in Bali, but I ended up in the Caribbean."

"Fascinating. I thought only men went on these sex vacations."

"Have you ever been to one of those locations?" I joke.

"I don't need to travel to Thailand and pay for sex. I can keep myself quite busy right here in New York City."

His hazel eyes go cold, but the slight grin suggests he was trying to shock me. I hold his gaze and continue with my story.

"Women now have the money and freedom to do the same thing men have been doing for decades. It was an incredible experience to delve into this unspoken world, but personally I wouldn't be able to maintain these types of relationships."

"Why not?" He tops off my champagne glass before topping off his.

"The women have the money and many become sugar mommies to these younger and sometimes destitute men. In Jamaica, I interviewed this guy by the name of Elroy. He was a tall man with ebony skin and Rasta hair. He was only twenty-two, so only a few years younger than me, but he already had a wife and four kids. He also had a so-called girlfriend in Germany who sent him gobs of money every month. They communicated daily via a live Skype chat and she would come to visit every three months for her fix. The worst part is Elroy's wife knows about the other woman, but she doesn't mind because the German girlfriend sends a lot of money— far more than any menial job could pay on the island. Granted, Elroy doesn't represent the reality of all Jamaican men, it was still quite shocking to listen to his story."

"What offends you the most?" His leg brushes mine and I instinctively bring my hand up to the front of my dress. It's as if I'm trying to hide the goosebumps on my chest.

"Good question," I say, searching the ceiling for an answer. "I couldn't deal with the idea of sharing a man. Not to mention after interviewing so many of these pseudo-gigolos, I realized none of them were take-charge kind of men. Some didn't have any ambition other than to wait around for a wire transfer to magically drop large sums of money into their accounts."

After dating my fair share of wishy-washy men and after the incident with Vince, it would be nice to be with a strong man who could sweep me off my feet and let me know he's in control.

Maximiliano studies me for a few long seconds before gulping down the amber liquid floating in his glass. He leans down towards the table and grabs the champagne bottle by the neck to top up both our glasses. He sits back, crosses one leg over the other and slides his right arm behind me.

"You like strong men?" His eyes sparkle when he asks the question.

Oops. I didn't expect he'd latch on to my comment. Maybe I should slow down on the champagne.

"I mean some men are ambitious and decisive, but not all." I pause, uncertain if I should continue down this potentially dangerous road. He's already disarmingly charming and it remains unclear why he's picked me out of all the beauties in this room. "Enough about me. What was the last place you visited, Maximiliano?" I change the subject to avoid revealing too much to this stranger whose sheer presence is making me lose my mind.

"I just got back from Brazil ten days ago after spending three weeks there."

This explains the tan. "Wow. Were you there for vacation?" I ask before sipping more of my champagne. *God, I've never tasted anything this amazing before, but then again, I tend to buy the cheap stuff. I could never imagine buying a bottle of Dom Pérignon.*

"Yes and no. I'm half Brazilian and half American. I also have a division of my business in Brazil that requires a bit more of my attention. I have a full team managing the day-to-day operation, but I'll confess, I'll use any excuse in the book to fly down there to visit my aunts and cousins."

"I hope I'm not prying by asking if Maximiliano is a Brazilian name?"

"Not at all, Candice. I inherited my names from my maternal and paternal grandfathers. My dad can trace his roots to England, which explains my last name and my second middle name, Adrian. My mom wanted me to still be close to my ancestors, which explains my first middle name, Tomás. Both my parents decided on my first name because they thought it suited me even though it's a Spanish name. My full name is Maximiliano Tomás Adrian Keller."

What an impressive name.

"Do you have a nickname?"

"Most people stick to Maximiliano, but my close friends call me Max."

"Oh. Max is short and sweet, but Maximiliano sounds so exotic."

"And do you have a nickname?"

"My friends call me Candy."

"Hmmm. Candy."

There's something extremely sexy in the way he says my nickname and I cross my legs in an attempt to ignore the desire consuming me. I know I'm out of my league here and I shouldn't lust over a guy I don't have a hope in hell of catching, but he's making it impossible for me to remain indifferent.

"I don't know much about Brazil, but I did watch the soccer World Cup when it was hosted there a few years ago. I'm clueless about sports, but I got swept away by the energy." I veer the conversation to a safer topic.

"Brazil is like paradise on earth. There's no other place in the world quite like it because of our mixed heritage and breathtaking scenery. I'm certain you'd fall in love."

"When I hear Brazil, I instantly flash to images of four distinct things," I say, narrowing my eyes.

"Really? And what are they?" he answers, matching the inquisitive expression on my face.

I reward him a cocky smile as I put up four fingers in the air. "One, wild carnivals. Two, beautiful beaches. Three, scenes from a very popular James Bond movie were shot there in the late seventies. And four, all women look like supermodels. You know, like Gisele Bündchen, Alessandra Ambrosio and Adriana Lima."

He tilts his head and laughs aloud. I immediately notice a few lookalike models glancing my way with envy.

Beautiful women envying me? Well, this is a new experience for sure.

"You got three out of four right."

"Hmmm, I was certain *Moonraker* was shot in Brazil," I say, uncrossing my legs and turning my body toward him.

"I think you're too young to know so much about such an old Bond flick, but you're right on the money on the movie location."

"Well, my friends and I have weekend flick marathons and we watched all twenty-three James Bond movies over the course of four weekends a few months ago. So which one did I get wrong?"

He slides so close to me I catch the sophisticated scent of his cologne. He brushes my hair back before speaking into my ear. Chills run down my back and my nipples harden so much it's painful. *Shit.*

"Most women in Brazil look exactly like you. They have delicious curves, full butts, wide hips, luscious thighs and heavy breasts," he whispers.

Oh, boy. I desperately want to fan myself to cool down. This guy is raising my temperature to dangerous levels.

"No way," I squeal. "Are you saying that to be nice?"

"Nice? You'd be shocked. My mother is from Brazil and she's as curvy as my aunts and my cousins." He winks. "In fact, they don't look too different from you."

"Maybe I was born in the wrong country or maybe I need to move to Brazil before the end of the week."

"Maybe you haven't met a man who appreciates curves."

I swallow hard and stop breathing. *This is not happening. Someone needs to slap me right now to reassure me I'm fully awake.*

Suddenly a voice behind Maximiliano breaks the tension.

"I'm sorry, Mr. Keller, but would you like to see the menu?"

Maximiliano peels his eyes from me and looks down at his impressive watch before looking up at the manager.

"Andrew, what a tempting proposition, but I have an early conference call at six o'clock in the morning at my office and since it's already nine-thirty, I should be heading home. Unfortunately for me, my Friday is booked solid until six tomorrow night. I haven't decided yet if I'm looking forward to another twelve-hour day, but what can you do?"

"It's not easy to take Manhattan."

"Those were last year's goals. This year, I take the world."

Both men are laughing at Maximiliano's joke, but I'm still so overwhelmed by what just happened I sit quietly hoping to God my heart rate slows down before I pass out.

"Perhaps Candice would like to stay longer and sample your delectable selections." Maximiliano turns around and I can tell from his boyish grin how amused he is at my obvious discomfort.

"Oh, no. I'm sure the food is amazing if the delicious appetizers are any indication, but it's late and I should also get home."

"Are you sure? Andrew will look after you and I can have a car waiting to drive you home."

Thank God for the food because I would be carried out of here if I didn't have something to absorb the superb amber nectar. Maximiliano kept pouring champagne and I kept drinking. "You're being very generous, but I should get home." I don't have anything urgent to take care of at home other than petting Leo DiCaprio and returning Devin's frantic text messages, but there's no way I'm going to sit here by myself.

"Andrew, it seems both of us will call it a night. Is the members' private VIP den busy at this time? I'd love to show my friend Candice the breathtaking view."

"I doubt it's busy, Mr. Keller. It's been quiet all week and since tonight is Thursday, most of our members are enjoying a relaxing evening."

"Can I still go up there?"

"Absolutely. You're one of our esteemed members. You can simply use your electronic access card to let yourself in. Would you like me to send someone up there with more drinks?"

Wow. He's a VIP member at this prestigious hotel?

"Oh, no, Andrew. I doubt we'll stay long."

"You're going to love the view at night. It's spectacular." Andrew's eyes sparkle when he looks at me and I'm already excited by the new adventure.

"I think I'm ready to settle my tab."

"Let me grab the bill." Andrew leaves as quickly as he arrived without waiting for Maximiliano's answer.

"I didn't want to assume, but I'm glad we'll have a chance to leave together. You won't believe your eyes when we get to the forty-first floor." Maximiliano has returned his full attention to me. "I hope you no longer consider me a stranger anymore. I think the last few hours together have allowed us to get to know each other much better." He brushes my arm with the back of his index finger and I widen my eyes, surprised by the intimacy of his warm touch.

Andrew's return saves me from having to compromise myself with an answer. *Thank God.*

"Let me pay and let's go upstairs."

Maximiliano gets on his feet, fishes for his wallet in the interior of his expensive-looking tailored grey suit before pulling out four one-hundred-dollar bills and flinging them on the table in front of me. *Yeah, I'm going to stick to the cheap bubbly for now.*

"Shall we?" He extends his hand to me and I know the second our palms touch, I'll melt inside.

It may be nothing more than a few hours in a swanky New York hotspot with a dreamy guy over expensive champagne, but this never happens to me. The evening could end right here and I'd feel like I spent two hours in heaven.

Devin, Lia and Lexi will die when I recount tonight's surprise encounter.

He could have spent the evening scanning the room for a chick to fuck, like many of my dates have done in the past, but he only seemed to have eyes for me. I don't want anyone to burst my bubble—not immediately, anyway. I want to be able to relive this moment over and over again in my head. As I suspected, the second our skin touches, I turn into a molten lava cake inside. *The man has such an effect on me.*

We walk hand in hand to the elevators in silence.

"Candice, I'm happy I didn't have to wait until Sunday and I hope you'll pop by Vanilla Beans to meet me again. I had a very pleasant evening."

"I had a lovely evening as well," I say shyly as we walk into the elevator.

When we arrive at the forty-first floor a concierge greets us.

"Good evening, madam and sir. Are you members? I'm sorry for asking, but I'm still new at this position."

"Not to worry, my friend. You're doing your job. Yes, I am." Maximiliano flashes an electronic card and the tall gentleman at the desk nods in approval.

"Please go right in. We had a few members earlier today, but it's pretty quiet right now."

"Excellent, I want to show my friend the spectacular view."

"I've been working at this hotel for six years now and I never get tired of this view. Your friend will be as dazzled as the rest of us." The concierge winks at me before flashing me a warm smile.

"Are you ready to be dazzled?"

I grab the hand Maximiliano extends and follow him inside the VIP members' den. When I step into the opulent space I bring my hand to my mouth, amazed by the luxurious décor. The grandiose room is decorated in an inviting neutral palette. Two decorative ebony-colored wood panels separate the space's three intricate areas and make the room appear bigger than it is.

"Is this a room where high-powered executives meet to hash out multimillion-dollar deals?" I'm speaking to him, but still scanning the room.

"Something along those lines," he mocks. "It's a place to connect with potential business partners. I belong to a few of these private clubs in New York and I must say, it does make a difference. Come to the back of the room with me. I want to show you a view of the city you've never seen before."

He doesn't wait for me to answer. He's already dragged me to the other side of the members' den and I gasp when my eyes land on the bright lights below me. "I didn't know Manhattan could look this beautiful." I turn around, still mesmerized by the city at my feet. He's taken a few steps back and he's casually leaning against a wall with both hands crossed over his chest.

"From where I'm standing, you're the beautiful one."

I instinctively bring my hands to my cheeks to hide how surprised I am by his compliment. He takes a long step towards me and pulls me against him before turning and forcing me to walk backwards until my back hits the same wall he was standing against a few minutes ago. "As I've shared earlier, my friends call me Max and I hope since we're no longer strangers, you'll also call me Max."

"Oh," I whimper, too turned on to speak. I can barely breathe because I'm afraid I'll kill the moment. *Get a grip, Candy.*

"I keep bumping into you, Candice. Wouldn't you say it's fitting I get to know if you are as sweet as your nickname?"

"Maximiliano…"

"No, no, no, it's Max," he says softly as he presses his body closer to mine. I'm trapped between the wall and his tall frame. *God.* I tilt my hips forward in the hopes of creating some distance between us before I combust of desire, but instead I end up brushing against his hard cock. *Jesus.*

"I… Well, Max, I don't want to sound ungrateful for the attention, but I'm sure there must be a mistake. I mean, maybe this is a fun night out after a long day at the office and you'll go home soon to your wife and twelve kids." I don't break his gaze.

"Twelve? You've given me quite a large family. Couldn't you have started with a more manageable number like two or three?" He leans in closer to my lips.

"Uh. Maybe I went overboard. Does it mean you only have two or three kids?" I try to swallow, but my throat is as dry as sandpaper.

"Candice, like you, I'm *very* single."

Oh, shit. Thanks, Lia, for sharing details of my personal life.

"Okay. Good to know," I respond nervously. "Max, there are at least two hundred beautiful and thin women at the lounge. What are you doing here with me?" I can't ignore the obvious—hot men go for hot women and unless this guy is blind, I don't know what game he's playing.

"I agree, there were quite a lot of gorgeous beauties at the lounge tonight, but it's a typical occurrence in a trendy place like the Brinkley Lounge."

"I see." I bite my tongue to hide my disappointment. Here I was thinking he only had eyes for me, but he's been checking out women all evening long. *You're so silly, Candy. You may scrub up nicely, but you're no supermodel.*

"Here's the thing, Candy, there's only one of those beautiful women who has sexy curves threatening to make me lose my mind and I'm looking at her right now."

He must be pulling my leg. After struggling for years with men and my self-esteem about my weight, I can't have possibly bumped into a hot guy who likes women with curves. For crying out loud, this isn't a Harlequin novel.

He glides his hand down my shoulder and stops between my breasts. "You've been teasing me since we met in the lobby by exposing your luscious full tits. Don't think I didn't notice your perfect pink nipples peering through the sheer fabric of your bra."

"It was an accident," I plead, caught between panic and insatiable desire.

"Shhhh." He brings his index finger to my lips and silences me. "I haven't been oblivious to the way your black silky dress clings to your round hips." He moves his hand to my hip so quickly I'm caught off guard. "Although the room was packed, your fragrance has been wrapped around me all night long."

"Max…" Fuck, this is so hot. I can't remember the last time I was this turned on. I swear I could scoop my juices trailing down my thighs.

"Yes, Candy?"

I want to beg him to stop, but I can't. I desperately want to continue engulfing myself in his sweet words. I don't care if I'll wake from this dream tomorrow. For now, I want to lose myself completely in him.

"Did you have something to confess?"

No. Please don't stop.

His eyes are burning mine and his gaze is making me feel so vulnerable—almost as if he can read my mind. He runs a finger down my cheek and I close my eyes for a second, savoring the moment.

"Your skin is as soft as it looks. I have a thing for beautiful curvy women with big green eyes and soft skin." *He does?* "I'm certain we were destined to meet tonight and discover more about each other."

I nod my head, unable to respond, and my eyes widen when it becomes clear he's going to kiss me. There's a part of me desperate to bust the doors to this VIP room and run down forty-one flights of stairs in my four-inch heels to escape this burning passion, but I don't even bother to pull away. This sensual electricity running through us is so strong, I can only offer my mouth to him.

He kisses me, soft and gentle at first, before demanding my mouth more forcefully.

Damn. He's an incredible kisser.

Without warning, Max pulls at the sash of my black wrap dress and he takes a step back to study me. I'm very aware of the dim lights in the room revealing every part of me and I flush. I look away, embarrassed by my own personal fears about my body image and by how much I want this stranger.

"Wow. You look sensational. Would it be too forward of me to reveal your suggestive bra and your sexy panties are making me hard?"

Would it be too forward of me to reveal I'd walk on my hands and knees to stick your cock into my mouth?

"You're going to make me blush with all your compliments."

He takes a step towards me and pushes open my dress. His gaze is burning mine as he sensually cups my breasts. *Damn.* Even through my bra, his fingers send a thrill through me.

"Ahhh." I exhale.

"You might be a little shy, but you're not completely indifferent to me."

Are you kidding me? Do you know how much I want you right now?

He pushes down my bra and reaches for my exposed breasts. A spike of arousal shoots straight down to my pussy.

"Your luscious tits are insanely sexy," he murmurs, his thumbs circling my hard nipples.

"Oh, gosh, Max, I don't know…" I met the guy a few hours ago and now I'm making out with him on the forty-first floor of a high-end hotel in a swanky private room overlooking one of the most beautiful cities in the world. This stuff never happens to girls like me.

"No, Candy. Don't even try to deny our strong mutual attraction."

"Mutual attraction?"

"Uh-huh."

My panties are dripping at this point. There's no going back.

He strokes my boobs, his palms so big he can hold my double Ds fully. "When I caught sight of these, I had to restrain myself not to reach out in the middle of the lobby and grope them like a horny teenage boy." He flashes a side grin. His fingers circle my nipples and then gently roll the peaks.

"Ahhh." I tilt my head back against the wall as his touch causes my pussy to clench hard.

His eyes on my face, he increases the pressure until I bite my tongue to alleviate the agony raging inside me. *Dear Lord.* He knows exactly what he's doing. He's painting me like one of Peter Paul Rubens' extravagant Baroque-style masterpieces, each stroke deepening the intensity of the moment. "Max," I whisper, shivering as new sensations travel throughout my body.

"Is it too much?" he asks softly.

"I'm about to erupt."

"Good. It wouldn't be fun if I was the only one taking pleasure here."

His hands are all over me and they're causing my body to flame out of control. *No, I can't succumb to the charms of a complete stranger.* Good girls don't fool around with men they barely know. Why do I want him inside me with more intensity than I've ever wanted any man before?

"Fuck, you're sweet," he grunts.

Without warning he grabs both of my arms and brings them over my head.

"Oh," I let out when his cock presses against my stomach.

Clasping my wrists with one strong hand, he pushes me against the wall. I'm a prisoner. There's nowhere for me to run. I struggle at first, unsure of this rough play, but his grip tightens. Fear swirls through me even though my pussy is tingling with excitement.

"Let me go." My voice comes out husky and unconvincing.

"Do you want me to or should I continue?"

"I don't know." I do know, but I'm afraid of admitting aloud how fucking turned on I am right now.

"If you're not enjoying this, we can leave right now. The choice is yours."

He doesn't wait for an answer. He's already shoved my bra up with his free hand. He runs his long fingers around my hard nipple then the other. He's merciless. My nipples tighten with every touch and my pussy pulsates with every breath I take.

"You... Oh... Your fingers..." I'm unable to string a sentence together because my brain is so occupied by the colliding sensations rushing through me.

"You like what I'm doing to you?" He plays with my boobs as his hazel eyes catch every flicker of excitement on my face. "You're so vulnerable in this position. You know, with your hands restrained, I can pretty much do anything I want to you."

"What do you mean?"

"I'm the one in control right now." He grins as he narrows his eyes.

Instinctively, I struggle. After a few seconds I realize I'm going nowhere. He's much taller than I am and his grip is unyielding, his strength overpowering. Each one of my futile attempts shoots a current of excitement through me until my aching pussy clenches with need.

"Don't worry. I like to play rough. I'm not going to hurt you."

I stare up at his intense gaze and I pant.

"I've been waiting all night long to suck on these." He chuckles before lowering his head towards my chest and pushing my boob inside his mouth while groping the other possessively.

"Fuck," I exhale. *God, Candy, what are you doing? You don't even know him.*

"I could suck on your tits for days without ever taking a break, Candy." He sucks my breast again.

I press my back so hard against the wall when he bites down carefully on my nipple. *Shit.* The sharp pain is so intoxicating; it sends a sizzling rush straight to my clit, hitting me with such force I want to pull at his hair for salvation, but then I remember I'm shackled. *Oh yes, God. Thank you.*

"Max, your tongue is going to make me forget my name."

He chuckles instead of answering me, unwilling to let go. He licks my swollen peak, his tongue hot, his breath cooling my feverish skin. I close my eyes and arch my back uncontrollably, pushing my boobs upward.

"Oh, yeah. Your beautiful tits are going to make to lose my mind," he murmurs, switching to my left breast until both are swollen. I'm burning up and drowning at the same time.

He lifts his eyes to catch mine and I can't help but notice the mischievous look on his face. "I'll have to buy you a new pair of these," he says.

Huh?

I don't have time to react. Taking hold of my turquoise panties, he rips one side, then the other, and yanks the shredded fabric from under me before tossing them over his head. The sliding sensation of the fabric pulling at my juices nearly sends me over the edge. *This is the most lascivious makeout session of my life.*

"They were nice and all, but your glorious pussy is far more delectable."

Oh, my God. This can't be happening. A hot single guy who happens to love curvy women is all over me like a drifter who hasn't had a sip of water in weeks.

"Mmmm." His eyes are locked into my pussy as he licks his lips, stroking his chin like a winner-takes-all at an international poker tournament. "Good girls don't shave bare. It seems there's a vixen inside you."

I turn my head to the side, trying to avoid the raw desire I read in his eyes, but he grabs my chin into his hands, preventing me from looking away.

"Oh, no, you don't. I want you to look at me. I want to be able to lose myself in your eyes when you melt into my hands."

What is he talking about?

I open my mouth to protest, but he drops to his knees in front of me. He pushes open my left leg and I panic.

"What are you doing?"

"I already told you. I want to find out if you're as sweet as your nickname. I love seeing you vulnerable and I want to look up at your beautiful face as I push you over the edge."

"You can't…" I squirm desperately, trying to convince myself I'm half as offended as I am pretending to be, but it's too late. He has me wedged against this damn wall. My panties are ripped to shreds and lying on the floor of this VIP den as a telltale sign of my misbehaving. My pussy is unshielded and begging for his tongue.

"If you don't want to continue, we can go downstairs and you can catch a cab home."

I open my mouth to respond, but I slowly close it instead, incapable of finding a valid reason to prevent this man from licking me. He smiles victoriously as he slides his hand down my stomach until he reaches the betraying wetness of my pussy.

"Oh, dear God," I whisper.

I look down at him and I immediately close my eyes against the amusement flashing in his eyes. *Bastard. He knows he has me.*

"You're so wet. I guess you no longer consider me a stranger," he mocks.

I can't help but smile with eyes half open. With one finger, he strokes down into my wetness and back up, circling my clit. Each circuit sends a gush of tingling sensation to my engorged nub. He teases me and I'm sure he's aware of the pain and pleasure he's subjecting me to by never touching my aching node.

"Sweet Mother of God," I whine and I thrust my hips forward hoping he flicks the tip of my impatient clit with his tongue.

"Don't rush me," he laughs into my pussy. "Enjoy every bit of it because I'm going to finger-fuck you until you're forced to bite your tongue in order to avoid screaming out my name."

"Jesus," I let out, caught between excitement and the fear of losing all control to this stranger. "But I barely know you."

"From the way your body is responding to me I'd say, you've been waiting for me your entire life."

"You're very cocky."

"Not at all. You keep betraying yourself, Candy." Without leaving my gaze, he pulls his fingers from my pussy and licks them. *Ah.* "You're so fucking wet it won't take me long to make you lose it."

"You think you have me all figured out."

Instead of responding me, he pushes his finger into my pussy, hard and fast.

"Oh," I gasp.

The exhilarating shots of pleasure make my head spin. *What's come over me?* My body has never responded like this to any man I've been with in the past. Nothing makes any sense anymore considering how out of control I am under the hands of a guy who has never explored my body before.

"Oh, Candy, you are sweeter than I expected." His fingers slide in and out of me in a ruthless cadence until my pussy clenches around his sweet intrusion, gripping him tight. *I never want to let go.*

I'm nearly delirious and I can't possibly imagine anything more intoxicating until he inserts another finger.

"Holy shit," I scream out.

"Candy, you're going to have to keep it down or else the concierge will run into the room to find your pussy exposed," he warns, grinning with satisfaction.

I shake my head to let him know I have no desire to be found out and he smiles before thrusting his fingers inside me again.

"Oh, Max," I moan.

He increases the rhythm of his naughty play and as the pleasure increases, the overwhelming intensity of the pressure building inside frightens me.

"Yes," I hiss, tilting my head against the wall. I push my hips forward, vying for more.

"Look at you. You're dying for me to give you more, aren't you? You look innocent enough, but there's a bad girl waiting to escape."

"It's your fault. You're doing things to me…"

"I'm pleasuring you as much as I'm pleasuring myself, sweetness."

His comment leaves my legs shaking. Little do I know there's much more to come.

"Your tight little clit is yearning for relief."

"Oh, hell yeah." I'm surprised I'm willing to admit so much.

Without warning, his thumb skates over my clit, gliding directly over it each time his fingers plunge deeper inside my aching pussy.

"Did your last boyfriend know how to meet your needs?"

Well, we can't officially call Vince a boyfriend, since I was fucking a married man, and George was a capable lover, but it was always about him. If he didn't make me come before him, I was screwed since he had the annoying habit of falling asleep right after ejaculating.

"Not like this," I confess, shaking my head.

Without losing a beat his thumb continues to toy with my clit. One, two, three strokes. *Jesus.* My body coils tighter as he relentlessly torments me. I'm gasping for air, shaking my head from left to right so violently my hair sticks to the pearls of sweat trailing down my face.

"Remember, sweetness, it doesn't matter how hard I make you come, you can't scream or else we'll get caught."

Devious man. He's taking pleasure in seeing me so helpless and so close to the edge.

I nod my head in agreement as I slide a finger into my mouth to keep me preoccupied and to prevent me from screaming my head off.

"Good girl. I can't wait to find out if your cheeks will flame up when you come."

"Ah." His words turn me on so much, I sink my hips lower against his hand, seeking more sexual healing. *Make me come.*

His thumb rolls over my clit and my orgasm explodes inside me like fireworks on Times Square on New Year's Eve. Here I am completely undone on the forty-first floor of a hotel with a dreamy guy on his knees giving me more pleasure than I thought possible.

"Oh, Lord," I murmur, biting my lower lip so hard I draw blood. My hips buck against his hand as a second and then a third wave of a dizzying climax tears through my trembling body.

"I love watching your wide hips pulse in response to my touch."

"Your touch is…" I try to find the words to describe what he's done to my body, but how can you ever describe ecstasy?

He gets back on his feet and straightens his impeccable suit before taking a step closer to me. "You look so dazed, sweetness. That was nothing. Had the concierge not been standing within hearing range, I would have made you lose your mind so much they would have heard you downstairs in the lobby." His finger is trailing along my jaw before tilting my head. I lose myself in his intense eyes and I don't even move when he takes my mouth hard.

Nothing? Is he kidding me?

"You're so sweet and so tempting," he sighs as he takes a step back.

"What about you?" He's made me nearly lose my mind, but I should return the favor.

"I should stop now or else I'll throw you against the couch over there and I'll slide my hard cock inside your luscious pussy. It might be wise to wait for another fortuitous encounter, don't you think?" He winks and my legs go so weak, I flinch.

It's not as if Vince was an inadequate lover, but he never left me so helpless, so vulnerable and so weak in the knees. Max has masterfully taken control of all my senses by using his tongue and his fingers. Compared to most men, he has a PhD in sexual pleasure.

"Perhaps it's best to wait for the next time I flash you." I lick my lips, savoring every ripple of pleasure, and I shrug at the idea I could dissolve so easily in the arms of a stranger.

"I do apologize again for the panties. But since you can't possibly wear these anymore, why don't I hold on to them. Since I promised you a new pair, it's going to make my job much easier if I know your size," he says, bending down to scoop up the panties he had casually discarded earlier.

I smile when he tucks my panties into his pocket and taps on the front of his jacket as if to confirm they're safely in his possession.

"Oh, I can't possibly get a new pair of underwear to you if I can't find you. Of course, I could wait until we bump into each other again, but I'd rather have the peace of mind of knowing I have your number."

"You want my number?"

"Of course, sweetness. I hope you don't think I've already had enough of you."

"Uh… I wasn't sure what would happen next," I confess, surprised he's making plans to see me again. I thought it was a one-time thing.

"Hand me your phone, I'll put in my number and you'll do the same for me."

I turn on my heel to grab the handbag I dropped on the coffee table in front of the couch he was threatening to fuck me on and I fish for my phone. He grabs it and pushes in seven digits and hands it back to me with a bad-boy grin. "I hope you'll want to see me again, Candy?"

Everything about his tone suggests he's not asking me a question, but rather confirming how things will unfold between us.

"It would be lovely to see you again, Max," I say so quietly I can barely hear myself speak.

"I'm glad you feel the same way I do. Now let's get out of here," he says, slapping my ass so hard I jump.

Chapter Five

I desperately tried to regain my composure during the ride home last night at the back of a chauffeured limousine Max hired for me, to no avail. My stomach was a ball of nerves the whole way back to my place. As I relived every detail of the evening, from the moment I stepped into the luxury hotel where I was supposed to meet my cousin Trish to the point where Max was on his knees in front of me licking and finger-fucking my pussy, I couldn't help but wonder if it was a dream. I kept waiting for the car zooming down Manhattan's deserted streets to turn into a pumpkin, the chauffeur into a mouse and the dress that witnessed our naughty interlude into rags. When I looked down at my turquoise high-heeled shoes, I knew what I experienced wasn't a fairy tale and I wasn't Cinderella.

It's not as if I've never climaxed before, but last night was more like a volcano erupting than a simple tickle—which is the only kind of orgasm I had known until I bumped into Max.

Fuck, I can't believe I allowed a stranger to make me come more strongly than I've ever come before.

I'm so upset at myself. How can I have fallen for a person I know so little about... especially when Vince's drama is still ringing in my ears? *God, why couldn't I have resisted Max more?*

"Candy? Earth to Candy?"

Carl Applegate, one of my fabulously gay male co-workers, is snapping his fingers in front of my face trying to catch my attention. I'm so surprised I blink a few times to remind myself I'm still at work.

"Child, where were you?"

I immediately straighten myself in my chair when I realize I'm spending more time thinking about Maximiliano than doing my job.

God, are Carl's glasses getting bigger and bigger? These new ones nearly hide his entire face.

Carl is one of our beauty editors at large. He's the go-to person for all beauty magazines for both the skinny and plus-size divisions. He has a thing for big bold glasses. Although he has twenty-twenty vision, he insists on using glasses to make a statement like some women use their overpriced Hermes Birkin bags.

"Sorry, I'm a bit distracted with personal stuff."

"Oh, I'm sorry. I hope it's nothing too serious?"

"Nah, I'll be fine."

"Well, it's good to hear because Maleficent wants you in the boardroom, pronto."

Shit. I roll my eyes, dreading an unexpected meeting with my boss, Jennifer.

I love my job and my co-workers. The only blemish on an otherwise perfect career is my new boss, Jennifer Lau. She's such an ice queen, the entire office calls her Maleficent behind her back because she makes the villain witch from Walt Disney's *Sleeping Beauty* look like a little lamb.

Jennifer is a petite Asian-American who runs this magazine with an iron fist. I doubt she could spell the word smile with a dictionary, but I've been stuck with her since my former boss, Christine, decided to become a stay-at-home mom after the birth of her third child six months ago. I know Jennifer secretly despises me, but there are three undeniable things playing in my favor—I'm very good at my job, the plus-size online and offline division has helped balloon annual sales by several tens of millions of dollars in advertising spending from some of the biggest luxury brands, and I've been voted best new voice for plus-size women by the influential online Bible for all big girls—The Curvy Fashionista. I ain't going away, no matter how many times she hopes a slender girl will replace me. *Bitch.*

"What? I wasn't supposed to have a meeting with her," I lament.

"It's not a meeting with her per se. She's sitting in the boardroom with a bunch of suits—the ad executives from Bard Advertisement, a tall slender woman wearing a fierce suit that would make Tilda Swinton weep and a mystery bigshot client. I couldn't see his face, but he has incredible hair."

Great, a meeting with a skinny woman who will remind me how not skinny I am.

"I'm not the one who usually sits with new ad accounts. I'm just the editor. I write pretty stories and I'm the cheerleader for our readers. I don't negotiate ad contracts."

"You're right, but Jennifer called for you because Denise had to run to the daycare and grab her twins who have chickenpox. Since she most likely won't be back for days, you've inherited her duties because the bigshot client wants to spend gobs of money on the plus-size magazine and website over the next two years. Jennifer wants someone who will be the liaison."

"Isn't the agency our liaison?"

"Jennifer said this client required a more personal touch."

What the hell? "Numbers are not my thing."

"Maybe, but the way Jennifer is batting her eyelashes at this client like a hyena in heat, I think she'll kill you if you don't get your ass in there and start catering to this guy's every need."

"Jesus." I stick my elbows on my desk and hide my face in the palms of my hands, unwilling to have to sit in a boring number-crunching meeting on a

Friday afternoon. "Can't Denise be patched in via Skype?"

"You're hilarious, honey. Maleficent is so tech-averse I'm surprised she can turn on her iMac computer."

He's right. Jennifer thinks no one notices, but it's so blatant how afraid she is of technology.

"Okay, I'll go," I say reluctantly, trying to pep myself up.

"Honey, look at you. She's going to freak out if you walk into a meeting with a potential big advertiser looking like you just rolled out of bed." Carl stares at me with a disapproving look before folding his arms over his chest.

"Carl, I didn't sleep much last night."

"Uh-huh. Perhaps a valid reason at nine this morning, but it's two forty-five in the afternoon and you should have done something to fix this disheveled look you've got going on." Carl scrutinizes me with his hand on his hip.

God, do I look so dreadful?

"What am I supposed to do? It's not as if I have time to run back home and change. I didn't expect to have to walk into a meeting."

"You still have fifteen minutes. Come on, get up. Let me see if I can work my magic."

"I don't think there's much you can do. I'm wearing simple jeans and a baggy black top since it's Casual Friday."

"Honey, maybe for people working at an accounting firm, but you should know by now, no days are casual days when you work in fashion."

"I woke up late because I couldn't fall asleep until four o'clock in the morning. I rushed out this morning so I wouldn't to be late."

"You're not wearing any makeup? Why?"

"I told you…"

"Hush, child," Carl interrupts me. "I don't care if Godzilla has descended upon us, a girl should at least put on a little makeup before walking out the door. You never know who you'll bump into."

Yeah. I bumped into a hot guy and did unspeakably dirty things with him. Then I tossed and turned all night, riddled with guilt at the same time as I'd give up a right kidney for a few more hours of saucy pleasure.

"Do you have anything in your handbag?"

"A red lipstick."

"I'll need to a miracle to make this happen," he sighs.

"Wait, I have a sample of a new mascara in my drawer."

"Now you're talking. Grab it, please."

I turn around and fish in my drawer until I find the mascara that's about to save my ass.

"Great. Let's get to work." Without wasting a second, Carl meticulously applies two coats of mascara before painting my lips. He dabs a touch of lipstick on each cheek before smudging it with his fingers. "Much better."

"Thanks so much, Carl," I squeal when he hands me a pocket mirror.

"I'm not finished, honey. Your hair is a disaster."

Tell me how you really feel.

"We need to put it up so it doesn't look so messy. Obviously, you didn't wash your hair this morning."

"No." There's no point in coming up with an excuse.

"Hmmm, I don't have time to run to the accessories room to grab something pretty to hold up your hair. Grab me the elastic on your desk."

Carl sweeps my hair back and fastens the elastic so tight I think I'm going to have a headache. Luckily he loosens the ponytail before wrapping the hair sticking out in a deconstructed updo.

"Now we're talking. All right, I'm going to bunch up this dreadful shapeless sweater you're wearing and tie it at your waist so it looks somewhat stylish."

"No. You can't."

"Why not?"

"It's going to reveal my wide hips. I don't want all these skinny women in the office staring at my hips. Oh, and my thighs…"

"Would you rather Maleficent have a shitfit over your wardrobe selection?"

"Crap. Let the skinny bitches laugh at my wide hips and my big thighs."

"You've got it all wrong, honey. Those skinny bitches wish they could fill a dress like you can. I've seen you when you make an effort and you're gorgeous. Honey, straight men would kill to catch a glimpse of your huge tatas." Carl is gesturing at my breasts with so much enthusiasm, I burst out laughing.

It doesn't matter if they're gay or straight, men are obsessed with big boobs.

"I'm happy to see you smile. Now, stop obsessing over your sexy curvy body, grab this notepad, and walk into the boardroom before Jennifer starts spewing fire and roasts all of us like marshmallows over an open campfire."

"Bring it on. I can take on this new client with my hands tied behind my back."

"Meow. You go, girl. Snap."

I match Carl's snap before turning on my heel.

I so can do this.

I sashay into the boardroom bursting with confidence from Carl's pep talk. Even though I'm wearing rider boots, I make my way to an empty seat to Jennifer's right with as much attitude as plus-size Australian model Georgina Burke.

As I stride in, I notice the typical agency people. *Hmmm, I've never seen her before.* The thin woman sitting to the right of the empty chair across from Jennifer must be the one Carl was going on about. Where is the high-powered client? I lift my eyes and notice a tall man standing by the window with his back to me.

"Ah. Candice. Thank you for joining us and replacing Denise. You already know a few members of the Bard Agency."

"I look forward to this meeting, Jennifer," I lie. "Of course, I know Jack, Trent, Cindy, Ashley, Drake and Donna." As I call out their names, the agency people take turns flashing me a contrived smile.

"Excellent. Let me introduce you to Deidra Summers. She's one of the VPs working with our new potential major advertiser."

"Pleased to meet you." Deidra stands up to shake my hand and I have to tilt my head back to take her tall frame in. Of course it doesn't help she's wearing three-inch heels.

She must be six-three in those killer shoes. God, do I ever feel short next to her.

"Deidra, I love your suit."

"Oh. Thanks. I'm so tall, I had to get it handmade," she says, polishing the expensive wool fabric.

"It was worth it, you look impeccable." It never hurts to pay a compliment here and there.

"Candice?"

"Yes, Jennifer?" I say, turning my attention to my detestable boss.

"I'd also like to introduce you to someone I hope will be part of the history in the making of the plus-size division, Mr. Keller."

Huh? I know a Mr. Keller.

Before I can put two and two together, the man standing staring at the skyline with his hands in his pockets turns around with a cocky grin on his face. *No way.*

My nerves hit me in one big rush when I gaze up at his beautiful hazel eyes.

Maximiliano?

"Mr. Keller, I'd like to introduce you to Candice Westerman, our editor on the plus-size sections of the magazine. She also takes care of the content on our web portal. She's done an incredible job at building such a loyal following for *Sassy* magazine."

Jennifer is still talking, but my mind is racing so fast at the sight of him, I can only take in her last sentence. *First off, what the hell is he doing here, and second, why is Jennifer kissing my ass?*

"Candice, it's a pleasure to meet you. I was admiring the view while we were waiting for you. I can never get enough of seeing New York at my feet."

Is he quoting what I said last night?

"Mr. Keller, it's a pleasure meeting you as well," I lie, shaking the hand he's extended to me.

If I were to kill him right now, would anyone else in the room notice?

"Please, call me Maximiliano. My father is the only Mr. Keller I know." He laughs and the entire room follows suit.

If I could crawl under the conference room table to hide, I would. This cannot be happening.

"Jennifer, shall we start?" He's speaking to Maleficent, but his eyes are locked into mine. I wonder if the other eight people in the room can sense the tension between us.

"Absolutely. Candice, why don't you take the seat next to me?" Jennifer says, gesturing at me.

Good Lord, there's no escaping him. I'll be staring into his eyes during the entire meeting.

I settle myself next to Jennifer and immediately lower my gaze to the notepad in front of me. Jennifer breaks the ice and starts the meeting.

"Mr. Keller…"

"Maximiliano." He flashes her a disarming smile. I notice his side glance and look away.

"Oh, of course," she coos, bringing her manicured hands to her chest like a debutante. "Maximiliano, it's unusual for the client to come to meet with us. We usually deal with the agency. I'm sure you must be an extremely busy man."

"Jennifer, you're right. I buy struggling companies and send a team to restructure the operation. I don't get involved much since I have very smart people working for me, like Deidra," he says, touching the forearm of the woman sitting to his right. *Great. I bet you he's also taken her to the forty-first floor and submitted her to all sorts of dirty things.* "These three divisions are different. They're personal," he continues. "I'm half Brazilian and when my mother's oldest brother passed away, I was the only one capable of reshaping the family legacy. My uncle died three years ago and I inherited Sexy Curves Lingerie, Splash Swimwear and Divine Curves Couture. These three lines were near and dear to my uncle's heart. He couldn't get enough of women with curves and he's spent his lifetime catering to these beauties."

What? He owns Sexy Curves? I see this is the part of the dream that turns into a nightmare. I knew last night was too good to be real.

"Maximiliano, you seem too young to be so accomplished. Along with these three companies, you own a fleet of other ones."

"I keep myself busy and I surround myself with good people. Don't be fooled by the boyish face, I'm thirty-six."

Jesus. I've never been with a man who was older than thirty-one. This is going from bad to worse. He's so much older than me.

"I was flipping the pages of the latest *Forbes* magazine edition and I noticed you made the list of Richest Under Forty. What an accomplishment. You're so young to be a billionaire."

No wonder he spent four hundred dollars on a bottle of champagne and a few appetizers.

"Jennifer, I'm lucky in many ways because my talented team has always been able to reshape the companies we buy. We either hold on to them and place new management or we sell them for a profit. It's been a lot of strategic work and thanks to my team, it's paid off big time for us."

"I can't tell you how impressed I am."

Oh, please, Jennifer, stop gushing all over him.

"The Sexy Curves Lingerie and Splash Swimwear divisions are finally profitable. Bless my uncle's heart, he was running these businesses into the ground. We have managed to turn things around and we're now ready to expand in America. We've had a phenomenal year because the mommy bloggers have been all over our collections, but we plan on opening stores across this beautiful country of ours and we're looking for additional exposure."

I'm pretending to take notes to avoid his gaze, but I'm dumbfounded to find out Max owns some of my favorite designer lines. In fact, I was wearing a turquoise combo from Sexy Curves last night when I bumped into him.

"You've come to the right place." Jennifer lifts her slender hands, sticks her elbows on the boardroom table and steeples her fingers under her chin.

"Deidra and the team have done quite a lot of research on your magazine and it seems you're among the premier publications celebrating women at any size."

"I do like the way you put it. Yes, Maximiliano, we believe a size zero should be made to feel as beautiful as a size twenty-six and vice versa."

Liar. She might not put it in words, but everything about her body language suggests Jennifer is allergic to plus-size women—myself included.

"It's good to hear, Jennifer." Max and his VP Deidra are both nodding in approval. "We were hoping to start by pushing the lingerie and swimwear first, given the season, but by end of year, we should be gearing up to launch our Divine Curves Couture collection. We have a team of designers working tirelessly to ensure we have the entire collection ready before the holidays."

No wonder he has a thing for women with curves. We represent a lot of money in his pockets.

"Our readers love sexy and flirty underwear designed with the plus-size woman in mind, don't they, Candice?"

Jennifer's question startles me because I didn't expect she'd seek my opinion.

"Oh. Yes, they do. It's not easy to find flattering lingerie past a certain size," I say, addressing Deidra, who is sitting next to Max.

"Perhaps in America, but in Brazil, where most women have beautiful curves, it's a common occurrence. We brought one of our most popular sellers to show you and we've agreed with the agency, it would be the best one to help us make our mark in the market. We envision this flirty little number everywhere. Don't we, gang?" Max addresses the suits sitting around the table and they all nod in agreement.

God, they're such bootlickers. It's sick.

"Deidra, do you mind showing Jennifer and Candice our Sensual Vixen collection?" Something flickers in his eyes and he represses a smile. Why is he so amused?

Instead of sliding the folder on the table, Deidra extracts her long and lean body from the chair and strides towards Jennifer with a dead serious look on her face.

"The Sensual Vixen is feminine, but it also allows the plus-size girl to let the vamp inside come out to play."

I swallow hard when Jennifer slides the folder towards me and I lay my eyes on the pictures in front of me. *No way.*

The Sensual Vixen is exactly what I was wearing last night. I didn't remember the name of the collection. I loved the color and the fact I could be a little flirty. I never imagined my underwear choice would come back to haunt me.

I look up at him, my cheeks burning, trying to understand why he'd be so cruel. I hope to God no one else in the room notices how uncomfortable I am right now. I inhale and exhale, trying to calm my speeding pulse. *This is not happening to me. I cannot have done unmentionable things with a potential bigshot client.*

"Candice, what do you think? Would your readers go nuts over this blue combo?" Before I can even answer, Max turns his attention to the woman sitting next to him. "Deidra, what is the fashionable name we use to describe this shade of blue? I can never remember these details."

"It's called turquoise, Maximiliano."

"Ah, yes, turquoise." *Is he mocking me?* "Our talented Brazilian designer added an element of naughtiness by replacing the usually bulky cup with a sheer fabric that leaves little to the imagination," he says, curling his lip. "It comes in other shades, but last night I had an opportunity to see the Sensual Vixen in turquoise on a luscious curvy model and she looked dangerously hot. I'm so proud of our risqué designs."

Bastard. He knew the second he laid eyes on my exposed boobs I was wearing one of his collections. *What was last night about? Was he conducting market research?*

"Candice, you seem tongue-tied. I knew you'd be taken aback by our sexy designs."

The entire room turns to look at me and I honestly could die right then and there of embarrassment. I clear my throat and take a sip of the water sitting in front of me before speaking.

"Maximiliano, I'm sure our readers will love the new designs and the orders will come flooding in."

I have no idea how I'm able to be so calm and collected given the outrageousness of the situation.

"I'm so glad to hear you approve of our design. I don't normally do this, but as I've explained, I'm much more involved than usual because this is a family business. I don't tend to spend too much time flipping the pages of women's magazines or searching the web to find out what curvy girls will want to wear for spring. I have an incredible research team who takes care of these things. However, I became fascinated with the way you engage with your readers. I've been following your columns in both the magazine and the online portal for months."

So he's not such a random stranger after all. He's more like a stalker. He knew exactly who I was when I met Lia at Vanilla Beans. I'm the idiot who had no clue I was making out with a potential client.

"Thank you, Maximiliano. I'm passionate about what I do. I love my job and I love my readers. I'm surprised you'd take the time to read what I write."

"I must agree with Candice. I'm equally surprised." Jennifer looks even more shocked than I do at Max's revelation.

"I must say, your photo doesn't do you nearly justice. You're much prettier in person."

Fuck him for being disarmingly charming while my whole world is falling apart.

"Thank you." I blush.

"Jennifer, I surprised myself as well, but I wanted to make sure the person who was going to review our products would be able to communicate her experience in a compelling and honest way. I believe Candice can do this well. And by the way, good call on Melissa McCarthy. What a brilliant scoop."

My God, he really has been reading what I write. "It was a lucky guess," I say shyly.

"Nonsense. You were predicting this for months. You're far too modest."

From the corner of my eye, I notice Jennifer's stern look. She's not a fan of people who pay me compliments. She must be sitting between a rock and a hard place since the person she's fuming at right now might end up injecting tens of millions of dollars in ad budget into *Sassy* magazine.

"I'm sorry, Maximiliano, you said I'd be reviewing your products? What do you mean?"

"If Jennifer is interested in doing business with us, we'd love a more experiential approach. Since we would be buying ads space featuring professionally shot sleek and glossy images, we still want the buyers to feel our collections are for them.

We'd be more than happy to send you a number of our top sellers for you to wear and describe your experience. There's nothing quite like touching and feeling lingerie to fully appreciate it."

Are we still talking about the magazine feature? "Seriously?"

"Deidra came up with the concept and now that I've met you in person, I can't imagine not running with it."

I gasp at the idea he'll be privy to what I'm wearing under my clothing. How the hell did this all happen?

"Maximiliano, I'm sure Candice will love every single item you send her." Jennifer leans in against the boardroom table and answers on my behalf.

What?

"*Sassy* magazine and our entire staff wants to work with you and we're happy to accommodate you in any way you'd like. Whatever you need is yours."

No. I don't want to be part of this deal. It's not fair I don't have a say in this.

"Really?" Max leans against the table and stares Jennifer dead in the eye. The tension is palpable in the room to the point where the suits lean in as well in order to be closer to the action.

"Absolutely."

Max has been manipulating me since I bumped into him last night. He knew full well he'd be sitting in our boardroom today and he knew exactly who I was.

"Anything?"

For crying out loud, spit it out. Maleficent said you can have anything. Obviously, my body is part of the deal. What more do you want?

"I'm glad to hear you say this, Jennifer, because I want her."

Dear God.

Jennifer flinches in her seat, unable to comprehend Max's request.

"What do you mean?" Both Jennifer and I ask the question at the same time.

"Deidra also thought it would be brilliant to document some of our big upcoming shows and fashion shoots in Miami and Brazil. We'd love a sort of candid-camera approach where Candice would give your readers an insider's look into our collections. Deidra was also thinking live Tweets and Facebook posts on your magazine's social media platforms. Essentially, we'd love for Candice to travel with us."

Jennifer nearly chokes and the three agency women shoot me envious looks. I know I should be enjoying this moment, but I'm too mortified to appreciate this victory.

"Well... I'm not sure. I'd... I'd have to check with management." I've never seen my boss babble before when answering anyone.

"Jennifer, it's quite simple. I'm going to spend an insane amount of money on ads with your publication over the next few years. I'm simply asking for one of your editors to document a few fashion shows. If this is a problem, perhaps one of your competitors would welcome our business."

Good Lord. He's playing hardball with a woman who's made it her mission to be known as a ball-crusher.

I've not been able to say a word since Max dropped the bomb. I'm afraid everyone will know what happened between us last night and I'm also scared of Jennifer's reaction. I don't want to lose this job.

"Candice will bring a lot of heart and soul to these types of features, Maximiliano. Let me have a quick word with the VPs to confirm, but I'm certain we can accommodate your request."

Beads of sweat are pearling down my temples. I brush the back of my hand against my forehead, trying to stay calm, but suddenly I feel faint.

"Candice, are you okay?"

Deidra is the first one to notice I must have turned white like a ghost at the news.

"I think I ate something that's not sitting well with my stomach," I lie. "I'm going to run to the fridge and grab a Perrier. I'm sure I'll be okay once I get some fresh air. I'll be right back." I grab my notepad, get up on shaky legs and do my best to leave the room with as much dignity as possible. When I'm close to the door, I ready myself to sprint back to my desk, but his voice stops me dead in my tracks.

"Candy? Are you okay?"

I turn around, infuriated by Max's questions.

"Don't call me Candy." I turn my back on him, determined to get as far away as possible, but he's faster than I am. He takes one long step and grabs my wrist in his strong hand.

"Why are you running away?" His face is inches from mine and I hate myself for being turned on.

"You played me for a fool last night. What do you expect?"

"I didn't play you. I texted you all morning and afternoon, but you haven't returned any of my messages. Who's playing who?"

I'm painfully aware of his numerous messages, but I was so paranoid this was another case like Vince, I didn't want to get my hopes up. Who the hell meets Prince Charming randomly in a big city like New York?

"Let go of me. Someone will walk by and question why our big advertiser is gripping my wrist in such a personal way."

"You're right. Let's find a quieter place to talk."

Huh?

Before I can even react, Max scans the hallway and heads towards a door marked Fashion Archives. He jiggles the handle, pulls me in, and closes the door before resting his weight against the door.

Great. I'm a prisoner. There's nowhere for me to go.

"There's nothing to talk about," I spit out, enraged.

"Then why are you so angry?"

"You want to know why? Let's start with the fact you knew who I was, but you never let on. Let's move on to the fact you knew you were coming for a meeting at our offices today and finally what kind of girl makes out with a stranger who turns out to be a client?"

"You're very sexy when you're angry." He closes the gap between us and he's so close, I can see every shade of green and brown in his sparkling eyes.

"Argh. You're impossible." I'm fuming. "I'm not going with you to Miami or Brazil. There's no way I'm spending any more time with you. I'll beg Jennifer to find a replacement."

"If you do, I'll pull the account right under her nose."

"You're bluffing."

"Try me." His eyes are cold as ice and I'm confused by how the man standing in front of me can be so different from the one I met last night—the one who rubbed my clit until I came hard.

"What do you want from me?"

"You haven't return my text messages and I'm crushed. To make up for things, have dinner with me tomorrow night." He trails his finger over my chin, sending an electric shockwave to the tip of my clit.

"I'm not having dinner with you." I shake my head to emphasis my point. "You can't buy me with all your money."

I refuse to ever be caught alone in a room with him again.

"I'm not trying to buy you. I'd love to explain why I didn't reveal too much about who I was last night."

"It's too late, Max. I don't care," I say, taking a step back. You've been lying to me since I met you."

"You do care or else you would have called me Maximiliano."

Damn. He can read me so well.

"It's not going to happen. I'm not meeting you tomorrow night. End of story."

"I always get what I want, Candy."

"You can't trap me in this room and make such demands." I'm insulted by his insinuation. "You can't force me to do anything I don't want to do."

"The choice is yours. Either you accept my invitation for dinner or I'll walk back in the boardroom and let Jennifer know one of *Sassy* magazine's longtime competitors just made me an irresistible offer." He grins mischievously as he narrows his eyes. "Your boss doesn't strike me as someone who would appreciate seeing such a big contract slip through her fingers," he continues.

"You wouldn't dare," I say, scandalized by the options.

"Are you willing to gamble? One phone call and I can have Caitlin Jacobi, the editor-in-chief of *Femme* magazine, on the line within the next thirty seconds. She's been wining and dining me for months now hoping I'll give them our business." He fishes in his pocket and he pulls out his phone. "Once she agrees to my demands, which she will in under three seconds, I'll waltz back into the conference room and I'll announce the unfortunate change of plans to

Jennifer," he says, grabbing the door handle. "So what will it be, Candy? Dinner or not?"

I can't tell if he's bluffing, but I'm not certain I want to take the chance. I wouldn't want to jeopardize a job I love, but the reality is—even though I'm pissed off at myself for even considering caving in to his demands—I'm dying to see him again. My God, it's totally inappropriate for me to have dinner with a powerful client. Isn't it?

I'm paralyzed with fear and I hesitate, still unsure how to handle this sticky situation, but when he opens the door and takes a step out, I nearly pass out from holding my breath.

Good Lord, he can't actually be serious.

****

Get Your FREE SECRET Chapters!

Thank you for purchasing this romance!

I'd love for you to lose yourself in more sultriness, sexiness and steamy passion!

When you sign-up today, I'll send you the following *Secret Chapter* for Part 1 of this serial:

You'll want to read how Max becomes totally enraptured by Candy the minute he sees her walk into Vanilla Beans! (This is Max's POV)

*** <u>PASSWORD FOR</u> Secret Chapter Part 1:
Vanilla-Beans

Note: the password is case sensitive!

Sign-up TODAY!

www.RomanceBooksRock.com

If you've already signed-up to my list from previous books, you can visit the same page to download the Secret Chapters for this romance

****

Curvy Girls Do It Better

Chapter One

I've been up pacing my apartment for hours now, biting my nails, waiting for the cavalry to come over to rescue me—again. I couldn't sleep last night, tossing and turning, reliving every moment of my interaction with Max inside the Fashion Archive room. *How could he have known who I was all along and never dropped a hint?*

I hate myself for having fallen so easily for another smooth talker right on the heels of my drama with Vince. Here I am one week later and I'm once again in turmoil over a guy. *I can't believe Max owns Sexy Curves—and he's so much older than I am.*

Lia, Devin and Lexi agreed to meet me at my place for breakfast at ten o'clock and I can't wait to see them. I desperately need to confide in my friends.

"You're so lucky," I say to my cat. Leo DiCaprio opens one lazy eye and looks up at my worried face before rolling on his other side. "Yeah, you don't have men troubles. No wonder you can sleep peacefully."

I've been up for hours because I've been so preoccupied by the fact I agreed to have dinner with Max tonight to avoid Jennifer's wrath. I mean what was I going to do? He left me no other choice.

I wanted to meet up with my friends last night after work to share the latest chapter in my soap-opera life, but the stupid meeting at the office dragged on for hours and by the time it was over, I was too exhausted to recount the last two days.

Thank God Jennifer invited Max to have dinner with two of the VPs after the meeting. I was able to escape a potentially uncomfortable situation. He texted me while he was at the restaurant letting me know how excited he was about seeing me again, but I'm not buying it. I'm sure he's buttering me up so I'll give his collection of plus-size lingerie and swimwear glowing reviews.

"They should be here any minute now," I say aloud as I check the time on my iPhone. I've avoided every mirror and shiny object in my home, unable to look myself in the eyes. I've been conflicted about this whole story with Max since I found out he wasn't a random stranger I happened to bump into over brunch with my best friend Lia seven days ago. Maximiliano Tomás Adrian Keller is now my number-one client and I'm to be at his beck and call because he'll be injecting a ridiculous amount of money into *Sassy* magazine.

If I could erase all the mind-blowing things he did to my body on Thursday night, I would, but every time I close my eyes, I'm transported back to the forty-first floor of a luxury hotel where a drop-dead gorgeous successful executive was on his knees pleasuring me. *This stuff only happens in movies and trashy romance books.*

I'm so lost in my thoughts, I jump when I receive Devin's text letting me know they're on their way up. *Thank God I can spill my guts to people who love me.* A few minutes later, Devin knocks three times before sliding his emergency key into the lock.

"Hey, sweetie, we're finally here," he announces once he opens the door.

"I'm so happy you guys are here," I say, running to the door to kiss him.

"I brought some fried-egg and bacon sandwiches from Witchcraft. When you texted me to let me know you made out with your secret admirer and he turned out to be your new VIP client, I figured it's best to get some ammunition."

"God, Dev, I'm salivating. I needed pork fat last week after Vince, but this week it's an emergency."

"Candy, how are you?" Lia walks in right after Devin with so much booze I wonder if she's planning on having a party at my place I wasn't aware of.

"Lia, why did you buy so much alcohol?"

"Honey, let's be honest. We've had to rush back to your place two Saturdays in a row because you keep randomly meeting *interesting* men."

"Point well taken. We might end up finishing all this by noon," I joke.

"Candy, don't listen to Lia. She's jealous a hot guy finger-fucked you while she's been celibate for a very, very long time."

"As if you've been getting a lot of cock. Listen, Lexi, I'm not afraid of washing your mouth out with soap." Lia and Lexi are at each other and Devin and I roll our eyes.

"Come on, ladies. We're here to support Candy, not to start a catfight."

"Devin is right. Candy, I bought some fresh Belgian waffles from Wafels & Dinges. They are divine reheated in the oven. I got us whipped cream, a huge basket of fresh raspberries and chocolate syrup as the toppings."

"Bless your heart, Lexi," I say, hugging my tall and lean friend. "I need sugar badly."

"We would have been here earlier, but we can't talk about such drama without food." Devin is already in my small kitchen opening cupboards, looking for plates and wine glasses.

"Did you sleep?" Lia hugs me and I dissolve.

"Not well. I got home last night an emotional wreck. You're right, one week ago I was dealing with Vince's baby-momma drama and now I find out my secret admirer is a billionaire stalker whose fingers are lethal. My life is a disaster," I let out before bursting into tears against Lia's shoulder.

Within a few seconds, Devin and Lexi run to me and all three of my best friends embrace me in a bear hug.

"Your life is not a disaster. Vince is a shit-head for doing what he did, but this client of yours didn't really do anything wrong."

"Lia, how can you take his side?" I step back, surprised by my friend's comment.

"Okay, first off, before anyone says anything else, am I the only one who picked up on the fact Candy got fingered by a billionaire?" We all turn around to face Devin and we all burst out laughing.

"Dev, you have the most comical expressions. Yes, the client is a billionaire."

"Oooooh." Both Lexi and Lia widen their eyes as if they totally missed that part of the conversation.

"I found out during the meeting yesterday afternoon at our office. I was sitting in a boardroom with eight other people—one of them was my bitchy boss."

"What's his name again?" Devin is scrolling through his text messages on his phone for an answer.

"Don't bother. I didn't include his name in the message I sent you guys last night. His full name is Maximiliano Tomás Adrian Keller."

"You remember the man's full name?"

"How can I not? I've never met anyone like him before. Here I was sitting in an upscale hotel with an elegant and eloquent man. It was a first for me and I soaked in every detail."

"His name is quite sexy."

"Yeah, Lia, but he insists on me calling him Max—like his close friends."

"Wow," Devin and Lia both say in unison.

"What's the problem, Candy? Why are you so upset? Max sounds dreamy. Is he married?"

"Lexi, he's not. He's very single, so he says, but what are the odds a twenty-four-year-old plus-size woman would magically bump into a hot billionaire who happens to love women with wide hips?"

"Honey, you tell us, because from your long text, there's not a whole lot to complain about," she winks.

It wouldn't have surprised me one bit if Lia had responded this way, but Lexi is the conservative among us. She's not a virgin, but she's not sexually active either. She keeps everything to herself and none of us have ever had the courage to pry. She's very reserved about her love life and since she's been through hell as a child, we don't have the heart to push her. She's always given off the impression she's not very interested in men—or women.

"Okay, let's get the food on the table, let's fill those glasses to the brim with wine and I'll start talking. Does anyone want coffee?"

"Yes, please." My three best friends respond in unison and we get ourselves ready for another Saturday morning heart-to-heart.

* * *

For the next ninety minutes, as we devour our succulent fried-egg sandwich from Wichcraft, I recount every single detail to my best friends. I bare it all from the second I stepped out of the elevator on the fourteenth floor of the Bymark hotel up to the point I nearly passed out in the boardroom when he revealed he wanted me to travel to Miami and Brazil with him.

"Shit, Candy, that's a pretty steamy encounter. The sexy stranger gave off a cocky flair, but who knew he was downright dirty?" Lia fans herself and we all laugh.

"I have to agree with Lia. Your hookup could win an award in the gay world." Devin is grinning at me from over his coffee cup and I can't help but roll my eyes at him. "I'm so thankful for the freak storm in Nashville. If Trish had showed up and laid eyes on your mystery man, she would have unleashed her slutty self all over him. Trust me, if the bitch had tried anything, I would have been on the first flight to LA to bitchslap her."

"Dev, you're so protective of me when it comes to my cousin. I'm also secretly happy she never made it."

"Trish has no shame."

Devin is right. Trish would have ruined it for me.

"Who knew a guy we met one week ago at brunch could turn out to be so delicious?" Lia is licking her lips so suggestively, I'm not sure if she's scooping up the drizzle of sauce at the corner of her mouth or reliving the story I shared.

"Doesn't it bother either of you he never mentioned he already knew me when he invited me for drinks?"

"Maybe he didn't want to kill the mood. God knows, I'm all work and no play. Hearing your story makes me want to run to your bathroom to take a cold shower."

Devin nearly spits out his coffee at Lexi's remark and Lia is so shocked she's looking at our friend up and down with her jaw dropped.

"Wow. Lexi, you're living vicariously through my story of shame."

"There's nothing to be ashamed of. You hooked up with a guy who obviously was interested in you. He had been following you via *Sassy* magazine and maybe he fell for your wittiness and when he recognized you at brunch a week ago, he thought, 'Damn!'"

"Okay, hearing those words come out of her mouth seems unnatural, but I have to agree with Lexi, this naughty encounter is pretty hot."

"But, Lia, he's most likely using me to ensure I give his product glowing reviews."

"You're assuming things, honey."

"Candy, once again I have to side with Lexi here. You have no idea why this guy couldn't keep his hands off of you."

"None of this makes sense. Max is drop-dead gorgeous, he's extremely successful, insanely rich and he has a phenomenal sense of humor. Why in the world would he be remotely interested in someone like me when there are so many other skinny options in a city like New York?"

"I thought you said he liked curvy women?"

"Vince said the same thing and his wife is a stick figure with a swollen belly. What if this guy is pulling my leg and taking me for a ride? What if eve-

ry woman he's ever dated is a freaking size-zero supermodel and he's only buttering me up because my
position at *Sassy* could help him expand his empire?"
Is Max more interested in what I can do for him than
in who I am? "I'm sorry, but handsome and rich men
go for slim bombshells, not average plus-size women
like me."

"You infuriate me when you talk like this,"
Devin shouts from the kitchen where he went to fetch
another cup of coffee. He looks at me in such a disapproving way, I lower my gaze, feeling slightly guilty
for what I said.

"Name me one powerful man dating a plus-
size woman," I say, tapping my nails against the stem
of my wine glass.

"You're blind."

"What do you mean?"

"You know what I mean," he responds in a
clipped tone.

"If I did, I wouldn't ask," I say, ticked off.
"Listen, if you're going to give me a pep talk, don't."

"I won't. I'm going to answer your question
because right now the only thing you see is how
seemingly huge your ass is as opposed to how phenomenal you are as a person. Pierce Brosnan, Ben
Falcone and Simon Konecki. Sexy Irish actor Pierce
is married to plus-size babe Keely Shaye Smith. Ital-
ian-American actor Ben is the father to your idol
Melissa McCarthy's two kids and yes, they are married, as you well know. Finally there's CEO Simon
who is Adele's baby-daddy. If you need me to name a

few other men who think meat on a woman is sexy, let me know. I'll be happy to oblige."

My apartment goes dead silent as Devin stares down at me from where he's still standing with scornful eyes while Lia and Lexi exchange side glances.

Jeez, no need to gang up on me. I want to believe him, but there's a part of me still struggling to accept I could be as lucky as Kelly, Melissa or Adele.

"Just because you've dated assholes, cheats and scumbags with small dicks doesn't mean all men fall in those categories. Maybe this half-Brazilian billionaire really finds you attractive."

"Dev's right, Candice." Lia squeezes my hand gently.

"Ditto, hun. I'm totally siding with Dev and Lia on this one. I'd kill for your luscious tatas." Lexi is desperately trying to push her breasts together to give the illusion of fullness and we all burst out laughing.

"Well, he does want to meet me for dinner tonight to explain why he didn't reveal who he was from the get-go," I say, biting my lower lip.

"What?" my three friends scream so loudly it sends Leo DiCaprio running to the bathroom to hide.

"Yeah. I might have forgotten to mention that part of the story," I say shyly.

"Fuck you for holding the best part to yourself. Let me pour some more wine in your glass. Start talking." Before I can respond, Devin is already marching to the fridge to pull out another bottle of California Sauvignon Blanc wine. "Don't wait for me to uncork the bottle, spill your guts, sister," he commands.

"At some point during the meeting, I felt nauseated at the idea I'd made out with one of our biggest clients. I excused myself pretending to have eaten something that made me sick. Once I burst out of the boardroom, my intention was to sprint to my desk and hide, but Max ran after me and he pushed me into the empty Fashion Archive room. To top it all off he had the audacity to threaten to blackmail me if I didn't agree to have dinner with him tonight."

"Oh, honey, this story is juicier by the second." Devin is filling my glass and I grab it and take a big gulp, letting the alcohol calm my nervousness.

"Devin, it's not. He's manipulating me."

"He can manipulate me any time if you don't want him."

"Amen." Lia and Lexi are high-fiving each other while giggling over Lia's comment.

"You two aren't being supportive," I scorn.

"You've accepted his invitation, right?"

"Dev, I didn't feel I had any choice in the matter. It was either accept or he was going to pull the contract and award it to one of our competitors in the marketplace. This would make Jennifer look bad and I'd most likely get fired."

"If Max didn't want to see you again, he wouldn't be playing hardball like he is."

"Yeah." Devin and Lia are both nodding at Lexi's comment with a huge grin on their faces.

"Honey, I hope you said yes."

"I did say yes. I didn't want to jeopardize my position at *Sassy*." I might not be willing to admit it openly to my friends, but I do want to see Max again.

"Great call," Devin says before bringing his wine glass to his lips.

"Were you only thinking of holding on to your job when you agreed to have dinner with him or were you having flashbacks to his impatient fingers against your clit?"

"Lexi!" we all say, shocked by her bold comment. She's never talked in such a raunchy way in the past and I'm curious to find out what or who brings out this side of her personality.

"What? If your first night was so hot and heavy, I can only imagine how sizzling tonight will be. Damn. Should we make plans now to meet on Sunday morning so you can share all the dirty details?"

"Honey, on second thought, she does have a good point," Lia says, winking at Lexi.

"I'm also happy you saw the light. You're totally blowing this out of proportion. Honey, you could give lessons to a few of my gay friends how to make out with a rich single guy," Devin says before snapping his fingers in the air.

"You guys really think I'm overreacting?"

A collective, "Yes!" fills my apartment, as my three friends lift their glasses to toast my decision.

Chapter Two

At seven o'clock, a sleek black chauffeured BMW rolls up in front of my building. Max texted me to let me know he'd send a car to pick me up, but I've been anticipating this evening so much I've been standing out here ten minutes already.

Terence, my chauffeur, is so elegant and I must say the BMW is a lot more impressive than the Lincoln Max hired to drive me home after our naughty interlude on the forty-first floor of the Bymark hotel.

As I slide into the back of the car, I can't help but wonder if I made the right wardrobe selection. *I hope he'll find me as irresistible as he did a few nights ago.* I opted for a curve-skimming wrap dress from plus-size designer Kiyonna. I would have bought this design in black, but lately designers are being daring with color and prints for curvy women. I must confess, it took me a while to get used to bringing attention to my figure, but I love this purple dress so much. I can't speak highly enough of the three-quarter sleeves, which allow me to feel more comfortable. The flattering neckline is low enough to warrant attention to my cleavage without being trashy. *I have big boobs and I might as well use them, as Lexi keeps reminding me.*

I paired the flirty dress with Christian Louboutin nude platform four-inch heels. Since I had to save for an entire year to get these as my twenty-fourth birthday gift, I bought them in a classic and versatile shade. *For the money I spent on these, I'll milk the investment for the next twenty years.*

When it came time to pick the lingerie set to compliment my outfit, I realized everything I owned is branded Sexy Curves. *Damn him.* I completed the look with a pair of simple gold earrings and a matching bracelet. Once again I have to thank Devin for forcing me to make an effort. As I caught my reflection in the mirror before rushing out, I had to admit I felt very pretty.

I'm a ball of nerves the entire ride, uncertain how the evening will unfold. Parts of me are yearning for more of Max and parts are scared shitless at the fact I'm infatuated with a man who holds my career in the palm of his hand. *It's already seven-thirty.* I look down at my phone to check the time when the chauffeur slows in front of a luxurious building on the Upper East Side. *Posh.*

"I'm sorry, Terence, is this a restaurant?" I lean in to ask the chauffeur if we have arrived at our destination.

"Mr. Keller requested I drop you off at his home."

"Oh, I see. Which floor does he live on?"

"He's arranged to have a concierge escort you to his floor, Madam."

"Ah, very well. I guess I'll get out then. Thank you so much, Terence." I fish inside my designer handbag to pull a tip, but the chauffeur stops me.

"Madam, I work for Mr. Keller full-time. He's already taken good care of me. Please enjoy your evening."

"Oh, yes, of course," I babble, regretting the faux-pas.

I reach out to grab the handle of the door with trembling hands and before I even step out of the car, a young doorman rushes to help me.

"Madam, you must be Ms. Westerman? My name is Ben, please allow me to help you. Mr. Keller has asked me to accompany you to his suite."

"Oh, thank you, Ben." I take the doorman's hand and slide out of the back of the BMW. Although night is falling, I can still make out clearly the superb building before me. *Wow. It's good to be a young billionaire.*

Max's building is the type of address you see in design magazines or on TV shows like *Million Dollar Listing New York*. It's located in one of Manhattan's most exclusive neighborhoods, surrounded by New York City's premier museums, retailers and restaurants, and if memory serves me correctly, we're a few steps away from the splendor of Central Park.

Everything about this tall, elegant and sophisticated building screams money.

I'm sure this must be a landmark, but it's clearly been impeccably renovated. I follow Ben into the lobby and stop when I take in the décor surrounding me—lush, opulent, refined. Everywhere I look I see beautiful white marble. The interior combines old-world comfort, avant-garde design and chic aesthetics. *Yeah, my renovated building isn't quite as glamorous.*

"Is everything okay, Ms. Westerman?" Ben turns around when he notices I'm no longer following him.

"Yes. I'm admiring this incredible space."

"It's extravagant, but it's well suited to our elite residents." *I bet.* "If you'll follow me. Mr. Keller is already awaiting your arrival."

"Of course," I say, taking a step forward.

As we walk by the concierge desk, I smile at the tight-faced woman staring at me. The petite redhead curls up her lips instead of smiling back. *Long day, I guess.*

As I step into the elevator, a vivid memory from last Thursday flashes in front of me—him touching me with his strong hands. I'm excited and worried at the same time about tonight. I was too shy to answer Lexi's question this morning, but she's right. The reason I accepted dinner with Max is because my body responded to his touch in such a hedonistic way. A part of me is dying to relive our naughty interlude. *How far am I willing to go tonight if he touches me again?*

"Ms. Westerman, we're here."

The doorman's voice wakes me up from my delicious dream and I gasp when I realize I've been riding in a private elevator. The door opens into Max's home and he's standing in front of me looking as incredible as he did a few nights ago.

"Candy, you made it." His bad-boy grin is devastating and I flinch when he extends his hand to help me out of the elevator. "Thank you, Ben, for accompanying Ms. Westerman to my penthouse. Have a great night."

"The same to you, Mr. Keller. Ms. Westerman, enjoy your evening."

"Thank you, Ben."

We both pretend to be fascinated by Ben's departure to avoid each other's gaze.

"Thank you for coming. You're looking stunning tonight," he says as my eyes are still fixed on the private elevator.

"Thank you. Your compliments always make me blush," I confess, turning to face him before bringing the back of my hand to my face to cool off my burning cheeks.

I was really hoping he'd make things easier for me by not looking so devastatingly handsome. His fitted unbuttoned dark grey Henley shirt drapes his muscular chest like a kid glove and reveals enough of his chest hair to seriously turn me on—thank God he's not one of those men who shaves his entire body. His long-sleeved shirt falls casually over his dark-wash jeans. They remind me of those sinfully skin-tight denims he was wearing when he was standing in line behind me at Vanilla Beans. Although more casual than anything I've seen him wear so far, his shoes scream expensive.

He's a very sharp dresser. The simplicity of his style speaks of elegance without trying too hard. His scruff is all too pleasing to the eye. *Damn.*

I'm sure my jaw must be hanging open when he breaks the silence. "Let me take your coat."

"I'm surprised you don't have a butler and a full staff of eight at your beck and call," I mock as I hand him my black trenchcoat.

"I remained in the shadows until the *Forbes* spotlight. I'm a little more popular these days, but I still prefer to keep things as simple as possible. I have a cleaning lady, a chef, a personal chauffeur and two personal assistants who keep my life organized. I don't need a butler and I have yet to use the services of a bodyguard. Have you read the *Forbes* article?" He's back near me, overpowering me. Even with me in my four-inch Christian Louboutin heels, he's so much taller than I am.

Worry hits me when I realize I've been so preoccupied with reliving every salacious moments of our Thursday night encounter, I didn't even think of doing a Google search to find out more. "I'm really sorry, but I didn't."

He smiles and brushes my hair behind my shoulders. A tingle of arousal runs through me as I lose myself in his sparkling hazel eyes. *No, you don't, Candy.*

"Don't worry if you haven't. I was going to ask you if you had noticed there was no photo. It was a request I made before agreeing to the article. I'm a businessman, not a reality star. Although I was very flattered, I don't need to be paraded in the pages of a publication to be validated for my hard work."

My God, he's so self-assured. What a far cry from other men I've known so far.

"You're so certain about who you are."

"I was blessed with incredible parents."

So was I, but I lost mine too soon.

"I didn't invite you here to chat about body-guards, butlers and *Forbes* articles. Come on in. I want to give you a tour," he declares before grabbing my hand to follow him.

"Wait, where are we going for dinner?"

"Right here."

"Your place?"

"I hope you don't have a problem with us having dinner here. I thought it would be a more private setting for us to talk since I promised you a few confessions. I'm not big on making revelations in public."

"Oh. I assumed we were going to a restaurant."

"Candy, you can wipe the worried look from your face. I'm not the one who cooked. My top-notch chef did a superb job at coming up with a menu you'll remember for a very long time. It's like eating at a five-star restaurant without the prying ears," he says, grinning.

"I'm relieved. I'm happy to know you won't put to shame my limited cooking skills."

"If you ask me to do more than cook eggs and toast bread, you've lost me. Come on. I want to show you the view before we tour the rest of my place," he says, lifting my hand and bringing it to his lips.

Surely the heat burning my face comes from the fact his penthouse is set at an extremely high temperature. *You can't give in, Candy.*

As we walk towards the massive floor-to-ceiling window, I catch a few glimpses of the rest of Max's penthouse apartment. Nothing surprises me given his level of success—sleek white kitchen with kickass appliances, modern and elegant furniture, warm dark wood floors and a media center that puts to shame anything I've seen in *Elle Décor*.

The man is loaded. His place makes mine look like a kid's treehouse.

"Your home is spectacular."

"Thank you. It's my oasis away from the frantic hustle and bustle of owning so many companies. I chose every aspect of this home and I went out and found the talent to execute my vision. I'm glad you like it."

Are you kidding me? Your home is a dream. I never imagined I'd be standing in such an outstanding apartment.

"Have you ever seen anything more amazing?" Max and I are standing side by side in front of his window overlooking Central Park. *Wow. I really wouldn't be able to believe some people were privileged enough to live like this had I not witnessed it with my own two eyes.*

As beautiful as this view may be, and it's majestic, there are only a handful of extremely rich people in Manhattan who can afford this view. I don't know what a million, let alone a billion dollars would represent, but suddenly I'm quite intimidated by his colossal wealth.

"You get to see this every day?" I ask shyly.

"Pretty much. I know you thought I was mocking you at your office yesterday, but I truly never get tired of seeing New York at my feet."

"Neither do I."

"We have something else in common."

"Oh, really? What else do we have in common?" From our first few encounters, I can't imagine he can find many similarities between us.

"I love beautiful women with sexy curves and you happen to have been blessed by the gods in that department," he says, dropping one arm against the window before leaning in and brushing my lips tenderly.

"Oh," I exhale in his mouth before returning his kiss.

Okay, Candy, resisting a guy means saying no to him kissing you.

I close my eyes and tilt my head back, shutting down the pesky little voice inside my head screaming at me to stop. After a few minutes of passionate embrace he pulls away from me and I already miss his lips against mine.

"Come on, let me show you the rest of my place," he says, pulling away from me.

Max gives me a royal tour of his penthouse. It's obvious a connoisseur has selected every single piece of furniture. His place leaves me jaw-dropped, but nothing astounds me as much as the art adorning his walls and the bronze statues lining the coffee tables. The massive canvases are painted with the same flair you'll usually find hanging in hip art galleries like Agora Gallery on 25th Street. I've been once or twice with Lia when we played tourists for the day and it's always been a dream of mine to own a signed piece. So far, I've had to content myself with fake reproductions I've found here and there.

"Max, your home is truly an oasis. The art is…" I really am unable to find the words to describe what I see. It's so new to me. None of my friends have enough money to afford even the smallest pieces in his home—even if we combined our savings, I still doubt we could afford the tax on some of these masterpieces.

"You like the décor?"

"I love it. It's so refined."

"My mom instilled a love of art in us."

"Us?" I ask, surprised. "You have siblings?"

"Yes, I have two brothers—Gabriel, the eldest and Lucas, the baby. I'm the middle child."

"If you're the middle child, your older brother must be a trillionaire, since they say the eldest of the family is usually the most ambitious."

"Actually, it's usually the eldest and the youngest since the baby likes to find a way of standing out."

"You redefine the rules."

"I always have, Candy." His eyebrow arches. It's clear we're no longer talking about family dynamics.

"Your parents must be proud of your extraordinary success." Since I'm determine to hold it together regardless of the fact he's oozing gorgeousness, I gently veer the conversation to a less suggestive topic.

"My mom does love to brag about her three sons." *He's being modest.* "I'm sure your parents must also be extremely proud of your accomplishments. You're a trailblazer in many ways."

A pang of sorrow hits me. I share a lot on my personal blog and with the readers of *Sassy* magazine, but only a handful of people on this planet know I'm an orphan.

"I'm sure," I whisper. I lower my eyes before he has time to read the sadness in my gaze. Thinking of my parents always brings back such painful memories.

"These stairs over here lead to the second floor. The view from upstairs is even more breathtaking than what you've seen so far."

"I can't imagine how anything can be more amazing than what you've shown me so far, but I'm willing to take your word for it."

"Let's go find out."

Before I even have time to respond, he's dragging me up a set of beautiful rustic-looking wood stairs.

"Wow, I've never seen anything like this before. What kind of wood is it?"

"It's reclaimed barn wood. It's old and it's full of character. I wanted to add more depth to this very modern space. I had to have this shipped from Canada, but it was worth every penny."

"Yes, it was," I say, unable to peel my eyes from the stairs. I'm so dazzled by the wood, I'm oblivious to the view in front of me. When I lift my eyes, I gasp in amazement. Even with night falling, the view is arresting. "This must be out of this world during the day. I mean, the sun must shine through this massive window and you're able to enjoy something few mortals will ever see."

"I'll often have my coffee up here. I'll sit on this couch over there and I'll admire the sun setting over Manhattan. It's truly like having a front-row seat to paradise."

"I have no doubt."

"Perhaps I'll have to invite you back for coffee one morning. Unless you'd like to stay tonight and catch the view in the morning." The burning lust in his eyes makes me nervous and excited at the same time.

His open invitation shocks me so much I take a step back. His boldness and forwardness silence me. I thought maybe Thursday's encounter was simply a way for me to help him move forward with his business goals, but I'm not so sure anymore.

"Max…" My voice sticks to my throat as I lower my eyes, blushing.

"Those rosy cheeks make me wonder if you're more surprised by my honesty or by the fact you might be open to the invitation."

I open my mouth, but before I can think of a retort, he brushes a loose strand of hair from my cheek and drops a finger to my lips.

He has a way of disarming me.

"You're right," he interrupts. "I should behave. At the very least I should explain a few things before inviting you to stay the night. Of course, I have two extra bedrooms other than my own, you're welcome to use either of them," he says, fighting a smile.

"Good to know. It's unfortunate, I didn't pack an overnight bag."

"Honey, what I have in mind doesn't require an overnight bag."

Holy. Shit.

My heart is beating so fast I fear he can see the palpitations against my chest.

"I hope you're hungry." I'm so grateful he changes the subject because I truly can't handle the raging passion filling me. I'm not used to men devouring me with their eyes the way Max does, nor am I used to men hitting on me like this.

"Yes, I am." I focus my gaze on the nocturnal view of the city to avoid the temptation I read in his eyes.

Since we had such a hearty breakfast, I skipped lunch. At least, I prefer this version of the facts rather than admitting to myself I was so nervously anticipating this evening I wasn't able to eat a bite all day.

"Good, let's go see what's for dinner."

Max grabs my hand to lead me down the stairs and I can't help look up contemplatively at the rooms on the second floor. *Which one is his bed-room?*

"Since there's still so much for me to discover about you, I asked the chef to prepare a classic American dinner. I'm not sure how adventurous you are when it comes to trying out new dishes, so I kept it simple."

"Oh. You didn't have to fuss over me so much, but you have me intrigued. What's on the menu?" I'm genuinely excited. George would have reprimanded me for even glancing twice at a dessert table.

"The chef left forty-five minutes before you got here, so it's ready and warm. I believe he mentioned we would be feasting on fresh brisket of beef *au jus* served with baby roasted potatoes drizzled with garlic butter, and he's also prepared a colorful assortment of heirloom carrots."

Hmmm. The last time those fancy carrots were on the menu was when I took ill-fated advice from Dr. Oz and ended up bumping into Vince—the mechanic-slash-wannabe-pilot. I hope this isn't a sign for me to run before a jealous wife gets off Max's private elevator and attacks me.

"You're right, this menu is worthy of a five-star mention." *Everything on the menu sounds exquisite. I can't believe he would have gone to all this trouble on my account.*

"I have chilled champagne in the wine fridge, would you like a glass?"

"Absolutely."

"I hope you like warm spinach dip." Max grabs a bottle of bubbly from his wine fridge and pops the cork with an expert hand before filling the flutes and handing me a glass.

"Thank you. It's one of my all-time favorite appetizers."

"We share something else in common." He winks. "I thought I had tasted a few great recipes, but my personal chef has taken a simple appetizer to celestial levels. Marcello is a real magician in the kitchen. I'm warning you, one bite and you'll be hooked. Every time he makes this for me when I have friends over, I can never convince my guests to go home. They want to camp at my door until Marcello returns the next day so they can beg him to prepare a new batch."

"I thought dinner sounded over-the-top delicious, but your description of this spinach dip is beyond insane."

"Should I call the paramedics right now before telling you about dessert?" he mocks.

"If it involves chocolate, you might as well call the cardiac surgery division at Mount Sinai Beth right now," I say dramatically. Anyone who knows me knows I'm a self-confessed chocoholic.

"I've spent quite some time reading your articles and I'm quite aware of your love of chocolate, which is why I asked Marcello to prepare his mouthwatering melting cakes. He's asked me to warm them up and top them with a scoop of vanilla ice cream and drizzle with a swirl of caramel sauce before serving them." Max narrows his eyes, awaiting my reaction.

"Call 911 immediately."

We both laugh.

"Seriously, Max, this whole menu sounds like a special feature from one of my favorite food-porn magazines."

"Food porn?"

"Cooking magazines. People like myself who can't cook to save their lives can still dream of impressing friends and family—that's why I keep renewing my subscription every year."

"I did good then by requesting the little cakes?"

"You did great."

"If you want to sit at the table for dinner, I'll bring the food over and we can dig in. It's very informal and I hope you're okay with things being so low-key."

My God, I never go to this length for my friends even for special occasions. We have a different definition of informal.

Chapter Three

Dinner is the second orgasmic experience Max has gifted me with in the last forty-eight hours. Every bite of the juicy brisket of beef is divine and I'll admit this meal might have changed my negative perception of heirloom carrots forever.

I expect dessert to be decadent, but the first bite sends my body into shock. The combination of warm chocolate cake, cold vanilla ice cream and sweet caramel sauce is truly a dessert food-porn dreams are made of. I've yet to enjoy a five-star meal at an upscale restaurant in New York or anywhere else in the world, but I'm certain this unforgettable meal rivals any one of them.

"I totally understand where your friends are coming from. I think I'm also going to have to start camping at your door and begging your chef to feed me."

"I'm glad you enjoyed the meal. I'll be sure to let Marcello know his efforts didn't go unnoticed.

Why don't we retreat to the couch? It will be far more enjoyable than these chairs. I'll put on some music and we can finish our espressos while overlooking the view."

"I love the way you think," I say, extracting my body from the dining chair. Max must notice my struggle since he rushes to my side.

Perhaps the second bottle of champagne was overkill.

"Those darn high heels of yours," he mocks, dropping his eyes to my feet.

"Right. The worst part is I'm addicted to them." I'll take any excuse in the book if it means feeling his hands wrapped around mine.

The plush dark grey L-shaped couch is conveniently located close to the window, allowing us to peek outside. Although Central Park is pitch black at this time of the night, New York never sleeps and the bright lights from the surrounding buildings illuminate the skyline. I'm so drunk with good food and tipsy from the bottles of Dom Pérignon, I kick off my high heels and stretch my legs out in front of me as I sink comfortably into the couch to rest my head.

"Who is singing?" I'm not a big music aficionado like Lexi, but I swear I've heard this song before.

"It's *Damn Your Eyes* by British singer-songwriter Alex Clare. This album is a few years old, but his music is timeless."

"I'm sure my girlfriend Lexi must own this album. She's really into music."

"And you?"

"I enjoy it and love discovering new artists, but I'm not hardcore like she is. My friend Devin is also into it, but I suspect it's because his boyfriend is one of the top DJs in the city," I say, closing my eyes for a second, soaking in this magical moment.

"I never meant to deceive you when we first met, Candy."

"I'm sorry?" His confession comes as a surprise given the mellow mood floating in the air.

"When you walked into Vanilla Beans and I caught a glimpse of your curves, I was mesmerized. When I took a second look, I realized I knew you, but I couldn't put my finger on it. I'm not sure what your friend and you were giggling about, but when she sucked in her cheeks and stomach in and both of you started laughing hysterically, it hit me. I grabbed my phone and there you were on *Sassy* magazine's website."

I guess this is confession time. I sit up on his couch and tuck my legs to the side before frowning. "Why does a successful billionaire CEO waste time on silly girly articles, Max?" I should be flattered a rich and powerful man would recognize me, but this makes no sense.

"My uncle loved his business with all his heart—he was practically married to those three companies. I needed to make sure we were forming the right media partnership. True, I could have trusted one of my talented staff members to do research, but this is too personal. After reading a few of your quirky articles, it became clear why the plus-size section of *Sassy* is so successful—it's thanks to you."

"There you go again, throwing compliments my way and making me blush."

"When I bumped into you at the Bymark hotel, I took advantage of the serendipitous moment to get to know you better. I felt keeping the conversation light and fun would allow me to get to know the real Candy as opposed to someone trying to pitch me. I needed the peace of mind of knowing my family's legacy was in good hands. I didn't want to be another corporate account with deep pockets *Sassy* magazine used to jump on the new trend of honoring plus-size beauties. I needed to know you were real."

"Was I real enough for you? Did I pass the test with flying colors, Max?" My ticked-off tone surprises me.

"You were very real. So much so, I couldn't keep my hands off of you." Without warning he slides his muscular body next to mine.

Damn. He had to go there.

"Sweet Candy." Max kisses the side of my neck, sending ripples of desire straight to my nipples. "I have a suspicion I won't be able to contain myself around you tonight either."

My heart is beating five hundred miles per second as my breathing turns fast and shallow.

Bending over, he places a hard kiss on my lips and leaves me panting.

"What happened on the forty-first floor was…" I place my hands against his chest, trying to distance myself from him as I desperately try to keep some sense of control over the situation.

"What I'd give to fill my hands with your full breasts again, Candy," he says, leaning so close he's inches away from my lips.

"Max, this cannot ever happen again between us. You're one of our biggest clients and I don't want to screw things up." I don't even sound convincing to myself.

The thought of his long fingers slick with my wetness, sliding into my pussy, pushing deep inside me, makes me want to strip naked, drop down on my knees and suck him like I've never sucked another man in my life. *Fuck, get a grip. One time was a mistake. Twice would be asking for trouble.*

"Nice sentiment, but it's a pretty worthless deterrent considering the look-at-me dress you've selected for the evening. Every flirty roll of your hips under this soft jersey dress is like an open invitation to seduce you again, Candy."

"Please don't," I attempt to protest, pressing my palm against his chest to stop him from getting any closer.

"Do you know Françoise Sagan?"

"Huh? I can't say I do." *Where is he going with his question?*

"She was a French playwright, novelist, and screenwriter. Françoise and I share a common belief. *A dress makes no sense unless it inspires men to take it off of a woman's body.* Honey, yours make me want to rip it off with my teeth."

Jesus.

"The consequences of us hooking up again are more than I can handle." I lick my lips and brush my hair away from my face. I'm suddenly burning up. His presence is overpowering.

His eyes are fixed on my lips and when they meet mine, I know he knows I'm bluffing. "Of course I understand your concern and that would be acceptable if I wasn't so attracted to you."

Oh, God. He's not playing fair.

"I can't put into words how much I enjoyed the hell out of having your warm, curvy body up against mine when I was claiming your lips. Between you and me, I wouldn't mind picking up where we left off."

"Max, you can't talk to me this way." I should be upset or even angry, but on the contrary, his naughty tease leaves me excited at the possibility of making out with him again—and frightened at the idea of losing my head like I did a few nights ago.

"I haven't been able to erase the image of your jade-green eyes watching me as I played with your sweet pussy."

"It was wrong. I shouldn't have allowed things to get out of hand." I force myself to block out how Max made me climax so hard my legs trembled for fifteen minutes straight. For the love of God, he's not helping here.

"You came so hard on Thursday, I want to see you lose your composure again."

Guilt slices through me the second he utters those words. I'm forced to relive the sweet moment his fingers plunged into my hungry pussy. He gave me an orgasm like I'd dreamt about for years, but I gave him nothing.

"Why the worried look?"

"I'm confused about Thursday."

"I doubt there was any room for confusion, but I'll humor you. What's troubling you?" He brushes my hair behind my shoulders.

"I was never able to…" I hesitate for a few seconds. I've never had this type of conversation with a guy before and I'm not certain how best to put into words what's been on my mind. "I thought men always wanted their needs met. I mean, you never came."

I'm not sure what I expected him to say, but I surely never thought he'd laugh aloud at my confession.

"Sweet Candy, Thursday was about taking pleasure in seeing you take pleasure. If you're so troubled, I can put your mind at ease. My cock is aching. The thought of teasing your soft pink nipples until you… Argh, your tits will be the end of me," he growls, cupping his cock. "I can pull down my jeans and I'm sure you won't feel this guilty once I come gushing into the back of your throat." He smiles. "Nothing would bring me more pleasure than to hold your head while you take my cock between your luscious lips."

"Max. Stop. I can't take this anymore. You're torturing me with your words."

"You know what I think about you? I think you've only been fucked by inexperienced boys who need a GPS system to figure out how to pleasure a woman like you. The sublime way you melted in my arms tells me you've never been with a man who can control you—dominate you."

"I don't need to be dominated," I babble. *What kind of woman does he think I am?*

"Why do you think you came so hard the other night? It's because I dominated every single one of your senses for my own pleasure while making sure you'd enjoy the ride."

He leans in again and threads his fingers in my hair. When he tightens his grip, I panic and try to wrench away. With a steady pull on my hair, Max forces me to lock eyes with him. I open my mouth to protest, but he beats me to it.

"No talking. From this point on, it's all about enjoying each other," he growls.

I press my thighs together to control my throbbing clit. His words are more potent than cocaine. Not only has he silenced me, he's managed to turn me on so much I'm sure he could ignite me with his breath.

"Much better. Look at you. Feisty. Spirited. Sweet. Vulnerable. How am I supposed to resist you?" Max releases me as suddenly as he fisted my hair and leaves me trembling with desire. He cups my chin in his hand, leaning in to brush my lips. "Your body is quivering in my arms, which confirms you want me as much as I want you."

Fuck.

"We can sit here all night and disagree on pros and cons of taking things further, or I can relieve my rock-hard erection inside your aching pussy. The choice is yours."

I'm completely under his spell. His hazel eyes pin me to his couch even as his strong hand keeps my head from moving. His voice, his command and his assertiveness keep me silenced.

God, I'm going to melt if these waves of heat keep raging inside me.

I stare up at him helplessly and I know deep inside my core, if he wants to take me right here in front of this massive window overlooking the calmness of Central Park, I'd let him without protesting.

"I want you so badly," I confess, unable to deny the yearning inside my soul.

"Good answer, sweetness."

His finger runs over my lips, and I realize my mouth is open, my breathing fast. His cheeks crease in a smile and I can tell he has me exactly where he wants me.

He gets off the couch and bends down to scoop me up into his arms. My first reaction is to resist. *God, I'm no lightweight.*

"What's wrong?"

"I can walk."

"I'm sure you can. Trust me, I've been salivating over your hips under your clingy dress, but I want to carry you upstairs and throw your curvy body onto my mattress before I have my way with you. If you have a problem with that, deal with it." The next thing I know Max flings me over his shoulder and he's climbing the gorgeous barn wood steps to his bedroom.

Chapter Four

To my surprise, Max carries me up the flight of stairs leading to second floor as if I weigh twenty pounds.

He's not huffing and puffing. I guess I'm worrying about my weight for no good reason.

We've barely stepped through the door of his bedroom when it's kicked closed behind us and I'm pinned against the wall.

"Take off the dress so I can see which one of our creations you're wearing," he says, reaching out to touch something against the wall.

How did he know?

I'm about to protest when I notice in panic that he's turning on the lights in the room before dimming them slightly.

Oh, God, I don't have sex the first time with lights on. I much prefer the safety of darkness until I'm more at ease being naked in front of a new lover.

"Whoa. Your bedroom is impeccable and is so well decorated." I latch on to the décor as a way out of this situation, but he reads me like a book.

"Candy, do you have a problem with me admiring your gorgeous naked body?"

Well, when you put it in such flattering terms, maybe a little light won't hurt. I shake my head, too shy to answer, and he grins from ear to ear.

"Good. Now, take the dress off. I want to watch you strip and to be seduced by your naughty lingerie."

Damn, he always finds the perfect words to make me feel so sexy. I smile from under my lashes, slowly turning around and gathering my hair over my left shoulder.

"What are you doing?"

"You asked me to remove my dress," I answer, confused.

"I want to devour you with my eyes as you slip out of your dress. Don't you dare deny me the pleasure," he says in a commanding voice.

"When you say such intoxicating things, it's impossible for me to refuse you." I turn around.

I pull at the sash of my wrap dress, conscious he's focused solely on me. I'm still determined to avoid his gaze when he takes a step and closes the gap between us. *My God, I'm so tiny next to him without my heels.* His first touch against my naked skin startles me. He caresses my neck with one hand while opening my dress fully with the other.

"Your touch is so sensual," I say softly.

"It's because your skin begs to be touched, Candy."

I pull my arms out of the sleeves, letting the dress pool on the floor at my feet without ever leaving his gaze.

He inhales sharply when he lowers his eyes. "You naughty, naughty girl. You're wearing garter belts."

"Maybe." I surely wasn't going to walk here unequipped. Garter belts are the most incredible creation ever. It doesn't matter if you're skinny or a voluptuous plus-size girl, men always lose it when they cast their hungry eyes on a pair of these babies. Since I only own Sexy Curves lingerie, it was a matter of selecting the design sure to stop his heart. From his reaction, I'd say he likes this vintage-inspired style, which marries sheer black and a delicate pale pink floral motif. I hope the see-through fabric revealing my nipples and hugging my ass gives him a hard-on.

"Holy shit, you look dangerous in these. I'm not even going to attempt to figure out which pieces of our collection you're wearing, but this is a heart-arresting combo on you. They are so seductively hot, I'm considering ripping them off with my teeth." He's trailing his eyes down my body and even more slowly back up to my face. I don't think I've ever felt more desired in my life than I do right here, right now.

"Please be gentle," I whisper, and for a brief moment, something raw flashes in his eyes.

"Hmph, perhaps that's a request you might have for one of the boys you've been with in the past, but you should know I don't do gentle. Life is too short to tiptoe. Your beautiful body is mine for the taking and I intend on having you the way I want—hard and rough." His finger traces the contour of my trembling lips.

"Oh." I exhale when the impact of his words fully hits me.

These are uncharted territories for me and he leaves me speechless. No one has ever been so commanding with me before. Perhaps I should be offended by his boldness, but I'm lapping up every second of it.

"Do I shock you?"

I nod instead of answering, locking my gaze into his.

"I'm about to shock you even more, sweetness." He fists my panties and rips them to shreds.

"Ah," I gasp, panting, surprised by how quickly my panties came undone.

"Remind me to ask my assistant to send you one set of each of our collections on Monday morning. You look too damn good in them and I have a bad habit of ripping them apart to have free access to your pussy." His smile is dangerous as his eyes devour me from head to toe.

"You don't have to…" I start, unsure I should accept his gift.

"It's not a suggestion, sweetness."

"Oh, of course." *Christ.* A part of me is scorning myself for accepting such an over-the-top gift from a near stranger, but another part of me is exhilarated at the idea of parading my new collection of lingerie for him. "I'm not sure what else you can say that would leave me more tongue-tied."

"Do you see the large mirror over there?"

"Yes," I respond nervously.

"I want you on your knees in front of it so I can fully take in your big round ass as I fuck your mouth with my cock. I want to come gushing into the back of your throat while I admire your wiggling butt in the mirror as I stand in front of you, dominating you."

I can't say I'm usually comfortable giving blowjobs to guys. It's always so messy and I feel awkward. Until this moment, I could have truly lived for the rest of my life without ever going down on another man, but Max is different—I desperately want to suck him dry. *What is it about this guy? Since meeting him, he's transformed me into this daring woman I don't recognize.*

"It seems I've shocked you again." He grins, reaching down to his waist.

I nod. My stomach is in knots, but it's an exhilarating sensation.

"Are you willing to submit yourself totally to me tonight? Whatever I want, you provide. No protests. No questions asked."

I've never considered giving myself so wholly to a man, but standing so close to his rock-hard body, I can't think of anything more thrilling than surrendering to him.

"Yes." I tremble like a leaf, amazed at how his raunchy words turn me on.

"Candy, are you sure you're willing to allow me to fuck your mouth until you can't take it anymore, pound your pussy with my hungry cock until you come screaming out my name and make you forget every other teenage boy who's ever pretended to fuck you?"

"I'm totally yours, Max," I whisper.

"Louder," he orders.

"Yes. Take me. Do with me as you wish. I want it all. I need it all. Please," I beg. God, I don't even recognize my own voice and I can't explain the source of this insatiable yearning.

Victory flashes on his face. "I love it when we're on the same page," he drawls.

I watch him watch me as he unzips his jeans and rolls them down before stepping out of them. Without wasting a second, he strips out of his boxer briefs and he stands in front of me—as gorgeous as a Greek god. My eyes bulge when I see his cock. *Mother of God, George might not be the best reference, but Max is huge.*

"I hope you like what you see," he declares, pulling his Henley shirt over his head before flinging it to the other side of the room.

I catch my breath. "You're massive." His impossibly hard cock is intimidating. As my eyes trail up his torso, I gasp.

If I were a gambling woman, I would have lost good money. Although dimmed, the light is bright enough to allow me to make out the tattoo running from the top of his left shoulder all the way down to his wrist. I'm so fascinated, I forget a drop-dead gorgeous guy is standing in front of me naked.

"Your arm…" I open my mouth, but I'm unable to explain my hesitation. Perhaps the fear stems from the fact I've never been with a man with tattoos before. *Men with tattoos are usually bad, aren't they?*

"Does it surprise you?"

"It does."

"Why? I don't look like the bad-boy type who would get inked?"

"Honestly, you don't."

"We all have something we're hiding, Candy. Something so deep and so personal very few people in the world know the secret we're so desperately trying to preserve. Does this make sense to you?"

Oh, very much so.

He strokes my cheek as I trace the outline of his chest. His face is extremely serious and I'm too intimidated to touch his intricate body art, so I stare, intrigued.

"There's a long story behind this tattoo, but right now, I want your lips around my dick so badly I can barely think. We'll have to wait until morning for me to share more."

He turns around and walks towards the mirror, giving me a prime view of his firm round ass. *Damn.*

"Remove the stockings and the garter belt. I want your pussy ready for the taking."

I obey, slowly undoing the snaps before rolling down the thin stockings. I drop each one of them on the floor near me and I wiggle out of the delicate lace fabric hugging my thighs. I'm quite aware his eyes are on me—analyzing every single one of my movements. I catch sight of his erection from under my lashes and I hold my breath.

If he fucks me with his massive cock, I won't be able to walk for days, if not weeks.

"Good girl. Now, I want you to slowly take off your bra. As pretty as it is, I want to be able to squeeze your tits while I fuck your mouth."

"Max, you're so raw." The words come out before I'm able to catch myself.

"It's a problem?"

"On the contrary. It's a turn-on. I don't think I can take much more."

"I'll decide what you can take and what you can't. Remove the bra and then come over here."

Reaching behind me with shaking hands, I unhook my bra and pull one strap down. As I ready myself to pull down the second one, my breasts fall so heavy against my chest they collide. I lift my eyes and hold his gaze flirtatiously before extending my arm to let the bra drop to the floor. We both follow the falling lingerie before locking eyes again. I'm not sure what's taken over me, but I cup my bare breasts, pulling my nipples, and arch my back with pleasure. His eyes are fixated on my fingers as I squeeze and pull my engorged boobs. I'm so taken by the moment, I lift one heavy breast and bring it to my mouth. I lick my hard nipple so daringly, I swear I feel the gush of my juices running down my thighs. I never leave his gaze. I want him to know how much I want him. *Je-*

sus, I've never done anything this sensual in my life in front of a man.

"Do you have any clue what you're doing to me right now?" His voice is strained and his eyes are filled with raw desire. "Come here, Candy." I get on my toes and I glide towards him. I barely have time to get close before he reaches out both hands to grab my breasts.

"Shit." I tilt my head back at his warm touch. "Fuck, I want you." My words leave me feeling more exposed than being naked in front of him.

"Do you?"

"Mm-hmm. Badly."

"Don't worry, you'll get all of me. Now, get on your knees, open your pretty mouth and make me come." He points down in front of him without another word.

I slide to the floor and I realize being naked in front of him for the first time doesn't bother me nearly as much as I had feared. As I steady myself, he fists his cock and it strains, massive in his hands, and I have to bite my tongue to keep from moaning. I'm certain he's going to rip me in half. But would I be able to resist him?

Max has so much power over me. If you had told me two weeks ago I'd let a man have this much control, I would have laughed because most of the men I've been with were wimps. I can't imagine it any other way now. I don't have to focus on anything else but the aching need possessing my body and the single, overpowering craving—for him.

"I doubt I'll be able to take you fully in," I say, mesmerized by his size.

"I'm sure you'll manage. Place your hands behind your back and interlace your fingers. I don't want to see your hands move. Do you understand me?"

I nod.

"Answer me, Candy," he growls.

"I understand. I can't move my hands."

"Good girl. Now open wide, sweetness."

Without warning, he plunges his dick into my mouth in one single stroke. He hits the back of my throat with such brute force, I nearly gag. *Oh my God, he's huge.* He doesn't stop, not for one second. He grips my hair in his fist and thrusts again, hungry, even savage, filling my mouth like no man has ever done before him, setting my body on fire like a volcano.

"Look at your big, beautiful, naked ass wiggling. What a fucking amazing view," he teases. "And it's all mine to enjoy."

I lift my eyes towards his face and I moan into his cock.

"Have you ever wrapped your pouty lips around a dick this thick, Candy?" he asks as he buries his hands in my hair, yanking my face down, controlling the tempo. "Those scrawny teenage boys with small dicks you've been fucking can't measure up."

I shake my head instead of answering, refusing to let go of him for even one second. What is there to say? He's the biggest man I've ever taken into my mouth—period.

"Hmmm," I moan, closing my lips around his erection and sucking, sucking, sucking.

I'm used to soft and steady blowjobs, but this isn't it. Max is delivering on his promise and he's fucking my mouth fast, hard and deep.

He's merciless.

"Take me in deeper," he commands as he rocks his hips back and forth.

I inhale into his cock to prepare myself for the next thrust of his hips and to my surprise I take him all the way.

"You're such a dirty girl. You're eating my big dick like a famished woman," he chuckles. He leans into me and pinches my right nipple so hard, I squeal as the intoxicating current travels down to my throbbing nub. My head is still spinning from the experience when he slaps my left breast so hard it jiggles against my chest, sending me into a sensual frenzy.

Shit.

"Yeah, don't ever forget it. From now on, those magnificently huge tits of yours are mine. I can suck, bite and tease them at will. I love how they're so heavy, they hang ready for me to wrap my lips around them." His words are so certain. "Since meeting you, I've been dreaming of fucking your tits and leaving my white mark all over them." He's not asking, he's warning me of things to come.

I don't care if he's demanded I keep my hands clutched behind my back. I don't give a damn if my body is rising and falling with every stroke he delivers. Who gives a fuck if I can't control his cadence or how deep he hits the back of my throat. All I care about is making him come hard.

"You look innocent enough, but you're good at this, Candy. I'm impressed."

I answer with a whimper. I can't believe he said I was good at this.

"I can't tell you how hard it makes me when you let out those helpless grunts. You're so vulnerable right now with your hands clenched behind your back, on your knees in front of me—it's a big turn-on."

My God, this man's dirty talk is going to drive me to the edge.

Armed with confidence from his naughty words of encouragement, I swirl my tongue around his cock before sliding my mouth down his shaft.

If I have to choke on his dick, so be it. At least I'll die content.

"Christ, Candy. Yeah, take me all in. Suck me dry."

Max thrusts into my mouth with force. I suck him like a starved woman and I take him in a little bit more each time.

"My cock is hitting the ridges of your throat and it's driving me crazy. You're so eager. Are you enjoying this? I want to hear you answer me, Candy."

Reluctantly I unwrap my lips from around his cock. "Yes," I say, catching my breath. "Taking you in deep is making me so wet I'm dying to touch myself to relieve the tension between my legs."

"Don't you dare stroke your clit. I intend on gorging on it once you make me come. Now put my cock back into your mouth," he commands. "Yeah," he lets out when I close my mouth around him. "How deep can you take me? Can you suck me all the way down to my balls? Are you going to stick your tongue out and lick my balls while my cock is down your throat? Jesus, you're even naughtier than I ever imagined."

I can only whimper. I'm so turned on my clit is aching for me to rub it until I come undone, but his power over me forces me to keep my hands locked behind my back.

"You're torturing me," he groans as he pumps harder. "I'm so fucking close. I know I'll never be as sweet as your pussy, but I hope you like the way I taste because you're about to taste a lot more of me, Candy. I want to spew so much of my cum inside your mouth it spills out of the side and I want to watch as you struggle to lick every last drop."

Holy shit, the man has a dirty mouth I can't get enough of.

Max's whole massive, throbbing length is buried deep. My eyes are on him as I watch him take pleasure. I blink twice, unwilling at first to see it, but when I blink a third time, there it is—the urgency, the ecstasy. I sob in an eager moan, unable to contain myself. *I can't believe I'm able to do this to a man.*

"Fuck, you're so hungry, Candy."

Christ, I'm so close to losing it. Each one of his sentences is acting like a tornado of lust, stirring every single one of my kinkiest desires. I can't lie to myself. I want it. I want it all and I'm willing to beg for it until he gives me every single last drop of his cum. I'm nearly feverish. Max is taking me to new sexual heights I've never even imagined.

"Christ, you suck me so well," he grunts, gripping my head tighter. "I'm going to fucking feed you, Candy."

I bob my head back and forth once, twice, three times, delirious from his words, and he comes with a savage cry.

"Fuck," Max roars, spurting his cum down my throat in a hot gush as pleasure ripples through me like a wave. To my surprise, his excitement causes me to clench my pussy so hard I come with his cock still in my mouth. *God. What has he done to me?*

For the first time since he ordered me down on my knees I dare to unlock my arms from behind my back and I hold on to his legs for support. My sudden climactic explosion has robbed me of all my strength. If I don't hold onto him I will tumble and fall.

I meet his eyes and I wipe the trail of come dripping down my chin. He reaches down to scoop up a few drizzles from my breast before forcing every last drop of him inside my mouth. *Fuck that's hot.*

"Damn, I've been gypped. Oh, baby, had I known you were this good at sucking cock, I would have forced you down on your knees last Thursday when we first connected so you could have made me come the way you just did. With your incredible skills, your ex-boyfriends must still be mourning the breakup. You can suck my cock any time you want." Max leans down to help me to my feet, but I'm so spent my legs give in and he has to hold me closer to him.

"Did I work you too hard?" He looks down at me with his piercing hazel eyes and I melt inside.

"Until today I never imagined taking a man into my mouth could become such an out-of-body experience."

He laughs before kissing the top of my head. "I'm not done with you yet, Candy. There's a lot more I want to offer you tonight."

"It could be my inexperience talking, but how can there be more?"

"It would be ungentlemanly of me not to make you come multiple times in my mouth after you've made me come so hard I nearly lost my mind."

What is this guy talking about? I've never climaxed multiple times in my life.

"I want to gorge on your pussy while your luscious thighs press against my head as you beg for mercy. My only response will be to squeeze your nipples so hard, the sweet sensation of pleasure and pain will silence you."

Jesus. How does he keep doing this to me—robbing me of my ability to retort to his saucy comments? His wicked words will be my undoing.

"Don't look so surprised, Candy, we both know you want to come all over my mouth."

"Oh." My cheeks flame up. *Am I so obvious?*

"It was sweet to watch you orgasm with my cock still in your mouth, but I can assure you you'll enjoy it a whole lot more when my eager tongue is rubbing your clit and toying with you until you climax."

I gasp for air, sensation running straight down to my clit like a shockwave. A deep pressure is building between my thighs. I'm aching to feel his lips wrapped around my throbbing node. I don't have a chance. Max is so close, murmuring such raunchy promises in my ear, the ache is unbearable.

"Do you remember how you dissolved in my hands the other night?"

"Uh-huh. How can I forget?"

Max flashes a victory smile before taking a step back and leaning into me. He reaches between my thighs, pressing hard against my clit with such deadly precision it sends me moaning as I tilt my head back for relief. "I know you like it when I touch you right there."

His fingers rub my swollen node with a torturous rhythm. The sensation sends pleasure ricocheting straight down to my toes and back again. My legs give way. I push my pussy against his hand, hoping to increase my arousal. I grab my boobs in my hand and I skate my fingertips around my nipples at the same mind-blowing pace Max is circling my clit. I've never been so in touch with my body.

"Fuck, it turns me on even more to watch you play with your tits."

"I want your mouth on me," I whisper.

"You want my tongue lapping at you like I've never tasted you before," Max "You dirty little girl, you want me to get down on my knees and lick you, don't you? You don't care if you have to beg for it because you know it will feel so good. Look at me, Candy. Don't close your eyes on me." He grabs my jaw with his right hand and forces me to lock eyes with him.

"Ah," I scream out. My legs tremble so much I grip his arm and dig my nails into his body art. *Oh God, his skin...* I can't describe the roughness and unevenness of his skin. I'm too far gone to figure anything out right now.

His fingers pulse harder with every word until he pulls away and I whimper out in frustration. I'm like an addict who's been denied and I can't stand the pain.

"Max. Please. Don't stop," I beg, not caring how much I have to grovel to convince him to continue stroking my clit the way he does so well. I sway my hips back and forth against his hand to entice him to continue, but instead he extracts his fingers from my pussy and forces them inside my mouth.

"Lick."

I obey. He watches me lick my salty juices, enjoying every second of forbidden pleasure.

"Now the real fun begins." Before I can react, he scoops me off my feet and flings me over his shoulder before walking decisively towards his king-size bed. He throws me against the mattress with such force, I hold on to the sheet to avoid falling to the ground. Without a word, he yanks me towards him. I lift my arms over my head and grip the sheets to slow my slide for a second or two. I'm no fool. I know nothing I do or say will prevent him from having his way with me.

"Oh, fuck, Max, touch me, lick me, suck me," I plead, desperate. He chuckles. *He knows he has me where he wants me.*

He doesn't wait for me to beg twice. Max dips his tongue inside my wet pussy and I cry out, bucking against his mouth. He reaches one hand up and pinches my nipples, sending me spiraling in a vortex of hedonistic pleasure. This is too much. He's gorging on my clit like a wolf on its prey. I need release so badly, I think I'm going to die.

Lord.

I lift my hips in the air, desperate, and he rewards me by sliding a finger into me, pulsating up against my wall, driving me towards the edge while he flicks my hard node with the tip of his tongue. Without warning, he pins me down, controlling my pleasure.

"Do you remember when I told you about your tits belonging to me now? Well, make that double for your pussy, and don't you ever forget it."

I'm so dazed, it takes me a few seconds to lift my head from the bed to meet his gaze, but when I do, he's already focused on eating my pussy again.

Max is lapping and plunging his tongue deep inside me so mercilessly, I can only shake my head from left to right in an attempt to temper the looming orgasm threatening to explode inside me. His lips crash down against my pussy as he thrusts a second finger inside me, stretching my tightness forcefully. His tongue is more demanding and rubs faster and faster until I yank my hips up, clamping my thighs against his head. I start to quake, my orgasm building, and I close my eyes. *Fuck, I'm coming.* I come undone against his mouth with a scream I've never heard leave my body before. The spasms ripple through me with such intensity, it's as if I'm freefalling from a cliff into heaven.

"Oh, Max," I scream out, reaching for his head.

He brushes my hand away before pushing his fingers into a place I've never explored before—my ass. His fingers are still slick with my own juices and slide in easily.

Mother of God.

How can something so wrong, so forbidden, so kinky leave me panting like this? It's like nothing else I've experienced so far. None of the men I've been with have ever dared to touch me there, but Max doesn't even ask—he simply takes.

"You're impossibly tight down there, Candy. You might need a few warm-up sessions before you're able to handle my big cock."

What? I tense, stricken by panic. There's no way I'm allowing him to go there. *Good girls don't have anal sex, right?*

"Don't worry. It's not going to happen tonight, sweetness. Relax, don't fight it—enjoy it."

My mind is resisting, unwilling to allow myself to soak in the pleasurable tremors, but my body has already given in. *Holy shit.* I shudder through another orgasmic shockwave as Max pushes his fingers deeper into my backside, all the way into the knuckle, while he presses his lips against my clit.

"Oh, oh, oh," I scream out as my body comes apart around his tongue. The climactic spasms hit me so hard I stop breathing for a second. *This is the most intense orgasm ever.*

I lie on his king-size bed with my eyes shut, savoring every ripple traveling through my exhausted body. My legs are wide open and I'm gasping for air while Max blows hot air against my fiery pussy.

"I hope you don't think we're done yet."

Good Lord, I need a minute or two.

"Huh?" I'm so spent, I can't even lift my head to look at him. "I don't think my body can handle another orgasm, Max."

"You can't possibly be serious. I'm certain you have at least one more in you, but I'm gambling on two."

"You're so ambitious," I tease.

"Candy, my cock is raging. I'm so hard I was practically fucking the mattress while I was tongue-fucking you. I need to lose myself inside you," he says, getting back on his feet. He walks to the night table near his bed and opens a drawer. He walks back to the bed where I'm still in a post-climactic semi-conscious state and hands me a box. "Why don't you help me sheathe my cock so I can slide into the warmth of your pussy."

I roll to my side and look at the box of condoms as if it's a dangerous object. *Oh, God, this is awkward.* I open my mouth a few times, but I'm not sure how to say what's on my mind without revealing how much I lack experience with men.

"What? You don't like this brand of condom?"

"I'm sure they're fine," I mumble. "It's…" I reach out and grab the box before getting up on my elbows. "Well…"

"I'm listening," he presses.

"I don't know how to put one on. I've never had to do it before," I whine. "The guy was always the one who took the lead." In an effort to avoid looking like a complete newbie, I attempt to open the box, but it's a disaster. I fumble to open the packaging as if I have six thumbs. "Crap." I finally manage to open it, but in my haste, the cardboard rips wide open and a flurry of condoms spill out onto the bed. I'm feeling pretty sorry for myself, but Max roars with laughter.

"Sweet Candy. Your innocence is such a turn-on."

"I was afraid you'd be upset."

"Why would I be upset?" he says, climbing back into the bed next to me. "Why don't we try together." He picks up one single packet from the spill and hands it to me before pushing the others onto the floor. "It's not complicated. Take the condom out and roll it down my dick."

I so can do this.

I give myself a silent pep talk and I obey. My hands shake, but I'm determined. I cover the head of his cock and try to roll the condom down his shaft, but it won't budge. I try to push harder, but still nothing is happening. He contorts his face in a grimace and I instantly know I've screwed up. He looks down at his cock and looks up at me before laughing again.

"You're almost there. It won't roll down because you have it the wrong way," he mocks. "If you keep tugging at my cock like this with the condom, I won't be able to fuck you because I'll be in so much pain. Try again," he says, reaching onto the floor to grab another one.

"Oh, okay."

I take the second condom he throws onto the bed and I unroll it with tentative fingers and place it on top of his very big erection. "Damn," I let out, annoyed. The whole process seems to take an eternity, but to my surprise, Max patiently strokes my hair. I take a breath to calm down and I finally manage to slide the darn condom over him, cautious to avoid ripping the shield along the way.

"Candy, you're rolling this so carefully—too carefully. It's as if you're covering a glass object instead of my hungry cock."

"I'm sorry."

"Don't be. I'm impatient to fuck you so hard the bed drops into the penthouse below us, but you're taking your sweet time."

"Oh, jeez." I blush.

"I love it when you come all over my mouth and looking down at your lips wrapped around my cock as I fist your hair is surreal, but nothing will replace being inside you for the first time."

Dang.

"I don't know what to say to that."

He smiles and strokes my cheek. "You don't have to say a thing, sweetness." He leans down and kisses my forehead.

"Good news, I got it all the way." I beam proudly, looking at his throbbing dick.

"You did, didn't you?" I'm expecting him to return my smile, but instead he flashes an evil grin before pulling the condom off and tossing it away. "Let's start from scratch."

"What did you do that for? I had it right. You said so yourself," I lament.

"You did, but do it again and this time don't be so tentative. I want you to put the condom on decisively so I can fuck you and unleash my fury on you."

His rawness catches me off guard and turns me on at the same time. I grab the third condom Max throws at me and I rip it open with my teeth. I slide out the shield from the packet and I cover his cock in one swift movement—without any hesitations.

"And now?" I ask anxiously.

He looks down at his cock and his cheeks crease into a huge smile. "Perfect."

"Yes! I got it right."

He straddles me and places his cock right at my entrance. Without even having to reach down, I know I'm dripping wet again.

"Slide my cock into your warm pussy, Candy," he whispers so low I barely hear him, but the electricity burning from his eyes is unmistakable.

"Damn," I exhale when the impact of his words hit me. Max pushes onto his hands to give me more space to slide my hands between our bodies until I reach his cock. My first instinct is to shove him deep inside me so I can be dominated by his power, but something takes over me. Instead of swallowing his dick with my pussy, I rub Max's erection over my wetness. "Ohhhh," I let out, closing my eyes, and a small moan slips from me before I can catch myself. "Your cock is going to be my undoing," I whisper.

"I feel the same about your pussy," he whispers back.

I lick my lips and I flutter my lashes open so I can look down at the space between us, watch myself play with him and observe his reaction as I tease my clit with the head of his dick. *This is insanely hot.*

"I could come just by rubbing your cock against my nub," I sigh.

"You could, but you'd be missing out."

I run my free hand up his chest and I cup his neck, murmuring, "I think you're right."

"I'm warning you, I can't be gentle. I want you too much."

"I don't want you to be gentle."

"Good."

Max slides in carefully at first, but once he's halfway inside me, he rams in with such force I gasp. As he thrusts in and out of me, crushing my body with his weight, I start my slow and blissful descent into the chasm of ecstasy. I look up at him, but I no longer seem to be able to see his face. Waves of pleasure take over me and I can only focus on one thing— feeling him filling me up.

"Look at you. Your eyes are glazed and I haven't even gotten started yet." Max has barely delivered his warning before he picks up the pace, sucking savagely on my neck, growling like a wild beast and grunting with each swing of his hips.

"Are you okay?" he asks, moving in a slower cadence. "I'm not too rough?"

"Is that all you've got?" I tease, knowing full well he'll make me pay for my cockiness.

"I was trying to be a gentleman, but obviously, you respond better to me when I'm an animal." He grins.

"I'll take you any way you want me to," I pant.

"There's no reason for me to slow down, then."

"None whatsoever," I whisper, turning into his hand when he sweeps a few strands of damp hair off my forehead.

"You know what?"

I'm expecting raunchy repartee that will make me blush, but he surprises me.

"You look so fucking perfect under me."

No man has ever said anything remotely close to this to me before. Instead of answering, I nod as a way of letting him know I feel the same way he does and I push myself up, unconsciously telling him with my body that I need more of him. Something shifts in his eyes and I know the sensual moment we just shared is over.

"Fuck, I want you, Candy. I want you so much it hurts."

Max pulls back, starting an easy rhythm before switching gear and turning feral on me. I grab his ass cheeks with both hands and press his body into me so he can penetrate me even deeper.

"Jesus, Max," I hiss.

Max's cadence is frantic and then he slows down and eventually stops, kissing me deeply. He sucks my tongue, stealing every one of my carnal sounds, swallowing them like a greedy bastard. *God, I love how he does that.*

He abandons my lips and returns his focus to fucking me. He shifts from lazy pushing into quicker, more forceful thrusts. I answer with mirrored movements of my hips, arching into him and squeezing my thighs around his waist as if I'll never let him go.

"Oh, yes, yes, yes," I plead as he pumps into me inexorably.

"Candy, I love your hoarse voice and the way you're begging for more."

"Max, make me come," I let out with eyes half closed, desperate for another release.

"You want me to make you scream out my name like you did when I pinched your clit between my lips a few minutes ago?" He presses his face to my neck.

He had to go there?

Too consumed to answer, I grip his ass and dig my fingernails sharply into his flesh.

"Argh! Bad girl," he growls.

Max pulls my right leg up, pushing my knee to my chest, and he lets loose as if to punish me for my boldness. He fucks me fast and hard, sliding in and out of me, demanding so much more than I thought I could ever give to one man. I bite his shoulder, hoping to containing the fireball-like meteor mounting inside me, but to no avail. *I'm coming.*

"Sweet Mother of God."

"You're close, baby?"

I nod, letting him know that I'm nearing the edge—again.

"Good. I want you to go off like a bomb when you come with me inside you—dominating you."

Yeah, that won't be hard.

Max thrusts in and out of me with such fervor, I fear he'll make good on his promise and fuck me until his bed drops to the floor below us.

"Shit, shit, shit."

It's explosive the way my orgasm builds beneath my skin, first as a flush, then a tightening of my muscles until I'm shaking. *How can this be so surreal?* I'm sweaty, my heart is beating hard against my chest and I beg unintelligible words beneath him, conscious I've lost all control.

"Don't hold back, Candy."

"Max…" I struggle to speak as my body starts convulsing underneath him.

"That's it," he whispers. "I'm not coming until you come, baby, and I can't hold back my own release much longer. You have to let go and succumb. Now."

His words are more than I can bear. I squeeze my eyes shut, fighting to tame the intensity of this third looming orgasm, but I can't. Max is fucking me so thoroughly, I can only let go and enjoy the ride. "Christ, I'm right there," I hiss.

My body bows off the bed as I scream out my climax. Max doesn't spare me. He moves through my hedonistic explosion, taking every single second of pleasure he can draw out from my exhausted body.

"God." I loosen my grip on his ass and let my arms fall onto the mattress. Max props himself up on his hands, looking down at me, smiling in victory. "You keep doing this to me."

"And it's bad?"

"On the contrary. It's all good—really good," I say with a languid drawl in my voice. "But you…"

"Shh." He shushes me gently by brushing his lips against mine. "I'm not done yet," he warns me. He caresses my cheek, his cock slowly sliding in and out. "One more?"

"You can't be serious."

"Every time you say that, I prove to you that I'm as serious as the dick fucking you right now."

I laugh, knowing there's no point in arguing with him.

Max moves one hand between us, rubbing my clit back to life. I'm going to be so sore after this, but who cares? This man is giving me more pleasure than I ever thought possible. If being sore is the price to pay, I won't object.

He strokes my node while pumping inside me rhythmically. To my surprise, after only a few minutes I arch and my hips start rocking faster with him. "Oh, Max…" *How can he ignite my body like this?*

I curl into him, biting down his shoulder to his chest. "Come inside me, Max," I gasp, dragging my nails possessively down his back. "I want to feel the weight of your body on top of mine once you've climaxed."

"Fuck," he grunts.

It's as if my words cut the last chain of his self-control. Max hits deeper and harder, prolonging my own release with his thumb pressed to my clit. I throw my head back into the pillow, hands back on his ass, pulling him forward while I rock up into him.

"I love seeing you undone like this—your lips parted, your hair wild all around your head against the pillow and you giving yourself completely to me."

Yes. I'm coming.

Unbridled pleasure floods my veins, hot and frantic. It's such a rush, it's as if I've been plugged into an electrical outlet—every inch of my skin is alive and buzzing with excitement.

Max collapses onto me, screaming out my name. "Jesus fucking Christ, Candy."

Wow.

We're both breathing heavy, trying to lower our heart rate. After a few minutes, he breaks the silence.

"Goddammit, Candy," he pants. "That was so insanely good... I can't... I can't even think straight anymore." He drops quick, sweet kisses all over my face and the contrast between the childish boy and the über-alpha male who just fucked me to the point where I think I'll never walk again makes him that much more endearing.

Holy hell. How can a casual encounter with a man who was a complete stranger a few days ago turn into the most mind-blowing, earth-shattering and toe-curling sex I've ever had in my life?

Chapter Five

Did this happen or was it all a dream?

I slowly open my eyes, afraid I might break the spell from last night. I turn to the right and there he is, sleeping like an angel with a possessive hand rested against my soft stomach. *I guess it really did happen.* I lift my head to scan the room and I'm shocked by the telltale signs of our sexual abandonment—my garter belt on the armchair next to the window, my panties swinging off of a lampshade, my dress still pooled on the floor where I left it, my bra lying on top of my silk nylons and a pile of his own clothing. *Jesus, it's worse than the set of a porn movie.*

I scan the room, trying to find the time. It's only seven-thirty. I lift his arm as gently as possible to avoid waking him up and slide my body quietly out of bed with the initial thought of wrapping my dress around my nakedness, but I decide against it when I flash back to a vivid scene from last night—Max spewing his cum all over my stomach and boobs after he fucked my pussy to the point of no return. *Maybe not.* I tippy-toe out of the room like a mouse in search of a bathroom to clean up and a robe. I can't possibly walk around in front of him without any clothes on in broad daylight. I need to cover up.

I close the door softly behind me and when I turn around, I gasp. I forget my quest when I approach the window, mesmerized by the view displayed at my feet. *My God, this is absolutely breathtaking.* Only the very rich can ever afford to admire Central Park from this vantage point—I guess for today I'm able to enjoy a view of the city very few will ever be privileged enough to soak in.

There's not a cloud in the sky and I'm able to see as far as the eye can see. Wow! This is truly outstanding. When I feel safe enough and realize no one can catch sight of me this high up, I get closer. I lift my hands up at the level of my waist and I place the tips of my fingers against the glass as I take in every possible angle of this magnificent city. *Maybe if I get all the way up on my toes I can see even further.* I swear if I squint hard enough, I could most likely catch a glimpse of Coney Island from Max's penthouse.

I'm lost in my thoughts, soaking in Manhattan's beauty, when his voice startles me.

"And here I was thinking I already had a spectacular view to wake up to every morning, but seeing the sun shine against your naked body is truly a vision."

His comment freaks me out and I immediately turn around, struggling to hide my body. *No, no, no, this cannot be happening. He can't see me without clothes on. It's too bright and I have too many lumps.*

"Candy, you can't possibly be shy. Surely not after the way I fucked you last night."

"Oh, I didn't expect you to catch me like this. I was trying to find something to cover up with."

"Why in God's name would you ever hide your gorgeous body from my eyes?"

"I don't usually walk around naked in front of men," I let out shyly before lowering my eyes. As I look down to the floor, I catch sight of his left arm and admire his body art from under my lashes. I wonder what the story behind it is and why his skin is so uneven under my touch.

"The boys you've dated in the past are fools for not demanding you expose yourself to them twenty-four seven. When you're around me I want to be able to admire your beautiful curves as often as I can—preferably naked."

As always, his words are intoxicating, but suddenly I feel very insecure about being here at his place. I'm starting to have serious doubts about last night. It might be best for me to leave now.

"Max, maybe last night was a mistake. Maybe we got carried away with the food, the champagne, the mood and the view. It's not too late to forget taking things too far," I confess, biting my lower lip.

"You want to call what we shared a mistake? Or are you too scared to acknowledge our strong connection?" He glides towards me and I turn away to avoid the sight of his budding erection. "Is it the age difference? I'm sure I'm older than most of the other men you've been with."

"Yes, you are, but it's more than your age."

"What is it? Tell me, because I can't see it."

"I'm sure you want to take good care of the legacy your uncle left you. Don't worry, I love your collections and it won't be too difficult for me to give them a positive review since they are so flattering to plus-size women." I switch into this detached corporate persona, hoping to protect my feelings when he also comes to the realization we moved too quickly last night.

He doesn't answer. He simply stares down at me with a dark and serious gaze. Even with my hands covering my breasts and my pussy, I feel more naked than ever in front of him. I'm so nervous right now, conscious of his disapproving gaze, and I continue to babble, unable to withstand the silence. "I mean really, look at me, I must be nothing like the women you're used to sleeping with. You must be on a steady diet of beautiful models."

"You're right. I do have a thing for models."

A sinking feeling hits me like a rock. *I knew it.*

"My uncle's divisions have given me plenty of opportunities to date a few gorgeous models—as long as they were plus-size beauties."

Huh? Did he say he's dated plus-size models?

"My father, who is as WASP and as Anglo as can be, has always worshipped women with curves. He's instilled in me the love of big tits I can suck on, a round ass I can slap at will, wide hips I can ride like a rodeo cowboy and curves wet dreams are made of. Interestingly enough, all three Keller boys have a thing for voluptuous women."

"You don't have to lie on my account, Max." I'm unwilling to accept his words. *I find it difficult to believe this could be this easy.*

"Are you telling me the way I fucked you last night leads you to believe it was all a lie?"

"I'll be honest with you, standing right here in front of you in broad daylight... I don't know what to believe anymore. There's a part of me dying to believe you really wanted to be with me, but there's another part of me riddled with doubt at the idea that any man can find my body remotely attractive."

"I'm very certain of what I want and what I don't want in life. Candy, I love every part of your body. I want to have something to hold on to when I'm in bed with a woman. Why the hell would I waste my time with a skinny bitch when I can gorge on a luscious full-size beauty like you?"

Why am I resisting him so much? His words are so disarming, I drop my hands from my breasts and let my arms fall to my side. Instinctively I lift my head towards him, seeking his lips. He solves my dilemma, gripping my hair and kissing me so hard he forces me to part my lips. The demanding thrust of his tongue makes me think of how much I lost it last night when he lapped at my clit so skillfully. *God.* His kiss is so passionate and each time he moves his rock-solid cock bumps against my stomach, each touch a jolt of sensation. My hands clutch at his sides and I don't know whether to pull him closer or push him away. *I really shouldn't be doing this.*

"Candy, you have no idea how much I wanted you last night... and that was just a warm-up. Today, I want to do dirty things you'll be ashamed to tell people about. Are you willing to go there with me?"

My fingers tighten around his waist as I try to find my eroding balance before giving in more and more into his desire.

"Max... I don't..." My body is flaming out of control and he's barely touched me. Although a part of me is protesting, I want his hands all over me.

"It's all right, Candy. I want you to lose it," he whispers as he lifts my chin with his finger. It's as if he can see right through me.

When he sucks my tongue into his mouth, I fear the aching need growing inside will take over all my senses. Slowly and passionately, he kisses me forever and by the time he raises his head to meet my gaze, my fingers are clawing his back holding on for dear life.

"I hope you don't kiss all the guys you meet like this. Please tell me you reserve this sort of passion only for men you flash in the lobby of luxury hotels."

I laugh into his mouth. "I reserve this display of affection for men who fuck me as well as you do."

"Good, because I need a lot of your affection." He lowers his eyes and I follow his gaze. I'm greeted by a massive erection I'm aching to jump on. "Do you see what you do to me? I can't even contain myself around you. I must have made you come at least four times last night, but I want more of you."

"Seriously?" I bite off a smile. Wow. Max's words make me feel like a queen. He strips me of my inhibitions and entices me to dare to explore a side of my sexuality I never even knew existed.

"Fuck, yes." His hungry stare melts me like a marshmallow over a campfire. His hand grips my head and he crashes my mouth against his. *How can he be so rough so early in the morning?* His tongue swipes into my mouth, his kisses eager and hungry. We're all lips and tongues as he sucks and bites my lip.

"Ouch." I laugh. The tiny pain is fueling my desire for him.

"Too rough?"

"You took me by surprise, but please don't stop," I beg into his mouth as I give my lips to him.

"Good, because I have no intention of slowing down until you scream out my name and come undone with my cock deep inside your hungry pussy."

"Please don't make me wait, sir," I answer flirtatiously.

"I was going to suggest we go back to bed so I can punish you for ever doubting I like your body just the way it is, but on second thought, I think we should both come with New York at our feet." His lustful gaze is on my face, his fingertip trailing along my collarbone, awakening nerves throughout my entire body.

"What did you have in mind?"

Suddenly, he threads his fingers into my hair and forces my body down to the wooden floor. We both lie at the base of this massive window, wrapped in a passionate embrace. I tangle my hands in his hair as he strokes my nipple with his tongue, pulling it into his mouth and sucking hard before releasing.

"Jesus Christ." I tilt my head back to contain the sweet pleasure.

"Mmmm, you taste almost as good as you did last night," he moans into my boobs.

"What's changed in the last few hours?" My eyes are closed to fully savor every single flicker of his tongue against my peak.

"My appetite for you is increasing by the minute," he chuckles. "It simply means I'll need a lot more of you in order to feel as satisfied as I did the first night I had you. I hope you won't have an issue with me fucking you more often?"

"I was worried for a minute. I thought you'd already had enough of me."

"I think that's unlikely to happen anytime soon, sweetness." His mouth moves to my left breast. He licks me with such vigor before flicking my nipple with the tip of his tongue. The thrilling sensation is like a rush.

"Ah." A deep cry storms from my core.

"What do you want me to do to you, Candy?"

Am I in control here? "What do you want to do to me?"

"I asked you a specific question and I expect a specific answer."

Hoping to avoid having to be decisive, I reach down and wrap my hand around his cock, hearing a sharp gasp from him as he grabs my jaw and pushes my head against the floor. Max shakes his head and gently brushes my hand away, causing me to frown like a child he's reprimanded.

"You grabbing my cock is not the answer I was looking for."

"I'm not used to telling a man what I want."

"Why don't we start right now? Tell me what you want and I'll let you know if I'm in the mood to give it to you or not."

Even when he asks me what I want, he's fully in charge.

"Okay… I like it when you lick me," I let out shyly.

"Much better. Where do you want me lick you?"

"Don't make me say it. You know exactly where."

"If you don't tell me right now, you can forget about it. I'll leave you here and I'll march downstairs to make coffee." His eyes are dead serious.

He can't possibly threaten me like this. He knows how I dissolved against his tongue.

"Max…" I close my eyes and inhale, mustering the courage to allow the words to leave my lips. "I want you…" *Crap.* "I mean…" *Breathe in. You can do this.* "Please lick my pussy until I come and then fuck me hard enough to make me forget every man before you," I let out in one sweep, afraid I'll stop myself from being honest with him. Slowly peeking one eye open, I find a gorgeous man grinning down at me.

"Was that so hard?"

"Yes, and you know it."

"You're in luck. My plans this morning involved gorging on your wet pussy and giving you a good fuck before breakfast."

Without waiting one more minute, Max slides down my body and spreads open my legs so quickly I barely have time to take a breath. He latches onto my clit and sucks hard. I groan loudly and arch my back, feeling his strong hands wrapped around my ankles, spreading me wide open before planting my feet flat down against the wooden floor. *For the love of God.* I'm completely exposed to him and I try to stretch out my legs, but he holds me in place with a firm grip.

"You asked me to lick you. Move again and I stop."

I lift my head and stare down my body into bright hazel eyes.

"You only get one warning, Candy."

I nod, letting him know I have no intention of robbing myself of this man's touch, and lay my head back down. *Jesus. I'm fully opened in front of a window in broad daylight. There's nowhere for me to hide. He can see every imperfection.*

He holds my gaze as he trails sweet kisses down my inner thighs. "You're trying to hide from me, but you have no idea how beautiful you are. Every part of you—your soft stomach, your luscious thighs, your incredible big tits, and especially here."

His hands brush between my legs and I whimper. "I want to see all of you. Now if you'll allow me to continue what I had started, or do you intend on stealing from me the pleasure of tasting your sweet pussy?"

His words dissolve my fears and I allow myself to let go of my anxiety. *I'm yours.* I open myself up to him, ready to come against his tongue.

He doesn't bother to wait for an answer. His fingers are already deep inside my wetness—my eagerness.

"Yes, yes, yes." I gyrate my hips against him as he slowly strokes up the length of my pussy and around my clit, licking me like a lollipop. "Oh, don't stop." I want him to pull me into his mouth and suck me hard, knowing perfectly well I will lose it completely when he applies enough pressure against my sensitive nub. But he doesn't. Max keeps up the rhythm of his soft caress, teasing slightly over or under my clit and driving me absolutely insane. He only flicks his tongue over my hard node just enough to make me squeeze his head between my thighs before he plunges his tongue inside my wetness.

"Oh, Max," I exhale.

"Are you close?"

"I'm going to explode." I can't believe he's able to get me there so quickly. My climax is looming and my body is already convulsing against the hardwood floor under his skilled mouth.

"Candy, you're pulsating against my tongue and it's driving me fucking nuts. I'm going to make you come so hard you'll think last night was a rehearsal." His devilish half-smile makes my pulse stutter.

He laps at my pussy slowly, swirling and dipping, brushing over my clit. *Jesus, he's killing me here.* I can't stand it anymore and I yank my hips up to make him go where I desperately need him, but his hand clamps on to my stomach.

"You're cruel. Please... a little lower," I beg, gyrating my hips in circular motions as I tilt my head back.

"Are you always so impatient in the morning?" he mocks. "Let's get one thing straight. From now on, I control your pleasure. *Lick.* "I'm in no rush to make you come." *Lick.* "This is too good." *Lick.* "I can continue to tease around your clit for the next thirty minutes to drive you out of your mind." *Lick.* "What do you think about my little idea, sweetness?" *Lick.*

"Christ, you can't be serious," I bark in frustration. *I'm going to go mental if I don't come now.*

Quickly dropping my hand to my pussy, I go to rub my clit with my two favorite fingers when he grabs my hand, forcing it down to the wooden floor.

"Fucking shit," I curse, irritated by his denial of my gratification.

"What are you doing, Candy?"

"Why are you punishing me like this?" I whimper, on the verge of tears.

"It has nothing to do with punishing you. I want to linger on the pleasure." His breath is so warm against my aching pussy it's intoxicating. "The more you rush me, the more I'll tease you." His cocky grin lets me know how much he's enjoying my agony. "Let go and I'll give you what you crave." As if to make good on his promise, Max licks my clit, rubbing the peak of my node with his tongue, and I pant. "Play nice and I'll play even nicer. Your orgasms are mine now and you come when I want you to lose it." *Uh, well, if you're going to put it like that, I'm okay with you taking the lead.* "You want to touch your pussy until you come? You know perfectly well you'll never climax as hard as you do when I tongue-fuck you." *Lick.* I shake. "You must know that by now?"

"Yes," I agree, nodding as the words leave my trembling lips. Vince was far better than most guys I've been with, but he's an inexperienced rookie compared to the guy between my legs inflicting on me the sweetest type of torture.

"Did the last guy you fucked make you come this way?"

"Not even my best sex toys make me come nearly as hard as your tongue, Max."

He stops, frozen between my shaking legs. I can't see his head, but I feel his hot breath against my skin but nothing else. *Damn, did I say too much? Great. I've ruined it for myself. Way to go, Candy.*

"Are you serious?" His question hits me after several long seconds of silence.

I close my eyes and I nod shyly as I cover my face with my hands. "I shouldn't have revealed such details."

"No. I'm flattered."

I open my mouth to take back my confession when he wraps his lips around my clit and pulls it into his mouth. He lets go of the pressure only to circle my nub with swift, deadly strokes. "Dear God," I cry out. Sucking hard, he growls against me and I go off like a rocket launched in space.

"You know why I love fucking a woman like you with generous curves?" *Lick. Lick. Lick.*

"No," I exhale.

"The thicker the thighs, the sweeter the prize." He's barely had the time to utter those words before he has his hungry lips wrapped around my clit.

"Good Lord," I yell as the first wave of orgasm hits me. Without warning, he lets go of my throbbing clit.

"Fuck, your body transforms me into an animal." I'm still sobbing in ecstasy. I'm so far gone, it's nearly impossible for me to make out his words.

He extends his arms and his hands mold to my breasts as I fist his hair, holding on for dear life as a second, even more powerful, wave of orgasm rips through me the moment he pinches my nipples. My eyes are glued to his arm and I marvel at the intricacies of his tattoo. Unable to hold back, I release my lip, only realizing then I've been biting it for the last few minutes.

"Your arm…"

"Shhh, not now," he whispers.

My eyes are locked onto his face, his chest and his mysterious body art as he gets up to his feet and takes a step towards me before stepping over me and straddling my body. He hovers his weight over my chest, balancing himself carefully. Each time he sways, his butt caresses my breasts. The touch is so hedonic and so sensual.

"Make me come with your mouth," he commands as he strokes his erection inches from my mouth. This close to me, he's even bigger than I had imagined last night under dim lights.

"Yes, sir." I smile. "I can't wait to suck on your cock until you come gushing into the back of my throat." Without protesting I lick my lips before parting them, ready to receive his huge cock.

"Open wide, sweetheart." Max rubs his cock against my lips, drenching them with his juices. I hang on to his strong thighs as he plunges deep into my mouth. *I need every inch of him.* He possesses my mouth so completely and he's buried himself to the point where his balls are flirting with my chin. I take him in, wrapping both hands around his hard shaft to control him. *I could suck him for days.*

"Have I created a monster? You dirty little girl," he chuckles, pumping harder.

Something inexplicable takes over me as he's thrusting in and out, fucking my mouth like he would my pussy, and I slide my hand under his dangling balls before squeezing.

"Fuck." Max yanks his hips up in the air and he enters my mouth so deep, I gag. As a response to my daring move he squeezes my nipples harder, sending shockwaves down to my aching clit. I cry out, closing my eyes, and cup his balls tighter.

"Look at me," Max demands, grabbing my face between his hands. He holds tight as he face-fucks me without giving any signs of slowing down. "I want you to lock eyes with me when I come, baby."

"Hmmm," I moan, nodding my head. Another ripple of pleasure is curling tight between my thighs and I can't believe I already need release.

The blinding light coming from the massive window to my left allows me to read the dark, dangerous hunger in his gaze. In the sunlight, his eyes are sparkling green with lust, full of fierce desire.

"I need even more, Candy," he hisses. Before I can react, he unfolds his right leg from underneath him and places the sole of his foot against the wooden floor before sliding deeper into my mouth. He fucked my mouth last night like no man before him, but obviously it was a mere warm-up. He must have been preparing me for this—him taking over me so completely. He thrusts into my mouth, back and forth, gently at first, but he quickly picks up his pace. *Damn. His cock is rock hard.* He pumps and pumps and pumps again until I'm so fucking turned on, it's like my clit is going to erupt between the trembling walls of my dripping pussy.

"I can't hold it anymore," he growls, pumping once, twice, three times before jerking up. "Fuck," he yells, yanking his cock from my mouth before grabbing it between his hands and squeezing every single last drop of his cum into my mouth.

Mother of God.

I clench my legs together so tight a climactic tornado rips through me. Max raises his hand and holds on to the massive window to prevent himself from collapsing on top of me.

"You're truly going to kill me," he chuckles while trying to catch his breath.

"Not if I die of kinky pleasure first." I breathe fast, my heart racing like a sports car.

Max brings his hands to the side of my head and lowers his body close to mine. His voice comes low in my ear.

"We've got the rest of the day to see if you can survive another naughty round of toe-curling sex."

"I'll hold you to your promise."

Chapter Six

As I fasten the sash to my wrap dress in his bedroom, Max's words are still ringing in my head and I blush at how he gushes over my body. Even after having lost some weight, I'm still all too aware of the fact that my body will never be wafer-thin as the frail supermodels I spent most of my teenage years worshiping.

I glance at myself one last time in front of the mirror. I'm trying to make sure I look good before running downstairs to join him for breakfast, but I'm too fascinated by the reflection of the room behind me.

Everything about Max's penthouse is spectacular, including his master bedroom. It was impossible to take in any of this majestic décor in the heat of the passion we shared last night, but now with the sun high in the sky over Manhattan, I'm in awe. At first glance, the room might seem understated, but a second glance reveals intricate details—the rich furnishing, the refined bedding, the silk drapery, the modern lamp hanging right in the middle of the bed and the perfect blend of neutral colors.

I shake my head as I run down the wooden steps to meet Max in the kitchen, still unable to believe he's made me come four times since we got up. After keeping his promise, he insisted on taking a shower with me and washing all of my naughty bits, which of course led to a very steamy interlude under the sprinkling water of his rainforest shower head.

When I walk into his kitchen, I'm greeted by the delightful smell of fried eggs and bacon. *I'm famished.*

"Good morning again. I hope you're hungry. I know I'm starved."

"I thought I didn't need to be intimidated by your cooking skills, but this all smells absolutely scrumptious. It seems to me you've been downplaying your culinary talents."

"You don't have to worry. I wasn't born to be a celebrity chef. I'm treating you to the only thing I know how to make." He laughs as he places two plates on the table nested in a nook with a great view.

"I'm relieved I don't have to run to New York's culinary arts school in order to freshen up on my cooking skills."

"Nah, I can think of better ways for you to spend your time." He flashes me a devilish smile and raises his eyebrows suggestively.

I stare a minute too long at his tattoo and we lock eyes.

"My tattoo intrigues you. Doesn't it?"

"It's very intricate," I say in an attempt to make up for the fact I might have made him feel uncomfortable.

"There is a very complicated story behind my tattoo."

"Max, I didn't mean to stare." Although the growling of my empty stomach is distracting, it's still impossible for me to move my gaze away from his body art.

"You should dig in or else the food is going to get cold. You want some toast?"

"Absolutely. I would love some and if you have butter that would be even better."

"Ah. A woman who eats real butter is a woman after my own heart. I'm glad you didn't ask me for margarine." He winks.

"Nah. I believe in eating real butter, full-fat cheese, velvety cream and I'm extremely partial to pork fat."

We both laugh. Although he's putting up a good front, something is different about his demeanor since I walked into the kitchen. *What's the big secret behind his inked arm?*

He slides four slices of bread into his state-of-the-art stainless steel toaster and we both fixate on the common kitchen appliance as if it's the most interesting thing on earth.

"This morning you were desperately trying to hide your divine body from my eyes. I'm still not sure why. I suspect there's a part of your story you haven't yet decided to share with me. I can't blame you, since we haven't known each other for very long."

"I wasn't…" I open my mouth to protest because his statement makes me feel so transparent, but I quickly realize he knows more about me than I thought.

He strolls back to the kitchen table with a plate of grilled toast and a sly grin on his face.

"You're going to make me feel very self-conscious if you don't eat the breakfast I slaved over for exactly fifteen minutes before you showed your pretty face." He drops his eyes towards my untouched plate and I immediately blush. I grab my fork and I dig in with much gusto.

Yum. "I think you underestimate your talents. Your eggs are slightly runny and the bacon is crisp—just like I like it." One bite is all it takes to awaken my hunger like a starved groundhog after a long winter of hibernation. I dig into my plate and I devour another bite.

"You must have noticed the unevenness and roughness of my skin." He grabs a slice of bacon and bites into it.

"Not really." I lower my eyes to hide the fact I'm lying.

Who am I to judge? It's not as if I have a perfect body.

"You might be extraordinarily talented at sucking cock, but you're a terrible liar, Candy."

Shoot. He caught me. "I mean it didn't bother me, Max."

"It's taken me years to feel comfortable with this blemished part of me. For the longest time my scar was all I could see every single time I stood in front of a mirror. It didn't matter how many hours I spent with a trainer sculpting every single muscle on my body, my scar defined who I was."

"What happened?"

"A terrible accident while I was away with my best friend on vacation in the Dominican Republic when I was nineteen." He smiles, but his eyes are filled with sadness.

"Oh. I'm sorry to hear that." Instinctively I reach out to grab his hand. I'm all too familiar with the deep pain inflicted by a sudden and tragic accident.

"I don't want to burden you with my story, but it's impossible to understand who I am without understanding how a simple trip changed the course of my life forever." Although, he's only taken a few bites, he pushes his plate to the side before leaning in on the wooden table. Suddenly, my appetite disappears and I follow his cue, pushing away the other half of my breakfast.

"My best friend Jonathan Meyers and I had worked an entire summer to save up enough money to go to the Dominican Republic on a wilderness trip we had been eyeing. We were both into sports and daredevil stuff and this seemed like the perfect excursion for a trip outside the US—neither of us had traveled abroad until then. The first week was a dream—we'd hike for hours and when our bodies couldn't take the exertion any longer, we'd find a safe place to camp for the night. We were part of a small group of adventurous travelers determined to remain unaffected by the rigorous conditions of the trip and the burning sun. By the second week, our bodies had acclimatized to the brutal conditions and we were accustomed to feeling the sun hitting the back of our necks as we trailed the countryside of this spectacular country." Max reaches out and grabs my hands in his. His touch is so warm and inviting. It's like a comforting blanket protecting me from the outcome of his story. "Have you ever been to the Dominican Republic?"

"No, I haven't. My editor-in-chief had considered adding that Caribbean island to our to-do list for our exposé on Western women willing to travel to poorer parts of the world in search of love, but it seemed the trend was stronger in Jamaica and Cuba."

"The island is rich with culture and you can't help but fall in love with the people. I'm happy I was lucky enough to visit at least once in my life because I doubt I would ever go back."

"Oh, God. This doesn't sound good."

"You don't know the half of it yet." He curls up his lips, but it looks more like a grimace than a smile. I can read the pain in his eyes.

I'm dying to know the outcome of his trip, but I'm too afraid to push. It's obvious from his discomfort the story doesn't end on a happy note.

"Jonathan, or Nate as we called him, and I decided to rent a Jeep during our last two days on the island. We wanted to spend the day at Playa Rincón after reading so many glorious reviews. *Condé Nast Traveler* hailed it as one of the top ten beaches in the Caribbean. As teenagers, we were hoping to hook up with a few hot babes and spend the day drinking beer." He chuckles.

"Is this where I'm supposed to feel sympathy for you?" I mock.

He offers a half smile before continuing to speak. "It was a perfect Caribbean day. The sun was high in the sky, there wasn't a cloud as far as the eye could see, the wind was blowing through our hair and we were carefree. The music was blasting on the radio and we were singing along like rock stars, bobbing our heads, snapping our fingers and feeding off of each other's energy. It was a magical moment—the calm before the storm."

"Then it happened. We didn't even have time to react. The truck swerved to avoid us, but it was coming at us too fast. Nate turned the steering wheel sharply to try to avoid an accident, but he didn't notice the cliff to his left. The front tire hit a rock and the Jeep tumbled down a steep cliff. I was lucky... I guess. The impact propelled my body out of the car and I landed on the side of the road before Nate plunged to his death in a ravine."

"Oh, my God," I cry out in horror, yanking my hands from his to cover my gaping mouth.

"Yeah. Apparently, a passing car dragged my unconscious body for miles before stopping. I found out after four days in a coma that my left arm was the only part of me seriously injured. I had some pretty bad scrapes and bruises, but they would heal. My arm, on the other hand... I still remember when I came to. My mom was so broken and scared. She must have been crying for days."

"How did they find your parents?"

"I was fortunate my guardian angel was on duty when the Jeep tumbled. My wallet was still inside the pocket of my jeans. My mom had insisted on inserting an emergency card just in case and her motherly advice allowed the hospital to contact my parents in New York and inform them of the news."

"I can't imagine how your mom must have reacted," I lie. I know too well how empty you feel inside when you get an unexpected call from the police to let you know your loved ones have been involved in an accident and you need to rush to the hospital.

He closes his eyes before continuing. "When my dad told me Nate hadn't survived, I went into shock. The ordeal changed me, as you can imagine."

"Of course. The death of a loved one create a monumental shift in your life." I should know.

"It does. It took me eight months to recover emotionally and physically. I couldn't fully use my left arm for nearly a year, but after months of physical therapy, I was almost as good as new. One year after the accident, I summed up enough courage to visit Nate's mom, Jasmine. When she opened the door, she was unrecognizable—she had aged at least three decades from the emotional toll."

"Was Nate her only child?"

"No. He had two younger sisters, but his mom pretty much checked out after his death. She fell into a massive depression. She locked herself in her bedroom and refused to come out for seven months straight. One day she snapped out of it, but her family unit was never the same."

"It must have been equally difficult for Nate's sisters and his father."

"The whole family was devastated. Our entire school was in mourning for weeks after my best friend's death. Nate was the kind of guy everyone gravitated towards. He was a top athlete and he had a great heart. What he lacked in academic ability, he made up for with his unbounded generosity. The visit with his mom was a turning point for me when I asked her what allowed her to keep moving forward despite her tragic loss."

"What did she say?" I ask, surprising myself by how engaged I am in his story. I guess a selfish part of me is dying to find out how someone else dealt with losing a loved one.

"One of Nate's teachers had returned some of his essays to his mom. She read one my best friend had written about friendship." For an instant Max fights his emotions. "Nate had written this long essay. I'll be honest, I don't remember all the words and he even admitted in his paper he needed some help from his girlfriend to fully express how he felt about us, but the conclusion remains with me to this day. He said our friendship had taught him how to live, love and matter. He was this star athlete who stood six foot five inches tall—a beefy guy with more muscle mass than any champion MMA fighter—and he was describing our friendship with such depth. Jasmine asked me to honor her son's memory by living, loving and by only doing meaningful things. Those three simple wishes I took to heart and I've been on a crusade ever since to make good on my promise to her.

Even though she died two years ago, I've still kept my word to her."

"You're right. They are simple wishes, but they are so meaningful."

He nods his head in agreement and brings my hands to his lips. The tenderness of his actions catches me off guard.

"I guess I still haven't explained how I got inked."

I shake my head and lean in towards him to listen to the rest of his tale.

"Nate died one week after I had turned nine-teen and for six years I hated my body. The scar was a reminder of my loss and the unsightliness of my skin made me feel disfigured, like a monster. For my twenty-fifth birthday, my older brother Gabriel suggested we take a trip to New Zealand and Australia. For a year, we picked up as many odd jobs as we could to save up enough for our adventure on the other side of the planet."

"Wow. You've been a globetrotter your entire life," I marvel.

"I wouldn't go that far. I shut down and refused to leave the US upon my return from the Dominican Republic. This was my brother's way of pushing me out of my self-imposed boundaries. After my South Pacific trip, I couldn't wait to explore more of the world."

"I envy you. I've traveled across the US, but I haven't traveled internationally as much as I'd like."

"You're still so young. You have a lot of time ahead of you. If you hang out with me more, I'll make sure you see more of this wonderful world we live in." He winks.

"If I decide to hang out with you more, I'll hold you to your promise." I wink back.

"You're feisty after some bacon and eggs."

"Funny."

"My brother was the one who initiated the trip and a few days after arriving Down Under, Gabe suggested I conceal the scar behind a tattoo. At first I thought he had gone mad. My parents would have been furious. It's not as if I was part of a gang or anything that edgy. I laughed it off until he revealed he had already talked to Mom and Dad about it and they were unanimous. They all felt I needed help to stop grieving my friend—six years was long enough."

"It's not fair someone else would put a time limit on your grief. You're entitled to mourn your friend as long as you need." Suddenly I'm quite irritated by the fact his brother and his parents tried to shake the sadness out of him. Trish and my aunt Caroline tried to push me out of my misery numerous times, but there was nothing to be done about it. The pain of losing my parents nearly ate me alive and there weren't enough pep talks in the world to make me see things differently.

"You're so spirited and passionate. It's almost as if you have firsthand experience."

Gosh. I'm so not ready to share such a tumultuous part of my past with him. It's too soon. I don't even know where this is going.

"I'm sorry. I'm being too involved—too empathetic." I'm suddenly riddled with guilt for allowing myself to transfer my own emotions on to him. *This is about his best friend Nate. Not about Mom and Dad.*

"Not at all. This is a very difficult part of my past. I felt compelled to share it with you because I could see from your eyes you were intrigued even though you didn't dare to ask."

"Why did your brother suggest getting a tattoo in New Zealand? Why not go down the street to any tattoo shop and get inked here in New York?"

"This tattoo was more about healing than making a statement of how much of a bad boy I was."

"I don't get it."

"Shortly after we set foot on the other side of the planet, my brother asked our tour guide to seek out a Maori tattoo artist to cover my scar with ancestral symbols of courage to change my perception of my past."

"I don't know much about tattoos and I know even less about the aboriginal people of New Zealand. I must confess you're the first tattooed man I've ever slept with." I blush at my own inexperience.

He smiles before tenderly stroking my cheek. "The Maori are the indigenous people of New Zealand. They have a form of body art, known as *moko* but more commonly referred to as Maori tattooing. The art form was brought to the Maori from Polynesia and it's considered highly sacred. For the Maori, tattooing was, and for some still is, a rite of passage, which meant it was highly revered and ritualized. The great thing about Maori tattoos is their uniqueness—no two tattoos are alike. Maori tattoos are one of a kind, like people. They are always highly intricate and detailed and display the craftsmanship and artistry of not only the artist but of the Maori culture."

"This all sounds so fascinating, but it must have been painful as hell."

"You're adorable. Your horrified look cracks me up. I won't lie, the first touch was biting, but every pinch of the needle moving over my skin reminded me of my commitment to my best friend's mother. Even when the pain threatened to devour my resolve, I remained stoic. The tattoo wasn't about me, it was about Nate's memory."

"Nate was lucky to have you as a friend. Your tattoo is magnificent. It's been hard for me to take my eyes off of it—it's like nothing I've ever seen before. It's so much sexier than a chick on a bike, a cartoon or a horseshoe."

For the first time since he started sharing his heart-wrenching story, he lets out a genuine laugh. "I love your flawless skin. You don't have any scars to hide, therefore unless you were a fan of tattoos, there wouldn't be any good reason for you to get inked."

It's too bad you can't tattoo an aching heart. Maybe it would have helped me deal with my loss.

Chapter Seven

I'm standing in line at Mazama coffee shop for my daily shot of caffeinated elixir. It doesn't matter how early you try to sneak into this place, it's always jam-packed with New Yorkers desperate for a cup of java.

Since seeing Max, I've had to rely on coffee a lot more to perk me up because he works me so hard I'm constantly exhausted from his sexual prowess. I can't believe I've seen Max every single night this week—it's still so surreal. It's taken me a little time, but I've accepted the fact I might be one of the luckiest women in the world to have accidentally bumped into a gorgeous and successful man who happens to adore women who have a little skin on their bones.

I never imagined submitting myself so wholly to a man could allow me to experience such heart-stopping orgasms. I was never confident enough to demand certain hedonistic pleasures from a man, which is why Max's domineering nature in the bedroom makes me lose it so much. It's as if he knows what my body craves even before I do. Everything about our sexual interludes is naughty, raunchy and downright dirty. The man is so gifted, I could climax simply by listening to him whisper in my ear. I still remember how Vince used to boast about how big an Italian stallion he was. Well, he's got nothing on Max. Vince never filled me up the way Max's huge dick does—Max could fuck me twenty-four seven and I still wouldn't get enough of him.

Someone is speaking, but I'm still too caught up reliving my frolics with Max and I don't catch the guy's question.

"Are you going to stand there with a grin on your face or are you ready to order?"

"Huh?" *Shit. I'm so not paying attention.*

"I have thirty desperate New Yorkers waiting in line behind you for their morning fix. What will you have, sweetie?" The barista's abrupt question wakes me up from my reverie.

"Oh. I'm sorry. I'll have an extra-tall, extra-hot, skinny chai latte with a double shot of espresso and I'd like it half sweet, please." Does anyone order a simple cup of coffee with cream anymore? Nowadays, coffee sounds more like a chemistry project than a dark cup of goodness.

I barely have time to order before my peevish barista is back. Something must've happened within the last few minutes because he's now smiling at me. Since I'm in such a good mood, and I've been fucked so well, I return his smile before paying and grabbing my salvation in a cup. I wish him a good day and wiggle my way out of the busy coffee shop.

I'm not usually an early riser, but since I stayed over at Max's place last night, I had to leave extremely early because he had to be at the office at an indecent time for a conference call with a German magazine. There's something quite invigorating about strolling down the streets of Manhattan this early in the morning while sipping on my favorite caffeinated drink. I might be tired as hell, but I'm determined to make the most of this day. Carpe diem, right? Being up and about alongside the Big Apple's movers and shakers makes me feel like anything is possible today.

As I ride the elevator up to my office, I can't help but marvel at how quickly things unfold. Eight days ago, I hadn't planned on a trip, but in forty-eight hours I'll be on a plane heading south. I'm really looking forward to visiting the Sunshine State for the first time in my life.

When I push through the doors, I'm taken aback by the quiet of the office. It's usually so noisy and animated, but most of my colleagues are still waking up while I'm ready to tackle a few unfinished articles for upcoming editions. *I might have to get to the office before everyone else more often.*

The workweek has been packed with the humdrum of working in the fashion industry while trying my best to stay out of the way of Maleficent— aka my boss, Jennifer Lau. The only remotely interesting thing this week, other than the multiple toe-curling orgasms Max rewards me with every time he lays his hands on me, will be spending the evening with my best friends. I love those three more than life. Since I'm leaving for Miami in a few days and I've been pretty much MIA because Max has been keeping me so busy, I haven't hooked up with Devin, Lexi, and Lia in what seems like an eternity. Tonight, we're finally catching up. Each one of my friends has been eagerly texting me to try to find out the juicy details behind my affair.

I get to the office ninety minutes early in order to get as much work done as possible before being cooped up in the conference room with eight of my colleagues to listen to Jennifer for an hour. Not only do I want to cross things off my list before the weekly meeting, I also want to get there early enough to snatch a spot as far away as possible from my irritating boss.

When I arrive at my desk, I'm greeted by a large box sitting on the edge on top of a pile of back issues. *Who left me this package?* I drop my bag and chai before opening a piece of paper folded and taped to the box. *It's from Jennifer. What does she want now?* Before I even read one word she wrote, I'm already rolling my eyes knowing in my heart this box will become a thorn in my side.

I read the note twice, intrigued by her unexpected request. She's suggesting I take this box home to test these new so-called cleansing pills. They are supposedly all the rage on the Internet and she claims our readers will, no pun intended, eat them up to help them deal with their weight issues. *I thought we were supposed to celebrate every woman regardless of the number flashing on her scale.* My former boss, Christine, frowned upon us testing any product we'd have to ingest. We'll gladly test makeup, perfume, skincare products, clothing, accessories and shoes, but we have never been allowed to sample diet pills.

Jennifer calls it a cleansing product for optimum health, but that doesn't change the fact this is another way of telling plus-size women they are not good enough just the way they are. *Great, my day hasn't even started and she's already managed to put me in a pissy mood.* I grab the stupid box and dump it on top of my filing cabinet, determined to ignore it until Jennifer waltzes by my desk to make sure I received her instructions.

I gulp down a steaming hot shot of my coffee and it instantly perks me up. I turn on my computer, ready to tackle an article I've been struggling with. It's been kicking my butt for the last week and I'm determined to get it done within the hour, but my phone rings. I lean across my desk to fish for my phone, hoping it might be Max calling. It's Devin.

"Hey, Dev."

"Hey, sex goddess. Did you sleep at his place or did you go back home last night to be with your long-time lover, Mr. Leo DiCaprio? Is it safe to talk?"

"First off, thanks for the compliment—Max has been sexing me up like a queen. Second off, my cat is totally jealous of all the time I spend with Max." I laugh. "Thirdly, I did sleep at his penthouse, but I'm already at the office ready to take on my day because Max had a conference call at a ridiculously early time."

"My God, the man has changed your ways in only one week. Have you ever been up this early in your life?" I can only imagine the grin on Devin's face right now.

"I take offense to your assumptions, Dev. I'm sure I must have been up at the crack of dawn at some other point in my life, I simply can't recall it at this very second."

We both laugh.

"Sweetie, I was calling because I got the text you sent me this morning and I couldn't believe the time stamp. I wanted to make sure another Candy hadn't hacked your account pretending to be an early riser."

"Yeah, I texted all three of you to make sure we're still meeting tonight at your place."

"Oh, trust me, we're so meeting tonight. King Kong attacking New York would be the only valid reason we would cancel hearing about your X-rated love affair with your rich boy toy. I've asked Lia to bring a lot of wine to ensure we keep you talking. I want all the juicy details, girl. You're not allowed to leave anything out. Your sex life is better than most gay guys'."

"Heck, I didn't even know it was possible to have this type of sex life."

"I'm warning you right now, Lexi is extremely jealous of the few cryptic text messages you've been sharing with us this past week. I think your story has awakened the dormant sex kitten in her."

"It's about time. I was worried about the girl. She hasn't talked about being with a man in ages and

I was starting to be quite concerned she might have renounced sex altogether. She spends way too much time working and not enough time having fun. She's too young to deprive herself of love and affection."

"I couldn't agree with you more. I've had this pep talk with her so many times, I simply can't go there with her anymore. She has to make the decision on her own. I understand about her horrible past and I do sympathize, but she's suppressing a very important part of herself."

"Don't worry, I'll remind her tonight."

"Are you going to be able to survive this day without seeing your man?"

"Well, he does have a meeting in a few hours on the top floor with the executives of the holding company, who apparently are extremely excited by his financial commitment for the next few years. Since Max was willing to buy full-page ads in *Sassy* magazine and advertisement banners on the website every single month for the next twelve months, the top honchos are beside themselves. I hope I'll be able to sneak out to have coffee or a quick lunch with him. He said he'd text me when his meeting was over. So I might be able to see him during the day and I won't have to wait until later tonight to steal a kiss from him."

"Good for you. Sounds like you've got it all figured out."

"I don't know if I have, but I'm psyched about the opportunity."

"Has he alluded to where the kinky relationship is heading?"

"If you're referring to us dating exclusively, he's not brought it up so far and I'm too much of a chicken to rock the boat. Things are great right now—scratch what I said, things are amazing—and I'm willing to be a little patient, which is completely out of character for me when it comes to men."

"Do you want more?"

What a loaded question. "I'd be lying if I said I didn't. Everything seems to be running smoothly—maybe too smoothly. Given my poor record with men, I'm kind of waiting for the other shoe to drop, Dev."

It's been impossible for me to stop daydreaming about Max and what we share. He's been preoccupying my thoughts every waking moment since I bumped into him at the Bymark hotel, but I've learned a harsh lesson from Vince—sometimes when things seem too perfect, it's because they are.

"Maybe the only shoe you'll hear dropping is yours as he fucks you hard until you forget your own name on his über-expensive dining room table overlooking Central Park."

"Don't be silly. You have the layout of his penthouse all wrong."

We both laugh.

"So we're definitely on then?"

"Abso-freakin'-lutely."

Chapter Eight

At ten-thirty, I head to the smaller conference room we usually use for team meetings with my iPad, my notepad and my third extra-tall coffee of the day. Max worked me so hard last night, there doesn't seem to be enough caffeine in the world to perk me up today. I cannot afford to doze off during Jennifer's important weekly team meeting. I don't need her to freak out on me in front of everybody.

Luckily, when I walk into the room, there are a few of my colleagues chatting and catching up. I take advantage of the fact they're busy socializing to find a strategic seat. Jennifer is standing in the corner of the boardroom laughing at something Molly Russell, one of the art directors on the plus-size division, said and I can't help but notice her striking red suit. *Have I ever seen Jennifer wear the same outfit twice since she started here six months ago? It's good to be her.*

Jennifer is a very privileged woman who has never known hardship—her dad still lives in Hong Kong and he owns a manufacturing plant that spits out millions of plastic bags for retailers from around the world every month. Since she's an only child, she's poised to inherit her father's colossal fortune.

Five years ago she married Seth Weingarten, one of the wealthiest real-estate lords in New York. Seth's grandfather is a legend in Manhattan. He came on a boat from Hungary with less than twenty dollars in his pockets and one change of clothes, but within ten years Yaakov Weingarten was king of the Big Apple's real estate market. Rumors flooded New York's papers and gossip blogs about tension and discord among the powerful Weingarten clan because Seth broke a tradition dating back centuries when he married outside of the Jewish faith. The only redeeming factor playing in his favor is the fact Jennifer is wife number three and the only non-Jew. Seth's other wives ensured the bloodline remained intact thanks to a brood of children.

As if being this privileged wasn't irritating enough, Jennifer's size-zero frame means she's never had to deal with body image issues. She's always the first one to gloat about how she's been able to maintain the same dress size since she was a teenager even after giving birth to her son Malcolm. *God, I want to puke every time she reminds us.* She might be well off, but it's too bad her personality sucks. *What's the point of having so much money if everybody abhors you?*

Jennifer has been awarded the name Malefi-cent thanks to her snooty and condescending attitude. She might be the queen bee around the office, but few of us trust her or even like her—I'm sure she wouldn't hesitate to throw her own son under the bus if it meant she'd gain favor with the big bosses of the holding company that owns this magazine. I guess you could say Jennifer is my own version of Meryl Streep in *The Devil Wears Prada*—except my devil wears Gucci.

She turns my way and I'm forced to lower my eyes, conscious of the fact I'm staring at her. *Fuck.* Without leaving my gaze she announces the meeting is about to start.

We all rally around the boardroom table like children about to start class. After going through the agenda, it's clear we're in for a long and boring meet-ing… or monologue, as I like to call them. *My God, I hope this coffee keeps me awake.*

* * *

Technically, I'm supposed to be paying a lot more attention during this team meeting than I actual-ly am, but Jennifer is going over the same rhetoric she always rambles about. *Jesus, this is painful.* If only her voice wasn't so monotone, perhaps it would help in keeping us somewhat interested in what she has to share. Just as I think I'm about to die from listening to Jennifer list a series of mundane goals we should reach as a division in the next quarter, a text comes across my phone. My eyes quickly dart down at my phone, which I strategically placed on my lap, and his name flashes across my screen. *Max.*

I grab my phone and slide it under my note-pad to be able to better read his message.

The meeting ended early and I was hoping to see you before I leave the building. Can you get away for a few minutes?

I look up at the clock on the wall and bite my lower lip. *Crap.* If I don't sneak out of here, I'll be stuck in here for another forty minutes and I'll have missed Max. I furtively scan the room. My colleagues are either extremely fascinated by what Jennifer has to say or they're sleeping with their eyes open. Most likely the latter given our past private chats.

Yes. I can get away. Where do you want to meet?

Good news. Let's meet in the Fashion Archive room where we snuck into a little over one week ago af-ter you stormed out of our meeting at your office.

What? Has he lost his mind? Why on earth does he want us to meet there?

You can't possibly be serious?

Sweetness, I'm as serious as
my hard-on. Get yourself here right
this instant to help me relieve it
before I go mad.

My eyes are glued to my phone and I'm still in shock at Max's words when I notice Jennifer is no longer talking. *Crap.* I slowly look up and meet her disapproving stare.

"Candy, is there something urgent I should know about?"

I was so focused on answering Max, I didn't notice Jennifer had turned her attention to me. As I look around the room, I'm mortified at the nine pairs of eyes darting my way. *I'm so screwed right now.*

Think fast. "I'm sorry, Jennifer. I didn't want to interrupt the meeting, but I just received an urgent text from our new advertiser and it seems there are a few things I should be aware of before I leave in a couple of days for Miami," I lie. *God, please don't let me blush.* "Can I step out for a few minutes to take care of this? I have a conference call with Sexy Curves Lingerie's team tomorrow to talk about their upcoming features in the magazine. There might be a few last-minute details I need to provide to them."

I hope I sound convincing enough. I fully expect to feel the weight of her wrath on me like a meteor hitting the earth on Doomsday, but instead

Jennifer's eyes light up and her lips curl up in a smile. *Lord, I've never even seen her grin. Money does talk.*

"Absolutely, Candy. Taking care of our top advertiser is your number-one priority. Why don't I fill you in on a few things you might have missed later today? Please, grab your things and go take care of this right now."

Did she actually use the word "please"? "Thank you for your understanding. I do apologize, but this is so unexpected. I'll see you later." I avoid making eye contact with anyone in the room, afraid my colleagues might read my deception, and instead gather my things and run out of the boardroom.

The second I step out of the meeting, I grab my phone again to answer his latest message.

Did I lose you?

No. Sorry. I had to find a way to get out of a meeting.

Thank God, because this raging erection is threatening to rip apart these new expensive trousers I bought last month on Bond Street in London and I'd hate for a good suit to go to waste simply because you're not attentive to my needs.

I'm on my way.

Come and get your quickie, Candy.

Fuck, I'm already wet.

Chapter Nine

I stand in front of the Fashion Archive room like a policewoman standing vigil at the door of a wanted criminal. I scan the hallway before I muster up enough courage to open the door to meet Max at our secret rendezvous location. *The man has balls.*

When I'm certain no one is paying attention, I knock on the door and he opens. I peer inside the room and when I finally step inside, a half-naked man greets me.

"How on earth did you manage to get in here?" I really should be locked into his beautiful hazel eyes, but his hungry erection is way too distracting.

"I rattled the handle of the door, and just like last week, it was open. I saw this as a sign we were destined to be misbehaving right here in your office," he says with a devilish smile.

"You're very lucky someone isn't doing their job properly because this door is supposed to remain locked at all times. We keep priceless archives of past issues and upper management is quite strict about protecting our assets."

"It's good to see you too, sweetness. We can stand here chatting about office policies or you can get down on your hands and knees. I want you to crawl all the way here and put my aching cock into your wet mouth," he commands.

The rawness of his words slaps me across the face with such force I take a step back. *Holy Jesus.*

"Tick, tock, honey. I don't have all day." His self-assurance is an aphrodisiac. "Where do you want me to leave my mark?" Max continues without waiting for my answer while his gaze zeroes in on my breasts. "That's a dangerously sexy top. I love how I can make out the outline of your bra. Damn, I'd give good money to see you strip right now and expose those luscious huge tits of yours." *His raunchy dialogue is going to set me on fire.* "You know, during my meeting, I could only imagine licking your nipples as my cock stiffened. There was no way in hell I was leaving this building without seeing you—or should I say fucking you?" As if his words weren't fuel enough, he strokes his hard cock and folds his lower lip into his mouth as a blatant invitation. "Perhaps I shouldn't be so forward, since you are at work. I'm sorry, but it's impossible for me to resist you."

"You really don't sound sorry and your erection negates pretty much every word you've just said."

"I'm really not and you're right, I do have a raging erection. I'm desperate to bury my cock deep down your throat and feel you shudder all over my dick, Candy."

Oh, hell, yeah. He was made to fit into my mouth.

"So this is what you've been fantasizing about instead of paying attention during the meeting with the executives?" I glide towards him like a panther after a prey.

He chuckles, but the sound dies when I hit my knees in front of him. Surprised by my suddenness, he shuffles backwards until his naked ass meets the edge of a filing cabinet. He braces both hands against it, trying to catch his breath. I unbutton his shirt, revealing his washboard abs, and I pause long enough to glance up at him and grin. My tongue flicks over the tip of his cock and then circles it, and he lets his head fall back with a groan.

"Holy shit."

After three long strokes up his dick, he's panting. *Good.* Once he's glistening with moisture, my hand curls around his base, my lips eagerly sucking his crown. Slowly. Inch by inch. I want to make sure I prolong the pleasure—his and mine.

"Jesus, Candy. I thought I had fucked you well enough this morning, but obviously I left you in need of more." He reaches down to open my V-neck jersey top before shoving his hand down my bra.

"Hmmm," I moan into his cock.

"Christ," he chokes out, threading his fingers through my mane. He grabs the back of my head and pulls me closer towards him and I whimper as he pulls at my hair. "Sorry," he whispers. "I can't stand it anymore. You suck me so well, it's surreal."

I haven't even started yet.

My tongue rolls around his shaft, teasing him mercilessly while my hand strokes him at his base. My other hand is busy cupping his balls and pressing hard enough to get another groan out of him. *God, I love his balls—heavy and full.*

"Fuck. My entire life is focused between my legs in this moment, Candy. Nothing else matters but your lips around my dick. I'm going to fill your pretty little mouth as punishment for being this good." He accentuates his words by pressing so hard on my right nipple, my body caves in and I stop breathing for a fraction of a second.

"Harder. Suck me harder," he commands in a low voice, pulling at my tangled hair harshly.

I take as much of Max as I can into my mouth, pivoting back on my heels to give me more leverage. I grip the base with my left hand as the right moves to caress his stomach.

He mumbles a string of inaudible words before letting out a muffled grunt. His hips bounce against the hard edge of the filing cabinets as he rocks himself into me inch by inch. I murmur around the thickness, relishing in the feeling of unbridled abandonment as my tongue runs over his cock in the most salacious way possible.

"Holy Christ." His hand moves to my neck and I flinch for a moment before I find my rhythm again. I pump him hard and fast, my mouth opening wider to take all of him in. I bob my head back and forth, overtaken by licentious horniness, oversexed by the most carnal love affair I've had so far.

"Damn, I'm going to have to sneak into your office more often and demand you get down on your knees and suck me so royally." His cock jerks in my hands the moment the words leave his lips. "Shit."

I slide my head back just enough so the tip of his cock is still inside my warm mouth, teasing and tempting it. *He'll never forget our smutty encounter in the Fashion Archive room.* I close my hands tighter around his balls and feel them constrict against my grip. *He's so close.* I tighten even more around his heavy balls as I firm my mouth around his cock. He grabs my hair so harshly it tingles. A small burst of his cum spurts onto my tongue followed by one endless stream of his warm release gushing down my throat.

"Jesus, Candy." His voice is deep, raw and low. I gently push him out of my mouth, relishing the moment, but a few drips of his cum land on my chin. I look up at him while I try to lick up the parts of him that escaped and I can tell he enjoyed this as much as I did. His eyes are still glazed from his powerful climax and he reaches down to help me scoop up every last drop, but he stops dead when we hear voices at the door.

"Shhhh, don't move," I whisper, placing a finger against my lips. *Fuck, fuck, fuck.*

"Hey, Stella, what are you doing on our floor? I thought you guys from the executive office only sent emails requesting stuff and the rest of us scrambled to get it to you pronto."

This is not happening to me. Carl Applegate, my colleague, is entertaining Stella Cavill, the executive assistant to one of the VPs, a few feet away from where I'm still in this submissive position in front of Max's dick. *Can I be more screwed right now?*

The only relief in this situation is the panicked expression on Max's face. I'm glad to see I'm not the only one worried to death. Both our gazes bounce from each other to the door. I'm so stricken with worry, I'm unable to move, afraid the slightest motion will call unwanted attention to us.

"Carl, nonsense. I'm here in the flesh to grab a few back issues to bring up to a meeting with the VPs. As usual they have big plans."

"Which issues do you need? I have a shitload of them at my desk because I'm planning a few special sections for the upcoming Christmas edition for both the magazines and websites."

"I need to grab a few wedding editions and bring them back up pronto for a meeting my boss is having with a few of the other VPs."

"Then I can't help you, child. You'll have to dig your way out of the Fashion Archive room on your own."

I hear Carl's boisterous laugh and I swallow hard.

Oh, my Lord.

I look up at Max, sweat running down my back, panicked.

"Didn't you lock the door behind you?" he whispers.

"No, I was too turned on when I saw you standing there with your pants down around your knees and your signature I'm-going-to-fuck-your-mouth grin on your face. It slipped my mind."

"This is not going to end well if one of the VPs' assistants opens the door and finds us in this compromising situation."

"You think?" I hiss.

I stop breathing the second I hear a key slide into the keyhole as Stella rattles the door handle to get into the room.

Oh, shit, we're totally busted. I'm going to get fired for performing lewd acts at work. How do I explain being down on my knees with a major adver-tiser's cock in my mouth and his warm release drizzling down my chin?

****

Get Your FREE SECRET Chapters!

Thank you for purchasing this romance!

I'd love for you to lose yourself in more
sultriness, sexiness and steamy passion!

When you sign-up today, I'll send you the following
Secret Chapter for Part 2 of this serial:

*You'll want to read about how Max gets ready to receive
Candy in his home for the first time!
(This is Max's POV)*

*** <u>PASSWORD FOR</u> Secret Chapter Part 2:
Central-Park

Note: the password is case sensitive!

Sign-up TODAY!

www.RomanceBooksRock.com

***If you've already signed-up to my list from previous
books, you can visit the same page to download
the Secret Chapters for this romance***

****

PART 3—CURVES ENVY

Claimed by An Alpha

Chapter One

I try my best to take a nap during the flight to Miami to make up for the lack of sleep, but it's been impossible for me to find my equilibrium in the last forty-eight hours. I usually never have any difficulties passing out cold on a plane, and I've been tossing and turning in my bed for the last two nights, but today it's impossible to even shut my eyes for a few seconds. I think I'm still quite shaken by my good luck.

What a surreal view. As I look out from my window seat, I can never get over how flying feels like you're able to touch the sky just by reaching out your arm. It's a perfect day to be this high up—the sun is shining and there are thousands of fluffy white clouds dispersed throughout the blue sky. I'm lost in the serene view when Deidra's voice brings me back to reality.

"You seem so far away."

Max's right-hand person is my travel companion, but I have to confess I've been as quiet as a mousse for the last hour, consumed by reliving every single scene since I overheard Stella's and Carl's voice in the hallway as I knelt in front of Max with his cum drizzling down my chin. Stella Cavill, the executive assistant to one of the VPs, would have opened the door and spoiled our raunchy sexcapade had she not been accosted by my colleague Carl Applegate right before she busted open the door to the Fashion Archive room.

"I'm sorry. I'm such a bad travel companion because there's so much on my mind."

"I know. Max told me about your close call."

"What?" I'm shocked by her revelation. *How can he share something so personal with someone who's practically a stranger to me?*

"Don't worry. Your secret is safe with me. Max asked me to make sure you have everything you need while you'll be with us in Miami. He trusts me implicitly because we go way back."

If her words were supposed to be comforting, they only make my insecurities flare up. Since the first day I laid eyes on the sultry Deidra Summers, one of Max's top executives, I've always wondered if there is a steamy history between the two of them. I mean, who could blame him for not being able to resist her charms? "I didn't think he was going to talk to anyone about the embarrassing situation we found ourselves in a few days ago."

"Max is like the brother I've never had. We've known each other for so long and although things never worked out between me and his older brother after I came out, Max and I remained the best of friends."

"Oh." I'm surprised by her revelation.

"Gabriel was a wonderful man. In fact, he was one of the best boyfriends I ever had, but during our twelve-month relationship, it became obvious I was running away from who I truly was and it wasn't fair to lead him to believe our story would have a happy ending. I've had conflicting feelings about women since I was fifteen years old and I kept dating men thinking if I could only find the right one, my feelings for women would dissolve. Gabe was everything a woman could ever dream of and then some, but he still wasn't able to fulfill a deep void inside me—I needed to be with a woman."

"I didn't know you were…" *She's gay?*

"You're not the first person to react that way. I think so many people have preconceived notions and stereotypes about lesbians, they're always taken aback when they find out."

We both laugh. Her comment calms the uneasiness that's taken permanent residence in the pit of my stomach since Stella jiggled the doorknob of the Fashion Archive room.

"Are you still on good terms with Max's brother?"

"It took a while for him to come around. I think he was hurt when I came out because he thought he wasn't man enough to please me. We didn't speak much for about a year, but my burgeoning friendship with Max allowed us to bump into each other and in time Gabe accepted the fact he was absolutely, irrefutably not responsible for my coming out to the world."

"It's amazing he was able to come around in the end."

"I value our friendship so much. I was willing to let him go had he not been able to accept who I truly was, but things turned out far better than I'd hoped. I'm lucky to still have him in my life."

"I understand about surrounding yourself with people who accept you for who you are. I'm blessed enough to have some amazing friends in my life. I really don't know where I would be without them."

The night after my second incident inside the Fashion Archive room wasn't supposed to be an intervention *per se*. We planned to meet at Devin's home for a relaxing evening where I was to entertain Lia, Dev and Lexi by spilling my guts about the best sex I've ever had in my life. The theme of the evening changed dramatically after I nearly got caught doing things I had no business doing at work. After escaping, I texted my three best friends to let them know I was in urgent need of love and support.

As usual, they came to my rescue and lifted my spirits. For a few hours, I was able to blank out the embarrassing event from my mind.

"I hope we might be able to be friends."

Deidra's confession takes me aback. *I didn't think she saw me this way since we haven't known each other for very long.*

"I'm a little younger than Max, but I'm still a bit older than you are and he thought you might need a guardian angel while you're away from New York. Since we'll be roommates over the next three days, in order to ensure no one suspects anything is going on between you and the CEO of my company, I figured maybe we'd get to know each other a little better before we land in Miami."

"I can't believe Max forced you to take on this responsibility."

"Let's get one thing straight, Candy. Max might be the boss at the office, but he's not the one who makes up my mind on such things. I willingly took this on after he shared how the two of you were spared public humiliation. I can't believe how lucky the two of you were."

"Tell me about it. One extra second and it would've been a disaster."

"I guess in your case, the wedding really did save the day."

"I love your perspective on this, Deidra. It's a good thing women love to gush all over their wedding day or else I most likely wouldn't be sitting next to you right now on my way to sunny Miami."

"Max told me you nearly turned as white as a ghost. But then again, who can blame you given the eerily close call? He said a photography assistant came to your rescue? We got interrupted as he was telling me the amusing details of your story and that part still remains a little fuzzy to me."

"Yeah. Stone Emerson's big fat Greek wedding saved my ass."

"Why don't we get the flight attendant to bring us a few drinks and you can tell me all about it."

"I'll be honest, a drink would help to calm me down."

"You don't have anything to worry about anymore. I scolded Max about his carefree behavior."

"You did?"

"Of course. When Max wants something or someone, it's like he has blinders on. It works well in the world of business, but when it comes to people, he forgets he can get them in trouble."

We both laugh.

Fifteen minutes later, Deidra and I are sipping on two gin and tonics as I spill my guts.

"Stone Emerson, a photography assistant on *Sassy*'s skinny side, happened to be waltzing by as Stella was about to walk in and catch us red-handed."

"Stone's your lucky charm." Deidra's laugh surprises me. She looks so put together, I'd never expect her to laugh like this.

"Yes. Thank God for her six-carat stone that shines brighter than the sun. Stella hadn't seen Stone since her wedding a month ago and as she was about to open the door, I heard her gasp at the sight of Stone's impressive ring. The next thing I knew, the two were commiserating in the hallway before deciding to go back to Stone's desk to look at her wedding album she kept on a personalized website. Since wedding blogs were still buzzing about the over-the-top wedding, Stella couldn't resist the invitation and temporarily forgot about her quest for archived wedding magazines. Max and I waited for a few minutes and when we didn't hear voices in the hallway, I quickly made my exit and he followed soon after."

"Wow. Talk about a timely encounter."

"More than you can imagine. I've never been more grateful to a man's wealth than I was trembling with fear on my knees in the Fashion Archive room."

"What do you mean?"

"Stone married big when she tied the knot with Dean Catsimatides."

"*The* Dean Catsimatides?"

"Yup. The one and only. Stone's new husband took over the presidency of Motor Oil Matides after his father Yiannis stepped down a few years ago. The company still operates in Greece, but the Catsimatideses hold several US base companies, including a network of gas stations and another very profitable division that sells fuel for airplanes. Apart from petroleum, Dean's family business has also invested in publishing, television and radio industries in America and in Europe, as well as a ferry company that serves the island of Crete. All these business interests have contributed to making Dean one of the richest men in Greece and in New York with an estimated net worth of thirty million. The downturn in the Greek economy eroded their fortune by seven million dollars and after a few challenging years, the patriarch of the family handed over the reins of his dynasty to his eldest son. Stone doesn't have to work, but she shows up at the magazine every day before most of us because she loves the fashion world so much."

"News of the wedding was everywhere in the media, but I didn't connect your Stone to the one who married Dean because I never imagined the Greek magnate's new wife would still be a working woman. Frankly, I became quite tired of it. Everything leading up to the big day seemed more like a circus than anything else." Deidra chugs down the last sip of her drink before smiling warmly at me. "It's all behind you now," she says, squeezing my hand in hers. "I hope you're ready to enjoy three days of sun-filled fun?"

"After the last few stressful days, I'm sure looking forward to enjoying a lot of cocktails by the poolside."

"I want to give you a fair warning, there will be quite a lot of work, but I think you know by now Max works hard and plays even harder."

Chapter Two

I slowly open my eyes, blinded by the early-morning sun filling the hotel room. I sit up to see if Deidra is still sleeping, but the rumpled blankets indicate she's already up and about.

"I haven't slept this well in two days," I tell myself aloud. I stretch my arms in the air like Sleeping Beauty awakening from her spell, feeling rejuvenated and excited to take on the day. "I wonder what time it is." I reach out to the nightstand to grab my iPhone and when I turn on my phone, I gasp. *How can it be eighty-thirty already? Crap. I'm going to be late. I need to skedaddle if I want to make it to the photoshoot by nine o'clock.*

I pull the sheets away from my body and jump to my feet, sprinting to the bathroom like an Olympian. I take a two-minute shower, put on a five-minute face, sleek back my hair into a low ponytail, grab the first outfit that catches my attention, slip into a pair of ballerina flat shoes, grab my bag and head for the door. I only allow myself to breathe when the elevator doors close behind me. I've been collecting a string of faux-pas like others collect trophies lately and I don't want to screw up this important day.

When I glance at my reflection in the mirror, I realize my understated look is quite pleasing. *Not bad for a woman who only had twenty minutes to get ready.*

When I arrive at the lobby, my phone flashes Deidra's number and I immediately accept her call. "Good morning, Deidra."

"Someone sounds quite chipper this morning. You looked like you needed the rest so I didn't want to wake you up this morning, since I was up before the roosters."

"I can't tell you how much I appreciate your gesture. I needed to sleep off the last few days. I must say, this morning, I feel like a new woman. What time did you get up?"

"I got up at six and I've been at the photoshoot since seven. I didn't think you wanted to wake up as early as I did."

"Yikes. You're right. If I had gotten up as early as you did, I most likely would be dozing off underneath a palm tree right now."

We both laugh.

"I'm going to send a car to pick you up to drive you to the mansion where we'll spend the majority of the day. We've rented an exquisite home and it will be the perfect backdrop for our next swimsuit collection. The chauffeured Benz should be there within fifteen minutes. I hope you don't mind waiting a bit?"

"The timing couldn't be better. It will allow me to grab a quick breakfast and a much-needed latte."

"If I were you, I'd keep it to the coffee only. As delicious as the food is at our boutique hotel, the spread here on location is outrageous. I've been stuffing my face since we got here and I can't stop."

"Oh, I'm really excited now. I'm starved. The last time we ate was when you and I snuck out of the hotel in search of local Miami delicacies."

"You're right. Even more reason for you to hold off until you get here. I can't promise the same exotic experience as last night, but the food here is simply sinful."

Deidra made reservations before leaving New York and she couldn't wait to whisk me to one of her favorite spots. CVI.CHE 105 serves the most exquisite traditional Peruvian dishes in a modern presentation. I loved everything about this Miami eatery, from the pleasant environment to the friendly staff, the excellent food and the kill-me-with-decadence desserts.

I'm usually not very adventurous when it comes to international foods, but something about Deidra gave me the confidence to dive into uncharted culinary territory. It was my first time trying ceviche, but to my surprise I thoroughly enjoyed the fish marinated in fresh lime juice, mixed with onions and a dash of cilantro, as an appetizer. We both opted for the *arroz con pollo*—an iconic Peruvian dish consisting of rice with chicken fragrant with touches of fresh coriander. If I could have licked my plate clean, I would have.

I was going to pass on dessert, but Deidra insisted on ordering the *lúcuma* cheesecake. She said it was an experience not to be missed and she was right. Deidra had to enlighten me on her selection because I had never heard of this exotic fruit before. It turns out the *lúcuma* is a Peruvian fruit. Although it's prevalent in Peru, only a handful of people grow it in California and in Hawaii. It was hard for me to pinpoint the taste, but I'd say it's a bit like caramel custard. The only thing I know is I could live off of this sweet creation.

The pastry chef at CVI.CHE 105 integrated the exotic fruit in a classic cheesecake over a base of chocolate cookies and with a fudge topping. I gripped the table when the first bite melted in my mouth—it was truly worthy of being featured on my list of food-porn faves.

"Since we finished dinner at nine o'clock last night, I've been fasting for the past twelve hours, but you've convinced me to be a little bit more patient." I laugh.

"Did you get Max's text messages?" Her question puts a dead stop to my giggling.

Shit. I was so preoccupied with not being late, I didn't even take the time to check my messages. "Shoot. I only got up thirty minutes ago and I was rushing to make it to the photoshoot on time. I didn't have the good sense to check and see if Max had been in touch."

"I most likely won't have an opportunity to speak openly to you because the set will be swarming with people and it will be nearly impossible to keep this conversation private."

My stomach churns. "Should I be worried?"

"Nah. Max came by our room last night. He wanted you to go up to his suite, but you were sleeping so soundly neither of us had the heart to wake you. He's not going to be at the photoshoot today, Candy. He has a full day of important back-to-back meetings with the top retailers in the city and with our local PR company. Since I'm here manning the fort at the photoshoot, his cousin Luana Monterroso, who manages our swimwear production in Brazil, will spend the day by his side. Chances are he's not going to reemerge until the party later tonight. I wanted to warn you in advance."

A flood of relief washes over me. I thought I was going to have to handle yet another crisis, but this I can accept. It will be excruciating to spend a whole day without seeing Max, but knowing he came looking for me last night makes me giddy. *This might turn out to be the longest day in history, but at least I'll see him later.*

"Thanks so much for the heads-up, Deidra. I guess I won't have to worry as to when he'll show up."

"You'll be so busy soaking up this new adventure, you won't even have time to miss him."

I know she's trying to make it easier for me to swallow this bitter pill, but I already know every minute away from him today will be agonizing.

* * *

When the driver slows down in front of the biggest house I've ever laid eyes on, I pull out my phone to double-check the address to make sure I'm at the right location. *Holy shit. Who the hell lives here? Lady Gaga?*

Once I double-check the chauffeur didn't make a mistake, I step out of the chic Mercedes Benz car. Although it's only ten in the morning by the time I arrive, the bombastic beat of an expert DJ fills the mansion. I immediately recognize one of my favorite songs from Justin Timberlake's 20/20 album. God, I love *Pusher Love Girl.*

I make my way to the garden where the photoshoot is to take place while still bobbing my head to the sultry vibe. The backyard is already packed with models, photographers, makeup artists, hairdressers and a series of people fretting as if we're on the set of a Hollywood movie. *Wow. They spared no expense for this swimsuit collection.*

Deidra waves at me from the other side of the pool as she sashays towards me. *She's thin and tall enough to be a top model and her gorgeous features don't hurt a bit.*

"You made it. You look fabulous in that adorable red dress with white polka dots. If you keep this up, we might have to include you as part of the lineup of models." She winks at me before hugging me.

Although it's warm, I draped myself in a matching red cardigan to hide my upper arms. If this heat keeps up, I'll have to ditch the cotton sweater in a few hours.

"There's no way I would allow anyone to take photos of me in a bathing suit." It would be easy to blame my flaming cheeks on the warm weather, but I know I'm beet red from embarrassment at the idea I could prance around in a skimpy little two-piece suit allowing the world to ogle all my lumps and bumps. *Yeah. It's not going to happen.*

"You, my dear, underestimate what you've got going on."

"You sound exactly like Max." It's hard to believe somebody as slim as Deidra could make this comment about my body. She's rail-thin. *She doesn't have an ounce of fat, how can she possibly understand?*

"I have a feeling by the end of the day you'll see yourself very differently. After watching our dangerously sexy plus-size models make love to the camera, I'm sure you'll have no choice but to face reality—you're as beautiful as all of the women we hired for today's shoot."

"Now you're really going to make me blush," I say, biting my lower lip as I drop my gaze to my shoes.

"Come on, I want to introduce you to a few of our models and introduce you to the photographer. I think if you spend a few minutes with them, you'll be able to find interesting angles you can inject in the articles." Before I can answer, Deidra grabs my hand and forces me to follow her. God, even in those heels she's walking fast. "Not that I'm one to start rumors, but word has it we might get a surprise visit from a reporter from CNN today. It seems plus-size model Tess Holliday's primetime appearance not long ago has the worldwide channel very interested in curvy women."

"Are you serious?" I speak so loudly I surprise myself.

"I'm not promising anything. I'm just saying there's a possibility we might have a very interesting guest on site today." She flashes me a mischievous smile. *I wonder if she knows more than she's letting on?*

"I hope the possibility turns out to be a reality. I would be beside myself to meet a reporter from CNN in the flesh."

"I wouldn't worry about reporters from prime-time channels for now. I promised you a spread fit for royalty and I believe we should start the day off on the right foot by indulging in delectable food before anything else. Once you're fully satiated, I'll introduce you to key people." Deidra's eyes are gleaming with excitement and she pulls me towards the kitchen by the hand.

I doubt very much I'll ever be able to forget this day.

* * *

I think I need to pinch myself. I can't believe I spent most of the morning interviewing some of the top models in the plus-size industry.

Since this is a rare opportunity to interview someone face to face as opposed to an email interview, a Skype interview or even a phone interview, I went to town. I quizzed these beauties on their beauty regimes, their makeup tips, their hair secrets and flattering wardrobe selections for plus-size figures.

Most of the models are sweethearts. I got along famously with nearly all of them, but I must say there was something slightly off-putting about Bruna Alvares. *Who cares if she was voted plus-size model of the year when she has such a snooty attitude?* I know she's an international model and she's graced the cover of *Sassy* magazine and of a number of other publications dedicated to plus-size women, but there's no reason to look down on me the way she does. I could easily chalk it up to our height difference, since the Brazilian model stands five-eleven before she slips into her five-inch heels and my flat ballerina shoes don't do much to enhance my petite five-four figure, but I'd be ignoring the obvious negative vibes she's been sending my way since we first met. I know I seem plain next to her glamorous goddess-like self, but if she clicks her tongue while rolling her eyes before answering another one of my questions, I'll scream. *Biatch.*

As much as I hate to admit it, Bruna is beautiful, although not in a classical way. Her nose is a little on the large side, her eyes may be too wide for her face, and her forehead is a little small, but combined with her olive skin, naturally pouty lips, and jet-black hair, it works. She also oozes sex. I tried to remain as inconspicuous as possible while Ken, the top photographer, was gushing all over her earlier, but it's impossible to be blind to how she manipulates people around her, especially men, with her sultry looks and her wide mouth. It didn't take long to confirm Ken was straight given how his eyes devoured every single one of her curves. I think he must have asked her to arch her back at least eighty times to better showcase her enormous tits. *I'm sure after this shoot, he's either going to fuck her or he's going to retreat to his room to jerk off salivating over her photos.*

I'm still pouting with my arms crossed over my chest, fuming at Bruna's condescending attitude, when Giovanna Rossi calls out my name. "Candy, I've been talking Brian's ear off about how I've never missed one of your articles since you took on the position of plus-size editor at *Sassy* magazine. After I went on and on about how you inspired me to send my headshots to an agency, he insisted on speaking to you."

"Oh, Giovanna, you've already made my day with your compliments. I can't believe you're spreading your gospel to strangers."

Giovanna Rossi and I have been email penpals since the day I published my first article for *Sassy* magazine. I still remember how shy she was about expressing her dream of becoming a model and how I encouraged her to go after what she wanted with gusto. I was the first person she contacted when Plus Models signed her on as one of their rising stars.

Today, she's one of the highest-paid plus-size models in the industry.

"Are you kidding me? I wouldn't be here today in Miami on one of the most luxurious properties in the country parading in my bathing suit for an obscene amount of money if it weren't for you. Brian was curious to meet the woman responsible for inspiring my success." She winks, pulling at the arm of the tall man standing by her side. "Brian Whitfield, please meet Candice Westerman."

Giovanna is flanked by a tall, good-looking young guy with piercing light blue eyes, dressed more to attend an Ivy League school than for a photoshoot. His gaze is as striking as his red hair. *Is her boyfriend with her on set?*

"Candy, Brian has at least one million questions to ask you. I hope you have a minute or two to answer them. I'll leave the two of you alone to chat. I have to go change for my next photo session." She laughs and turns on her heel. Before I can even thank her for the introduction, Giovanna meshes with the rest of the bodies on the set. *I guess Brian isn't her boyfriend after all.*

"It's such an unbearably hot day, do you mind if we seek shelter?" Brian asks.

"I couldn't agree with you more. I must have guzzled down three gallons of water today, but I'm still dehydrated and if it wasn't so unladylike, I'd admit I've been sweating profusely all afternoon. I'd much prefer sitting in the shade." Armed with the confidence of seeing so many gorgeous curvy women strutting their stuff clad only in bikinis, I ditched my red cardigan a few hours ago, shoving it at the bottom of my tote bag. *I can either continue to be self-conscious or I can avoid passing out from the insane heat.*

"Three gallons of water? I'm surprised you haven't spent the better part of the day running to the bathroom." He laughs.

"I tend to exaggerate when I want to drive a point across."

"The mark of a great writer." He flashes me a complicit smile.

"Why, thank you, sir."

"One little confession. I'm sure you can't possibly have perspired as much as I have."

We both laugh aloud.

I like this Brian guy and I don't even know who he is.

Brian and I make our way to the gazebo near the pool to hide from the harshness of the beaming sun.

"Giovanna is so forthcoming with her accolades about you, I'm hoping I might be able to interview you and include our discussion in an article I'll run on our website."

"I must admit, I was completely unprepared for Giovanna's eloquent comments," I say, taking a seat across from him. "Which website do you write for?" *I should ask in case it turns out to be* Hustler *magazine or some other site for horny men.*

"Oh, my gosh, this heat is affecting my brain. I should've mentioned I'm a writer for CNN.com's Living section."

What did he say? "What do you mean CNN.com?" I can hear the panic in my voice. *Surely this is a joke.*

"From your reaction, you're either pleasantly surprised or you're the only one on the planet who's never heard of CNN."

The air is completely sucked out of my lungs and my head is spinning so fast I have to bring my hand up to my face to slow things down. *I could blame my sudden affliction on the weather, but I'm pretty sure Brian's place of employment is responsible for causing my body to go into shock. This cannot be happening.*

"Are you sure you want to interview me?" I ask incredulously.

"I gather you've heard of CNN.com." He smirks. "You're hilarious, Candy. I have a sneaky feeling your enthusiasm is contagious and it will fuel the article I write about you."

"We're really doing this?" *Shit. Is he serious?*

"Unless there's another Candy Westerman who is the editor of the plus-size division at *Sassy* magazine and the voice of curvy women in America, I'd say I'm sitting across from the right person."

Mother of God! If I'm dreaming, please don't wake me up.

Chapter Three

Brian and I have been chatting animatedly for over ninety minutes. We're removed enough from the busy set to keep our conversation private, but close enough for me to catch all the action. Every time Brian asks me a question, I secretly pinch myself under the table, still unwilling to believe Lady Luck could be on my side like this.

Brian is getting ready to ask me another question when he stops with his mouth wide open. His eyes shift above my head and I turn around to discover what's caught his attention. The sun is so bright, even with my designer shades I have to squint before making out Deidra's slender figure. She smiles warmly before addressing Brian.

"I'm sorry to interrupt your interview, but I was wondering how much longer you'll be. I received a text message a few minutes ago from Mr. Keller and he's very eager to meet with Candy to go over the article she's writing about this photoshoot for *Sassy* magazine."

Mr. Keller? Why is she being so formal?

"Deidra, I've had a wonderful conversation with Candy and I'm certain I have more than enough insightful facts to craft a story about her passion and dedication to positively influence plus-size women across America. We exchanged numbers and I'm sure I can be in touch with her if I have further questions. Chances are I most likely will, since it's only when I start writing I'm able to discover the missing gems. If Mr. Keller requires Candy for a meeting, I would hate to keep her any longer."

Positively influence? Wow. I don't remember wording it quite like he does, but sure, let's roll with his version. I guess CNN knows best, right?

"I'm happy to hear you were able to gather enough information. Mr. Keller has been trying to reach our dear Candy here, but I believe her phone is off."

Huh? Oh, shit. "Oh, no. Did I turn off my phone instead of switching it to vibrate?" *I'm such an idiot sometimes.* "When the videographer asked everyone on the set to make sure no phones would be ringing while he was shooting the footage for the promotional video, I must have shut off my phone."

"Mr. Keller has been impatiently trying to reach you. Since these days are so hectic and I'm running around all over the place at the same time, I've been letting my messages go to my voicemail and he hasn't been able to reach either of us in the last few hours. Needless to say he's slightly ticked right now."

"Oh, gosh," I babble. "I was under the impression Mr. Keller wouldn't be able to make it to the photoshoot. I feel terrible about being unreachable." I pull my shades from my nose, grab my bag and stick my hand to the bottom to fish for my phone. I fumble to turn it on. *Why didn't she warn me he'd be in touch later in the day?*

"Deidra, I don't want Candy to be in any kind of trouble. If she's expected in an important meeting, please don't let me hold her back." Brian's uneasy smile confirms he's as worried as I am about Deidra's announcement.

"Thank you, Brian. Candy, do you mind following me?" Deidra's request is more a command than a question. I quickly gather my belongings and push back my chair with such force it tumbles behind me and causes somewhat of a ruckus on the set. Deidra folds her tall body and grabs the chair before placing it back in its place. *I'm so clumsy sometimes.* I silently scorn myself.

I turn to Brian to mutter a few parting words. "I really don't know how to thank you for such an amazing opportunity. This day was already surreal as is, but the last hour and a half has taken an already perfect day to celestial levels. Thank you so very much for being willing to listen to my story."

"You were a riot to interview, Candy. I'm sure I'll be in touch soon. Enjoy the rest of your stay in sunny Miami."

I wave goodbye to Brian before following Deidra's quick steps.

"I'm really sorry Max has been trying to reach me. I didn't mean to be missing in action," I say, trying my best to salvage the situation even though I was completely unaware I was to have a meeting with Max this late in the day.

Deidra stops so abruptly I nearly bump into her. "He wants to see you privately. If he walks into the mansion he'll be attacked by a mob of eager industry people wanting to talk to him hoping to advance their career. He doesn't want to bring too much attention to himself or to you, so he's waiting for you outside in a SUV."

No way. "This little ruse is because he wants to see me? I thought he wasn't supposed to come to the mansion today."

"We're talking about Maximiliano Keller. What Max wants Max gets, and right now he wants you, love. He told me over the phone he was calling it a day so the two of you can spend some time together before the big party tonight because he hasn't seen you since the little incident at your office."

"Oh my God. In my twenty-four years on this planet, I'd say this is the most indescribably wonderful day of my life." I beam, reliving the highlights of today.

"If you're going to hang out with Max, you'd better get used to it," she says, raising her eyebrows as she flashes me a perfect set of pearly white teeth. "Come on, let me get you out of here before he calls me again looking for you." Deidra is pulling my hand and dragging me across the opulent house.

"Wait," I let out, panicked, as we near the front door. "How am I going to know which car is his?"

"When you step outside, you'll notice a chauffeur standing next to a big black SUV. You can't miss him. Now off you go." She pushes me out the door with a little tap against my butt. *I guess I'm on my own now.*

Deidra was right. It doesn't take me long to spot a man standing guard near an impressive-looking shining black SUV. *I've never seen anything this massive on four wheels before.* I walk towards the vehicle and quicken my step when the man built like a bodyguard gestures my way.

"Ms. Westerman, my name is Manuel. Mr. Keller is waiting for you."

"It's a pleasure to meet you, Manuel. Please call me Candice."

The chauffeur nods in agreement before extending his hand to help me inside the car. When he opens the door, I'm face to face with the sexy, gorgeous, and entirely delicious man I've desperately missed all day. *He's even more disarmingly seductive than I remember. Not seeing him for the past forty-eight hours has been more difficult than I ever imagined.*

My excitement quickly turns to worry when I notice how high the vehicle is set on these enormous wheels. *How the hell am I going to get up there with my short legs?* I look up at Max and I can read his amusement. *Bastard.* I think Manuel must have read my mind because he speaks the magic words. "Please allow me."

With a little help from Max's chauffeur, I gracelessly yank my body next to Max's.

"Why are these vehicles set so high up?" I huff. "They are absolutely not built for short people."

"God, I've missed your sense of humor today." Max is flashing me his utterly yummy smile—the one I can never resist.

Before I can even answer, Max is already busy giving instructions to Manuel. "Why don't you go inside the mansion? Enjoy the spectacular view of gorgeous women covered in nothing more than a few pieces of fabric, sample the amazing spread—I've been told the food is exceptional. Have some fun and I'll see you back here in about an hour. Please make sure to text me to let me know you're on your way."

"Of course, Mr. Keller. I'll see you back here a little later. Ms. Westerman, enjoy the rest of your afternoon."

"Thank you. Mr. Keller is right, the spread is to die for."

We both wait patiently for Manuel to close the door behind him before locking eyes with each other.

"How was your day today, sweetness?" Max slides his body so close to mine I hold my breath. I'm already turned on by his proximity and he hasn't even touched me yet. "Deidra might have alluded to the fact you've officially become a celebrity." He grins as he loosens his tie and undoes the first three buttons of his pristine white shirt.

Even though the SUV is air-conditioned, my cheeks warm when I think of all the incredible events that have unfolded in the few hours since I set foot in this mammoth residence. "An hour isn't nearly enough time for me to describe the astonishing day I've had."

"I'd hate for us to waste an hour chitchatting about every aspect of your day, as amazing as it might have been. I'd much prefer to show you how much I've missed you." Without warning he grabs the back of my neck and crushes my lips with a passionate kiss. *Oh, Jesus.*

"I've missed you so much, Max," I answer between kisses. *My God, I can't believe how much I crave his touch.*

"You've been on my mind all day." As if to punctuate his words he grabs my hand and forces me to cup his hard cock. "I couldn't stand being trapped one more minute in another dry meeting when I could only think of losing myself inside your pussy." He removes my other hand from his forearm and brings it to his mouth. As he nibbles on my fingers, I can't help but reminisce how his lips tightened around my nub the last time we were together. "Have you ever been fucked in the back of a car before, Candy?" The rawness of his question startles me.

"When you said you wanted to skip the chit-chat, you weren't joking." I chuckle.

"Honey, I haven't been able to fuck you in over forty-eight very long hours. Do you know how excruciating it's been for me? I must have jerked off at least twenty times yesterday and twenty times more last night after I went to get you and I realized you were sound asleep in Deidra's room. I'm not even going to bore you with how many times I've already jerked off today. Let's just say at this rate I won't be able to use my right hand. What I do know is if I don't stick my hungry cock inside your burning-hot pussy, I'll lose my mind."

Christ. I struggle to find the words he's knocked out of me. "Oh."

"Fuck. You're adorable enough to eat. I'm very lucky you decided to wear a flirty dress today. I thought I was going to have to struggle with a pair of pants before I was able to slide between your luscious thighs. The red screams naughty. I like it."

"Well, since I woke up late..."

"Shhh." He presses his index finger against my lips and I widen my eyes, surprised by his sudden reaction. "The only words I want from you are 'yes', 'more' and 'fuck me hard'. You can tell me all about the details of your eventful day later tonight when you sleep in my bed. Am I clear?"

I gasp with delight when a quiver runs through me from my toes all the way up to the tight peaks of my nipples. "Yes, sir."

"Good girl." Max strokes my cheek softly before kissing me, allowing me to feel his overwhelming warmth. Without warning he grabs my legs and flings them over his. "Which one of my creations are you wearing under your red dress?"

I'm about to answer his question when a devious thought runs through my mind. "I decided to slide into a pair of Jabe Curves underwear today instead of one of yours. In fact, I don't think I packed any of your lingerie for this trip." I pucker my lips to tease him further.

"You can't possibly be wearing a design from one of our biggest competitors. You're joking, right?"

"Maybe," I say like an innocent angel before bursting into laughter.

"You had me going for a few minutes. Let's take a look at which cock-hardening lingerie you slipped on this morning," he says, glancing down the length of me. "God save me if your underwear matches the color of your dress. I may not be able to contain myself." Before I'm even able to muster up an answer he's already pulled my dress all the way up to my waist and he growls at the sight of my crimson panties. "Oh, you naughty, naughty vixen. Jesus, the ruffles hugging your round hips are going to drive me mad. It's a good thing I can get you another pair of these…"

"Why would I need another pair?"

I gasp when with one quick movement Max tears my panties off. The rip of the fabric echoes in the silence and we both lower our eyes to take in my exposed pussy. *Mother of God, people from the set could be passing by Max's SUV and they might catch us in this salacious act.*

He smiles with satisfaction, slips two eager fingers into my wetness and parts my lips. Instinctively, I squeeze my legs together, flushing with embarrassment at the idea of being so vulnerable in a man's hands. When I look up at him through my lashes, he frowns until I open my legs wider, enough for him catch a glimpse of my bare pussy yearning to swallow him whole.

"Very nice, sweetness. I can't wait to tease your pretty little clit. God knows I've waited all day long for this moment."

My nipples tighten and a drizzle of my own juices slides all the way back to the crack of my ass. *This is so dirty and so wrong, but how can I say no to him?*

"We only have a few precious minutes together and I want to make the most out of every single second. Once I'm finished playing with your pussy, we'll have just enough time for me to pound you hard to make up for the last two days of abstinence. After the party tonight, I want you to come straight up to my room. I want to fuck you over and over and over again until you pass out. Do you like what I have planned for you?" I'm completely under his dizzying spell and I'm so taken by every raunchy word he's uttered so far, I can only nod in agreement. "I love it when we're on the same page." Max slides his fingers into my pussy again, tracing a circle under the hood of my lips, increasing my arousal very quickly to near-climactic levels. My body quivers uncontrollably as he fondles me, skating his fingers over my clit until it throbs. When he pushes a finger inside me again, I clench his arm to avoid yelling aloud. *No man has ever touched me so intimately. He's caressing me as if I have no right to deny him.*

My nipples nearly burn under the satin fabric of my bra, begging to be released, touched and sucked.

As if he can read my mind, he reaches his hand down my dress and yanks out my breasts. No part of me is sheltered from his hungry eyes. The sensation of his lips wrapping around my erected peak sends me into a frantic euphoria. *Yes, yes, yes.* I shake my head left to right against the back seat, desperately trying to contain the wave of desire threatening to completely wash over me.

My head comes up and I stare at him. "Your mouth is going to be the end of me," I mutter before dropping my head against the seat as quickly as I lifted it. Every ounce of my being is focused on my clit and I don't have any energy to say more.

"I bought you a little gift. Do you want to see it?"

"You bought me a present? Max, you didn't have to, but I'd love to see it."

He pulls his finger out of my wetness and I whimper, already missing his touch.

"Don't worry, sweetness. I'm not done with you, but I do need my hand to pull out the little trinket I got for you from inside the pocket of my jacket." He flashes me a bad-boy grin and my heart skips a beat. Something about his playful eyes tells me his gift might be more for him than it is for me. "Have you ever seen one of these?" He's waving a little purple rubbery item shaped like a cone.

"What is it? I've never seen anything like this before," I say, scrunching my nose.

"Are you telling me you're a virgin?" He smiles.

I yank myself up to rest on my elbows to take a better look at the little item he's dangling in front of me. I'm completely stumped. "What do you mean? I think you've been inside me enough times to know I'm not a virgin."

"Technically you are if no other man has ever claimed your ass before me."

I open my mouth to protest, but my heart is beating so fast I choke up. "What? I mean... Are you serious? There's no way." I string together a few words to express my sheer panic, but I'm too much in shock to share my growing fear.

His eyebrows draw together, his hazel eyes turning cold. "Are you refusing me?"

No, no, no. Whatever he has in mind, it's not happening. Lia confessed anal sex hurts like hell. "No. You can't go there."

"Do you know what I'm going to do to you, Candy?"

I shake my head. "But you talked about..." I can't even allow the words to escape my mouth.

"Do you think I'd hurt you? I love nothing more than to see you come undone in my arms when I make you climax. This little butt plug will bring you more pleasure than you've ever thought conceivable."

"I'm not a girl who would allow a man to do such dirty things to me. Goddamn, Max, you can't just do stuff to me without asking me." I struggle to slide my legs off his lap, but he's much stronger than

I am. I'm a helpless prisoner. His grip holds me firmly in place despite my tantrum.

"Have I ever steered you wrong so far?" His jaw tightens and a quaking jolts inside me.

"No, but…"

"No, but what?"

I can't look away from his intense eyes. Even though the windows of the SUV are tinted, his eyes have turned bright green. Despite the cool temperature in the vehicle, pearls of sweat break out all over my body.

"You either trust me or you don't, Candy. We can stop this now, you can get out of the car and walk right back into the mansion. The decision is yours."

I don't want him to stop. No. I want him to hold me, caress every part of my body and lick me until I come screaming, banging my fist against the cushion of the seat to sustain the violent climactic waves. I want his hands all over me, not a sex toy inside my butt.

He awaits my decision with a blank expression on his face, looking down at me. He's making me feel extremely self-conscious, even naked, although he's not fully disrobed me. *God, I don't want to walk out the door.* Even as my mind screams no, I'm already defeated by my desire for him. "I trust you implicitly."

"I'm happy you feel this way about me, because without trust, there's so much you won't be able to discover."

"Max, is this… I mean, am I going to be in pain?"

"Nah. I don't want to see you suffer, sweetness. I bought an anal plug well suited for beginners like you. I've also made sure to buy lube to ease your introduction to one of the most enjoyable and sinful pleasures you'll ever experience in your life. Since this little baby here is a nice small size, it should slide as effortlessly inside your ass as my cock slides into your wet pussy," he says, raising his eyebrows as he shakes the sex toy in front of me. "I want you to turn on your stomach, get up on all fours and spread your cheeks wide." Max must have sensed my hesitation because he frowns. "Now. We don't have all day and my erection is aching for relief."

"Oh." My breath comes in small pants of excitement and worry as I flip my body over and land on my knees. I hear the sound of rustling fabric behind me and I turn my head slightly to catch him undoing his belt buckle before he unzips his pants. Folding towards me, he clamps his left hand against the roof of the SUV to steady his body. He flings off his shoes and uses his right hand to pull down his pants and his boxer briefs in one clean sweep before kneeling on the seat, straddling my naked ass. I keep my eyes on him the whole time, too mesmerized to look away. He wraps his hungry cock before meeting my worried expression.

"You really don't have to look so terrified. I bet you'll be begging for more of this once you realize you've lived this long without experiencing the most mind-blowing orgasm of your life. If you turn your head around it will be a lot more fun for both of us."

I slowly pivot my head and move my gaze away from his ruggedly handsome face. *He's never steered me wrong so far. I should allow him to take my body where it's never been before.*

Max squirts a cold liquid between my cheeks and I gasp. Then something presses against my rectum, trying to poke inside my hole from behind, and I whine, "Noooo." He remains unmoved by my sudden burst of panic. Instead, he presses one of his hands against my ass, while the other decisively inserts the... kinky toy.

To my surprise, it slides in, stretching me open as the butt plug pops in smoothly. *God, it's inside me—foreign and hard.*

A sudden thought sends me into panic mode again. "You're... Max... Your cock..." I try my best to find out if he plans on fucking me there once he removes the toy, but I'm so terrified, I'm unable to express myself.

"Relax. I'm not going to take you there, not today anyway. I'm using the anal plug to stretch you a tad because you're a sweet virgin. You're still too tight, and I'm way too big to fuck your ass without any prior training. This gives you an idea of how amazing it feels."

"Okay." Relief washes over me and I calm down a bit.

"I guess I should've also told you I got you a second little gift."

Consternation grips me as I take in his words. I swivel my head behind to look at him so quickly it loosens my ponytail. "What do you mean a second gift?" Every muscle in my body tenses. It's as if my insides are liquefying.

"I can't possibly ignore your clit. I bought a tiny vibrator I'm going to press tantalizingly against your node while I pound your pussy with my dick. And of course, during this whole time, my free hand will be pushing the butt plug deeper and deeper," he says, tapping the little purple plastic cone stuck inside me. "When I'm done with you, not only will you think you've seen God, but you might never walk again." He grins and I shiver. "The only unfortunate thing is the fact I only have two hands. As I'll keep your clit and your asshole busy, I won't be able to fill my hands with your huge boobs. I guess I'll have to make up for that tonight by fucking your tits and leaving my cum all over you."

His words ignite something inexplicable in me and instead of fear I'm overpowered by wanton indecency, willing to allow him to use my body for his pleasure as long as he pushes my climax over the edge.

Max folds his body on top of mine and presses his chest against my back. In this position he feels so heavy. *Yes.* Even though he kept his shirt and his jacket on, the warmth of his body seeps through me. When his cock caresses my behind and his hand touches my pussy simultaneously, I jump forward, surprised by how much I've missed him.

He remains true to his promise. He turns on the vibrator before covering my clit with his strong hand. *He must have turned the thing on with his teeth since both of his hands are on me.* His cock slides in gently before he picks up his cadence. The slow grind turns into a frantic assault on my pussy. He pounds his dick in and out of me, slick with my own juices, teasing my hunger. I push against him as I match his frenzied rhythm. Max ruthlessly flirts with my sensitive nub even as he thrusts his thick cock into me. *Don't stop.* He hammers me over and over again as he presses the anal plug deeper, sending me near the brink. I moan as the excruciating and yet delightful pleasure increases. When he circles my clit with the vibrator, I muffle a scream as a climactic tide tears through me.

"Holy Jesus," I pant. Explosion after explosion rips through my body, shattering me into pieces with exquisite abandonment.

"Fuck," Max roars behind me. His fingers grip my hips in such a commanding way he stops my body from bobbing forward. My muscles spasm around his hard length as another wave of pleasure ripples through me. Somehow the air in the SUV has disappeared and I gasp, unable to catch my breath. "Oh, baby, I missed this with you." Wrapping his arms around my stomach, he starts into the inexorable tempo I've become used to. Only somehow it seems more intense.

He's going to rip right through me at this rate. I'm not sure if it's the raunchiness of having sex at the back of a vehicle parked in the middle of a residential street, but he rams me like a beast. It takes me a few seconds to understand why all my senses are still tingling. *He's left the butt plug in.* Every thrust inside me moves the plastic cone deeper, filling me and sending odd sensations thrumming through me. Hedonistic thrills I've never known before. Ones I don't want to like... but I do. He's broken me in.

"Are you ready for round two?" Max slows down his cadence, throttling himself down, moving his cock in and out very slowly. "I've got a lot more to give and I know you can take it," he says as he leans down to cup my breasts. "God, your tits are gorgeous. They're so full and I love how they spill over my hand."

"Max, I don't think I can take more," I pant between breaths.

"Of course you can. Don't think about it, relax into it. It wouldn't be fair if I gave you a quick fuck. I want your eyes to roll into the back of your head when you climax."

He doesn't give me a chance to protest a second time. Gradually he angles himself so his cock hits a part of me I didn't even know existed. He grinds into me when I stiffen. "Did I hit your G-spot, baby?"

"I don't know, but I'm going to lose my mind." This is all new to me, I probably wouldn't be able to recognize my G-spot if it were looking at me in the face.

"I didn't realize you are also a virgin in that department. For a woman, hitting the right spot is like striking gold because your G-spot is as sensitive as the peak of your breasts."

I shake my head, refusing to believe his cock can do this to me, and I try to move away from him.

"Oh, no, you don't." His commanding voice halts my escape. Instead of moving my body forward,

I clench uncontrollably around him as I realize my own vulnerability. *He knows more about my body than I do.* At this moment, my control is in tatters and I give over my will to him. My body is evidently his—why would I want it any other way? He pushes my legs farther apart to emphasize my helplessness.

"Your closed fists hurt my feelings because they indicate to me you don't trust me fully. You may say you do, but Candy, you're not willing to let go."

His words challenge my resolve and surprise me at the same time. I didn't realize both hands were closed into fists.

"I do trust you, but you're stirring a flood of overwhelming feelings that reach down deep into my core. If I let go entirely, I fear I may never be able to recover."

"The intense pleasure you're so desperately trying to rob yourself of is exactly what I want to inflict upon you."

"But…" I open my mouth, but nothing comes out.

Without asking for further permission, Max forces me to submit by driving into me. Slowly I allow myself to let go and instinctively tighten around him. My thighs, wide apart, tremble like leaves in a winter wind as my orgasm builds. I'm close. Max pushes back on his knees and slides his hand down my stomach, anchoring me in place and putting pressure on my clit at the same time. With the other hand, he pushes the butt plug deeper into my defenseless ass. He wiggles it, increasing the delirious sensation, increasing my submission to him.

"Argh," I hiss. My whole body quivers in shock, and I let out an indescribable noise. "Lord." My hips jerk, inadvertently rubbing my swollen node against his hand. "This is too amazing," I whimper, yielding to ecstasy.

"Come hard for me, Candy."

"Oh, Max, I'm... I'm..." The words escape me as I come undone. Something this transcendental must be forbidden.

Max thrusts with his cock and slides the soft naughty sex toy out of me without so much as a warning. *Bastard. I was so close. He can't deprive me now.* "No," I cry out as my body craves more of him to fill the void. Suddenly, he pulls his cock out and pushes the plug in. My legs turn rigid, my back arches, thrusting my butt up higher. As he continues his mischievous game of alternating the thrusts in my wetness and ass, my needy pussy clamps down on his cock, tighter and tighter, and seconds later I lose it. "Yes. God. Please." I convulse, wailing my climax in short cries corresponding to each rippling spasm of my pussy.

"Fuck, Candy, I love your unrestrained response to me."

I'm so far gone I can't answer. I can only focus on one part of my body right now. I'm too busy enjoying the tight milking sensation around his cock. I squeeze down hard and I milk him until I can't stand it anymore.

"Holy Christ." Max pushes the butt plug firmly inside me before grasping my hips with both hands and pounding into me. "Shit, shit, shit." His own climax boils up and out of him like a violent tornado.

Our heavy breathing fills the SUV. *I'm spent.* I'm still holding on to the backseat cushion as if my life depends on it, lost between Planet Earth and Nirvana.

"You did good." Max wraps his arms around me, burying his face in the nape of my neck. "You surprised me, sweetness. I didn't think you were going to allow me to expand your sexual bliss. If I could, I'd stay deep inside you forever."

And I'd allow your beautiful hard cock to remain inside me like this until the end of time. Max is the lover I've always dreamed of. This afternoon's kinky escapade has robbed me of my strength, my will, my speech and I can only shudder in his arms in response. *God save me. I think I'm falling for him.*

Chapter Four

After our raunchy rendezvous, I try to slip back into the mansion as inconspicuously as possible, fearing everyone around me will know I got fucked in the middle of the afternoon at the back of a SUV by a god of sex. I tiptoe inside the home and run straight to the bathroom so I can pull myself together.

Holy Jesus. I look like I got caught in a raving storm. I'm bewildered by the telltale signs of my little romp with Max—smeared lipstick, mascara running down my face like a Goth devotee at the end of a night of feverish clubbing in one of New York's trendiest spots, hair looking like I rolled out of bed a few minutes ago and no matter how many times I tried to smooth down my dress at the back of the car before stepping out, I still look disheveled.

I guess I should be grateful, because if I didn't look like such a hot mess, I'd never believe I allowed Max to corrupt me to this point. *Damn, I loved every single second of it.*

Once I feel secure enough, I waltz back on the photoshoot set as if nothing happened. Luckily for me, everyone around is so busy fretting, no one notices I disappeared for over an hour.

I try to locate Deidra in the sea of busy bodies, but after thirty minutes, she's still nowhere to be found. I look around hoping I might be able to continue my conversation with Brian, but he's disappeared as well. After forty-five minutes, I give up searching for both of them. *Maybe it's time for me to go. I want to dazzle Max tonight.* Since I've already collected more than enough material to cover one week's worth of articles, I call it a day. I grab a cab and head back to the hotel to get ready for tonight's big bash.

* * *

I'm standing in front of the tall mirror in my hotel room and I'm admiring myself from every angle. Luckily for me I have the room all to myself since Deidra left me a note letting me know she has to be at the party before everyone else. I have carte blanche to pamper myself like a princess before a ball and I haven't skimped out. I've spent the last two hours primping myself for the VIP party Max is hosting tonight.

Usually, I walk into a party expecting everybody will look better than me—and everybody will be wafer thin. But after spending the afternoon at the mansion ogling curvy body after curvy body, I know tonight I won't feel out of place.

I have to stop biting my lower lip or else I'll end up ruining my lipstick. I've been fidgeting nervously, hoping I look good enough to hold Max's attention despite the parade of beauties. I'm not a fool, I know I'm in for some steep competition tonight—the other women will be gorgeous plus-size models and I'm well, me. Of course, my agitation is only amplified by the fact I've finally admitted to myself I want a lot more with Max. *If I confess to him how I feel, I might drive him away since he hasn't made any promises of forever.*

Given Max's penchant for curvier women, I can't ignore the fact his eyes will travel tonight unless I look arresting. I was so worried about messing things up, I patched Devin in on a Skype video call so he could walk me through all the secret steps top stylists rarely reveal to the public. After our two-hour conversation, during which I was getting ready under Devin's watchful eye, I became a believer because right before my eyes I had transformed from an ordinary and forgettable woman into the kind of head-turner I've always wanted to be.

After fanning myself and reciting a few silent prayers, I muster up enough courage to grab my evening clutch and head to the party.

Although Max and our team are staying at the luxurious Four Seasons Hotel Miami, the swanky affair will take place at Smith & Wollensky. I was quite surprised when Deidra told me Max refused to use the meeting rooms of the acclaimed hotel chain in favor of one of Miami's most sought-after eateries in order to keep some sense of privacy. He wants to have the privilege of leaving the party behind when he's had enough. What Max wants, Max gets.

As I sit at the back of the chauffeured car, I pull out my phone and Google the party location. I'm quite impressed by the reviews. Quoted as one of the best places to watch the sunset in Miami, Smith & Wollensky is the ideal destination to watch cruise ships sail by as they leave Port of Miami while sipping on cocktails or enjoying one of their award-winning wines. TripAdvisor claims nothing beats the experience of strolling through the nearby parks admiring the sky being washed with shades of tangerine, lavender and pink.

I hope Max will be able to get away. I'd love nothing more than to watch the sunset hanging from his arm.

I barely have time to complete my search before the car slows down in front of the high-end steakhouse. It looks more like a prestigious estate than a restaurant and I'm already excited by the idea of rubbing elbows with some of the top names in the fashion world. I don't even have time to set one heel outside of the vehicle before an eager man rushes to help me out. I open my mouth to thank him, but a familiar voice interrupts me.

"Candice, what an interesting choice for an evening dress for such an important party."

The minute I recognize her strong accent, my stomach churns. *Did she really have to be the first person to greet me?*

Until Bruna made her disparaging remark, I thought my dress looked amazing. But the way she's staring down at me, from what seems to be twelve-inch heels, with both fists on her hips and a look of disdain, I start doubting myself. *Oh, God. Devin would never steer me wrong. This is his profession and he knows how to play up a woman's best features, but this bitch has me worried now.*

"Bruna, I see we've arrived at the same time. What a coincidence," I say, trying to deflate her attack. I'm not sure a slender actress like Gwyneth Paltrow would be caught dead wearing such an in-your-face design, but Bruna doesn't seem to have any qualms about exposing her giant tits under her couture. I'm not exactly sure how to describe what she's wearing, but in my opinion the combination of sequins and see-through fabric that runs down each side of her body, hugging her enormous ass, is over the top and clearly denotes how she's desperate for attention. In fact, the dress is so short, it should really be called a tee-shirt. "Black is such a classic selection for evening wear. Who's the designer?"

"It's a Brazilian design," she retorts, rolling her r. "Americans are far too conservative to allow a curvy woman to showcase her assets. Fuller women in this country dress like frigid nuns, but in my country we believe if you have it, why not flaunt it," she continues before tilting her head back and letting out an almost evil laugh.

We're not conservatives, you idiot. We have a sense of dignity. "It does seem Brazilian women are bigger... how can I say this... risk-takers than we are.

We Americans are a little shy in baring it all for strangers to ogle freely." I look up at her and I'm met with a pair of cold brown eyes. It's still not clear what I've done to irritate this woman so much considering I only met her earlier today for the first time, but everything about her suggests she can't stand the sight of me.

"What does 'ogle' mean?"

"Oh, I forgot English is not your first language. It is simply another way of saying 'admire,'" I lie through gritted teeth.

"Ah." Suddenly she's beaming like a peacock. "Thank you for the compliment." *If you weren't so dense and so full of yourself, you'd realize it wasn't a compliment at all.* "I guess your dress suits you, but I would never choose something so... saintly. Your dress covers eighty percent of your body."

I wish I were tall enough to be able to bitchslap her.

"Why don't we go inside? I'm sure a lot of familiar faces have already arrived and we can mingle with new people." I choose to take the high road and put an end to this conversation or else it might get ugly between the Brazilian model and I.

I don't think I've ever been so grateful to have short legs in my life. Since my strides aren't as long as Bruna's, I'm forced to walk several steps behind her and I'm able to avoid the embarrassment of walking into the party with a woman who lacks in class and sophistication.

It doesn't take long for me to lose sight of the bitch. She melts into the crowd and I'm left standing at the entrance of the room. *Thank God.* I quickly scour around, eager to spot him. At first, I think he might not have arrived, but when a tall man steps aside, I notice a mob of reporters and camera people surrounding Max. *It sucks being so short in circumstances like these. I could have easily missed him.* I take a step forward to make my way to the back of the room to meet the gorgeous man of my dreams, but Giovanna shouts my name so loudly, it stops me in my tracks.

"Candy, you look gorgeous, darling." I barely have time to turn around before she has me locked in a bear hug. "I love the jade color of the flowy skirt and the matching colored print against white at the bodice is simply adorable," she says, pulling away from me to take a better look at my outfit. "And I like how the deep V-neck is low enough to reveal your fabulous boobs, but not so low it looks trashy. It's chic, but flirty. It's so you," she concludes. Giovanna's effervescence is contagious and I forget all about Bruna's scornful words. Giovanna lowers her eyes and I follow her gaze to my feet. "Oh, I almost forgot. The nude Louboutins are the perfect accent,"

"You think I look okay? I bumped into Bruna outside the restaurant and she compared my dress to what a conservative nun would wear," I say, worried.

"Please don't tell me you believe anything that comes out of her mouth. Look at her." Giovanna and I follow Bruna with our eyes as she gets acquainted with every single man in the room. "Her skanky dress is going to get her a lot of action tonight, but not the kind of action you and I are looking for.

Whoever she ends up with tonight, the poor sucker won't remember her name in the morning."

"Thanks for reassuring me. She had some bitchy things to say about the way I looked and it ate at my confidence. I shouldn't let her get under my skin the way she does, but she irritates the hell out of me."

"Are you serious?" Giovanna laughs. "You are going to turn heads, darling. I hear there are loads of eligible bachelors here tonight. Who knows, we might both score big time."

I don't care about any eligible bachelors. I only want Max.

"Giovanna, you're going to leave them begging in your royal-blue creation. All eyes will be on you, not me."

"I don't want to hear such nonsense from you. No one here tonight will know you're not one of the models," she says, fixating on my ears. "Honey, your dangling gold earrings are so vintage. Where did you get them?"

Her question flushes my cheeks. "They belonged to my paternal grandmother."

It's still so difficult for me to elaborate when it comes to my dead parents and grandparents. Since tonight is all about celebrations and festivities, I can't bring myself to reveal to Giovanna that the earrings I'm wearing, a handful of gold jewelry hidden at my place and the apartment I own are the only things my grandmother Barbara left me. She fought the good fight trying to prove my parents' deaths weren't an accident, but in the end, she was no match against a company with very deep pockets and shark attorneys.

"Well, you look like the belle of the ball and the only thing missing is for you to find your prince. Come on, let's order a few drinks and then we'll work the room."

We turn around to head to the bar where Brian, who interviewed me earlier today, is hitting on Josephine. Josie is a tall black model with the most flawless skin I've ever seen. Her smooth complexion is only surpassed by her beautiful heavy breasts. No wonder Deidra had her sporting their brightest and most colorful swimsuit selections. She wears her loose curls in a stylish high Afro that accentuates her well-defined cheekbones. I'll confess, I'm jealous of her gorgeous full lips and her outrageous high ass. There's no two ways about it, the woman is drop-dead fantabulous.

I'm so focused on Josie, I nearly miss Brian's transformation. The CNN reporter has ditched his buttoned-up look and his studious glasses for an edgier style. I love how his black leather jacket hugs his slender frame so well. His fiery red hair contrasts with his head-to-toe black outfit and brings even more emphasis to his pale blue eyes. *Damn, he looks like a freaking model.*

When Brian sees us, he waves in our direction and gestures for us to come join them. I'm about to take a step forward alongside Giovanna when my phone rings. I quickly open my clutch and when his name flashes across my phone I stop breathing for a second. *Max.*

"Giovanna, why don't you go ahead without me? A text requires my attention and I need to make sure I respond, as it relates to an article we're running on the website in a couple of days," I lie, hoping she won't be able to see right through me.

"Honey, you have to turn that thing off," she says, waving at my phone with a disapproving look. "It's eight o'clock at night and it's party time. You shouldn't be working this late in the day."

"I know. Unfortunately the web is twenty-four seven and never sleeps. It's only going to take me five minutes and I'll be there before you even have time to miss me."

"Promise? If you're not standing by my side in the next five minutes with a drink in your hand, I'll come and grab you by the back of your neck and I'll drag you all the way to the bar." She smiles.

"Cross my heart."

"Good. Five minutes and no more. I'm turning on the timer on my iPhone and keeping a close eye on you." Giovanna gives me a quick hug before turning on her heel and heading to meet Brian and Josephine.

I get on my toes and I quickly look around the room to spot him. *Where is he?* When I can't see his handsome face in the crowd, I return my focus to my phone.

You're the most alluring woman here tonight. When you walked into the room all the others seemed to

```
fade in the background. How dare you
look so divine?
```

Oh. I was hoping I looked good, but his words take me aback.

```
        You don't look so bad your-
self.
```

Even though Max was surrounded by a mob of people his impeccable three-piece suit didn't go unnoticed. Honestly, I thought only older men or grooms-to-be wore a waistcoat, but the way he works his three-piece suit, you'd think he jumped out of the pages of *Details* magazine.

```
        Can you find a quiet spot to
hide so we can talk instead of tex-
ting?
```

```
        Give me a second to step out
of the room. Where are you now?
```

```
        Outside on the deck. Why don't
you head to the lobby? Since most of
our guests have arrived, it should
be quiet there.
```

Okay. Call me in a few minutes.

I quickly head to the entrance and I barely have time to close the door behind me before my phone rings. It's Max.

"You're too eager, buddy," I say.

"Can you blame me? You're radiant."

"Stop, you're going to make me blush."

"You know perfectly well I can't resist you when your cheeks flush. If I could get away right now, I'd kidnap you, lock you up in a bathroom and fuck you senseless for making my cock this hard."

"You can't get away?" I'm so disappointed to hear I won't be able to see him until later.

"Not for a while, sweetness. We have press from all over the country, plus Brazil, the UK and Germany, and they're all very interested in our three plus-size collections. It's a wild night because all of these media outlets are eager to spread the good word to their readers."

"Why are you hiding on the patio while I'm hiding in the lobby to have a conversation?" I ask, slightly irritated.

"I'm afraid if I get too close, everyone in the room will know how aroused I get around you be-cause I'm certain it will be written all over my face. Don't worry, I'll make up for this charade when I have you all to myself."

I wish I could be by his side right now. This hide-and-seek game isn't doing it for me. I want him to wrap his arms around me and crush my lips until I nearly stop breathing.

"It's unfortunate you'll have to wait until later to find out which one of your creations I'm wearing under my dress..." I hope my cockiness motivates him to find some time for us to escape from the prying eyes of the partygoers.

"You dirty girl. You're teasing me and you know I'm going to have to punish you for being so daring. I'm dying to touch you, kiss you and pound you, but given how many reporters are swarming in the room, it's best if we keep our distance until later tonight when we're behind closed doors."

"I hate it, but I understand."

"You can't possibly hate it as much as I do. I'm going to have to exert a Herculean effort to avoid focusing on what you might be hiding under your emerald-colored dress."

"It's naughtier than you think."

He lets out a low grunt. "Please, don't tempt me any further. I want to protect you from the unkind eyes of the press. If they spot us together and suspect something is going on between us, they'll have a field day—at your expense, since I'm immune to this sort of garbage by now."

"I get it. I'll see you later. You can text me when you want me to come up to your room."

"Did you leave your things with the concierge?"

"Yes, I left my suitcase with Charles."

"Excellent. I'm sure he already has it up in my room. I'll make sure we leave together. Before I go I want you to know one thing, sweetness."

"What?" I ask hesitantly.

"You do know I'll only have eyes for you tonight?"

How in the world am I supposed to respond to that? "There must be at least three hundred attractive women in the room."

"Yeah, but there's only one of you," he interrupts.

"Max…"

"Every time we lock eyes, you'll know I'll be counting the minutes until I'm able to have my way with you."

Holy hell.

No man has ever made me feel as unbelievably sexy and as utterly desired as he does now.

Chapter Five

After my short conversation with Max, I meet up with Giovanna, Brian and Josephine at the bar. For the next hour, we have our own little private party amongst all the industry people. The flowing drinks mellow me out somewhat, but not enough to ignore Bruna's attempts at catching Max's attention. *She's looking him up and down like a lioness eyeing a baby gazelle. Bitch.* She's tried everything—flipping her black mane, yanking up her giant boobs to make them more obvious, pulling up her already indecently short dress to expose more of her long tanned legs, and she's even resorted to reapplying her red lipstick as if she's performing a crude act in public. The woman won't give up.

Luckily, Max has been too busy with the press and top retailers to pay the bitch any attention. It becomes so hilarious at a certain point during the evening, Brian starts betting on her next moves. Every time he predicts her next ploy, Giovanna and Josephine burst out in laughter.

Unfortunately, my stomach is tied up in a knot for me to enjoy myself. *What the hell is she up to?* I'm so troubled, I stand up from my stool and take a few steps forward with my arms crossed over my chest like protective armor. I want to make sure I keep a close eye on the human piranha and the man who makes my heart skip a beat.

Although the music has been playing in the background all evening long, the sudden change is unmistakable. The smooth vibe from Mexican superstar duo Camila changes to a sultrier and more provocative beat. Were it not for the fact Lexi is half Latina, I'd know very little about Spanish music, but I recognize a feverish tune she played last summer every time we visited her home—*6 a.m.* by J. Balvin.

The next thing I know, Bruna is gyrating her sinful body theatrically in the middle of the restaurant. It comes as no surprise all eyes are glued on the Brazilian as she undulates her hips to the cadence of the music. She's making such a spectacle of herself, even the media who had been focused on Max turn their attention to the tall model. I'm fuming with jealousy as she approaches Max in front of everyone. *What the fuck is she doing?* My mouth is still gaping open when Brian behind me summarizes my exact feelings.

"She's such an attention-seeker. I'm sure she must have masterminded her plan all night long so that she could bewitch everyone as she works her dirty-dancing moves on Max. The poor chap has no choice but to play along given how many reporters are crammed in this room and how many cameras are pointing at him."

I really don't need to hear this.

"Yeah, you're right. It's not as if he can brush her off in front of so many people. The next thing you'll know we'll read on the cover of every newspaper in the country tomorrow morning, *Sexy Curves' CEO Rejects Plus-Size Model On The Dance Floor!* I know from firsthand experience the media can twist pretty much anything to sell more papers or get more page views online." Giovanna's observation should calm me down, but I feel so sick to my stomach right now, I could run to the bathroom and puke my guts out.

"Well, she did say in passing on the set earlier today she was determined to get to know Max a lot better before the clock strikes midnight..." Josephine's words send me into sheer panic. *No, no, no.*

Unable to hold back any longer, I turn on my heel and face the group who has so accurately been commenting on the unfolding events and I dare to ask a question that might expose me. "What do you mean, Josie?"

"I've done many photoshoots with Bruna and I've seen with my own eyes how she plays men to her advantage. I'm not saying she's not a beautiful curvy model—she is and she knows it. What I am saying is the reason she gets called back for photoshoots so often is because she's not afraid of putting out. I've caught her quite a few times in compromising situations with photographers, representatives from the company who hires us, videographers and pretty much any human being walking around with a cock. The girl has no shame. In my opinion, she's going to get him before the end of the night because she's been hinting at it since we've arrived in Miami yesterday morning. I should know, since I'm her roommate. What Bruna wants, Bruna gets."

God, please make it stop.

"I didn't want to bring it up, but since Josephine let the cat out of the bag, I can share that Bruna cornered me earlier today and rubbed her tits all over me hoping I'd write the same kind of feature story as I'm crafting for Giovanna and Candy. I would have been flattered, but I caught her with her hands down the photographer's jeans about an hour before she approached me. Frankly, she's so obvious a blind man can see her coming a mile away."

Jesus, this is my worst nightmare coming to life. There's no way I can compete against her—she's a star in the industry and I'm only me.

"At least we didn't have to deal with Benita being on set this time around. I've dealt with the double-trouble duo before. It's excruciating."

My head turns in Giovanna's direction so quickly I fear my neck might snap off. "Who's Benita?" I ask in a higher voice than normal.

"Her twin sister," Giovanna and Josie both answer together.

Fuck, there's more than one of them? "I didn't know she had a twin."

"Benita's super-popular in South America and she's gaining popularity here. I'm sure you've seen her in ads for Tremendous Splash swimsuits," Giovanna continues. "You haven't put two and two together because they're fraternal twins and not identical. Also, Benita dyes her dark hair blonde. This has helped her get bookings where she doesn't have to go head to head with her sister."

"Giovanna is right. The next time you see Benita's photo in a magazine, you'll immediately see the resemblance." Josie's words do little to comfort me as I rack my brain to remember the lineup of models under the Tremendous Splash brand. "Benita goes by her first name only, which is why you might not have connected the two sisters. She thinks she's the Madonna of the modeling world. Whatever. Like Giovanna, I've also worked with both of them and they are indeed a nightmare. Here's the other twist to the story—when they're together, they never shy away from seducing men with the promise of a hot *ménage a trois* with two plus-size Brazilian bombshell supermodels. As they love to gloat, few mortals with a cock can resist such illicit temptation. To be honest, I know a lot of men who've bagged both sisters during an evening of debauchery where no kinks were off the table. Yeah, the Alvares twins are something else."

For the love of God. Is there no end to this?

Although I haven't missed one word Josephine and Giovanna shared, I still have my eyes glued to the dance floor, fearing the worst, and when Max wraps his arms around her waist and Bruna slams her tits against his chest, I lose all my composure. By the time she rubs her boobs up and down Max's torso, I've officially had enough. I'm certain it would've been less painful if someone had poured a bucket of salt on an open wound than to watch Bruna grab Max by the back of his neck and crush her lips against his.

When the crowd roars with excitement, I concede defeat. *Maybe he'll stick the butt plug he bought for me earlier up her ass while teasing her clit with the vibrator as he pounds her with his hungry cock. See if I care.* In an attempt to stop the agony, I turn to the trio still sitting at the bar with a proposition to allow me escape this hellhole.

I fist my right hand against my thigh to give me more courage. "There are tons of long black limousines in front of the hotel. Why don't we jump into one of them and go discover Miami's vibrant nightlife? Why would we stay here and watch her make a fool out of herself?" To my surprise I manage to muster up a tight smile. I can't believe I was able to say those words in a steady voice considering how fast my heart is beating right now.

My idea takes them aback at first, but Brian's beaming smile lets me know he's on board. Soon after, Josephine and Giovanna both jump to their feet, excited by my suggestion.

"Candy, let's hit the town and let's go find ourselves a few hot eligible guys, since Josephine and Brian seem to be so smitten by each other."

"I wouldn't be averse to the idea of sharing my bed with three luscious women. Perhaps we should skip the club scene and head directly to my room." Brian grins from ear to ear and earns himself a slap on the arm from both gorgeous models.

I need to get the fuck out of here. Now.

Chapter Six

Just like New York, Miami comes to life when the sun goes down. My goal was to do whatever it took to erase the earlier traumatic scene of watching Bruna and Max embrace so intimately in front of hundreds of pairs of eyes, and if I'm willing to lie to myself that I don't care, then I've somewhat succeeded.

After hitting six different high-energy nightclubs where we danced our heads off, where I flirted with any stranger willing to look my way and guzzled down probably more booze than I should have, Giovanna, Josephine, Brian and I are sprawled inside the limo like spoiled rich kids at the end of prom night on our way back to the hotel. The four of us are resting our heads with eyes closed against the seats until Brian breaks the silence.

"I wonder how many bottles are in the mini fridge."

"Why don't you open the door and do an inventory, Mr. Inspector?" Giovanna laughs and Josephine and I join her.

"From what I can see, it's fully stocked and there's enough to last us until we make it back to the Four Seasons."

"Great. Can you grab me a bottle of white wine if they have one?" Even with my eyes closed, I can feel the shift of energy and I crack my eyes open. I'm met with three puzzled faces. I'm in such a cocky mood, I decide to ignore their stares. "What? Don't they carry white wine?"

"They do. I didn't take you for a person who could party this hard. Candy, you've surprised the heck out of me—in a good way." Brian makes his confession as he folds back up with a mini bottle of wine in his hands.

I grab it and hold their gaze. "Don't stare at me, get your own drink." I twist the cap before taking a massive gulp, letting the alcohol burn away the memory of Max's betrayal.

It doesn't take long for all three of my party companions to follow my cue. Since we ventured far away from the hotel, our trip back gave us enough time to clean house. Each and every bottle from the minibar is emptied—we even take care of polishing off the bottles of water, and the mood inside the stretched car elevates with each sip.

At some point Josephine selects a playlist on her iPhone and suddenly the moving vehicle becomes a nightclub on wheels—there's dancing, laughing, and Giovanna, who cracks us up by reenacting Bruna's slutty moves. When we're all tipsy, giggling in the back of the car and falling all over each other, the limousine comes to a screeching stop.

"Oh, my God. This was so much fun it should be illegal," Giovanna chokes out, wiping the mascara running underneath her eyes.

"Giovanna, darling, you deserve an Oscar nomination for your rendition of dirty Bruna." I burst into laughter. I'm way past the point of tipsy, as are my three partners in crime, but I'm still sober enough to feel a pang of sadness when a thought flashes through my head—Max might be upstairs right now with Bruna in his bed.

"Giovanna, Candy is right. You're hilarious, girl, and I wish you were my roommate instead of bitchy Bruna." Josephine is folded in half as she does her best to keep it together.

"Well, I hope for tonight I can convince you to be my roommate, Josie." Brian's unabashed confession earns him a few whistles of admiration from Giovanna and I. *The man has guts.*

"It's a good thing I'm already bunking up with Sarah, the curvy Texan model, and Candy is sharing a room with one of Mr. Keller's top executives. You haven't hurt our feelings by not including us in your sultry night of passion."

"Since he's writing an article on us, I think it's a good thing he doesn't know more than he has to, Giovanna. By tomorrow morning he'd have way too much incriminating information if we were to spend the night with him." My witty repartee earns me high-fives from the group.

Hysterical laughter fills the limo as the door opens, prompting Giovanna and I to climb off the floor where we slid some time during our joyride. We hold on to each other for support as we make our way into the hotel and head for the elevators.

Luckily, we catch an empty car and we all cram inside, determined to keep the party going until we separate. Given the speed and the efficiency of this luxury hotel's ride, it doesn't take long for each of us to debark to our respective rooms for a much-needed rest.

Since I'm on one of the top floors, I ride the rest of the way solo and I can't help but reminisce about our night of misbehaving in Miami's hottest clubs. The morning after should be quite interesting to say the least, considering I have to be back on set at the mansion before nine.

Crap. That only gives me four hours of sleep if I want to leave here by eight o'clock to arrive on time. I'm going to look like shit in the morning. I totter off the elevator with an unsure step and for the first time this evening, I curse my high heels. Unable to continue, I kick off my designer shoes and stroll barefoot to my room. When I get to my door I tuck them under my armpit to free up my hands to fish for my keycard. When I locate the little gold and white plastic card, I slip it in the hole and crank the handle to push open the door. *I guess I'm not nearly as tipsy as I thought because I didn't even fumble, nor did I drop my shoes. Bravo to me.*

My only saving grace is the fact my cousin Trish taught me how to drink. Without her simple yet astute formula, I would have probably ended up a blubbering drunk by now. As long as I keep the ratio right—one eight-ounce glass of water for every two drinks—I can avoid making a complete fool out of myself. *Thanks, cousin.* I'm still grinning to myself as I step into my hotel room, but I don't linger in my festive mode for too long. I can't, because Max's frame is filling the hallway—his very tense frame.

As I focus on his face—the hard lines, the frowning eyebrows, the tight jaw, and those hazel eyes heavy with disapproval—I'm quickly reminded of what I must look like after a night of wild partying with my three accomplices. *Oh, shit. He doesn't look happy.* I can practically feel Max's irritation boiling off him despite the fact the room is air-conditioned. I instinctively smooth my dress and comb my fingers through my hair, trying to look semi-decent. I open my mouth, but he precedes me.

"Where the hell have you been all night?" His eyes are cold, his jaw rigid, and I'm suddenly aware of how furious he is right now.

I defuse his question by looking past him to spot Deidra. "Where is my roommate?"

"Candy, perhaps you didn't hear me. I asked you a very specific question and I'm expecting a very specific answer." He narrows his eyes in such a menacing way I take a step back. Just in case I needed it, I'm fully sober now.

"What's it to you? Weren't you busy doing the lambada with Bruna?"

Max's eyebrows drop in an intimidating way as he squints at me. He doesn't have to say one word. It's clear he's pissed off. My temporary victory is short-lived, his eyes piercing my brave front and erasing my smug smile. *This would be a lot easier if he didn't look so delicious.*

"Frankly, I'm surprised to see you here. I expected you to be lying next to the Brazilian model's curvaceous body after a few hours of wild fornication," I continue, determined to ignore his dangerous stare. I refuse to use the word "sex" because that's what I've shared with him so far. I want to use a word so crude it can't possibly be associated with any of our sensual interludes.

"What the fuck are you talking about?"

I guess that last part hit a nerve. Good.

He must think because I'm so much younger than he is, I'm a complete idiot to the ways of the world. It was so blatant how much she wanted him and I'm pretty certain very few men escape Bruna's claws.

"Oh, please don't take me for a fool. I saw it with my own two eyes. You were eating her up like a beggar wolfs down a hot meal with your arms wrapped around her waist."

"Did you get any help in concocting this far-fetched story or did you make it all up by yourself?"

His words sting so badly, I nearly bring up my hand to my cheek to soften the blow.

"Listen, Max, I get it. You're a very rich and eligible bachelor. It's normal women trip all over themselves to be noticed by you. Let's face it, it's not as if what we have is much more than..." Even though I know exactly what we share, I'm unable to say it aloud. I'm unwilling to put the words out there because I fear once I do, our mind-blowing sexual escapade may never amount to much more.

I turn on my heel and grab the door handle, ready to storm out of the room and escape this unbearable tension, but his strong hand slams the door shut. I'm trapped.

"You're not going anywhere until we talk. Now turn around and please face me."

I obey without any objections. *My God, he's so pissed off.* I'm sure there is no other man who can command attention the way Max does, especially when he's this upset. I glance up at him from underneath my lashes, connecting briefly with his stormy eyes before dropping my gaze and allowing myself to take in his casual yet outrageously panty-melting outfit. I guess he must have jumped out of his smoking-hot three-piece suit in favor of his form-fitting black tee shirt and these thigh-hugging dark jeans.

"I don't have anything more to say to you, Max." *It's best if I keep in mind how he was all over Bruna on the dance floor instead of salivating all over his good looks.*

He stares at me and then inhales, and his anger disappears. "Good. I'll do the talking and you can listen. When I'm done you can decide if you want to walk away or not." He steps into me, flattening my body against the door and letting me know he's about to rip the hell out of me for leaving his VIP party early without telling him. I gasp as he presses his lips to my forehead. "I've been trying to reach you for the past five hours and you've been avoiding my calls and my text messages. Why would you ignore me like this without knowing the full story?"

What does he mean by full story? The entire room saw the bitch kiss him. End of story. "She was all over you and you did nothing to push her away. You even allowed her to crush her lips against yours in front of everyone." I spit out these words through clenched teeth.

"Had you stuck around for a few more minutes, you would have seen Deidra come to my rescue."

"Why would Deidre need to rescue a grown man like you from a woman?"

"I couldn't push Bruna away from me under the scrutiny of over twenty-five of the top media outlets in the country and a dozen international reporters without raising suspicion. I wasn't going to make it easy for the press to spin this stupid incident into something it wasn't. Deidra rounded up a couple of handsome men who were more than happy to cut in and continue dancing with Bruna, making it possible for me to exit the dance floor without ruffling any feathers."

"So what? You were able to get away for a few minutes. From what I understand, Bruna doesn't take no for an answer. When she has her sights set on a man, he inevitably succumbs to her charms."

"Bruna's reputation precedes her. It's a very well-known fact in the industry she's willing to do anything to advance her career. From what I hear, her sister is also a handful. I guess we were lucky because we only had to deal with one diva on the set today," he says, looking away for an instant. "Both Deidra and I hesitated in booking Bruna, but it's hard to ignore her popularity and her legion of adoring fans. On her Facebook page alone she has over seventeen thousand fans from around the world and most of those are women we want to reach, not to mention she's a heck of a lot easier to book than megastar supermodel Ashley Graham. I was willing to make the sacrifice of forcing our crew to deal with a diva because she's worth it and I knew I'd rarely cross her path."

I turn my head and look at him sideways, still trying to size him up. *Is he telling me the truth or is he lying to me?* "You could be blowing smoke up my ass." I defiantly cross my arms over my chest to create some sort of a barrier between us.

"Honey, why would I waste my time blowing smoke up your behind when I could fuck your ass instead?" *Holy shit. I didn't see that coming.* "What was the last thing I told you when I called you at the party?"

I'm still so intoxicated by his dirty talk, it's impossible for me to think straight. I search his eyes for an answer, but his raised eyebrows greet me.

"I don't remember. A lot has happened tonight," I murmur, regretting I've allowed Bruna and my blinding jealousy to allow me to forget parts of our chat.

"I guess you weren't paying attention... unless my words meant nothing to you." *Oh, God. What did he say that was so important?* I rack my brain trying to replay our conversation in my head, but I'm afraid it's been too long of an evening to recall our brief exchange. "I told you tonight I'd only have eyes for you and I meant it. I know what we share started out in a kinky fashion on the forty-first floor of a luxurious New York hotel, but in time I've found myself impatiently looking forward to seeing you again. Heck, most days, I'd start my mental countdown after lunch." *Seriously?* "I was hoping we could have slipped out of the party early so I could have whisked you up to my penthouse suite. I would have been able to confess to you behind closed doors how I want much more than what we've shared so far."

Did he say he wants more?

"Max, none of this is making sense to me. I know you haven't made any commitment to me and we're seeing each other casually, and I'm okay with that." I'm babbling aloud, afraid my decision to leave the party early might have caused him to reconsider what we share.

"I was hoping we might be able to change things."

"Change what?"

"Since we're both single... I was thinking we might want to share something less casual." He grins from ear to ear and I melt inside. *Oh my God, is he saying what I think he's saying?* "Neither of us is seeing anyone else and we're a pretty incredible match in the bedroom, or at the back of an SUV, and I thoroughly enjoy your company." We both laugh. "Candy, if we make things a little bit more official, we'd avoid having to sneak around when we're out in public, don't you think?" I'm so tongue-tied, I can only nod in agreement. After a few seconds of pure bliss the impact of his words hit me and I flash back to the conversation we shared earlier.

"But what if the press catches us together? I thought you were so concerned right before the party started?"

"Other than Deidra and your friends, no one knew we were seeing each other then, but if everyone knows, the press won't have as much leverage to twist things in their favor to sell more papers or to get more hits to their websites."

"Now I understand why you were being so protective earlier."

"Exactly. I didn't want you to get hurt," he says caressing my cheek. "There's only one question burning my lips now that I've shared how I feel about you."

"Which one?" I smile.

"I hope when you accepted your position at *Sassy* magazine, you didn't have to sign any contracts precluding you from becoming a client's girlfriend."

No way. This can't be happening to me.

My heart is beating so fast I can nearly see it jump out of my chest. I open and close my mouth a few times before attempting to speak.

"Did you... Are you saying..." I'm so shell-shocked, I can't string a coherent sentence together to let him know how utterly happy I am.

My sudden joy turns to worry when I soak in his last words. *Oh, no. Is there a clause preventing me from dating clients?* I know we can't technically date colleagues, but our employee contracts have done little to stop a string of office hookups amongst both gay and straight co-workers.

"What? No feisty repartee?" He wraps his arms around my waist and pulls me against him tighter. Harder. The moment our bodies collide, I feel his desire for me. "It's been a fight for me all night— between being mad as hell at you and wanting to fuck you so badly my cock aches."

I bite my lower lip, unable to contain my smile. *I can't believe I had it so wrong about him and Bruna.*

"Max, do you really mean what you said?" I'm impressed I have the presence of mind to ask this question considering how intoxicated I still am by his words.

"Which part do you want me to repeat? The part about having a hard-on all night long or the part about us making what we share more official?"

"You're really asking me what I think you're asking?" I press, still trying to make sense of it all. "Maybe I misunderstood. I'd hate to jump to conclusions and make a fool out of myself."

"Since you keep asking me questions and you haven't said yes to becoming my girlfriend, I'm starting to think this whole confession was a bad idea."

"Oh, no, you don't, mister. You can't drop such a bomb on a girl and not expect her to be bewildered. I didn't see this coming at all. I thought we were casually fucking each other and..." I really never imagined he wanted so much more from me. Although I dreamed of this and even confessed my desires to Devin a few days ago before leaving New York, I never wanted to rock the boat by blurting out my feelings for him. "I thought I was the only one who had started to…" Even now standing in front of him, I am unable to say the words aloud. *God, if this is a dream, do not wake me up.*

"Is it not obvious, Candy? I've been smitten by you for weeks now, but I was waiting for the right moment to share my feelings with you. Why do you think I've been making so many excuses to see you nearly every night since we met at the Bymark Hotel? I thought tonight was perfect to declare my intentions, but I didn't foresee Bruna's little attempt at capturing everyone's attention as the incident that would unravel my best-laid plans." His hand on my cheek warms my skin and keeps me from turning away from him. His eyes penetrate me, gaze deep inside me. I'm so overtaken right now, I'm sure he can feel me trembling.

"I think I've fallen for you since the first night you invited me to your home… but I didn't think it could ever be mutual."

"Shhh," he whispers, dropping two fingers against my lips to silence me. "Now you know it is." He smiles before dropping a soft kiss on my lips.

"I do." I grab him closer to answer his kiss. The passion burning inside me threatens to consume me whole. *He wants me as much as I want him.*

"I'm glad we're on the same page, but I can't possibly let you get away with what you've done to me tonight. You had me worried out of my mind. Your phone was off all night and there was no way for Deidra or I to reach you. We had no idea where you were or if you were alone." *What have I done?* "Luckily, Deidra texted me a couple minutes before you walked through the door when she finally received a reply from Giovanna, who confirmed you had been out on the town partying with her, the CNN reporter and Josephine."

I swallow hard, my throat dry as sandpaper. *Oh, shit.* "When I saw you with Bruna tonight, I figured I didn't have a chance in hell. She's a model and I'm not. She's Brazilian and I'm not. She stops traffic and I don't. Why wouldn't you fall for her? I couldn't stand watching the two of you anymore, so I asked Giovanna, Josephine and Brian to join me to paint the town red, because standing there made me feel helpless. I figured if I could escape, I wouldn't have to know more than I needed to."

"Earlier today inside the SUV you promised you trusted me implicitly. What changed?"

"I... well..." I mumble, riddled with guilt. My insecurities prompted me to act like a hothead. I wasn't even thinking straight. I could already picture Bruna fucking Max's brains out. I only had one thought in mind—get the hell out before I get hurt.

"You storming out like you did is like saying you don't trust me." His voice roughens. "Turn around."

"Wh-what? Why?"

"As I said earlier, you had me worried sick and there's no way I can allow you to get away with that."

"But what are you..."

"Turn. Around. Now." His voice is so domineering and so certain, it strips away my ability to
think along with my willpower to argue back. Slowly,
I do as I'm told. Without warning, he grabs my hands
and places them over my head, pressing them against
the door.

"Don't move," he growls.

When his hands glide down my body, a gush
of arousal runs through me. He angles his body to the
side and pins my wrists together, preventing me from
moving. Although generous, the entrance to my hotel
room feels like a tiny closet right now, with both of us
filling the space. I open my hands and flatten them
against the door, hoping he plans on fucking me from
behind with my clothes still on. When he lifts the skirt
of my dress with his free hand, a cold breeze from the
air conditioner brushes across my exposed bottom and
I wiggle my ass in anticipation. *Yeah, take me.*

"Hmmm. Nice lingerie selection and good
call on matching your underwear with the color of
your dress. The emerald-green satin and the black
lace aren't helping my hard-on. It's a good thing I can
easily replace these or else your sexy collection would
cost me a fortune." He wraps my panties around his
fingers and pulls the fabric apart.

Jesus, I love it when he's such a tyrant. I
close my eyes and lick my lips, readying myself, but
instead of his cock, I jerk forward the second the first
slap hits my cheeks. *What the fuck? He's spanking
me? No way.*

"Max, have you lost your marbles?" I squeal.
Slap.

"For the love of God. I'm not a child," I protest.

Slap. The third slap hits across my right buttock and stings like crazy.

"Ouch!"

He pauses. "This will be far more enjoyable if you relax," he says, as if I haven't even spoken, as if he hasn't noticed me struggling to escape.

Slap. Slap. Slap.

"Damn you."

"The boys you've fucked in the past never spanked you? It's a real turn-on for me, especially when I'm pissed off."

"No. No one's ever slapped my ass."

"Twentysomethings have so much to learn about satisfying a woman," he hisses into my ear.

Slap. Slap. Slap.

Oh, Lord. I really screwed up.

He strokes my bottom gently, temporarily relieving the pain from the assault.

"I don't think I like this game, Max. I much prefer the butt plug."

"You think I'm playing? Did you know Manuel and I circled the hotel and the adjacent streets in the SUV for ninety minutes looking for you? Deidra had her own search party frantically trying to retrace your steps. The funny thing is, no one in the hotel remembered seeing you slip out."

Ah. The group of Japanese tourists. "We walked out as a bus parked in front of the hotel and a sea of Japanese tourists mobbed the lobby. I guess it was the perfect getaway since it became so chaotic no one seemed to care about us. Even the bellboys and doorman were busy at work taking care of the new guests."

He went looking for me? I never imagined he'd be so concerned. My mind was haunted by one thought—avoid pain and humiliation at all cost. I can't believe I acted like such a brat. My anger withers and dies, and my resistance with it.

"Max, I'm sorry," I whisper when I come face to face with how my selfish actions have affected others. "Please... I'm sorry. I'll apologize to Deidra first thing in the morning."

My answer must have calmed him. He lets go of my hands and allows my dress to fall down.

"Turn around. I want to see your pretty face."

"I didn't mean to worry you or Deidra."

"In case you need any further clarification, Candy, I want to fuck you. No one else. I've been thinking of fucking you since you left the SUV earlier. It's as if my cock needs to be inside you twenty-four seven." His hands glide down my thighs and suddenly they are traveling higher up, underneath the fabric of my dress. His eyes lock onto mine. "Got it?"

"Yes." I lower my eyes.

"Good. Spanking you turned me on even more and now my cock is still raging and begging for your pussy, but this isn't what I had in mind," he growls as he unzips my dress. The fabric pools at my feet and he wastes no time freeing my breasts from their confinement. Instead of hiding my body with my hands and shielding myself from the light, like I'd normally do, I daringly hold his gaze. "You're beauti-

ful. I can't get enough of your luscious curves."
Damn, I love how he worships every part of me.

"Really?" I can't believe he thinks I'm beautiful.

In lieu of an answer, Max lifts me in his arms, throws me over his shoulder and carries me to my bed. He drops my naked body against the mattress and walks to the desk to pick up a lighter. He circles the room and with each step, he lights a candle, brightening the space. *Where the hell did these come from?* Pleasantly surprised, I prop myself up on my elbows to watch as he illuminates the room.

"Who placed these candles here?"

"I did. They were in my suite along with a few other things designed to seduce you, but it became clear at about midnight we were going to have our heart-to-heart right here. After securing Deidra another room, I asked the hotel staff to help me bring these down. It was all part of the master plan Bruna screwed up," he mocks with a dangerous sparkle in his eyes. "The whole setting was far more elaborate in my suite simply because it's much bigger than yours, but I figured this would still work." He approaches me, stands over me and stares down at me for a few long minutes, taking every part of my body in like a religion. *If he continues to look at me like that, will my skin ignite?*

Without turning his gaze away, Max slowly strips out of his casual and oh-so-fuckable outfit. *Damn, I'm insatiable when it comes to his chiseled physique.* His intricate tattoo is so edgy and so sexy under the candlelight. It's not like I've never seen him naked before, but something about this moment prompts me to close my eyes against the sight of him. He's so gorgeous. A condom wrapper crinkles and the growing lust between my legs flames up. When the bed sinks under his weight, I open my eyes.

He lies besides me, propping his head up on one hand.

"Isn't it too late for this?" I tease, knowing I'll get a reaction from him. His eyes narrow as he studies my face, and his jaw slowly turns to stone.

"Do you see this erection?" he says, bringing down his attention to his cock before locking eyes with me again. *Fuck, is he bigger than usual?* "Since you stepped out of the SUV earlier this afternoon, I've already jerked off three times. If you think I'm going to go to sleep without fucking you, you've got another think coming." He grins.

"Well, maybe I have a headache or something," I lie, pulling up the covers on the right side of the bed and wrapping myself snugly.

"Bullshit." He lifts my chin and gives me a look that sears all the way to the tip of my toes and makes my stomach quiver. "I can call the concierge to get some Advil sent right up and we can take care of your fictitious headache in no time."

His knuckles rub gently against my nipples and my entire body shivers. His pitiless smile betrays him and I know he undoubtedly feels the taut peaks. *Bastard.*

"I was going to be gentle because I did rough you up this afternoon with the two little gifts I bought for you, but you've lost that privilege with your smart comment. Instead, I'm going to take you for my own pleasure since you've made me wait for you while you were partying hard. I'm going to ravish you until you can't breathe anymore."

My mouth drops open, but before I can speak, he rips the covers out of my grasp and he rolls me on my stomach. Max ruthlessly shoves my legs apart. *What just happened?* He yanks me onto my knees, putting my butt in the air. His finger assaults my pussy, swirling through my wetness despite my squirming. He lets out a satisfied grunt. "You're impossibly wet, sweetness. Is your headache gone?" The mockery in his voice is unmistakable.

Something pushes against my pussy, and then he hammers into me with such power, I cry out as my body jerks forward. My hands fist in the white cotton sheets as I quake around his hungry dick in shock. His knees shove my legs outward, opening me even farther, and he thrusts inside of me so deeply, it's as if the tip of his shaft brushes against my womb. I am still in awe from his assertiveness when he starts to move.

No gentle, sweet seduction. This is rough, raw and urgent. His hands are on my hips, taking all the control for himself as he drills into me so hard, tiny grunts break from me. No one has ever been this ruthless with me in bed—ever. In spite of the unyielding way he takes me, my insides heat up like a kettle, threatening to burst from the inexorable pressure. My clit swells and throbs as my need for him grows. I bury my face in the pillow, turning just enough to get air, realizing that's all I can do. *Jesus, he's going to take me as hard as he promised.* Overpowered, anchored in place and imprisoned, I can't even push back. I can't do anything else except but take him. Take all of him. *I wouldn't want it any other way.*

The more he pounds me the more I tighten around him until shivers spiral through me. My legs begin to tremble like crazy as I hold on for dear life, unwilling to let go. Max has touched my desire so acutely it's become despair. *He's ruined it for every other man after him.* I bite my lip, trying to muffle a whimper. He picks up on my plea and responds with a short laugh. He slides a hand down my stomach until he strokes my clit with a finger against my aching nub. My hips jerk, trying to move away from him, but he leans forward, pressing his chest against my back, bracing himself over me with one arm on the headboard, the other between my legs, flicking, teasing, stroking my node with a mind-blowing cadence... *Fuck, I'm unraveling.*

"Mother of God," I scream out when his heavy balls slap against my pussy, sending shock waves through me. His balls swing back and forth like a pendulum. Every rhythmic hit ignites an earthquake-like tremor inside me, each pulse increasing the smoldering tension. My hands nearly rip the sheets off the mattress as I pant, out of control. "Yes, yes, yes," I chant with my eyes closed as I pull myself closer to allow him to fuck me deeper. Max pulls back, almost all the way out, and I whimper in frustration.

"Oh, baby, you want more?" He laughs behind me before pounding inside me. "Don't worry,

I'm not done yet." His entrance into my swollen pussy brings out a cry from me. He remains deep inside me as he rubs my clit, bringing me close to the brink, then he lifts his fingers and pulls his cock out again.

"What kind of maddening game are you playing with me, Max?" I steady myself on my elbows, wiggling my ass in discontentment.

"I want to make sure you never walk out on me ever again, love." He accentuates his words by repeating his demoniac game over and over—pounding me hard then retracting, fingers on and off my clit.

"You're going to kill me," I shout, unable to focus on anything else but the feeling of his fingers and his dick entering my impatient wetness. "Oh, shit," I exhale. I clench him tighter inside me and the pressure is so surreal, I nearly lose my mind. *How can this get any better?* "Aaaah!" I fist the sheets when he traps my clit between his fingers, using a firm pinch as he drills into me like a wild beast. "Oh, oh, oh." Arousal shoots through me, and my insides coil as I approach a powerful orgasm. *God, oh my fucking God.* My back stiffens and then everything stops. My body tenses and my fingers dig deep into the sheets beneath me. I try to fight it off at first because it's so shatteringly amazing I fear I may never be able to enjoy sex ever again unless I'm pushed this far, but as soon I let go as the pressure of the stalled climax recedes and I sob when my orgasm shoots through me. "Argh," I yell, my vision blurry from tears, desperately trying to catch my breath. My hips buck against his hand, but Max's fingers only tighten, gripping me as my pussy spasms around his cock, milking all of him in unending deluge of pleasurable waves.

He slows his cadence, stops and waits, allowing me to soak in this perfect moment. His next thrust sends an explosive surge through me as my insides clench his shaft hard in a spiraling and heart-stopping climax. *Another one? So soon?*

Then he opens his fingers and I let out a carnal scream of desperation as a gush of blood shoots back into my clit. Max pulls out of me for a fraction of a second before he slams his cock back into me with such violence another release bursts through me. *My skull is going to burst.*

"Oh, Lord. Oh, Lord, oh, Lord," I wail with the last breath I have remaining in me. I bury my head in the pillow in front of me and I bite it hard, hoping to curtail the mind-blowing sensation of my powerful climax. My legs are shaking too hard to hold my weight and I collapse on my stomach, depleted of all my energy.

Max lands right on top of me and snarls, "Tonight, there is no mercy, honey." His unyielding hands grip my hips before yanking them up, and the pounding starts again, short and fast, his hands controlling my every movement. He angles my body exactly where he wants it, and then he picks up the pace. Max's thrusts rattle the bed so much, I fear we'll end up flat on the floor if he doesn't come soon. I'm so far gone it's only when he growls my name I realize he's close to losing it.

" Goddammit, Candy." He comes with epic force as he pulls my hair back and crushes my glistening forehead with his lips. I feel his thick cock jerk inside me at the same delirious rhythm as the pounding of his heart against my back. *I'll never be able to walk again after this.*

Afterward the room is so quiet you could hear a pin drop. Max rests his spent body on top of mine and doesn't move for a minute. He holds me against him with a possessive arm across my stomach, keeping me pinned against his hot, sweaty body. His breathing slows down, and then he tips both of us over, keeping us spooned together. I'm still sobbing, unable to come down from this high.

"Baby, are those tears of joy or pain? There is nothing more perfect than your face when you come."

I struggle to breathe, hoping to calm down my heart rate enough to speak. "You… You… This…"

"Too much?" he mocks as he brushes my damp hair away from my face.

"How can I ever accept vanilla sex again after today? I mean between the interlude in the SUV and this…" I didn't even know it was possible to feel like the earth had opened beneath you and was swallowing you whole.

He kisses my lips with such tenderness, it's a sharp contrast with the way he was ravishing me a few minutes ago. "You're mine now, and you should know by now, I don't do vanilla sex."

I can't foresee ever getting tired of hearing him say those words—I'm his.

Chapter Seven

God, my head hurts. I'm never drinking again. Although Trish's formula is perfect to prevent me from making a fool out of myself when I've had a few too many drinks, it does little to lessen the hangover the morning after.

I thought I was doing so well. It's clear from the pain that's overtaken my body I might have underestimated how much I drank last night. My head is pounding, my stomach is rolling, and my head is so heavy I can barely lift it off of the pillow. Slowly, I open one eye and blinding sunlight greets me. I extend my left arm, hoping to caress Max's warm body, but the bed is empty. *Where did he go?*

I roll on my back and painstakingly lift my heavy body from the bed. When I sit up, Max is sitting bare-chested with a white towel wrapped around his waist at the desk, already busy at work. Without even turning away from his laptop, he dispenses his words of wisdom.

"Too much partying and too much pounding doesn't do the body good the morning after. Considering the fact you've been moaning for the past couple of hours, I'm surprised you haven't thrown up all over the bed."

"All right, I might have had too much to drink last night and you pounding me like a caveman surely didn't help." I brush my unruly hair off my face.

"I had a sneaking suspicion you'd have a rough time this morning, so I took the liberty of ordering a bottle of liquid capsule Advils, a dozen bottles of filtered water, some plain yogurt with a side order of raw sugar and muesli to help soak up the alcohol from your stomach," he says, swiveling in his chair to face me. "My mom always gave us yogurt sprinkled with a little sugar when we had the slightest tummyache. She's convinced yogurt coats the stomach and heals everything. I've relied on her tried and tested recipe every time I've had too much to drink and what can I say? Mother knows best. Although yogurt is not part of the Brazilian culture or that of our Portuguese and African forefathers, my mother has adopted the superfood since the first time she tasted it in Geneva when my father took her there for their honeymoon. She might have been one of the first women in America to make it a staple on her grocery list." He chuckles, shaking his head.

"Your mom sounds like a caring woman and quite the pioneer."

"I'm sure she's as caring as yours, sweet-ness."

Ah. I'll have to tell him about my parents.

"Come on. Get up, sit over there and eat a spoonful or two of food. You'll feel much better in no time," he says, getting up to help me out of bed. I'm too weak to protest and I hold on to him like a crutch as I wobble my way up, but when I stand to my feet, I feel the sudden urge to run to the bathroom.

"Oh, wait," I say, bringing one hand to my mouth and the other to my stomach before running from the room.

For a second, I'm certain I'm going to puke, but miraculously once I close the door behind me, my tummy settles and the urge to throw up subsides. I'm about to turn on the faucet to splash cold water on my face when I hear him knock.

"Candy, are you okay in there? Should I get a doctor to come over?"

"No," I yell. "I felt nauseated when you lifted me from the bed, but I'm better now. Let me wash my face with cold water and I'll be right out."

"Are you sure?"

I hear the concern in his voice and I remem-ber the last words he uttered before we both passed out cold. *You're mine now.*

"I'll only be a few minutes. I promise."

Fifteen minutes later, I open the door to the bathroom and reappear wrapped in a white terrycloth bathrobe. After taking two Advils from the stash in my toiletry case, washing my face with cold water, freshening up and combing my hair, I feel like a new woman. He gets up immediately when I set foot in the room again.

"Should I be worried?" His brow furrows slightly.

"Max, I'll survive. I needed to bring back blood to my face. I might not drink for the next sixty days, but for now I'm okay," I say, meeting his concerned look.

"I'll take your word for it," he says, closing his arms around me and locking me against his chest. "Good. Now you have to sit down and eat something." Max lets go of me and grabs my hand to drag me to the small table near the window. As I approach, I notice the beautiful spread of foods, the adorable bouquet of blue petals and the cutest little red box with a floral pattern and gold-embossed lettering. When I make out the brand name, I bring my hands to my mouth. *Pomellato?*

I pivot to face him, still gaping, and I blink rapidly a few times before speaking. "Max. What have you done?"

He flashes me his bad-boy smile before brushing my hair behind my shoulders. "Nothing, love." He grins. "When I went shopping for your toys, I thought it would be unfair if it was all about my pleasure, so I grabbed these for you. I had them with me all night last night and I intended on giving them to you, but you ran away from me."

I never thought I'd ever own any piece of jewelry from this prestigious Italian brand. The closest I've ever gotten to this luxury designer has been through the pages of fashion magazines—I've never even had the guts to walk in either of the two flagship stores in New York. I'm still so bewildered, I can only shift my eyes from his gaze to the small box I'm cradling between my palms. *Seriously, God, if this is a dream, please don't even think of waking me up.*

"The box comes free when you buy something. I'm sure you'll find what's inside the box much more appealing than the package itself," he mocks with a half smile.

"Wiseass." I breathe in and out a few times before mustering enough courage to open my present.

When I lay my eyes on the dazzling gift, I gasp at the sight of a pair of small drop earrings in rose gold. I've never seen anything so delicate. The dangling ball isn't solid, instead it's an intricate filigree of ornate designs all meshed together. "They are exquisite, Max." I exhale.

"You like them? Deidra came out to shop with me and she said they are so you."

"When did you go out shopping with Deidra?"

"While you were having your chat with Brian the reporter from CNN. We figured you would be too caught up in the moment to notice Deidra escaping for a few hours."

"Thank you. I absolutely love them. They are the most opulent pair of earrings I own now."

"What about the ones you're wearing now? They're eye-catching and they suit you so well. If I'm not mistaken, they're also solid gold."

My heart sinks when his fingers caress my grandmother's earrings and I lower my eyes to conceal the spark of pain.

"Candy, what's wrong, honey? Your mood has shifted dramatically. If you don't like the earrings, I can get you anything else your heart desires." Max bends over to try to catch my eyes, but as hard as I try, the first tear rolls down my cheek. "Baby, what's going on?" He wipes my tear away with such tenderness. "It's not about the jewelry, is it? Did I say something to upset you?" Max is backpedalling, puzzled by my reaction. I take a few seconds to compose myself before speaking.

"Max, there's something you need to know about me."

"This sounds serious."

"It's more than serious. It defines who I am."

"Whatever it is, I'm sure we can work it out. Why don't we sit down at the table? You can tell me all about what's causing you so much grief and you can take a bite of food," he says, pulling a chair out for me before circling behind me and sitting across from me with his back facing the large window.

"These earrings are the most beautiful thing I've ever seen, Max." I lower my precious gift on the table next to me, teary-eyed. I sigh before scooping up a few spoonfuls of yogurt from a silver bucket resting on a bed of ice cubes and dropping the creamy cloud in the bowl in front of me in the hopes of settling my queasy stomach. I sprinkle the raw sugar and the muesli on top and I take a few bites under his watchful eyes.

After a few minutes, Max breaks the silence. "Candy, how bad can it be? You've shut down on me and I feel helpless. What prompted the tears?"

"It's about my family."

"Are they okay? Did something happen before you left New York?"

I shake my head and close my eyes before allowing the words to escape my lips. "I've been an orphan for the past five years—since I was nineteen."

"Baby, I'm sorry to hear you lost your mother and father. Did your siblings also pass away?"

"I don't have any brothers or sisters. I'm an only child. I lost both my parents during a freak accident. My maternal grandparents passed away when I was a small child and I never really knew them. My paternal grandfather Randolph had a heart attack six months after he lost his only son. My paternal grandmother Barbara survived him by only one year. She passed away eighteen months ago. I'm certain she died of a broken heart over the death of my father. Other than my cousin on my mom's side, who now lives in Los Angeles, and my aunt, who moved to Maine right after my mom died, I don't have anyone else left who is related to me by blood. I don't get along particularly well with either of them. My pillar of support and strength in the past five years has been my three best friends—Devin, Lexi, and Lia. You've already met Lia. She's the one I was having brunch with at Vanilla Beans…"

I'm so afraid I might choke up, I don't even dare to take a breath. I blurt everything out in one sentence hoping I've shared enough for him to understand the depth of my sorrow.

"I didn't want to pry, but you've been as silent as a clam when it comes to your family since we've met. I only knew of your cousin Trish because she was the catalyst to us bumping into each other again before the meeting at *Sassy* magazine's office. I had no idea you were dealing with so much emotional turmoil over the loss of people you loved."

"Yeah, it's been a devastating road to have to navigate. I'm much better at dealing with my past now, but it's still very much part of my life. I've healed somewhat, but I can't forget."

"Of course. What do you mean by freak accident?" Max pulls his chair closer to mine and caresses my thighs. His touch brings me comfort and makes me feel safe.

I sigh and flash a mechanical smile. "They say in life everything happens for a reason. If that's true, how can you explain death?" I say, putting my elbows on the table before resting my chin on top of my folded hands. "I've asked myself this question at least a million times and I have yet to find a logical answer for losing my parents at such a young age."

"My God, what happened to them?"

"It was a horrific accident, Max." I've been haunted for years by the mysterious events surrounding my mom and dad's final hours. I've even somewhat made peace with it all after my grandmother died, but it's still an agonizing exercise to voice so much pain. "I lived an idyllic life as an only child of two adoring parents. It's funny because until my parents' death, I had dealt with very few devastating moments in my life. I guess the price to pay for such a privileged childhood was to experience the worst kind of suffering possible—losing both parents at the same time."

I shut my eyes to muster up the strength to continue, but I don't think I have the courage to tell Max what happened to the two people I loved the most on this planet. *Too many emotions. Too many bad memories. Too much sorrow.*

"No, Candy, look at me. Don't shut me out." When I finally look up at him, he strokes his warm hands up and down my arm. "You're mine now and I'm here for you. Please talk to me."

Okay, you can do this. Under his anxious gaze, my words spill out of me, ugly and raw. I confess things I haven't been able to share with Trish or my aunt Caroline.

"That summer, my parents put me in the back of their Volvo for a road trip to Connecticut, where I was to spend the summer with my paternal grandparents who owned a home there. Once they dropped me off, my mom and dad planned on driving cross-country to Colorado. The drive from New York was absolutely breathtaking and the short trip locked in the car gave the three of us a chance to bond as a family, since we were all so busy with our hectic lives. I was always swamped with assignments and papers for school. We only spent a couple days with my grandparents before they hit the road again. On an early Sunday morning, they waved goodbye to my grandparents and me before heading west."

I shrug, barely moving my shoulders an inch to brush away the bad memories.

"I never saw them again. I vividly remember the life-changing knock from the police on my grandparents' door at one o'clock in the morning—it had taken them a while to connect the dots and to contact family members. Had it not been for the fact my dad paid with his credit card at Sweet Sally's, we might never have found out what had happened. Since Dad had parked right across from the eatery, the cops were able to piece the puzzle together when they interviewed witnesses." I shudder.

"I can't believe you had to live through this. Did the police investigate the accident?"

"The news claimed it was a freak accident—a downtown crane parked in front of a new real-estate development malfunctioned and an enormous steel cylinder dropped like a brick right on top of my parents' parked car. My mom and dad had gone to the same place for Sunday-morning brunch for as long as I can remember—everyone knew them at Sweet Sally's. They had stopped for a quick bite at their favorite spot before their long drive. They never expected it to be their last meal. There was nothing left of my parents. The crane destroyed their car and crushed them to dust. The puzzling thing to this day is how the steel cylinder dropped on top of their car like a missile, barely denting the cars parked in front or behind them—it seemed too precise."

"Jesus Christ." Max has shifted from his seat to sit at my feet. He's hugging my legs and dropping soft kisses against my skin. I can read the devastation in his eyes as I recount my catastrophic tale.

"My grandparents nearly died when the police broke the news to us, but they found the strength to fight back after the development company offered me a pittance to keep me quiet—they didn't want us talking to the press. My feisty grandmother sued the hell out of them, but after a nine-month court battle and a frightening legal bill, she resigned herself to the fact she had sunk all her savings into this—she even remortgaged my parents' home. The police's case went cold and they stopped cooperating with our attorneys. We were left alone against a giant with deep pockets—the classic case of David and Goliath, but this time, the monster won." I sigh again and drop my shoulders, relieving them from the tension of having to dig so deep.

"I can't believe the police didn't pursue this further."

"Me too, but I was a teenager back then. What was I going to do? I simply retreated into myself and I suffered in silence."

"It's unfortunate your attorney couldn't dig up anything incriminating on that development company."

"Yeah. I thought we might have had a lucky break a few months before my grandmother died, but I was wrong. My grandmother told me the lawyer had been in touch after not hearing from him for a long while. Apparently he had located a source who had some really important details about the case. Nothing ever came of it. He was in contact with my grandmother up until a few weeks before she gave up on life and then she said he never returned her calls so she figured he had hit another dead end."

"Did you follow up with the guy after your grandmother died?"

"No. After her passing, I was too consumed with grief to chase after another pipe dream. My parents were dead, my grandmother was dead, I was alone. I resigned myself to the fact I'd never get a resolution to this sordid tale."

"My God. What a heavy story," he says, kissing my hands. "Was there anyone who wanted to harm your parents? Did your father have problems at work he never told you about? I'm speculating here, but I can't imagine this came out of the blue."

"Everything surrounding the death of my parents is so strange and that's why my grandmother fought so hard. I can't imagine anyone wanting to harm my parents. My mom worked in an accounting office as a clerk and my father was part owner of a pharmaceutical company. He was a lab nerd who found pleasure in complicated chemistry experiments. Dad had been approached six years before his death by an investor with deep pockets who was looking to diversify his business assets and he was eager to tap into the fountain of youth industry."

"The what?"

"You know, the booming industry that's selling women all sorts of creams, lotions, potions and pills of eternal youth."

"I see."

"My father's business partner, Quintin Grayson, offered him something he never had in his previous job as head of research at a prominent biotech lab—freedom. That's a dream for any geek. My father could spend his days playing around with formulas and pushing the envelope, something he could never do at his old job. In his mind, although he was still a scientist, he was no longer forced to work in a restrictive box. Quintin had bought out a fledgling pharmaceutical company a few years before meeting with my dad. He was looking for the type of partner who could help him take the company to the next level and a chance encounter at a conference connected the two men. My parents were also grateful for the boost in my dad's income and they used most of that extra money to pay for my expensive university studies. Living on the edge for my parents meant trying out Greek food instead of steak and potatoes or taking an impromptu salsa class instead of playing cards with their friends in the middle of the week. My dad was doing well at his job, but we weren't gazillionaires. He didn't have an enemy in the world and neither did my mom. None of it makes sense to this day," I say, shaking my head.

"My sweet Candy, you're no longer alone and from what Deidra tells me, she's taken quite the liking to you. I've known her for many years and she doesn't like everyone, but she adores you."

"Those words mean so much to me, Max."

"Get used to it. I can't erase the dreadful day your parents died, but I can protect you from now on."

"Oh." I'm so moved by his comment, I can't believe he feels so strongly about me. I'm so utterly happy right now the words fail me.

"You're all mine now."

Max is still sitting at my feet. He grabs both my hands in his and brings them to his lips and I fold my body to kiss the top of his head.

I love hearing those intoxicating words roll off his tongue.

Chapter Eight

Since Lexi is stuck at work, I decide to have lunch with a few co-workers. It's always fun to get to know people outside of work and I welcome the chance to take a breath of fresh air after my stifling meeting with Maleficent.

After a much-needed break and a venti latte with a double shot of dark roast espresso, I do my best to immerse myself back into my work, but I find myself counting the minutes. Max should be back in Manhattan from his seven-day trip to India any time now. I can't wait to spend tonight cuddled against his warm body.

I've already packed my weekend bag and I plan on sprinting from work at five o'clock sharp so I'm home in time to transform into a vamp before Max's chauffeur picks me up at six-thirty. I want to make sure he flings me over his shoulder and carries me to his bedroom for a raunchy interlude the minute he lays eyes on me. *God, seven days without his cock has been the worst punishment.*

I open a few folders on my computer for upcoming articles I need to write, hoping I can quiet my mind and spark the inspiration I need to get some work done, but my phone vibrates on my desk. I glance down and my heart stops. *Max is back.* I pick up and try hard to contain my excitement in order to avoid bringing any attention to me.

"Are you back?" I whisper, covering my mouth so my voice doesn't carry.

"Sweetness, I've missed you like crazy. Yes, I'm back in NYC."

I'm thrilled beyond words. "Did you get in early?"

"We did. We wrapped things up as quickly as we could and we took a chance on being able to catch a flight a couple of hours before our scheduled departure time."

"I'm already counting the hours until I see you," I say, glancing at the time on my laptop. *Only four more hours.*

"Yeah, about us meeting later…"

Is he cancelling on me? "Did something come up?"

"As a matter of fact yes. I'm afraid, if I have to wait another four hours before fucking you, I'll die from blue balls."

My eyes widen and I place my free hand over my mouth again to hide my grin. "It's not that long, baby. We've already waited a whole week. What's a few more hours?" *I love how he never seems to be able to get enough of me.*

"I don't think you understand me, Candy." His domineering tone puts an end to my laughs.

"I did, but…"

"Can you get away for a little while?"

"Uh… Well, I think so. My boss is gone for the rest of the day. Where should I meet you? I can catch a cab."

"You don't have to travel far," he interrupts. "I came to you."

"Huh? Is it the jet lag or are you not making any sense right now?"

"I swear someone in your office needs to get fired for never locking the door to the Fashion Archive room. This is the third time in a row I've been able to slip in here."

"Wh-what?" I nearly choke. "You can't be serious."

"Honey, I'm as serious as my hard-on. Now don't make me wait. Get your fine ass over here for your quickie."

"Wait. You mean now?"

"I believe now means immediately. So yes, now."

My heart is racing and there are five hundred questions bouncing in my head. How the hell did he pull this off again? I mean you'd think a few women would ogle a tall, hot and sexy guy walking around in a well-tailored suit, but no… not at *Sassy* magazine. "What if…"

"We're smarter." He answers my question before I can finish asking it. "We'll make sure to lock the door this time. Stop stressing and come and relieve my aching cock." Max ends the conversation before I have time to reply.

Oh my God. This is so dangerous. What if this time we're not as lucky and we do get caught? What then?

I look around the office. Since everyone knows Jennifer is gone for the rest of the day, some people are chatting away while others have opted for an extended lunch break—half the seats are still empty. The ones who are here are way too preoccupied to care about my disappearance. *Good. I can sneak out without anyone noticing.*

I slide my phone inside my handbag, grab a few magazines stacked in front of me, plop a notepad on top of the pile and stick a pencil behind my ear as if I'm on my way to an extremely important meeting. I head to the elevator and I avoid breathing just in case I wake up any suspicions.

When I get off on the floor where Max is waiting for me, I scan the hallway a few times before gently knocking on the door. *I can't believe I'm doing this. Again.*

Max opens the door and peeks his head out and the second I lose myself in his eyes, I know the reward will greatly outweigh the risk.

"Come in," he whispers, grabbing my arms and pulling me inside the room. He locks the door and slides a chair under the handle to barricade our makeshift love shack from the outside world.

Max closes the gap between us, takes a deep breath through his nose and throws the pile of magazines I'm holding in my hands to the floor. *Shit.* He leans forward and presses his lips against mine and digs his fingers into my hair, pinning my body against an empty wall.

"Goddammit, I've been craving to taste you since I left," he lets out between kisses. He's so turned on his cock throbs against my tummy as my hands mirror his own and grip the base of his hair, fisting it roughly.

"You know, we should find another place in the building to meet," I tease.

"I've become attached to this room." He pulls my dress up along my thighs and groans into my mouth as his fingers travel to the lace edge of my thigh-highs. *Had I known he'd be fucking me in the middle of the afternoon, I would have slipped into garter belts and silk stockings this morning instead of wearing these stay-ups.* "Oh, Candy, you do this to torment me. I've gone without for seven painful days and you're wearing this little number?" I'm too consumed by lust to answer and I respond by running my tongue over his lips as Max's fingertips brush the warm and drenched material of my panties. "I assume these are part of my collection." He clenches his hold around the fabric and gives it a rough tug.

"I'm not going to have anything left at this rate," I laugh.

"I'm sure I can replace these and all the others I intend on ripping apart," he hisses, pressing his tongue between my lips and into my mouth.

"Damn, I've missed you." I groan as he thrusts two fingers inside my eager pussy.

"Christ, you're wetter than ever."

I break away from his lips with a gasp. "It's your fault. Every part of me has been yearning for you."

"Don't worry, I intend on making it up to you over and over and over again."

I tilt my head back, freefalling as he fucks me hard with his fingers, his thumb rubbing addictive circles on my clit. "Fuck me," I plead. "I need your cock in me. Now."

He narrows his eyes, studying the effect he has on me. "Say please, Candy."

I've been waiting for over a week for this. I can't believe he's making me beg. "Fuck me now, please," I respond more urgently.

"Much better." The look of victory in his eyes is such a turn-on. "Baby, are you on the pill?"

"Yeah."

"Good."

"Does it mean I get to feel your warm load deep inside me?"

"Did you actually say that?" he asks, surprised.

I nod defiantly, holding his gaze.

"You naughty girl. I'm going to fuck you like an animal and you'll definitely feel me explode inside you." Max fumbles with his belt and pants, pulling them down to his feet before lifting me up and thrusting hard inside my pussy. "Christ, Candy, you feel amazing. No wonder I couldn't get you out of my head. There was no way I was going to be able to wait four more hours for this."

"Ah." I gasp and I clench tighter around him, my breath ragged.

"I've been dreaming of this every night since I left you."

"Mmmm, so have I." I bite into the shoulder of his jacket and I wrap my legs around him as Max begins moving into me hard and fast against the wall. Any moment someone could break down his make-shift barricade, enter this room and catch my boyfriend fucking me in the middle of the day, and I couldn't care less. *I need this more than I need to breathe.*

"Oh, Max," I exhale as I lift my head from his shoulder and I bite my way up his neck before taking his bottom lip between my teeth. *I've never been this aroused ever.* "Argh, I'm close," I hiss and tighten my legs around his waist to pull him deeper into me. "I'm so fucking close."

"Damn," he mumbles. "Look at you. I love watching as you dissolve in my arms, sweetness."

His words trigger the final clench I need to come.

"Christ." I push down against his cock, rubbing my hard nub against him, and I let go. My climax takes over me in such a delirious way it reminds me of how long it's been since I've felt this satiated.

Max pumps into my throbbing pussy a few more times before letting out a deep low growl. He buries his face in my neck to muffle the groan as he comes hard and suddenly inside me, squeezing my ass in his hands.

"I've missed this," I let out between breaths.

"So have I. You were ravenous, baby. You worked me so hard I thought I was going to have a heart attack. I'm sweating like crazy."

"You know what Madonna says? No sweat, no candy."

"In that case, I've earned the Candy I got to-day."

We both laugh.

We stay locked into each other for a few minutes before he gently puts me down on unsteady legs. Dazed, I stumbled away from the wall, kiss him and prepare for my incognito exit.

"I have to go."

"I have to get to the office, since I came to you before checking back at my headquarters. I'll see you at my place in a few hours. This was just a little snack to hold us both until I can ravage you at will." He grins and I find myself grinning back, already looking forward to round two, three and four.

"Of course." I steal one last kiss before dashing off. "See you soon."

Instead of grabbing the elevators, I hike up a few flights of stairs into a restroom located on another floor to avoid bumping into anyone who saw me before I met up with Max. When I enter the bathroom, I do a quick check under all the stalls to make sure they're all empty and then I turn the lock on the main door. As I approach the bathroom mirror, I wince. I look like a woman who's been fucked hard at work.

Candy, you look like a raving mess. Next time, I hope Max warns me in advance. *Wait. What? Where the hell did that come from? Get a grip, girlfriend.*

I slam my fist on the counter and move closer to inspect the damage. My hair is a nightmare, my coral lipstick is smeared, my lips are swollen, my black eyeliner is all smudged, my thigh-highs have a telltale rip and I'm once again missing my panties. *There goes another pair.*

"There can be no next time at my office. We can't keep fucking like this at my work place. I'm playing with fire here," I scorn myself aloud. This has to stop but how am I supposed to resist Max's big hungry cock deep inside me when I've gone without for a whole week?

I smile in the mirror when I realize how much I'm lying to myself. I wouldn't give up the exhilarating thrill of a quickie with Max—even if it means chancing getting caught.

Chapter Nine

I sneak back into the office at three o'clock, according to my iPhone. Everyone still seems to be having too much fun on this Friday afternoon to care about little ol' me, but I won't hesitate to lie if anyone inquires about my whereabouts. I'm giddy and still grinning ear to ear when I turn the corner to head to the kitchen to grab another coffee. My euphoria ends when my colleague Carl Applegate frowns at the sight of me. He raises his eyebrows and inspects me from head to toe. Panicked, I open the fridge and stick my head in, pretending to search for something.

"Oh, Candy…" The second he chants my name, my heart sinks. *Fuck, am I busted?* I slowly lift my head and face him.

"Yes?" *Did he change his signature big-ass glasses after lunch? I swear he wasn't wearing these over-the-top red frames when I last saw him.*

"Child, I don't know what's going on with you, but lately you look sassy as hell. You've been walking around with a bounce in your step since returning from Miami and today you're glowing so much it's as if you got a total makeover during lunch."

Yeah, I got a makeover all right. I smile and steady my voice before responding. "Carl, thanks for the compliment. I've been experimenting with a few new things since Miami and may I say, it's done me a lot of good." I roll my eyes and curl my lips in a half smile as I flash back to Max and I at the back of his black SUV where he was pounding my pussy while pressing a vibrator against my clit and teasing my asshole with the butt plug.

"Good for you. I'm happy you're opening yourself up to new adventures. Keep it up. You look positively radiant. Any plans for the weekend?"

"I'll be dashing off at five to meet a friend." I smile. "And you?"

"I'm going to Chicago to connect with this new guy I've been seeing. He was here last weekend and it's my turn to fly to him."

"Awesome."

Carl opens his mouth to continue the conversation, but his phone rings. He fishes in his pocket and when he sees a number on his phone, his entire face changes. *My God, I've never seen him look so vulnerable.* Carl is always so stoic and he's a master at concealing his emotions, but the guy standing in front of me looks like a lovestruck puppy.

"Speaking of the devil. It's Trent. I'm sorry, but I'm going to have to take this. I haven't spoken to my honey since this morning." Before I can answer, Carl is already waving goodbye and walking away from the kitchen.

Did he say "my honey"? I shake my head, bewildered, and remember why I entered this room in the first place. "Okay, back to coffee," I tell myself before opening a cupboard in search of the biggest mug I can find. *After this impromptu romp, I need a burst of energy.*

The second the piping-hot coffee touches the bottom of my cup, I grab the mug in a hurry and I take my first sip. *Heaven can be found in a cup of java.* With my latte in hand, I march decisively to my desk, motivated to make the most of the next two hours.

I barely have time to turn my computer on before my phone rings. I'm hoping with all my heart it's Max calling to tell me how much he already misses me, but when I pull out my phone from my bag, I realize it's my cousin Trish. *What does she want now? She only calls when she needs something from me.*

"Hi, Trish, to what do I owe this call?"

"Hey, coz, how are you? We haven't spoken in weeks. It's been way too long."

Really? You've gone six months without enquiring to see if I was dead or alive and now a few weeks seems like a lifetime? "Has it been already been so long? How have you been keeping?"

"Good. Busy. I've been getting so many incredible parts lately on smaller-budget films, a few up-and-coming TV shows and commercials. You might have seen me in a few of them."

Nah, I'm not into the slasher movies you get booked for and I have no desire to surf the net to find the commercials shot for the international markets you seem to get all the time. "Great news. All your hard work is finally paying off."

"Well, I'm sure if I had a chance to get a feature on a major media outlet like CNN, my career would shoot off the charts."

Ha. I see why she's calling.

"Oh, are you talking about my tiny feature on a small website no one knows?" I pretend to play it coy, but I'm loving this moment so much.

"Tiny? Are you kidding me? You said you were an editor for a magazine, but it never occurred to me your job was so important you'd make the front page of CNN.com Living. Congrats."

Of course it would never occur to you since you weren't listening when you asked me about my job. You quickly moved on to some self-centered topic and you showed little interest in finding out more about me. "Thanks, Trish. I appreciate the compliment."

"We're going to be able to see each other soon. I landed a career-changing role in three episodes of a series they say will be bigger than *Friends* and it's shooting in New York. I've been meaning to call you for the last three weeks to tell you, but it's been crazy between my acting jobs and my waitressing gig. I'll be out there next week and I'll stay in the

Big Apple for about fourteen days. Maybe we can meet when I arrive."

"Sorry, Trish. Bad timing. I'm off to Brazil to cover the Rio Moda Week. I'll be there for eight days and I guess I'll catch you at the tail end of your stay."

"God, you're the international maven now. It's a deal. Let's connect when you get back. Maybe we can finally go to the Bymark hotel for drinks since last time I couldn't make it and you probably ended up going home right after we spoke."

Not this bullshit again. "I actually stayed. Remember, I told you I hooked up with a hot guy."

"Yeah, but I thought you were joking. I mean..." She laughs on the other end as if she's sitting front row at a comedy house.

Really? "No, I was quite serious, Trish. In fact the sizzling, sexy and extremely rich man I bumped into while making my way to meet you invited me for drinks when I found you were stuck in Nashville... and he's now my boyfriend." *Snap.*

The phone goes dead silent. Trish must be dying inside. *Wait for it. Four, three, two, one.*

"Candy, you actually met someone at Bymark? For the love of God, the legendary place is crawling with eligible, handsome and outrageously wealthy men."

"Exactly. And if you recall, I used those same adjectives to describe the man I'm dating now."

Another long silence follows as Trish gets over the shock of my revelation and processes her worst nightmare—her plus-size cousin ends up with the type of man she's always dreamed of being with.

"My, my, my. Good for you." *I'm sure those words must have hurt like hell. She's never been happy for anything positive in my life. Why start now?* "Things have changed a lot since I left New York..." Trish launches into a long spiel that will most likely ended up with her insulting me with a sly remark about my weight or the man I'm dating. I prepare myself for the blow when I notice Charlotte Jones, our receptionist, trying to catch my attention.

"One second," I mouth, lifting my index finger to indicate I'll be with her as quickly as I can get Trish to shut up.

Trish is still going on without any signs of taking a millisecond to breathe. When she finally takes a short pause, I grasp at the chance to cut short my conversation with my self-absorbed and condescending cousin.

"I have to go. One of my colleagues is standing in front of me and it looks important. Who knows, maybe CNN is calling for a follow-up interview."

"Oh, of course. I'm sorry. I can't believe my cousin might be featured twice on CNN.com," she gushes.

"It's still so surreal to me as well." I know I shouldn't lie like this, but I relish hearing Trish grovel on the other end because a family member is basking in her fifteen minutes of fame. When I hang up, I look up at Charlotte with a sigh of gratitude. *Thank God I didn't have to keep listening to her monologue.* "I owe you for saving me from that drawn-out conversation."

"I'm happy I was able to help." Charlotte winks. "Candy, a messenger came and dropped this off for you while you were away from your desk. It came about an hour ago and I tried to find you, but I couldn't. Since Maleficent is away so many people are taking advantage of this freedom, I assumed you were laughing it up with colleagues."

"No. I was away from my desk for a few minutes, but I wasn't too far."

"Gotcha," she says, surprised by my answer. "Well, while you were away, this came for you." She hands me an envelope and walks away.

"Thanks," I call out and she turns her head and waves.

I glance at the envelope. There's no return address. *Strange. Who is this from?* I get up from my chair hoping I can still catch Charlotte, but she's disappeared.

I'm troubled by the big blue envelope I'm holding in my hands for a few reasons. One, this is an unusual color and deviates from the common yellow or craft-paper envelopes I usually get. Two, my name is written out in exquisite penmanship instead of it being a label. Three, there's no return address. And four, it says "confidential" in big black bold lettering. *Maybe the return address is on the delivery slip.*

I run to the reception area to find out which courier company delivered my mysterious package.

"I'm sorry to bother you, Charlotte, but there's no return address. Did you keep the delivery slip?" I know I could easily open the package in my hand and find out who it's from, but something is quite strange about it's appearance and the word "confidential" is ominous. I immediately cast off the possibility it's from Max, and since I hung out with my three best friends last night, I don't think it's from one of them. Not to mention I doubt they'd pay to send a courier over with a note or an invitation—they'd text me instead.

"Strange. Give me one sec. I'm sure I've already filed it." Charlotte swivels on her chair and opens a cabinet behind her. She reaches to her far left and pulls out a folder and places it on her lap before leafing through the tabs to today's date. "Here it is," she says, holding up a yellow slip. "Hmmm."

"What?"

"It's blank. Weird. There's always a name and return address. I've seen thousands of these and they are pretty standard. I didn't pay attention when the courier dropped this off. I'm sorry, Candy."

"Yeah. I figured as much."

"You should open it. Whoever sent it took care in selecting an awesome-colored envelope. All that buzz from CNN.com is getting you a lot of attention. Maybe it's from a secret admirer."

Something tells me she's wrong, but I don't let on. "Good idea. Let me see who sent this. Thanks for your help." I turn on my heel and head back to my desk. When I get to my cubicle, I immediately open my drawer and fish for my scissors to open my package, but I hesitate. *Why are you hesitating so much? Open the damn thing.* I can't put my finger on it, but something about all of this is quite eerie.

It's a letter. I unfold the piece of paper and scan the words. As my eyes bounce from one sentence to another, it doesn't take much time for my heart to sink in shock.

Dear Candice,

I'm sure you won't remember me, but I used to work with your father at the lab. I've hesitated in getting in touch with you for the past few years because I felt awkward. I was quite close to your parents—especially your father. I've been following your progress and both your parents would be so proud of you. I can't believe your CNN.com feature story. Congratulations.

I've been reading your blog for a few years now trying to muster up the courage to contact you. I know from your columns on the Sassy *magazine website you're off to Brazil in the coming days. I hope we might be able to meet face to face for coffee upon your return. I'm still shy in approaching you, so I'll send another package when you get back in Manhattan with a location where we could potentially meet— if you feel comfortable. I'll hold off on sharing my real name for now, but you can call me Annie Smith.*

— Annie

PS: It might be best to keep this letter between the two of us. I know you're no longer in contact with your father's former business partner, but I thought I'd mention it just in case.

PPS: I'm sorry about the passing of your grandmother. You should know her fight to claim justice for her son and his wife was an honorable one. She deserved her day in court because there's far more to your parents' deadly accident than her attorneys were able to dig up.

What the fuck? Who the hell is this?

I reread the letter six times while holding my breath. By the last read, cold sweat is dripping between my boobs and all the way down my spine. I'm on the verge of tears because I don't know what to make of this. I knew something was creepy about this envelope and now it's been confirmed. Who the heck is this Annie Smith woman?

Is she trying to blackmail me or was there more to my parents' death? Could my grandmother have been right all along?

****

Get Your FREE SECRET Chapters!

Thank you for purchasing this romance!

I'd love for you to lose yourself in more
sultriness, sexiness and steamy passion!

When you sign-up today, I'll send you the following
Secret Chapter for Part 3 of this serial:

*You'll want to read about how Max plans the dirty Miami
car scene & the revelation!
(This is Max's POV)*

*** <u>PASSWORD FOR</u> Secret Chapter Part 3:
Miami-Heat

Note: the password is case sensitive!

Sign-up TODAY!

www.RomanceBooksRock.com

***If you've already signed-up to my list from previous
books, you can visit the same page to download
the Secret Chapters for this romance***

****

PART 4—CURVES ENVY

Curvy Conquest

Chapter One

My thoughts wake me up so violently, it's as if the flashbacks are suffocating me. *Am I having a nightmare?* I sit straight up in bed, trembling. I can't get Annie Smith's words out of my head.

I look around the room, dazed and confused. It takes me a few seconds to realize I'm in Max's luxurious penthouse and not in my own bed. *Oh, yeah, I stayed at his place last night.*

Yesterday was a freaky day of thrilling highs and shattering lows. I texted Devin, Lia and Lexi in a panic after receiving the mysterious package from one of my father's former employees. Once they calmed me down, I called Max to share the latest development in my family saga. He was so dumbfounded by my news, he got behind the wheel of his Benz and drove to my place to pick me up instead of sending a chauffeur. He felt we needed time alone to talk this out.

When I was safely hidden away at his place, I broke down. I spent the last night either spilling my guts out about what I could remember or bursting into tears at having to relieve some of the most gruesome moments of my life. Max was incredibly compassionate and caring. He allowed me to sob as much as I needed while consoling me into believing Annie might be the key to helping me make sense of the last five years. *For the life of me, I hope he's right.*

I look down at Max, sleeping so peacefully next to me, when I flash back to a conversation I had with my grandmother on her deathbed. I widen my eyes, shocked as the words resonate in my head. *I must have blocked this off until now.*

I take a hasty breath before reaching out to wake Max up. "Wake up. Please wake up," I plead.

"What's going on, Candy?" Max pops his eyes open and looks up at me with a concerned gaze.

"I just remembered my grandmother compiled so much information on the real-estate giant who tried to intimidate us while she was fighting for justice. It must still be with the lawyer she had hired to represent us."

"Baby, we're one step closer. How come you never mentioned this last night?"

"It only now flashed in my head. I've blocked out so many episodes during the last five years in order to diminish the pain."

"I understand, baby," he says, kissing my arm. "Do you remember the name of this lawyer?"

"I still have him listed in my contacts on my iPhone. My grandmother made me swear I'd never get rid of this guy's name."

"Great. Bless your *avó*'s heart."

"What does *avó* mean?" I ask, perplexed.

"It's grandmother in Portuguese. I called my mom's mom *avó*. As a child it was much easier to pronounce than the English translation." Max smiles warmly at me as he caresses my thighs.

"It's such a sweet way to refer to a granny."

"Let's jump out of bed and get in touch with him. He might be able to shed some light on some of the things Annie said in her letter. Let's hope we can meet today instead of having to wait until Monday."

I throw the covers off my naked body and I rush downstairs to grab my phone. I flip madly through my contacts on my screen until I find his name—Nathaniel Carpenter of Carpenter and Associates LLP. *Got it.* I run up the stairs back to Max's room with a triumphant grin on my face, waving my phone at him.

"Someone looks like they've found gold," Max says, getting out of bed.

"Not quite, but pretty close."

"Let's go to my office and we'll do a quick Google search first. This way we can find out what your grandmother's attorney has been up to since you last saw him. Once we gather a few details on him, let's call this guy. Lawyers usually have an after-hours service for evening and weekend emergencies. I'd say your case is pretty pressing."

"Let me grab a robe and I'll be right there."

Before I can turn around, Max grabs my wrists and holds me firmly. "Why? You don't expect me to start my weekend without royally fucking you? Once you and I are done speaking to this lawyer, I think we should play strip poker. Since you're already naked the only thing left is for me to do is poke you with my cock." He looks like a boy when he smiles like this.

"You never seem to be able to get enough of this," I say, waving my finger between us with my eyes fixed on his growing erection.

"Enough of your curves? Never." Max pulls my body into his and I close my eyes. *Thank God he's in my life now and I didn't have to spend the night alone, nor do I have to deal with this dreadful situation by myself.*

* * *

Max turns on his iMac computer and types Nathaniel's company information into Google. My initial excitement turns into worry when I read the devastating words on the screen over his shoulder. *Nathaniel Carpenter of Carpenter and Associates LLP Dies In Car Accident at Fifty-Eight.*

"Oh, shit," I whisper. "This doesn't look like good news at all."

"Let's click on the link before we jump to conclusions. Perhaps Mr. Carpenter has a daughter or son who's taken over his law firm. In many cases lawyers work with business associates who take on their roster of clients when it's time for them to retire or when they pass away."

"I pray you're right."

Max scrolls down the page and with each paragraph my anxiety grows. The new law firm that has taken over Mr. Carpenter's business published a dry press release reassuring Mr. Carpenter's active clients they'd gladly take over their affairs. It seems Mr. Carpenter died eighteen months ago in a car accident during a hellish stormy night.

"Eighteen months ago? He would have died around the same time as my grandmother. I guess that explains why he stopped calling."

"What an eerie coincidence." Max looks up at me and I can tell I'm not the only one worried here.

"It's way too close for comfort. Wait a minute, Max." I catch an alarming sentence on the screen. "Did you read this paragraph?" I wave my hand at the screen. Max brushes his hair with his fingers and when I pick up on his jittery reaction, I officially panic. "I can't believe the new law firm is unwilling to take on older cases. They're leaving us hung out to dry."

"I don't think that's exactly it. It could simply be a question of return on investment—some cases are too dated to make it worth their time."

"What am I supposed to do now?" I nearly scream.

"Candy, there's a good chance this new law firm still owns Nathaniel Carpenter's archives. If they are able to track down your file, you can still hire a phenomenal lawyer who will help make sense of all of this. Sometimes starting fresh is the best way to go."

"But Max, I don't know of any lawyers, let alone a phenomenal one."

"How many times do I have to tell you you're not alone anymore?" he says, taking my hands into his and kissing them gently. "My older brother is an astoundingly sharp attorney. Let me call Gabriel and ask him to come over. There's no point in both of us trying to figure this out on our own. We might be smart people, but from what I've read in Annie's letter and from this latest discovery about your former attorney's death, it's clear we're way over our heads and we need help from a legal top gun."

* * *

Ninety minutes later, Max, his brother and I are huddled around the kitchen table finishing a heavenly New York-style breakfast while going over the facts of my life since my parents died.

Gabriel showed up at the penthouse with the perfect feast to calm my nerves and start the day off on the right foot. It was only when he opened the bag of freshly baked goods that I remembered I had been far too distraught to eat dinner last night. I was absolutely famished.

He's brought an armful of Montreal-style bagels from the number one shop in New York. Black Seed Bagels is a tiny spot located near Grand Central Station subway. On weekends the lines are insane, but the sometimes-excruciating wait is well worth it. These outstanding Eastern European breads are hand-rolled and baked to perfection in Black Seed Bagels' wood-fired oven. What makes these so irresistible is the heavenly dough infused with honey. It goes without saying these delicacies are made in-house, which makes them even more sinful.

Gabriel gained a lot of brownie points with me when he showed up with my all-time favorite— their signature black seed bagel stuffed with beet-cured salmon. He really won me over when he announced he had also brought dessert—*sufganiyot*. These ridiculously fluffy and golden small doughnuts ooze with sweet jam. My love of homemade doughnuts runs so deep, I nearly jumped up and down when Gabriel pulled out the box he was hiding in his shopping bag.

Lucky for us, Marty Vogelstein, one of Gabriel's prominent clients, owns Sugary Treats along with a fleet of successful eateries. This little gem is one of the few Jewish pastry shops in New York that makes these deadly-delicious doughnuts just like they would in Israel, where people make *sufganiyot* of this caliber on a daily basis. One call to Marty's assistant and Gabriel was able to jump to the front of the line on a busy Saturday to bring these to Max's penthouse.

Before I started working at *Sassy* magazine, I used to work for a woman who would do a weekly run to Sugary Treats on Fridays and she'd always grab a few extras for me. One bite and you start hearing angels sing.

Damn, these are amazing. I'm still licking my fingers when Gabriel launches into another round of interrogation. He's already asked me what seems like one thousand questions about the events surrounding my parents' accident and the reasons why my paternal grandmother felt so strongly about avenging her only son and her daughter in-law's gruesome deaths, but this time he pulls out his iPhone to record my answers.

"Candice, may I call you Candy?"

"Of course, Gabriel."

"To friends and family, I'm Gabe. Seems you're family now." Max's brother raises his eyebrows and tilts his head. Although I'm not ashamed of what I share with Max, Gabriel's reaction makes me blush.

"Careful, bro." Max smiles at his brother and wraps me lovingly in his arms.

"Candy is adorable. I'm teasing."

"Consider yourself lucky, baby. My brother only mocks people he likes."

"Thanks for clearing things up for me, Max," I respond jokingly. "I'll gladly call your brother Gabe."

"On a more serious note, Candy, I want to go over key questions and I also want to record your answers. My penmanship is atrocious and since my days are filled with millions of little details, my head is constantly going a mile a minute. I want to be certain I don't miss one small thing that could turn out to be crucial a few weeks from now. I'm going to try my best in the next hour or so to gather as much as I can.

These are the preliminary stages, but on Monday morning, I'll put two of my top legal minds on your case. Sheena Wagner and Francis Kraai are both brilliant attorneys and they've helped my office win many cold cases we've reopened when new evidence surges. Francis has a particular affection for damsels in distress and I strongly believe we need a passionate, unwavering, and unyielding force to go after the bad guys who've robbed you of your parents' love."

"Let Francis know Candy already has a boyfriend."

We all laugh at Max's possessive remark.

"Gabe, I really don't know how to thank you. This means the world to me. My grandmother and I were no match for those monsters who destroyed my peaceful existence a few years ago."

"I'm sure your grandmother and Nathaniel Carpenter did the best they could with what they had, but Annie's letter and the facts you've shared so far suggest there's a lot more to this story. It would have been extraordinarily expensive for you to go after them. Unless Nathaniel was willing to draw blood, your Goliath would have quickly dismissed you. My team of attorneys are like pit bulls—relentless, ferocious and inexorable when it comes to seeking justice for our clients. They won't back down until they've flipped the case in every possible direction like a master Rubik's cube player. Of course, we always work within the American legal system, but sometimes it's a question of having the right insider contacts…"

"I appreciate all this, but…" I hesitate, uncertain how to let Gabe know I don't have the means to pay for such accomplished lawyers. *What am I talking about, I can't even afford a junior attorney.* "My only valuable assets are the jewelry and the apartment my grandmother left me. My parents' estate went to pay our astronomical legal fees. I'm not sure how…" I let my words trail off, fearing I might be so close to discovering exactly why my parents died, but yet still so far—given I'm unable to afford to foot what sounds like another colossal legal bill.

"Gabe, I'll take care of your fees on behalf of Candy." Although Max is addressing his brother, his eyes are locked into mine. "Baby, we can't let these monsters get away with this." His words touch the deepest part of me and a tear of relief rolls down my cheek.

"I can't believe I'll be able to avenge my loving parents."

"I know my brother and he's never afraid to draw blood. I think we need this in your case."

"God. I want nothing more than justice."

"And you'll get it. We'll make sure of it."

"I wish my grandmother was still here."

"She'll be celebrating up above when all this mess is over. Right, Gabe?"

"Max, it won't happen overnight, but Sheena and Francis are ferocious in cases such as these."

"I couldn't ask for more."

"Candy, we have a long haul in front of us. I know you're supposed to leave with my brother for Brazil in a few days and my best advice is for you to enjoy yourself. Our country is majestic and the best place for you to recharge your batteries. There's no point in worrying about anything more because you're now one of our top clients. I promise we'll take good care of you."

"Thank you, Gabe, from the bottom of my heart."

"Candy, you heard the man. A few days in Rio is exactly what the doctor—I guess I should say lawyer—ordered."

Chapter Two

The week in Rio is indescribable. How can you use simple words to depict heaven on earth? I still can't believe we're leaving this paradisiac land in less than forty-eight hours. I've so thoroughly enjoyed myself during these last eight days, it wouldn't take much to convince me to stay forever.

Travelling alongside Max has been a real eye-opener. I'd be lying if I said I wasn't utterly impressed by the swanky private jet with full service and personal chef. I honestly felt like I was in an episode of the eighties smash drama *Dynasty*. Although I doubt my parents had even met when the show first aired on TV, my mom was a huge fan of the gloriously over-the-top trials and tribulations of the fabulously wealthy Carrington and Colby clans. Just like she needed her weekly dose of *Murphy Brown*, she also had to keep track of Alexis Carrington's latest bitchy moves. She watched the reruns for years with me on her lap.

Max definitely has a "champagne wishes and caviar dreams" lifestyle. His penthouse in New York is breathtaking and it's no surprise his place in Rio matches such opulence. Max's luxurious apartment in Rio is located in the Lagoa area—the third-most expensive neighborhood in all of South America and the most exclusive neighborhood in the capital city. Not only is this one of the most idyllic spots I've ever visited, Lagoa is also home to an insanely beautiful water bed known as the Lagoa Rodrigo de Freitas, which is surrounded by a four-mile path encircling the lagoon. Since the adorable little open-air cafés and quaint local restaurants offer stunning views of the lagoon, Max insisted on us indulging in as many as we possibly could. After our delicious and satisfying meals, we'd stroll hand in hand every night admiring the enchanting sunset until Max's need to devour me became too overwhelming and we'd have to rush back to his place so that we could give free rein to our carnal desires behind closed doors.

Enjoying the scenery hanging from Max's arm and reveling in multiple mind-blowing orgasms night after night was only half the fun. Work was equally entertaining, since I had a blast at Rio Moda. Although not as illustrious as Rio Fashion Week, this dazzling event is still the second most important fashion event in South America's largest country. I was shocked to witness how curvy Brazilian women flaunt their assets without any shame and these Latin beauties don't hesitate when it comes to draping their delicious bodies with very revealing couture. Everywhere I turned, there was a constant reminder that being a big beautiful woman was something to celebrate. All in all, my work vacation in Rio has been dreamy, and I would have been fully satisfied had it stopped right there. I was floating on air relishing every blissful moment thinking nothing could surpass the last week when a last-minute goal from a rookie player changed everything a few hours ago. Nothing could have prepared me for the last few days in this vibrant South American city—not even a psychic.

When the news broke at one-sixteen this afternoon that the Brazilian team has qualified for the *Copa América*, the entire country went bonkers at another chance to claim the coveted South American Football Championship. The fervor of the Brazilian people was fueled by the fact their team came this close to not making it. Young goalie Fernando Hernanes put the winning goal in their long-time adversaries' net with five seconds left before the whistle, ending a long battle between Brazil and Argentina for the last spot in the championship. The twenty-year-old has now officially been crowned a national hero for his strategic kick.

It's such a big deal even the president, Marcela Luisa Lucas, went on television to declare today a day of unbridled celebration. Offices, shops and restaurants closed immediately after the announcement was made and all of Rio is now having the party to end all parties.

Since I was a bit taken aback by this madness, Max had to enlighten me by explaining why the country was so overjoyed—for Brazilians this victory is like the Super Bowl final times three hundred. By four o'clock, Max decides to throw all caution to the wind and join the festivities.

We're making our way through the city along with the rest of the inhabitants by foot. Even cab drivers are far too busy enjoying the moment to attend to customers. I'm sure my beaming face must reveal my excitement because Max jumps at the opportunity to tease me.

"Have you ever been to a Brazilian party, love?"

"I don't think I ever have," I tease back.

"You know the American expression, 'what happens in Vegas, stays in Vegas?'"

"Of course, who doesn't?"

"I'm warning you right now, a Brazilian party makes festivities in Vegas look as tame as a choir practice. You've not walked on the wild side until you've partied here."

His words detonate inside me and a million feelings rush through my body as he holds my gaze. *Am I ready to walk on the wild side?*

After what seems like an eternity, we finally arrive at the heart of it all. When I look around me, I'm dumbfounded. *How the heck could they make this happen so fast?* I haven't got a clue how the Brazilians managed to pull off a major concert within such a short window, but here we are crammed into a sea of tens of thousands of exuberant fans inside the Maracanã Stadium—home to some of the most historic games in history.

Since I know little to nothing about football, or soccer as we call it, Max gives me a crash course as we push our way through the partygoers. When we arrive inside, I'm amazed at how many jubilant people surround me, but at the same time, I'm delirious at the idea of experiencing this moment with the man of my dreams.

As a stroke of genius, Enrique Iglesias happened to be in Brazil when the news broke and he agreed to feature in this star-studded concert. When the MC steps on stage to announce the first act, the crowd goes mad and so do I. Since Lexi has single-handedly been responsible for my Latin music education, I immediately start swaying my hips following the cue of the sexy bodies encircling me when the guitarist plays the first few chords and I nearly lose my head when Alexander Delgado, lead singer to the Cuban reggaeton group Gente D' Zona, calls out for the drop-dead gorgeous Spaniard singer to step on stage to perform their monster hit *Bailando*. To honor the hosting country, Enrique invites local sensation Luan Santana to perform the Portuguese version of the song. *I didn't think anything could top this week, but this takes the cake for sure.* I'm completely in my zone with both eyes closed in some sort of a musical trance when Max whispers in my ear.

"I didn't know you could dance."

I slowly open my eyes before turning around, still inebriated by the spicy rhythm. I look up at him and I can't help but smile flirtatiously. "I don't know if I'll ever win a dance competition any time soon, but I can hold my own."

"Clearly you can."

I turn to face the stage again and I step back just enough to brush my ass against Max. I'm greeted by his growing desire and my body shivers.

"Hmmm, I like your ass against me," he murmurs, low and warm into my ear.

I daringly reach behind me, slide my hand between us, and palm him right there in the middle of the stadium. He exhales a warm puff against my neck, whispering, *"Foda-se, sim, baby."*

"What did you just say?" I can't understand a word of Portuguese, but whatever Max uttered in my ear sounded dirty as hell.

"Fuck, yes, baby."

"You like?" I respond, turning my head to the side.

"From the rolling of your hips and the boldness of your actions, I bet there's a vamp inside you dying to come out and play."

"You know me too well by now."

The music fades to a mere note and the change on stage causes us to unlock our gaze. The MC runs back to let the audience know Enrique and his band need to take a quick break to adjust a few instruments and to keep the saucy groove going strong they're going to play one of the most popular Salsa songs of all time—*Valio La Pena* by Marc Anthony.

The minute the Latin singer's voice blares through the speakers, the crowd's passion intensifies and couples lose themselves in some of the most outrageous and vertiginous dance moves I've ever seen.

Women are undulating their hips and flipping their hair while their partners are grinding provocatively against their thighs. Glistening skin is exposed as the tempo increases and women lift their skirts up indecently to bring more attention to their tempting curves. The couple to our right is so wrapped up in each other they're nearly fucking in plain view, but everyone around them is as bewitched by the moment as they are and no one seems to notice but me. *Maybe sex in public in Brazil isn't as taboo as it is back home.* When the chorus hits again, men spin their partners at such a velocity it's nearly dizzying. The air is filled with an indescribable energy that flames up my clit like a fireball.

I want him inside me now. I turn around and look up at him with eyes half closed. "We can stick around or you can help me unleash my wild side."

The heat emanating from Max's stare could burn straight to my soul. I catch my breath when he grabs my waist and slams my body against his. *Jesus, his desire is palpable.* Despite the bright sun peering through the roofless stadium, his hazel eyes are darker than I've ever seen them. "Come with me."

"Where are we going?"

"You gave me a challenge and I'm willing to take you up on it. I've been in this stadium hundreds of times since I was a kid visiting my family and I still catch a game whenever I'm in town. I know where we can go so you can make good on your dare. I hope you're ready to walk your talk, Ms. Temptress."

Without waiting for my answer, Max drags me by the hand past the dancers and lovers through the entrance before taking the first left and whizzing down a deserted hallway all the way to a door. I climb the stairs behind Max without saying a word until we finally reach the top. I'm breathless from the unexpected exercise and from all the electric energy surrounding us. We walk a few steps until Max swings open another door leading to a luxurious hallway. *What a contrast from the lower levels.* A tall, slender ebony-skinned man with greying hair immediately rises to his feet when he sees us approaching.

"Pare, por favor." The man in front of us lifts his left hand like a police officer and stops us in our tracks. I would freak out were it not for the words *guarda de segurança* engraved in white on his navy blue shirt and hat. *He must be a security guard.*

Max and the man—whose nametag is embroidered with the name Jorge Tavares—exchange a few words in a foreign language and before I know it, the two are laughing it up like old friends. When the tall Afro-Brazilian flashes his perfect white teeth and shakes Max's hand, I know we're in the clear to continue on our journey.

"What was that all about?"

"I hold VIP season passes and given the festivities, the management has decided to block off this entire area. Our friend Jorge was doing his job by making sure partygoers stayed away from these luxury suites. When I showed him my VIP card and explained how shameful it would be for my lovely American companion to travel all the way to Rio without seeing the stadium from atop, he agreed to slightly bend the rules… Oh, the crisp one-hundred-dollar bill I slipped in his palm might have also helped." Max grins. "Follow me."

Max pulls me by the hand while waving and bidding Mr. Tavares goodbye. As we walk past a few closed doors, I can't help but notice the upscale and modern décor of this entire floor, but in good Brazilian fashion, there's an unexpected pop of color—the bright yellow marries nicely with the dark grey. Max finally stops in front of a room and pulls out his electronic key and slides it in to open the door. He pushes the door open and drags me behind him until we reach the tall glass windows overlooking the crowd crammed inside the stadium.

"This room is insane." I take in what resembles an uptown condo—streamlined Italian black and white leather seating, sleek furniture, museum-like art on the walls and contrasting vintage-looking chandeliers hanging from the ceiling.

Max responds with a half smile and in one fluid motion, he pins me against the coolness of the windows with his body and crushes my lips. For the next few minutes we're all tongues as his hands explore every inch of me. He pulls away just long enough to give me a lustful glare. "I want the dirty girl in you to come out and play with me." His handsome face is only a couple of inches from mine, his breath coming out in sharp bursts against my cheek. "Candy, what happens in Rio, stays in Rio." He exhales, bending into my neck. "I want to do raunchy things to you you'll never have the guts to tell your best friend."

I pull back as much as I can. "I promise you I can take dirty." The sound of the stadium all around us fills the VIP lounge as we continue to stare at each other. Max caresses the side of my face with the back of his fingers. The ache from his contact against my skin begins to build up, first in my navel and spreading lower, between my legs and all the way to my throbbing nub.

"Are you sure?" Max bends forward, licking my jaw before covering my lips with his, and an involuntary groan rumbles in my throat as his hardened cock presses against my stomach. My body begins acting on instinct and my leg wraps around his as I press myself closer against his arousal.

"Fuck, yeah," I let out so softly I can barely hear the words escape my mouth. My hands find their way to his wavy brown hair and I pull back just long enough for his fingers to flick at the bejeweled clasp at my waist. My hot pink wrap dress drifts apart in front of him, exposing the matching lingerie panties and bras embroidered with bright orange lace. *God, I've come a long way.* I don't even turn away nor do I attempt to shield my body. Instead, I stand like a provocateur siren.

Max devours me from head to toe. "You know I adore every part of your decadent lusciousness—your curves, your huge full breasts, your big round hips, your full thighs, your soft stomach and your plump ass," he says, trailing his long fingers down the side of my body. "You're not as shy as you once were. I love your fearlessness. It suits you, love," he whispers. Placing his hands on my shoulders, he looks into my eyes and slides the fabric to the floor.

Goosebumps spread along my skin as he takes my hands and invites me to step out of my fuchsia dress pooled at my feet. He brushes my lips softly before turning me around. I yank myself up on my toes with my fingers slightly touching the window to admire the partygoers below me and when I look to the side, he wraps his hands around mine, forcing me to press my palms against the glass surface. Reaching up, Max removes my vintage tortoiseshell comb from my mane, letting my hair fall down on my naked shoulders. "This is pretty."

"Thank you. It belonged to my grandmother," I respond in a breathy voice.

"In that case, I'll make sure to keep it safely inside the pocket of my jacket." Taking my hair in his hands, he roughly pulls my head to the side, giving him free access to my neck. Max drops hot, wet kisses down my spine and across my shoulders. His touch ignites a flurry of electric sparks over every inch of skin he touches.

"Sweet Mother of God," I moan when he slides his body down against mine. On his knees behind me, he grabs my ass with both hands and presses his teeth into the flesh, eliciting a sharp gasp from me before he stands back up. He grabs on to the back of my bra and he slowly undoes each hook one by one before removing it from my body. I look up at him, tempted to cover my bare breasts from the glances of the crowd dancing in the stadium, but his disapproving gaze quickly changes my mind. With a calculated grin on his face, he twirls my lingerie in sensual circles around the index finger of his right hand before letting it fall to the floor, turning the moment into a lingering foreplay. Holy hell, how does he know how to make me lose it without even touching me?

"I don't remember seeing this two-toned little combo in our collection. It looks positively scrumptious on you. Is it one of mine?"

"Of course," I exhale. When I think I'm about to combust, Max fists the fabric of my panties and leans closer.

"Good. It's a shame you won't be wearing it for much longer."

"Ah!" I let out when he rips my panties right off of me, leaving me gasping for air.

I'm not only naked for his eyes, but my body is exposed for anyone down below us to see. For the first time in my life, I don't give a damn if strangers lay eyes on my nude body.

"It's almost as if I can't help myself. I'm in too much of a rush to get to your delicious pussy and the underwear was in the way." His fingers press and pull at my breasts. "Do you like being bitten on the ass while Rio is at your feet?"

"Yes," I answer coyly.

"You come off all innocent, Candy, but in reality, you're such a filthy girl."

I yelp, surprised, when his hand smacks hard where his teeth have just been. My only response is a moan of pleasure while I press my face against the cool window for salvation. The pressure from his touch causes me to arch my back, my fingers sliding down the glass, leaving me deprived. *Jesus.*

Moving lower, he stops right at my entrance. "You're so wet. What do you want me to do to you, baby?"

"I... Well... Oh..." I gasp as his finger pushes inside my pussy, urging me back into him.

"You might want to try that again." Although he's standing behind me, I can hear the mockery in his voice. "Tell me and I'll give you everything your kinky heart desires." A second finger joins the first, and the sensation causes me to cry out. *He's killing me here.* I shake my head, unable to let the words out, but my body betrays me because it knows exactly what it needs from Max.

He's asking me a question, but he's the one running the show. He's humoring me by allowing me to believe I'm in control so I can pretend I don't know he's been in charge of my orgasms since we snuck up on the forty-first floor of the Bymark hotel.

I close my eyes, trying to clear my thoughts, but everything is just too intense. The feel of his clothed body against my naked skin, the sound of his rough voice, and the feeling of his long fingers plunging in and out of me have me teetering on the edge of reason. His other hand reaches up, pinching my nipple, and I moan loudly. *Damn him. He owns every part of me.*

"Say it," he grunts into my ear as his thumb rolls over my clit.

I give in finally, whispering like a desperate soul, "I don't care how you take me as long as you fuck me until I come screaming out your name."

He lets out a low, strangled moan and his forehead rests on my shoulder as he begins moving faster, teasing, feathering and circling. His hips grind against my ass, his massive erection rubbing against me.

"Fucking Lord," I moan, the coil tightening deep inside, my every thought focused on the pleasure taking over.

"I want to take you with Rio at our feet, love. I want to fuck you in front of this large window overlooking the stadium. I want you to climax knowing someone could look up and see you come undone."

A small gasp escapes me.

"Did any of your past boyfriends take you like a raging animal in front of a crowd of people?"

"No," I answer, looking at him from the side.

"I didn't think so." He gives me a smile that makes me fear for a second that I've handed my soul to the devil.

Max's hands run up along my body, over my hips, across my stomach, up to where he cups my hanging breasts.

"Fuck, you're so soft, sweetness." One of his hands glides down my side and between my legs until he reaches my wetness. Max moves his hands away, clearing my head for only a beat. Behind me his belt clicks as he unlatches it, followed by his pants running down his legs.

"You're really going to do this?" I barely process the words, listening to him behind me.

"You asked me to help you unleash the wild child in you. Well, welcome to the jungle."

I'm too far gone to answer, caught between his delirious words and the torrent running through me at the idea of becoming the main act at a peep show. *God, can I do this?* I'm terrified. But I'm also buzzing, every single neuron firing, my blood pumping wildly in my veins as I get ready to allow the more feral side of me to frolic.

Just as I'm about to speak, without warning, Max rams right inside me and I hold my breath. I'm so goddamn wet he doesn't have to tease, stroke, or tantalize me. He just had to talk dirty in my ear to get me off.

"Don't you dare close your eyes. I want you to look down at the crowd. I want you to own this," he commands, pumping me frantically. He's so hard, so long, so perfect.

I bite my lip as Max slides his hand around my hip and between my legs, teasing my clit. "I can't," I whisper. I can see the entire stadium from here and if the mega-projector lights start dancing and hit my naked body, tens of thousands of people will witness my Brazilian debauchery. *If I close my eyes, I can't meet their stares.*

"Sure you can," he says, as if he's suggested I simply lick my lips. His fingers sweep across my clit again and again and again. He's mercilessly forcing me to submit. "Keep them open or we can stop right now."

Bastard. I throw him a dark, icy look over my shoulder and ignore his silent laugh.

"Please," I beg. My voice comes out shaky as I dread and welcome every brutal thrust.

"Christ," he gasps. His fingers dig into me and he swells inside me. Max shudders behind me, igniting the bad girl dormant in me. "Candy. Touch yourself."

"What?"

"I want to see you stroke your clit until you dissolve all over my cock." In true Max fashion, this isn't a suggestion, it's a command.

I brace one forearm against the fogged window and reach between my legs with my right hand, eagerly rubbing my node. The exhilarating thrill of pleasuring myself knowing full well anyone could catch us right now serves as a potent aphrodisiac. *Yes. I'm coming.* I've been so swollen, so heavy with the weight of my orgasm pressing down on me since we've been standing here that I explode within seconds.

"Fuck me, fuck me, fuck me," I chant like a mantra.

Ecstasy slams through me like a shot of cocaine. This must be what addiction feels like. Max's thrusts grow frantic, unwavering and more demanding, and then he grips my hips tighter. He roars like a warrior as he pumps hard, riding out his abandonment as I struggle to steady myself against the slippery window. I rest on my forearms, shuddering beneath him, unable to believe I've allowed him to take me in such a primal and audacious way.

"Max," I let out, spent.

When my legs stop trembling, he thrusts hard into me a few more times and then stills, stifling his groan with his mouth pressed to my neck.

"Goddammit, Candy."

The VIP suite is completely silent, and I realize I have no sense of how loud we've been. *Did the security guard hear us?* The music is raging below us, but did the noise muffle the sounds of my carnal voracity? After all, Jorge is sitting a few feet away from this room.

Max pulls out of me, releasing a grunt before whispering in my ear. "Fucking you from behind while holding on to your round hips and feeling the slap of your divine ass cheeks against my body is pure decadence. Your luscious curves make me come so hard I always fear I'll pass out." He kisses the back of my neck. "Mmmm. I want to take you again before we leave here. Outside this time."

I turn my head back so quickly I nearly give myself whiplash. "Huh?"

He watches me with a twinkle in his eye. "Looks like you had an insane orgasm. You wanted wild and from your dazed glance I'd say I've over-delivered. Why stop at one?"

"Yes. You did hold up your end of the bargain." I'm still struggling to catch my breath.

Lord. I'm falling so fast for this man. He possesses every part of me and I wouldn't want it any other way.

Chapter Three

As I stand in front of the window in my apartment sipping a cup of piping-hot coffee bright and early on this Monday morning, I can't help but reminisce about my last unforgettable days in Rio. *What a dreamy week.*

I got back to Manhattan on Friday morning, but since Max had a full afternoon of meetings and I dreaded the thought of going back to the office, I decided to work from home to catch up on my notes from Rio Moda and tackle a sea of emails from coworkers and readers. After another weekend at Max's where he fucked me against every wall in his penthouse, I'm surprised I'm able to walk today. *This man's appetite is insatiable.*

My head is still spinning from Max's demanding kinkiness in Brazil. After he took me in front of the floor-to-ceiling window overlooking the Maracanã Stadium, we went back down to continue the festivities with the other partygoers. At some point, Max pressed his hungry cock against my ass and before I was even able to react, he was already dragging me by the hand outside of the stadium.

He held true to his promise, like he always does. We traveled around Brazil's temple to soccer, passing thousands of amorous couples, to a small alleyway leading to the side of the building. The nightfall was the perfect intimate backdrop to allow Max to fuck me outside against a wired fence without raising any suspicions. I still remember holding on to the fence for dear life with my hands above my head as he rammed into me like a tank en route to a military convoy. The thrill and exhalation of doing something so risqué, so kinky and so dangerous made me come so hard, he had to clamp his hand over my mouth to avoid bringing too much attention to us. He's the most delicious lover I've ever had and I doubt I'd be able to resist any of his sexual demands.

"Oh, God, Leo, I'm going to be late." My white fluffy cat snaps me out of my reverie and I look at the time on my iPhone. I have an early-morning meeting with Max's brother to go over their latest findings surrounding the death of my parents. "Okay, Leo, be good today. I know you're pissed off at me because I've been leaving you with your uncle Devin, but Mommy has a really amazing boyfriend."

* * *

At seven o'clock in the morning, I'm seated in a conference room with Gabe, my two appointed attorneys, Sheena Wagner and Francis Kraai, and two paralegals, Suzette Warren and Regina Baez.

I reach across the mahogany wood table and grab one of the decadent morning pastries to calm my hunger. *God, I need to put an end to this rumbling in my stomach.* I'm just about to bite into a scrumptious-looking blueberry muffin when Gabriel turns his attention to me.

"Candy, I hear you enjoyed yourself in Rio."

My mouth is gaping with the muffin still hanging in the air. Five pairs of eyes peer at me, waiting for an answer.

"It would be impossible for me to describe how amazing the past week in Rio was. It's the most beautiful place I've ever been to so far in my life."

"I warned you that our ancestors' country on our mother's side was majestic—and the best place for you to recharge your batteries."

"I'm definitely ready to take on anything you throw at me."

"Well, I'm happy you're ready for anything, because we have quite a lot to share with you. We've made some amazing progress in some areas but we've also hit a few walls, but I promised you a debrief the minute you got back to New York and I always keep my promises. Since Francis is the one leading this case I'll let him share with you what's transpired."

"Welcome back, Candice."

"Thank you, Francis. As much as I adored Rio, it's good to be back."

"Let's start with the good news first. We've been in contact with the firm who took over Nathaniel Carpenter's roster of clients. It's none other than Baxter, Rufus, Lloyd and Associates LLP."

I shake my head. "I've never heard of them."

"They are fierce attorneys—some of the best in New York—but it's really all about money with them. A case like yours would require a lot of output of cash on their end and they'd most likely have to assign a full-time paralegal without any guarantees they'll see a cent of profit when and if your case gets settled. Unless you walk into their offices with pockets lined with cash, it's unlikely they'll give you the time of day. We requested a transfer of your files over a week ago, but they took their sweet time and we only received the boxes yesterday morning at our office."

"Boxes?" I'm surprised. "I didn't realize our case had so much paperwork attached to it."

"We received five boxes and two USB sticks with scanned documents. I've assigned both Suzette and Regina to your case to support Sheena and I, but you can understand we've not gotten very far. There's just too much to take in."

"No, I understand. I'm grateful for everything you're doing to help."

"Regina did stumble on something quite interesting."

"Oh?" My stomach is tied in a knot and I push the muffin away, unable to continue eating.

"It seems Rock Axel Development, the real-estate development responsible for the accident, declared bankruptcy one year after your parents' deaths."

"Crap."

"But Regina found some old documents on one of the USB sticks indicating they were part of a conglomerate."

"What does that mean?" I ask. All this legal mumbo-jumbo is way over my head.

"A conglomerate is a combination of two or more corporations engaged in entirely different businesses that fall under one corporate group, usually involving a parent company and many subsidiaries."

"I'm sorry, Francis, but this sounds Greek to me."

"It means although they're no longer in business, the company that owned them might still be operating."

"It's good news, right?"

"Candy, it's excellent news." Gabe jumps in the conversation to reassure me. "When Francis informed me of this twist, I was thrilled. We can keep swimming upward. Thank God the buck doesn't stop at Rock Axel or else we'd be seriously screwed."

"Gabriel is right. The only problem is we'll need to hire an expert who can figure out how this conglomerate was structured and dig as deep as humanly possible. We have some great people, it's a question of getting in touch with them."

"My friend Lexi can dig out anything on any company."

My statement catches everyone in the room by surprise.

"What does Lexi do for a living?"

"Gabe, she's a top broker on Wall Street. She takes care of analyzing IPOs. She has an MBA and a masters in finance. She eats numbers like others eat popcorn. She's a brainiac when it comes to this sort of stuff. She knows my case well. Maybe she can help?"

Both Francis and Gabe look at each other before returning their attention to me.

"Candy, I'd rather if we used our own contacts, but I'd love to involve Lexi. If she has access to software that can dig deep into the history of companies, she might be an invaluable resource for us to expedite things."

"I can patch her in right now."

"Candice." Francis clears his throat and readjusts his red tie. "It's twenty past seven in the morning. She may be just getting up. I'd hate to disrupt her."

"I bet you Alexis has been crunching numbers since before you got in your office. She gets to work by five-thirty every morning and she always does a few hours of analysis before the market opens. The woman is a machine and she's as sharp as a whip."

"If Alexis is awake, I say let's patch her in." For the first time since the beginning of the meeting Sheena speaks up and earns herself the attention of the entire room. "Someone out there is dropping not very subtle hints to Candice about the death of her parents. We don't know who we're dealing with and we haven't got a clue yet as to who is behind Rock Axel. The faster we collect data, the faster we can react the next time this Annie Smith contacts Candice."

"Oh my God, you think she's going to contact me again?" The idea of receiving another disturbing letter from a stranger is unsettling.

"Yes, Candice, I do. It's unlikely she'll drop one hint and run away. This person knows a lot more than they've revealed in the first letter they sent you. Francis, Gabriel and I believe it's a matter of when, not if, she gets in touch again."

"God. I can't believe this nightmare is still haunting me."

"I'm sorry, Candice. I'm sure this must be brutal for you, but maybe this person is your lifeline in uncovering the truth."

I shake my head, afraid of opening this hellish Pandora's box. One part of me wants to storm out of this boardroom and run and hide under my bed next to Leo DiCaprio, but another part of me wants to know exactly why my parents died.

"If anyone can figure out who's behind this conglomerate, it's Lexi."

"Let's not waste any time, then. Patch her in and Francis will explain exactly what we need from her. Sheena will still be in touch with our own experts, but the faster we move the faster we can resolve this."

God, I hope Gabriel is right.

* * *

Right after my meeting with Gabe, I hop in a cab and head to Max's headquarters across town for the first time. I spend the morning cooped up in a boardroom with six eager members of his team for a much-anticipated debrief after the Rio Moda Week. I was already excited like a kid going to the fair, but after three hours of brainstorming over creative angles for future stories to catch the attention of *Sassy* magazine's plus-size beauties, I'm totally pumped.

Unfortunately, neither Deidra nor Max are part of this pow-wow. They are attending meetings with the other VPs to discuss expansion plans, given the amazing press coverage Max's brands have received since the Miami party. My boyfriend promised he'll do his best to carve out a few minutes with me and I do hope I'll be able to steal a kiss or two before I go back to the office, but if I don't, I know I'll have him all to myself tonight.

Right before we break for lunch, Deidra pokes her head in the meeting room and beckons me with her finger. I grab my handbag and rush to meet her.

"How are you?" Deidra smiles down at me from what appears to be another pair of eight-inch heels. She's elegantly clad as usual, but today she seems a little more buttoned up than usual in her dark navy pantsuit. The only rebellious touch is the bold pattern of her floral Christian Louboutin heels.

"I'm good. It was an incredible meeting. I can't wait to get started. I already have at least six or seven great articles floating in my head."

"That's great to hear, Candy. I'm glad you seem to be getting along nicely with the rest of the team. We can't wait to get the word out about our three collections for plus-size women."

"Are you coming for lunch with the rest of us?"

"No. I'm not. I'm here to take you to Max. He wants to have lunch with you. He tried texting you, but your phone was off."

"Oh, yes. I didn't bother checking my messages because I thought you were in an all-day meeting."

"No, we were only meeting this morning. Max and I are spending the rest of the day in a planning session together, but I'm flexible. He's ordered lunch for the two of you and he wants to see you. Now."

"He does?"

Deidra smiles and rolls her eyes. "Grab your stuff and I'll take you to him."

"Give me a second." I run back into the conference room and gather the rest of my things at the speed of light before running back to the door where Deidra is still waiting for me.

"You have everything?"

"Yes."

"Let's go."

We get into the elevator and ride to Max's office in silence. I'm too eager to see him to engage in any sort of conversation and I suspect Deidra might have picked up on that, unless she's going over the thousands of things she has to do.

When we arrive on the top floor of the building, I follow the tall and lean woman in front of me until she comes to a stop in front of an impressive door.

"Here we go. This is his office and he's expecting you."

"Okay. Where's yours?" I'm a bit anxious and ask this silly question to buy myself some time. Although Deidra is one of the few people outside of my friends to know I'm involved with the billionaire CEO of an illustrious company, it still feels weird that she's the one taking me to him.

"Mine is right over there," she says pointing to a door that's diagonal to the one we're standing in front of. "Go on in. Max is waiting for you and I have a conference call starting in five minutes."

"Okay. Thanks, Deidra." I barely have time to finish my sentence before she's already marching to her office. I turn around and face Max's door. I take a breath before knocking. I'm so nervous because this is the first time I've met him at his office.

"Come in."

I push open the door and Max greets me, perched on the corner of his desk. *Fuck, he looks incredible.* I clear my throat and step closer to him, completely bewitched by his dazzling smile.

"Lock the door behind you. I want our time here to be private."

I obey without even questioning. *I guess he has more than lunch on his mind.* Suddenly the things I was carrying seem so heavy. I glance around me before deciding to drop them on a small table near the door.

"How's your day so far, sweetness?"

"It was an amazing morning with your team," I start, bringing my attention back to him. "We had a brainstorming session that will lead to a lot of incredible articles for both the website and the magazine. I'm sure our readers will eat up all of your collections."

Max tilts his head and strokes his jaw. Pushing off the desk, he bridges the gap between us. "Interesting choice of words." He brushes my hair off my shoulders. The sensual gesture causes my stomach to knot up. "You know what I'd like to eat up right now?"

I laugh. "Didn't you get enough all weekend long?"

"I can't believe you're asking me this question." His chest heaves as I run my fingers up his arms and stop at the lapel of his jacket, smoothing it down before flickering my eyes up to his. "It's Monday and I haven't had my Candy yet."

"Come to think about it, I haven't had my candy yet either." My fingers trail up to the length of his tie. Gripping it in my fist, I pull him back behind his desk and push him down into his leather chair. "I was going to go for lunch with the rest of your team, but all of a sudden I'm dying for something sweet," I declare boldly.

"What did you have in mind?"

"Oh, I don't know. I was thinking of your warm release for starters." Kneeling before him, I steady myself on my high heels. *Thank God I'm wearing a dress today.* I slip my fingers into his cognac belt, loosening it and unzipping his expensive-looking navy pants.

"You naughty girl."

"Uh-huh."

I grip his hardening shaft and pull him out. *Come out to play.* I lock gazes with him before folding my body onto his cock. I flick my tongue across the head and glance up into his lustful eyes. My tongue swirls around the tip and down his length, licking every inch of his gorgeous dick. I lap the few drops of his pre-cum escaping as his eyes stay glued on my tongue, his lips parting and his breath coming out in quick bursts. *I've got him.*

"Holy Christ. You do this so well, baby."

I smile and wrap my lips around him, guiding him to the back of my throat as he lets out a groan while pushing my head down against him. I want to take all of him in, but his massive cock will never fit. Wrapping my hand around his base, I stroke him with my mouth, sucking and licking as he grabs my hair tightly.

"Oh, honey, suck me hard." Max's hands control the pace. Up and down, I lick around his peak before I swallow him whole. My hand strokes him tightly, traveling along his slick shaft as my mouth continues teasing him. His fingers brush down my temple, along my warm cheek, across my jaw line. My eyes are still locked on his handsome face in awe as the muscles in his neck tense and the veins throb with each suck. "Yeah," he exhales, tilting his head back on to his chair when I close my lips around his tip. "Shit. Take me deeper," he begs.

"Hmmm." I'm too focused on making him come to answer.

Max moans, thrusting his hips to match my cadence as he holds my head in place. I've always doubted my ability to please a man by giving him a blowjob, but the raunchy noises coming from Max right now are boosting my confidence and turning me on. Not only am I getting him off, my clit is aching badly for relief. My thighs press together as I contort my lower body to contain my arousal. *Damn, my panties are drenched.* Sucking harder, I pull Max deeper and let him hit the back of my throat as I loosen my jaw slightly and relax my muscles. *Bullseye.*

"Jesus. I'm going to shoot my load inside your warm mouth. Would you like that, Candy?"

"Uh-huh." Fuck, how can a question act like rocket fuel against my clit? The man could make me climax with his dirty talk and the only thing I have to do is squeeze my thighs harder.

"I don't think I can hold it in much longer," Max pleads like a desperate man.

I can't believe I'm giving my boyfriend a blowjob at work before lunch. I pump him with my hand, one, two, three times and his juices gush out. I hold him trapped inside my mouth as I swallow all of him. *Damn. This is so illicit and so hot.* I've truly never felt more powerful than in this moment.

"Arghhh," he grunts as his legs tense under me, earning him a few extra sucks as I pull every bit of him out. Max loosens his grip on my hair and gently combs it away from my face. "You should come over for meetings at my office more often."

"You're simply inviting me back in the hopes I'll suck you again." I say, sitting back on my heels before flashing him a victorious smile.

"I'd be crushed if you told me you've done this with other men before me."

"You mean making a guy come apart with my mouth while kneeling in front of him at his workplace? Nah. Never. You're my first." I smile. "You're making me do a lot of kinky things, but it's worth it. Nothing compares to tasting you like I just did."

"I'm not sure what's sexier, your words or peeping at your exposed panties thinking of all the things I'll do with my tongue to your clit."

I follow Max's eyes and realize my legs are spread wide open, revealing my bright yellow lingerie. "Oh." I smile shyly and bite my lower lip, beaming inside.

Without even pulling up his pants, Max leans down and grabs me off the floor and plops my body on top of his desk.

"What are you doing?"

"I told you, I'm in the mood for some candy. Not to mention your lingerie is an obvious call for me to devour you. You didn't expect I'd allow you to make me come without returning the favor?"

"Uh…"

Max has a way of leaving me speechless. He reaches the edge of my panties and slips his fingers under the silky fabric.

"God." I let out a stifled groan when he grazes my clit before pushing his finger inside my wetness.

"You're so wet," he growls. He closes his eyes and tilts his head back and he seems to be battling the same overpowering desire as I am. I glance down at his lap and I can see his cock hardening. Without opening his eyes, he withdraws his finger and fists the thin lace of my panties in his hand. "Did you know these are my favorite ones in our Rio Carnival collection?" I open my mouth to respond, but it's too late. In one quick movement he tears them off, the rip of the fabric echoing in the silence of his office. "I'm going to eat you with such voracity you'll have to retreat to the bathroom later to touch yourself when you relive this moment."

Fuck. Max pulls my hips toward him roughly before spreading my legs in front of him. "Ah." I allow an involuntary groan to escape as his fingers return, sliding between my thighs and pushing into me again. *Damn, he's incredible at this.* My head falls to the side as I lean back on my elbows, feeling the surge of my impending orgasm approaching fast. *Already?*

"Oh, please," I whimper.

My words cause him to stop moving. "I can't tell you how much I love hearing you beg," he chuckles, pulling his fingers back and sliding them into his mouth. *Mother of God.* I sit up, grab his navy silk tie and pull his mouth roughly against mine. His kisses are like honey and I could lose myself in his perfect lips. *Yum.* I bite his lower lip as my hand fists his hair.

"Make me come."

He smiles, proud of seeing me come undone this way. "Don't rush this, baby. Your orgasms are mine now and I'm not ready to make you climax." He slides his strong hands up my stomach and over my breasts, thumbs slipping back and forth across my taut peaks, his intense stare fixed on my expression the entire time. His big hands rub over my body in such a pressing way it's nearly painful, but instead of wincing or backing off, I push eagerly into his warm palms, demanding more and harder.

He leans close enough to bite my shoulder through the fabric of my dress, whispering, "Candy, you fucking tease. Yellow panties?"

The way he hisses those words unleashes a torrent of unadulterated lust. He forces my dress higher up my thighs and pushes me back on his desk. Before I know it, Max takes hold of my ankles, grabs his cock, and takes a decisive step forward, thrusting deep inside me.

"Jesus," I yell. I'm horrified by the moan I let out. *What if someone hears me?*

"What's that?" he hisses through clenched teeth, his hips slapping against my thighs, driving him deep inside. "You've never had a man fuck you like this before lunch?"

Until meeting Max, I had never had sex anywhere but on a bed, and it never felt like this, but since this stud came into my life I've been having the raunchiest sexual interludes in the most forbidden places.

"I don't think so," I answer between breaths.

"Of course not. You've been dating inexperienced boys. You need a real man to uncage the filthy vamp dying to come out."

"How can you keep doing this to me? Your mouth and your cock will be the end of me," I exhale, closing my eyes.

He laughs, a quiet mocking sound. "Look at me."

"I can't. It's too much. Too strong." *I'm so close.*

Max pulls out just as I'm about to go over the edge. His devilish gaze suggests he's ready to leave me this way until he grabs my arms and yanks me up off the table, lips and tongue pressing against mine.

"I asked you to look at me," he says. And, finally, with him no longer inside me, I slowly open my eyes. "Good girl. Now, ask me to make you come."

"Huh?" I drop my voice and stare back at him. *Is he trying to make me lose my mind?* "I've already begged."

"Do it again," he says, swerving me around.

"Please," I say in a soft, unrecognizable voice, pleading for his cock.

The next thing I know, Max rips open the buttons of my dress and pulls my breasts out from my bra with such a swift hand I barely have time to blink. He pushes my body against the cold floor-to-ceiling window, squashing my boobs, and I groan at the intense contrast in temperature between it and the heat emanating from his skin. *How the hell can he move so easily with his pants still down the middle of his legs?*

I'm on fire. Every part of me yearns to feel his rough touch.

"You have a thing for fucking me in front of windows. First Rio and now Manhattan?"

"There's nothing like the adrenaline rush from fearing being seen," he snarls into my ear before biting my shoulder. He slaps my ass. "Spread your legs open, sweetness."

I part my legs and without hesitation he pulls my hips back and thrusts forward into me.

"Oh, oh, oh." His cock fills me so fully I can't imagine anyone ever fucking me again.

"You don't fool me, you wicked girl. You damn well know I can't resist your delicious curvy body and you taunt me with a heart-stopping blowjob and sexy yellow underwear. Don't you dare complain about my fucking you like this because we both know down deep inside, you like being watched, don't you?" he murmurs, taking my earlobe between his teeth. "You came hard when I took you in the stadium and now you're relishing every moment of this— anyone in those office towers could look up here and see you getting fucked, and you're loving every minute of it with your huge salacious tits pressed against the glass."

"I beg of you, stop talking. Your mouth will cause me to combust." My heart is beating so fast and I can only blame it on his chocolatey voice.

"You like my dirty mouth nearly as much as you like the idea of all of New York watching you come." He laughs and I shiver.

I groan in response, unable to form words with each repeated thrust into me, pressing my hardening nipples against the glass. *Christ.*

"Don't you? Answer me or I'll stop," he hisses, driving himself deeper and deeper inside me with every thrust.

"Oh my God, Max."

He reaches around, moving his fingertips across my clit with the perfect pressure, the perfect rhythm, the perfect stroke. *He owns me.* Although I can't see him, I know he's taking a lot of pleasure in this because I can feel his smile press into the back of my neck, and when he opens his mouth and sinks his teeth into my skin, I'm done.

Yes, yes, yes. An ecstatic current spreads down my spine, around my hips, and between my thighs, jerking my entire body back into his. The palms of my hands slam against the glass, my entire being quaking from the climactic tornado rushing over me, leaving me gasping for air. When this intoxicating ecstasy finally subsides, Max pulls out and spins me around to face him.

"Same time, same place tomorrow?" he whispers, biting off a smile.

Chapter Four

I'm sitting in the same boardroom in Max's office as yesterday, trying my best to focus on what Pamela Fletcher is saying, but reliving our evening of non-stop sex is so much more pleasurable.

The little appetizer we had in Max's office didn't sustain us long. After a busy day, I rushed to Max's place and he spent most of the night ravishing me. When we woke up this morning, Max declared it would be inconceivable for him to go to work without another round. I've been so unlucky in love so far in my life and I still pinch myself every day that an ordinary girl like myself could end up with a devastatingly sexy boyfriend who loves and appreciates my curves. I guess Devin was right all along— there are rich and powerful men who want a woman who's not all skin and bones.

I'm still daydreaming when all of a sudden I realize the room has gone quiet and Pamela is staring at me. Her lips are moving, but I was so taken by my daydreaming, I missed what she said. *Crap.*

"Candy, what do you think?"

Pamela is one of the senior project managers who worked with Deidra organizing the Miami photoshoot last month and right now she's looking at me with a puzzled face.

Huh? I was so totally not paying attention.

"Pamela, I'm sorry. I was thinking of a few story angles and obviously I got carried away," I say, trying to save face.

"No problem. I get it. There are so many incredible possibilities with these new lines. Not to mention these brainstorming sessions always leave me buzzing with creative ideas. I was wondering what you thought of doing a tandem feature about the swimsuit and the model wearing it. You know, as a way to get the readers to connect more with our curvy models?"

"Oh. Yes. What a great idea. It would be awesome to do an email interview where the models would answer a set of specific questions about themselves and we could share those tidbits with our readers. They'll jump at the opportunity to know more about their plus-size idols."

"Excellent. I'm happy you agree."

Since Rio Moda happened on the heels of the photoshoot in Miami, Max's team and I haven't had a chance to hash out the editorial angles until today. Yesterday's three-hour meeting was far too heavy to keep going. Luckily, Deidra booked these two meetings one day apart to give us time to process our creative sessions. Although Deidra is a no-show again today, this meeting is running smoothly without her. Even my few moments of distraction haven't affected the tempo of this animated meeting.

Deidra and Max are meeting with buyers from Saks Fifth Avenue and Macy's this morning to discuss expanding their collections in both retail giants, so obviously, they couldn't be present for the brainstorming session. I much prefer it this way. *If Max were in the room, everyone would be able to feel the insane energy between us.*

Pamela launches back into a lively spiel when my phone flashes a message. I furtively look down, hoping no one will notice my eyes shifting. Max's name pops up on my screen. I don't want to be too blatant about it, so I quickly scan his message.

We're heading back to the office right now. Your meeting should end in about thirty minutes. I expect you to be knocking at my door right after.

I beam. If today's appetizer is as decadent as yesterday's, I'll leave here with two if not three additional climaxes under my belt. I casually drop a notepad on top of my iPhone to avoid attracting too much attention as I type a few words.

Can't wait.

* * *

One thing I admire about meetings at Max's office is how efficiently they run. At *Sassy* magazine, an hour-long meeting can easily run over by twenty minutes and sometimes more by the time everyone adds their two cents. I think it's because we're all so passionate about fashion, but at Max's office meetings always conclude on time and we're all assigned a specific set of tasks. Any additional feedback must be shared on a virtual chatroom. When Pamela announces everyone is invited to the lunchroom for refreshments, I take that as my cue to go up to Max's office.

Luck is on my side because I'm able to ride solo all the way to the top floor. When I get off the elevator, I turn to the left and then to the right to make sure no one might see me heading towards Max's office. Although we're officially boyfriend and girlfriend, I still get nervous at the idea of people in his office seeing us together. When I feel the coast is clear, I dash to the location of our midday rendezvous and knock three quick times. He opens the door and greets me with his signature sexy smile.

"I came up the minute Pamela announced the meeting was over."

"Good. Why are you whispering?" Max grabs my arm and drags me inside his office before locking the door behind me.

"I don't want people knowing we're together."

"This is the executive floor, Candy."

"Exactly my point."

"My assistant and my top people know we're dating, love."

"Huh?" *Did he just say he's confessed to people we're dating?*

"Yes. I don't want anyone bumping into us and making up their own story."

"But yesterday you had Deidra come to get me and bring me to you."

"Simply because your phone was off, love. Had it been on, you would have read my text messages like you did today. I didn't want to walk into the room where you and my team were meeting because that would have been way too distracting."

"So people know about us?" I'm so shocked. I mean, I love the idea of being his girlfriend but for some reason I thought he was keeping what we shared a secret. "I assumed you wanted to keep the fact we're dating private…" I trail off, lowering my eyes.

"Look at me, Candy," he commands. "Do you remember in Miami, I told you I didn't want us to play hide-and-seek anymore?"

"Yeah, but…"

"But what? I'm happy to keep things quiet when it comes to your work because I don't want anyone to confuse what we share with the fact I'm spending a boatload of money with *Sassy* magazine, but it's okay for my people to see us together."

"It is?"

"Absolutely. Why in the world would I want to hide what we have?"

"Oh."

"Don't ever doubt the way I feel about you," he says, trailing the contour of my lips with his finger.

"I'll try not to," I answer shyly, focusing on his impeccable shoes.

Max is such a sharp dresser. His tailored dark grey suit fits him like a glove. I must say his colorful silk tie complements the classic VIP look. His calmness is such a contrast to the raging wild man who devoured me this morning before leaving for work.

"We don't have much time together today. I have an important call in about forty-five minutes and I can't possibly make it through the rest of the day without tasting you."

"Wasn't this morning satisfying enough?"

"Oh, it was, but I'm greedy. I want more."

"Max…"

"Candy, you can't possibly refuse me the pleasure of enjoying your curves."

The raw energy I read in his eyes surprises me. No man has ever made me feel so wanted before.

"Well…" I start.

Max interrupts me before I can finish my thoughts. "I have big plans for you, baby."

"You do?"

"Oh, yes."

"What did you have in mind?" I ask flirtatiously.

"I'm going to start by fucking your mouth like a beast and then I'll shove my cock right here so I can mark you as mine," he says, trailing his finger between my breasts. "Just thinking of what I'm going to do to you is making my cock very hard, sweetness." I read the carnal desire in his eyes as he squeezes his cock with every word. "I want to watch you lick the head of my dick while I fuck your tits."

"Max, you know what your dirty talking does to me." He's barely touched me, but his words have a potent effect on me.

"I want to see you lose control at my mercy," he hisses, grabbing me by the waist and grinding against me.

"Um, I think I'm already losing control."

"Good, because I needed you an hour ago but now I'm dying," he whispers, ducking his head to suck my neck, my jaw, my lower lip in one sensual stroke. *God, I love his hands on me.*

"I don't think we should make this sex at work a habit," I gasp, turned on like a lightbulb. "Why don't I give you a quick peck on the lips and let you get back to your day." I chuckle as I squeeze his cock.

"You know, you're such a tease—"

Max is cut off as the phone on his desk rings. We stare lustfully at each other, both of us breathing heavily.

"Damn phone. I'm sure it can wait."

By the fourth ring, it's clear whoever is trying to reach Max isn't going away. When his eyes turn somber, I seriously think he's considering throwing me down on the desk and taking me before he even answers his call. Still glaring at me, he sighs and takes a step back before he reaches for the phone.

"Yes," he barks sharply into the receiver, his eyes never leaving mine. "Alicia, of course I'll speak to Mr. Hatcher if he has an urgent matter and he can't make the scheduled call. His call is forty-five minutes early, but I can't wait another week before speaking to him. Put in through immediately."

Alicia Blackstone is Max's personal assistant. She's a perky thirty-four-year old brunette with two sets of twins—all boys. I still don't know how she finds the energy to hold down a full-time job and juggle motherhood, but she assures me it's all about hiring great help at home. Not to mention her husband's income as a professional comedian doesn't always cut it when it comes to feeding four hungry mouths.

"Mr. Hatcher. No, these things happen. I don't mind booking another longer meeting next week, but I feel strongly about us touching base today." Max lowers himself into his leather desk chair, and I linger to see if he wants me to stick around until he finishes his call or if I should head out for lunch on my own. I gesture to the door and he holds up his index finger for me to wait before he slides it over his pen and starts scratching a few notes.

"Are you sure you want me to stay?" I ask quietly, tracing the side of his desk with my finger.

He nods once before speaking into the phone. "Brandon, I'm aware of this, but right now I need to find a way to cut back on my shipping cost for my garments because it's eating into our profits." The deep commanding tenor of his voice vibrates down my spine and up again. "We're a great client and I'd hate to have to get my guys to look for a new carrier company." *God, he sounds so powerful.* I fan myself to bring down my body temperature. Standing here in front of him while he conducts business makes me feel like an undisciplined schoolgirl who's been summoned to the principal's office. *Sure, I'll just stand here looking pretty.*

I fold my arms across my chest and exhale. He looks up at me and does a slight double-take, his eyes dropping to my hem. When he looks back up, his lips part slightly, as if he would ask me something were he not busy speaking to Mr. Hatcher. He grabs a wooden ruler from the top of his desk that looks more decorative than practical and uses the edge to push aside the hem of my wrap dress. His eyes widen when he sees my new garter belt.

Oh, yeah, he left before I got into the shower and he had no idea I was ready for our kinky lunch. When Max left his penthouse for another early-morning meeting, I took advantage of the quiet time to make myself pretty for our lunch date. I selected a teal dress that cinches at the waist with a thin belt. The bell-shaped sleeves are particularly flattering and hit me right above the elbow. I love this design from Max's collection because it was cut on a woman who has ample curves and it shows in the way it fits me so well. I paired the bright wrap dress with white lingerie. I selected this one because I knew the little blue bows adorning the garter belt would drive Max insane. I guess you could call it virginal white with a touch of naughty.

"I'm sure your people can work with my people," he murmurs into the phone, letting the lower part of the dress fall. "I'm sure you can appreciate as those divisions grow, the burst in our sales will greatly benefit your company as well." Max's eyes move up my body, darkening along the way. My heart pounds like crazy as wanton abandonment washes over me. *I don't know if he's upset or incredibly turned on right now.* It's as if he's wearing a mask. When he looks at me like he's about to eat me alive, I want to drop to my knees and crawl on all fours all the way to his cock.

"I like your suggestion, Brandon. I think we should look at other more cost-saving routes. I'd hate to ask our clientele to fork out more for our designs to cover these sky-high shipping fees and I'd hate to disappoint our sexy buyers by considering alternatives that will add to our delivery time."

This man is transforming me into someone I barely recognize. I step to my left and I take a seat in the chair across from him. He raises an eyebrow, interested, and then slides his index finger between his teeth, biting down.

Do I have the guts to push the envelope much further than I've dared to try? There are a million and a half dirty thoughts bouncing in my head as heat blooms between my legs. *Jesus, I can't believe my clit is on fire.* I reach for the hem of my dress, sliding the fabric up my thighs, exposing my skin to the cool air surrounding me, and to the hungry eyes of the man sitting behind the desk across from me.

"I'd like to have something in place before our next delivery is scheduled to leave Brazil," he says, but his voice is much deeper than in was a few minutes ago.

He's always in control and I wonder what it would feel like to turn the tables. My fingertips trail over the lines of the garters, along my skin and to the satin of my lingerie. I stop at the bows and toy with them with a devious grin on my face, hoping like hell he's as aroused as I am. No one has ever made me feel as sexy as he does. It's as if he's erased all my past self-critical views of my plus-size body. When I look at myself through his eyes, I feel like the most beautiful woman in the world.

"Yes, of course," he says. "I also believe it's the ideal path forward for all parties concerned."

I couldn't agree more. I spread open my legs, exposing myself to him. *Take a good look, honey.* I smile at him, biting my lip, and he gives me a mischievous half-smile in return. One of my hands travels higher, cupping my boobs and squeezing. The other pushes the center of my panties aside and I run two fingers across my wet skin.

Max coughs as he widens his eyes and fumbles for his water. "Brandon, it sounds like we'll be able to meet in the middle."

Damn. I begin moving my hand, thinking of his long fingers grasping the glass, those very same hands grabbing my full hips and waist and thighs when he pounded me yesterday in front of the floor-to-ceiling window right behind him.

I move faster, tilting my head back against the chair and closing my eyes. I do my best to muffle the sensual sounds coming from me by biting down on my lip, but my body betrays me and a tiny moan escapes. I imagine his strong hands, his muscular forearms tensing as his fingers move inside me. I vividly remember how I came apart when his tongue lapped at me yesterday on this same desk, his gaze locked into mine the whole time as my body climaxed.

I slowly meet his gaze. Max isn't watching my hands, he's taking in every single expression flashing across my face as I'm about to lose my mind. His hazel eyes are dark and nearly indecent. They're solely focused on observing me take pleasure.

"Argh," I groan.

Sweet Mother of God. Even though my climax is overwhelming, it still pales in comparison to the way I lose it when Max teases my clit with his fingers or his lips. *He really owns my orgasms.*

At some point, Max must have ended his call with Mr. Hatcher because my breath sounds too loud in this silent office. When I regain my senses, Max sits across from me, his mouth gaping and his hands gripping the arms of his chair as if he's riding the scariest fairground ride.

"What the hell do you think you're doing?" he hisses.

I grin, brushing a loose strand out of my eyes. "Do I have to spell it out?"

His brow lifts. "I guess not," he says, getting up and circling the desk to stand over me. "If you think I'm going to allow you to tease me so merciless-ly, you're dead wrong," he continues, gripping my arm and lifting me up before slamming my body against his. "You think your little performance was amusing? I have a raging erection I'm dying to re-lieve, love."

"From what I can tell, you enjoyed my little performance," I answer defiantly.

"You're right. And I'm sure you'll love it when I take your ass as punishment." With one swift movement, Max flips me over and pins me face down on his desk.

"What? You can't be serious."

"You've pushed me and it's now time for me to return the favor."

Before I can answer, we hear a knock on the door and we both freeze. And then a voice speaks.

"Max, it's Elliot. I have the urgent report you needed for your upcoming call with Mr. Hatcher."

We both hold our breath for a few seconds until my boyfriend breaks the deafening silence.

"My VP of finance just saved your ass—literally."

Max takes a step back and straightens his ex-pensive suit. I pick myself up and follow his cue by smoothing my dress back down my thighs and comb-ing my fingers through my hair.

"I guess I got lucky."

"For now, anyway." His voice trails as he runs a finger between my breasts. "Just thinking of what I'm going to do to your tight little asshole to compensate for the fact I had to watch you come all over your hand while I was on an important call makes the waiting so worth it." He grins.

God, it was supposed to be an innocent tease and now he wants to claim every part of me.

Chapter Five

I'm floating on air by the time I return to *Sassy* magazine after my little saucy show at my boyfriend's office. This is the second day in a row Max and I spent lunch enjoying each other. I guess today, I was the one enjoying myself.

I have a sneaking feeling my performance and the fact that he wasn't able to come prompts him to send this text message at forty-thirty this afternoon. It read like a plot in a mystery novel.

I'm conducting a phone interview with an up-and-coming plus-size designer from Boston when the message flashes on my phone. I grab my iPhone as I prop the landline securely between my ear and my neck. For a few seconds I forget all about the person on the other end of the line because I'm engulfed by Max's invitation.

You're not getting away with murder. What you did this afternoon is a blatant call for punishment. Let's finish what you started. Meet me tonight at seven. I'll have the driver pick you up. Wear those naughty white garter belts with the blue bows you had on earlier today. You want to play? Let's do it right.

I have to bite off a smile in order to avoid being too obvious about how excited I am about Max's saucy plans. Right after work, I rush home to get ready for my impromptu rendezvous with Max at a secret destination in the city. After taking a few minutes to reapply my makeup and coif my hair *à la* Adele, I slip into an elegant navy blue dress, which I pair with hot pink sandals adorned with sparkled high heels and platforms. The shoes are playful enough to offset the demure and classy dress.

As predicted, Max's driver arrives at six-thirty sharp to take me to meet my boyfriend. The chauffeur swerves through the side streets to avoid traffic and to my surprise the drive is smooth and I don't have much time to get lost in my thoughts.

When I arrive in front of a renovated building in the fashion district, I grab my phone and text Max to let him know I'm outside. As I wait for him to come down, I anxiously focus on my high heels. My head snaps up at the sound of the heavy metal door sliding open. As he approaches me, he flashes me a radiant smile and I instantly melt. *I can't believe this handsome and dashing man is my boyfriend.*

"Max."

"Baby, you look stunning," he says, bending to kiss my cheek. "And you smell amazing—like a bouquet of gardenias. God, my girlfriend is hot."

I didn't think it was possible for him to get even more attractive, but the proud grin that stretches across his face right now does just that.

"Thank you," I respond shyly.

"Come on, let's go inside." He smiles at my reaction as he pulls me in the direction of the door.

I'll admit although I've been seeing Max for months now, we've never met at a strange deserted location like this and I'm a bit nervous at what he has planned for me. I suspect he might have picked up on my uneasiness. We ride the short elevator ride in silence and I can't help but glance sideways at him to see if he's also consumed by this heavy sense of anticipation pulsing all around us. Each floor heightens my excitement and I can't wait to discover what he has planned for the night.

The doors open directly into a warehouse, but instead of moving forward, I turn to face him.

"Max," I say, nodding toward the large room in front of us, "I know you talked about punishing me for my naughty ways, but I'm not walking into a dungeon with whips, chains or nipple clamps, am I?"

His boisterous laugh fills the space. "What do you know about nipple clamps?"

"I know plenty. I've had my fair share of discussions with my friends and I know all about this kinky world of Doms and subs."

"Jesus, Candy, you shock me. As much as I like sex rough, raw and relentless, I promise, tonight there will be no shackles or whips." He grins and slaps my ass before he walks past me to lead us inside.

"Wow," I say, blushing as I cross the threshold. "What is this place?"

"This whole building belongs to me. This is our storage facility, but this upper floor has always been empty for some reason. It's such a contrast to the rest of the floors, which are crammed with merchandise."

"It's beautiful." I take in the room.

"You like it?"

"How can I not?"

"It was last-minute, so it's not as elaborate as I would have liked it to be, but I think it will do for tonight. I called in a favor from a set designer I know and she sent her team to spruce up the place and transform it into a romantic wonderland."

I walk into the room and turn slowly, taking in every corner—the raw silk purple drapes against the cement walls, gorgeous antique furniture, the round table at the back of the room decorated like something you'd expect to see between the pages of *Elle Décor*, the large silver bucket filled with ice and bottles of champagne, the bouquets of flowers propped on little tables, the large gold mirrors and a velvet grey chaise in the middle of the room. It takes me a few minutes, but I recognize the beautiful melody playing in the background. "It's *Take Me To Church* by Hozier."

"Yes. I love this song and his entire album."

"You did all this for me?" I gasp, turning around to face him and holding my chest.

"Of course," Max responds, closing the gap between us.

"Why?" The word escapes my mouth before I can catch it.

He smiles down at me warmly. "You said something earlier when we met at my office. It bothered me so much because it made me realize perhaps you don't understand how I feel about you."

"What could I have said that would give rise to this royal treatment?" I ask, puzzled. "You spent most of your time talking to Mr. Hatcher while I played with myself," I add daringly.

"I'm not about to forget that conversation anytime soon. The imagery of you coming all over your hand in front of me is etched in my memory forever, love."

"Your text suggested you were going to punish me tonight. If this is your definition of punishment, bring it on."

"I was going to teach you a lesson tonight, but your words haunted me too much. I couldn't ignore them. Right after you left my office, I called a few key people who started the ball rolling and set the stage for this magical night."

"I can't remember what I said. Please refresh my memory." As much as I try, I can't recall what I might have said that would cause Max to pamper me like this.

"Before I pulled you into my office earlier today, you confessed you didn't think I had told anyone about us. You seemed to believe I was keeping you as my dirty little secret, but I'm not." He tucks a strand of hair behind my ear.

"Oh."

"Candy, from the moment I saw you walk into Vanilla Beans on a bright Sunday morning, your luscious curves have been the only ones I've craved."

"Uh…"

Max frowns and cocks his head to the side. "You and I seem to have this ongoing misunderstanding—I know exactly how I feel about you and you seem determined to think I don't."

"Well…"

"Isn't it not obvious?"

"Max…" I'm so overwhelmed by the moment, I can't continue. There's a part of me that believes him, but there's still a small part of me that doubts such a dreamy guy could fall for a girl like me.

"You can be so stubborn at times, Candice."

He hasn't called me by my full name in such a long time. Why is he being so formal?

"I'm not. It would have been okay with me if you felt it was more appropriate to hide our relationship from the people you work with." It's not as if it would be the first time a boyfriend has kept me as his little secret.

"Yeah, but it wouldn't have been acceptable for me to keep the woman I love in hiding. I want everyone to know how crazy I am about you."

"Wh-what?" I choke on those words as I take a step back. I'm so astounded by what I thought I heard, I stumble. Max leaps towards me and catches me like a white knight and brings me back to my feet.

"Is it something I said?" he mocks.

"You... Are you joking? I mean... You do realize..." I don't even know how to approach this.

"Yes, I'm fully aware of the fact I brought you to this romantic location to declare my love to you, Candice. I don't want you to ever have any doubts about the fact you've been occupying my thoughts since I first tasted your lips on the forty-first floor of the Bymark Hotel."

"Did you really say you loved me or am I dreaming?"

"Well, I guess a little of both since you're the woman of my dreams and I do love you very much."

His words are like fuel to a fire. I open my mouth to respond, but I'm so utterly shocked, I can't string together a coherent sentence.

After a few seconds of silence, Max searches my eyes for an answer, but I'm so taken by the moment I let my tears speak on my behalf. "Baby, you're crying. I hope they're tears of joy."

I inhale deeply and find the presence of mind to finally speak. "Max, I think I fell for you the morning you shared the story about how you ended up with such an intricate tattoo on your left arm. There's such a dichotomy about you—you're the sweetest man I've known and you're the raunchiest lover I've had. I love you so much."

"You were so quiet there. You had me worried."

"You caught me by surprise, Max."

"Good. I hope you'll never doubt how I feel about you again," he says, gazing at me with such intensity.

"I promise."

He leans in and brushes my lips with his. I can never get enough of his sweet kisses. I pull him closer into me and I respond voraciously to his passion.

A clink in the background interrupts the romantic mood. Since I've arrived it's the first time I've taken in the smell of food and I realize we're not alone in this spacious room. "Is there someone else here?"

"Yes. You didn't think I was going to cook dinner myself, did you?" he teases.

"We're having dinner here?"

"I couldn't possibly declare my love to you on an empty stomach."

"Of course not." I grin.

"I could have made reservations at one of the finest restaurants in the city, but I wanted something more original. Not to mention it's impossible to find a place in Manhattan that would have accepted this chaise," he says, pointing to the large lounge chair in the middle of the room.

"I can't imagine this beautiful piece of furniture would fit in many eateries in New York." I smile back at him.

"Seriously, it was too late to find a decent caterer at such short notice, so I called my personal chef Marcello and I asked him to whip up something sinful and simple."

"Hmmm, it sounds delicious. What's on the menu?"

"Since this extravagant set-up is last-minute, Marcello and his sous-chefs are preparing an exquisite Italian menu. The *pièce de resistance* is a succulent plate of creamy pesto pasta with garlic butter shrimp. Marcello ran to his favorite fishmonger to grab us some big fat juicy shrimp from Chile. I think we're in for a treat."

"I have a feeling I'm going to have to ask for seconds."

"I have a feeling I'll be doing the same." He winks.

"The food sounds decadent and it smells divine. I can't imagine how anything can top this meal. What's for dessert?"

"Marcello has prepared his famous tiramisu. You won't be disappointed, but I have to be honest..." Max reaches out to wrap his arms around my waist. "The only thing sweet I truly want is you."

"Tell me more," I coo.

"I intend on making good use of this chaise the second Marcello and his crew leave," he says with such carnal lust in his eyes, my clit tingles.

"I'd be disappointed if you didn't." *Wow, I feel like the luckiest girl in the world right now.*

This must be the most surreal and delightful moment of my life. This is the kind of day sweet dreams are made of. I can't believe the man I've fallen for weeks ago has declared his love to me. Devin was right all along—big girls can have hot boyfriends who love them.

Chapter Six

I can't believe it's already been ten days since I got back from Rio and it's been so crazy busy I've only been able to text Lia, Lexi and Devin. Tonight is the first time in a long time we'll be able to hang out together. I can't wait to tell them all about Rio and all about Max's declaration. I was tempted to text them a few hints, but I know they'd kill me.

It won't be long now before my friends find out about my magical love story. The timing couldn't have been better, since Max has dinner tonight with some old friends from college who are in town visiting from Colorado. It's one of the first Fridays where we won't end up sleeping next to each other in a long time, but tonight it's all about my best friends. I can connect with my man later in the weekend once his friends have left. While I'll be enjoying a leisurely brunch tomorrow morning with Lia, Max will be playing a few rounds of golf with his university buddies in the Hamptons.

The day started easy, but around three-thirty, I got slammed by an insane amount of work for my column in the next issue of the paper edition of *Sassy* magazine. I was practically chained to my desk all afternoon until I realized I had to get out of there or else I would be seriously late to meet with my friends. At seven, I shut down my computer and I grabbed my handbag ready to make a run for it when Jennifer cornered me at the elevators looking for an update on her stupid diet pills. Were it not for the fact her five-year-old son, Malcolm, called looking to know when she was coming home after she'd been talking my ear off for twenty minutes, I'd still be standing there listening to her yap about how revolutionary the cleanse is for consumers—especially women.

Of course, by the time I hopped in a cab, I was trapped in New York's legendary gridlock traffic and I only got home a few minutes ago. With little time to spare, I quickly touch up my makeup and trade my dress for a pair of black pants and a gorgeous bead-trim coral tunic with three-quarter-length sleeves I bought in Brazil. I'm rushing back to the bathroom when I notice the time.

"Crap. I can't believe it's a quarter past eight. I need to get out of here."

I put the finishing touches on my hair and run to the kitchen to grab my phone I had plugged in to recharge. In my frenzy, I knock off the bottle of diet pills Jennifer has been pestering me about for weeks now and the lid pops open, spilling little gel capsules all over the floor. "Shit!" I bend down and scoop the pills into a corner. I grab an empty box and place it on top of the mess.

"Leo, don't touch this. I'll sweep it up when I return. I'm going to leave you in the bathroom so you're not tempted to play with these." I grab my cat to place him in a secure location far away from the pills. I'm just about to close the bathroom door behind me when my phone rings. I look at the name flashing on my screen and I instantly know I'm in trouble. *Devin.*

"Hey, Dev."

"Where the hell are you? Are you ditching us for your god of sex? We've been here for twenty-five minutes and you're a no-show, Candy."

"Dev, I'm on my way. It was a stupidly busy afternoon at work and Jennifer insisted on a pow-wow right as I was leaving. I swear I have my handbag on my shoulder and I'm about to leave."

"It's going to take you at least thirty minutes to get here."

"I might be lucky. Maybe traffic has slowed down."

"Honey, this is New York on a beautiful Friday night, not Omaha, Nebraska. Get here fast. Lexi is already on her third drink and the girl doesn't look like she's going to slow down."

"Tell her not to get tipsy without me. I'll be there before you know it."

* * *

I slowly pry open my eyes after a night of partying with my friends and turn my face away from the bright sunshine. "We really party way too hard," I lament to myself. I roll to my side, ready to pet Leonardo DiCaprio, but I forgot he's still under lockup. I was too tired last night to even remove my makeup and I crashed the minute I got home. "Leo, I know you're mad at me for locking you in the bathroom. I'm going to let you out soon. I promise," I yell, hoping to catch my cat's attention before selecting a playlist from my phone and dropping it on my music dock. *Oh, well, he can be upset at me all he wants. I'm not ready to get up yet.*

I'm basking in a lazy Saturday morning listening to a new soulful bossa nova compilation Devin made for me before I left for Rio when my phone rings. *Lia.*

"Did you drink too much last night and are you calling to cancel our brunch date?" I ask.

"Nah, I can hold my liquor." She chuckles on the other end. "I was calling to make sure you were okay, since it seemed you were intent on matching Lexi. I guess you have a lot to celebrate, given the fact you've snatched one of the most amazing boyfriends in Manhattan."

"I do have a lot to be happy about, but I stopped well before Lexi and you know it."

"I'm teasing. I'm so jealous now. I need to get my act together and get my profile on one of those dreadful dating sites again or flash my tits in the middle of a swanky hotel like you did."

"You're hilarious this morning," I tease.

"I do my best. On a serious note, is it me or does it seem Lexi had a really hard week and she needed those drinks to unwind?"

"Yeah, I think you're right. She's been crunching numbers because of all these upcoming IPO deals and on top of it, she's been helping me dig out more details for my case."

"So how's that going? Is Max's brother still representing you?"

"Yes, Gabriel is officially my legal counsel. He's assigned a couple of legal eagles who are doing their best to get to the bottom of this messy ordeal. I wish I didn't have to reopen this nightmarish Pandora's box, but Annie left me no choice when she contacted me out of the blue with her message."

"Since we spent most of the night talking about your sexy boyfriend and your red-hot international love affair, maybe you can fill me in about your parents' case during brunch. I really hope you'll be able to get some kind of resolution even if it's taken too many years. I'm crossing my fingers. Perhaps this Annie Smith woman, or whatever her real name is, might be the one who helps you crack this case wide open."

"From your lips to my grandmother's ears. She fought hard but we were no match for this conglomerate with very deep pockets."

"True, but now you have one of the top legal firms in Manhattan helping you. I'm sure they'll make headway your former lawyer would have never been able to achieve."

"I hope you're right, Lia. I don't want to get my hopes up. I'd hate to be disappointed again if things didn't work out and the bad guys eluded us again."

"I know, sweetie, but it seems like Annie has information you didn't have a few years ago."

"And that's the only glimmer of hope I have right now."

"I have faith things will work out this time. Let's talk more about this over brunch. I was calling because I wanted to know where you wanted to eat today. I'm debating between three different new restaurants we haven't tried yet and I spent the last thirty minutes Googling each one. I've done my analysis and I'm ready to give you a summary so we can make a decision."

"You kill me. You really take eating out seriously, don't you?"

"Of course I do. It's one of my favorite activities in New York City."

"I have a sneaky feeling your restaurant critic review will take a while. Why don't I get out of bed and I'll stroll to the kitchen to prepare a cup of coffee while you give me the lowdown on our three eatery options." I chuckle while flipping the sheets over my naked body. I jump to my feet and stretch before walking to my closet to grab a robe. I look around, still hoping to see my finicky cat's beautiful white face, but then I remember until I let him out of the bathroom I won't be able to cuddle him. "I have to let Leo out."

"What do you mean? Where is he?"

"I was rushing to meet you guys last night and I accidentally knocked over the bottles of those stupid diet-slash-cleansing pills Jennifer is forcing me to ingest. Since the mess happened in the kitchen, I locked Leo up in my bathroom all night so he wouldn't be tempted to play with the pills."

"Man, your cat is going to be so mad at you. First you ditch him for a god of sex, then when you're not spending all your time getting fucked by him at his swanky penthouse, you're locking Leo up before running out to meet your best friends. Your cat has a hard life."

We both laugh.

"Hmmm, strange," I say as I walk through my apartment. "I swear I shut the door to the bathroom behind me last night right before I ran out to meet you guys. When I got back at the wee hours of the morning, I couldn't be bothered removing my makeup and I dove straight into bed, but now the door is wide open and there's no sign of Leo anywhere."

"Did he jump out the window?"

"Are you crazy? My cat is way too pampered to even think of doing such a foolish thing."

"I don't blame him. I wouldn't either if I was treated like a king."

"Don't be jealous of Leo. I found him. I don't know how he got out, but he's sleeping exactly where I didn't want him to be. Silly cat, I told him to say away from the pills." I squat down to pet my furry best friend. "Did you miss me? Come to Momma—" I stop talking and bring my hand to my mouth in a gasp of horror.

"What is it, Candy?"

"Oh my God, Lia. It's Leo."

"What happened?"

"I don't know, but he's lying on my kitchen floor as rigid as a board with his eyes wide open." I jump back up to my feet, panicked. "I swear I barricaded him in the bathroom. God, could I have forgotten to close the door when Devin called me to find out when I was getting to the bar? Oh, no. I think he's swallowed some of the pills, Lia. There's powder on the floor and he's not moving," I wail, scared out of my mind.

"Candy, calm down. Get dressed and get Leo to a vet."

"My vet is closed on weekends."

"This is New York. Someone is open. Let me do a few Google searches and I'll text you an address close to your home."

"Lia, what am I going to do if Leo is dead? I'm already an orphan and now my best—"

"Honey, you need to get him out of your apartment immediately and get him some help. I'm going to jump into a cab and come to join you. I don't want you to be alone right now."

"Lia, what have I done?" I cry out.

"Candy, don't panic. You haven't done anything. You need to rush your cat to a vet. Do you hear me?"

"Yes," I say, bursting into tears again.

Chapter Seven

Nine days later

"I have to stop crying," I whisper under my breath, aware the cab driver is looking at me suspiciously through his rear view mirror.

I'm on my way back to the vet. Dr. Victor Mills called me on Sunday as I was having brunch with Max to ask me to come into his office first thing. Max wanted to come with me, but I assured him it had to be a technicality, since there was nothing more the doctor could tell me that would shock me.

It's been a little over a week since my beloved cat, Leonardo DiCaprio, died. What more news can there be? I thought I had developed enough to no longer feel pain, but from the hellish week I've had to live through, I know nothing could be further from the truth. *Death sucks.*

Everything happened so fast last week. I couldn't think or feel. I guess I was lucky in many ways, because Lia found the address to a caring vet not too far from my home and I didn't have to deal with driving around the city with a dead cat in my lap. Dr. Mills gave his diagnosis very quickly and when he did, I broke down and collapsed on the floor. Lia and the doctor picked me up and took me to an empty waiting room where I cried my eyes out for thirty minutes straight. Lia sat next to me hugging me and caressing my back. She did her best to reassure me, but my heart was broken and I was inconsolable.

Once I stopped crying, Lia declared she need-ed to get me home. As we were leaving, Dr. Mills asked me to take a photo of the label of the BoostaSlimz-X30 Green Tea & Ginger Cleansing Total Body Cleansing System pills so he could com-pare the ingredients to what they'd find in Leo's stomach to confirm cause of death. He said something didn't add up given the details I had shared with him and his preliminary analysis and he wanted to get more accurate tests done at a lab. I must have looked at him blankly because Lia was the one who respond-ed, assuring the vet she'd send him a photo and drop off some of the pills lying on my kitchen floor.

I was so disorientated by everything that hap-pened last Saturday, it took me a few hours to call Max and let him know of my latest tragedy. He was so shocked, he put an end to his weekend with his old university buddies and his round of golf to rush to my side. When he got to my place, Lia, Lexi and Devin were already at my apartment comforting me, but I was a total mess. Here I am, a twenty-four-year-old woman who's lost every person she's ever loved in the last five years, and now I've lost my furry best friend. Why does this keep happening to me? What have I done to deserve so much pain and suffering?

I spent the weekend and eventually the entire week following my cat's death at Max's penthouse because it was unthinkable for me to spend one more second at my place without Leo. Devin and Lia helped with burial details because I had been to too many funerals in the last few years to deal with another one. Max took such great care of me. He allowed me to grieve. I locked myself in one of his guest rooms and I spent the entire weekend watching movies—I needed to find a distraction to numb the pain. Every few hours, Max would check up on me and he'd come sit next to me and force me to eat. By the time Monday rolled around, I dreaded going back to work because deep inside I know had Jennifer not pushed me to take those stupid pills home, Leo would still be alive.

I was ready to confront the bitch, but to my surprise her secretary told me she had an unexpected trip to Hong Kong due to a family emergency and left first thing Sunday morning. Apparently she was due to be out of the office all week long and she should be there by the time I get back from my appointment with the vet.

I spent the week trying my best to get work done, but it was extraordinarily hard. I regretted having to wait and not being able to unleash my fury on

Jennifer, but this was not the kind of conversation suited for an email. I needed to look her in the eyes.

When I got to work last week after Leo's death, I was too shaken to talk openly about my loss with my colleagues, but I did muster up the courage to write a post on my personal blog to update my followers. Unknowingly to me, Cori McDaniel, one of the personal assistants to Erik Buchanan, one of the VPs, read my confession and the next thing I knew, the entire office was rallying around me to comfort me.

Last week was right up there with the worst moments of my life.

* * *

The drive to Dr. Mills's office takes longer than nine days ago. There's nothing quite like Monday morning traffic in New York. As I ride alone in the elevator to the vet's office, I can't help but wonder why he's summoned me so early in the day. I already know Leo is dead. What more can there be?

To my surprise, when I open the door to Dr. Mills's office, there are already quite a few anxious pet owners waiting their turn with their furry best friends on their laps.

I guess Dr. Mills's assistant must have read my mind. "It's crazy how many accidents happen on a Sunday."

"It's quite surprising."

"Is your dog or cat outside?" the assistant asks, searching for my pet.

"Ah, no. Not quite. I'm here because Dr. Mills wanted me to come in to share results from tests about my cat."

"Yes, you must be Ms. Westerman."

"Candice, please."

"Candice, go right ahead. Dr. Mills is waiting for you."

"Are you sure?" I blurt out, looking in the direction of the busy waiting room.

The young woman sitting behind the desk smiles compassionately. "Don't worry about those guys. There are three other vets on staff on Mondays. They'll all be taken good care of." She winks.

Before I can respond, Dr. Mills opens the door to his office and greets me.

"Candice. I thought I heard your voice. Please come inside my office," he declares, gesturing for me to follow him.

"Good morning Dr. Mills."

"Good morning. Please take a seat," he says, pointing to a chair across from his desk.

"How was your weekend?"

"Busy. I worked Saturdays, as you know, but I spent all day yesterday reading the reports I received from the lab about your cat."

"Oh." I didn't expect Dr. Mills to dive right into the heart of the matter without the customary chitchat.

"Candice, where did you get the pills your pet ingested?"

"I'm an editor at *Sassy* magazine. A few weeks ago, my boss told me a potential advertiser wanted to run an advertorial in our magazine and it would be a good idea for me to test these cleansing pills. She's been pushing me for weeks and finally I caved in and took the pills home ready to test them."

"What's an advertorial?"

"It's when an advertiser buys ad space in a publication, but we wrap it within an article to make it look more informative than sales-y."

"I see. So you didn't take any of these pills?"

"No. I've been traveling and I didn't have time to start. In fact, I only brought the box home a few days before Leo died. To be honest, I've been resisting the idea of putting a substance I know little about in my body. Maybe that's the real reason I've been procrastinating."

"Thank God."

"You look worried, doctor."

"I'm extremely worried, Candice. We've found a list of ingredients that are not approved by the FDA and in many cases are considered illegal for consumption in America in the pills your cat ingested."

"What?" I'm scandalized at the idea I could have put Leo in harm's way by taking those stupid diet pills home.

"A lot of these ingredients are not only illegal here, but also in Canada, Australia and many European countries. The most troubling part of this is the fact the label says these pills were manufactured in the US, but many of the ingredients can only be found, to my knowledge, in China. There's no way a lab in this country could produce these without raising serious red flags."

"This doesn't make sense."

"Precisely. It doesn't... unless the manufacturer in involved in illegal activities."

"My God."

"My niece is in the fashion industry, like you, and a few years ago she lamented about how China was taking over the world of fashion production. She said a few clever Italian brands were cutting costs by producing as much as they could in China and then shipping the merchandise back to Italy, where they'd put the finishing touches and slap a 'Made in Italy' label on the garment even though ninety percent of the product was made in Asia. I was horrified by such practices, but then again, I'm not a businessman—I'm a doctor."

"I can't believe what you've shared. It's terrifying to think we could be vulnerable as consumers."

"Candice, I've been obsessing over your case since you came in because your cat was clearly poisoned, but I didn't want to alarm you until I had more facts."

"Poisoned?"

"Yes. I'm sorry to have to drop this bomb on you."

"So Leo didn't die because they were ordinary cleansing or diet pills?"

"No. Had they been capsules you had bought at a drugstore or a natural food shop, your cat might have had cramps, vomiting or in the worst case diarrhea, but the ingredients he ingested were lethal. In large enough dosage, they are so potent they could kill an adult hippo. Your case has gotten me wondering if the company behind these pills aren't getting ninety per cent of their production done in China and smuggling the goods in the US and adding a few FDA-approved ingredients before slapping on a 'Manufactured in America' label and fooling everyone."

"Ha," I scream out before clamping my mouth shut with my hand.

"I hate to be the bearer of such bad news, but I thought it was important for you to know. It was also important for me to find out exactly where you had purchased these."

"Are you saying anyone who might have taken these would be looking at a death sentence?"

"These things are never clear-cut. Some people will feel ill soon after digesting them and others might require a higher dosage. That said, in the long run, there's no way of surviving this list of ingredients."

"I'm distraught by this news."

"That's exactly how I felt all day yesterday."

"There's something more, doctor."

"What?"

"When my boss gave me pills she assured there were loads of medical studies and pages of testimonial from happy customers, but I couldn't find anything at all and I spent hours doing Google searches. My gut was uneasy about these pills from day one and it's almost as if I was trying to buy myself time."

"It's a good thing you trusted your gut in this matter or else your life could have been in danger."

He's scaring me here.

Does Jennifer know any of this? She was so pushy with these pills, I have to question her motivation.

"Your words are alarming, Dr. Mills."

"They should be. If these pills are sold anywhere in America or online there are tens of thousands of people potentially at risk. I was so concerned about these findings last night, I put one of my junior assistants on this case and she's trying to track down retailers and online merchants who are selling these. The public must be warned."

Chapter Eight

I'm too disheartened to face anyone at the office. I call Maleficent, who's back at the office from her trip to Hong Kong, to let her know I'm going to work from home because I have a terrible headache from all the emotions. To my surprise Jennifer doesn't fight me.

I'm grateful to push back my confrontation with her by another day. I need to calm myself down or I'll risk saying things that will get me fired. As I frantically type the words to an article and pretend my world is still intact and Dr. Mills didn't share overwhelming news a few hours ago, I play over my short conversation with my boss in my head. Contrary to her usual take-no-prisoners attitude, she was incredibly understanding and almost warm, which shocked the hell out of me because the queen of mean has never had one kind word to say. Maybe she feels guilty because she's the one who insisted on me taking these stupid pills home to test.

"I need coffee," I say, stretching and getting up out of my chair. I take a few steps towards my kitchen, but my phone rings. I quickly turn on my heel to see who's calling me. *Lia.*

"Hey, are you calling to check up on me?"

"Yes and no." Her voice is unusually cold.

"What's up? You sound different."

"Candy, have you heard the news about Damon West's mom?"

"Lia, I've had a few things on my mind other than an arrogant rapper's drama, let alone what happens in his mother's dating life." *What the hell? Has she forgotten Leo died nine days ago? Why would I clog my head with gossip?*

"I think you need to Google her name immediately, Candy."

I'm about to protest, but something in Lia's voice suggests I should do as I'm told. "I don't understand why you're pushing me to do this," I say as I type Marvel West's name in the search engine. "I despise Damon West and his baby-momma TV reality trash star Kaliah Darnadovich. I don't care how much money they have, they are tacky and lack class…" I stop talking as I make out the words on my screen before gasping in disbelief. "Oh my God, Lia."

"Exactly, Candy. She died the day after Leo and the shocking news was all over the entertainment tabloids and gossip websites, but the newswire about the cause of her death came in fifteen minutes ago and it's already gone viral."

I read aloud the headline flashing on my screen slowly, unable to believe my eyes. "'The LA coroner's office confirms Damon West's mom, Marvel West, is dead after having taken a diet pill by the name of BoostaSlimz-X30 Green'—" I trail off. "This woman died from ingesting the same pills as my cat." I'm so devastated, I can't contain the torrent of tears rolling down my face.

"Candy, I'm sorry to force you to relive this, but when I saw this monster news come in, I knew there was more to this. Apparently, Marvel bought the pills online."

"I met with Dr. Mills this morning, Lia. These pills were filled with poisonous ingredients that are illegal in the U.S."

"What are you talking about?"

During the next thirty minutes I recount my conversation with the vet. I barely take a breath, afraid my courage will fail me and I'll hold back details. By the time I'm done, I'm exhausted and I have a pounding headache.

"I can't believe this story and I can't believe your boss has been pushing you to take these. I'm so happy you never—"

"—took the pills." I finish Lia's sentence and we both remain silent at the realization of my words. "I've been thinking about this ever since I left Dr. Mills' office. Jennifer was trying to push me to take a product that had never been approved by the FDA. I could never understand why she was such a cheerleader for this company. I guess I'll find out tomorrow when I confront her," I sigh.

"You plan on approaching her with the vet's findings?" Lia asks, panicked.

"Yes, of course. This is all her doing. Not to mention she's the only one right now who knows who's behind these pills."

"Candy, has she mentioned anything to you since your office found out about Leo's death?"

"She was dealing with a family issue in Hong Kong."

"Is that an excuse? The woman could have emailed you to say she was sorry for your loss. Have you heard anything from her?"

For the first time, it hits me Jennifer is the only person in our company who hasn't called, texted or emailed me about Leo. Her assistant knows and all of the top executives know, so I'm sure she must have heard all the gruesome details. Not to mention I spoke briefly this morning and she still didn't extend her condolences. "No. Not a word, Lia."

"I'd keep this close to your chest for now until she brings it up. I know she's a bitch, but I find it strange she's the only person who's not extended her condolences. A few of the VPs who were overseas reached out to you, but your boss can't take thirty seconds to send a quick email?"

"Yeah, you're right."

"You should call Dr. Mills and inform him of this latest development. He doesn't strike me as the type who follows celebrity news, although at this point the medical community must be buzzing about Damon West's mom."

"Why? Leo is dead. Marvel is also dead. What's the point?"

"Call me crazy, but something tells me Dr. Mills would want to know about this if he doesn't already. These pills are lethal, he said so himself, and the company behind them needs to be stopped before they kill more innocent people or pets."

Lia's words send a chill down my spine. I was so consumed by my own grief, I didn't think of the fact other people could potentially end up six feet under if the truth doesn't come out. Dr. Mills was speculating this morning, but Marvel's death is far too real.

"You're right. Dr. Mills needs to be made aware of this," I whisper. "Let me call him now."

"Do you want me to come over later when I'm done with work? I don't think you should be alone."

"I'm going to go back to Max's place tonight. I wanted to come back to my apartment after Dr. Mills' autopsy report, but I find it hard to sleep here without Leo's presence."

"Good, as long as you're not alone, because this is a lot to process in one day."

"This day has been brutal."

"Big hugs. I have to get back to work, but call me if you need to talk."

"Thanks, Lia, for being such a great friend."

I hang up the phone and I place it on my desk before hiding my face between my hands. This news is so heavy and it's eating at me. *I still don't know what to make of Jennifer's reaction, or lack thereof, to the death of my cat or her involvement with these deadly pills.*

"Coffee. Now I really need more coffee." I peel myself off my chair and march to the kitchen area to get a fresh cup of coffee before calling Dr. Mills with the latest bomb Lia dropped on me. "I can't handle any more drama without caffeine."

Thanks to the magic of Nespresso, it takes me no time at all to sip on a strong dark roast espresso. I walk back to my desk with a lump in my throat. I decide to finish my cup of coffee before dialing Dr. Mills' office because I have a suspicion there's more bad news coming my way once I share the latest chapter in my drama.

I open the window to my browser to continue reading about Marvel West's tragic death when I notice I've received a new email. *What now?* With the day I've had so far, I'm tempted to ignore the email, but this one comes from one of my blog readers. The support from my incredible fans has been a blessing and I've made sure to answer each and every one of the heartwarming messages I've received. I click on the message and after reading the first few lines, I stop breathing.

Candice,

I read your blog post and I'm sorry for the loss of your beloved pet. I had no intention of contacting you so quickly, but Marvel West's death and the latest news that's already gone viral have expedited things. I'm sorry to say this, but there is a direct link between your cat's and Marvel West's deaths.

Unfortunately, those two tragic deaths are also tied to your parents'.

I wasn't planning on revealing my identity so soon, but there are a few things you need to know urgently. My real name isn't Annie Smith, as you know. It's Laurie Paddington. I was your dad's biomedical lab assistant and I worked very closely with him on most of his research and testing. After your parents died, I quit my job at Bio-Cytrax Cosmeceuticals and I went into exile. I needed to hide because I couldn't handle things and I knew too much. I mustered up the courage to reach out to your grandmother's attorney eighteen months ago, but he abruptly stopped returning my calls. When I read about the details of his death, I went deeper into hiding, fearing for my own life. I knew too much to believe it was an accident.

I'm putting myself in grave danger by contacting you like this, but I can no longer live with the secret I've been harboring for five years.

I'm including my cell number below. I know this is scary, but if you want to meet, there are a lot of things you need to know.

I can't force you to do anything you're not comfortable with and I'll respect your decision.

Whatever you do, don't let your boss know I've contacted you.

—Laurie

Laurie Paddington? I remember her well. There was so much going on when my parents died, I forgot she had disappeared off the face of the planet and I remember how my grandmother's attorney tried to locate her for months without much success. Was his death more than an accident? What does she know that links Marvel's, Leo's and my parents' deaths together? What does she know about Jennifer's involvement with these poisonous pills and why is she warning me against my boss? *God, my head hurts.*

Once the severity of the situation fully hits me, I run like a scared rabbit to Max's penthouse.

I'm so disturbed by Laurie's words, I stuff my belongings in a weekend bag and I grab a cab. I only call Max to let him know I'm on my way after twenty minutes of riding in silence at the back of the taxi. I'm beyond shocked by my dad's former assistant's claims and scared by the idea that the people who harmed my parents could still out there. I'm unable to wrap my head around her last sentence. *"Whatever you do, don't let your boss know I've contacted you."*

By the time I arrive at Max's home, Gabe, Francis and Sheena are there anxiously waiting for me. Max has summoned all three to his home so we can get to the bottom of things. All five of us take turns to reread Laurie's message, hoping to find a missing clue between the lines.

After two hours of debate, Gabe declares I'm to avoid contact with Laurie at any cost because being seen with her could be life-threatening. When the members of my legal team leave, I roll into bed and cuddle inside Max's arms, praying there's a reset button I can press to erase the last five years of my life.

Chapter Nine

I can't sleep a wink and when Max gets up at five to go to the gym before an early-morning meeting, I decide to head to the office and spend the next three hours in solitude drowning my sorrows in work. I think of going back to my place and working there for the day, but the solitude would kill me, not to mention Jennifer will have a fit if I don't show up again today. Although I've been staying at Max's penthouse for over a week now, it still doesn't feel like home and I need to be in a more familiar setting to process the last ten days.

Max insists on dropping me off in front of *Sassy* magazine, but instead, I ask him to drop me off at the Perfect Grind. Since I barely slept more than a few hours, I need a booster and the short walk to the office will help clear my head. *Thank God I live in*

New York. Where else can you buy a decent latte at this early hour?

There are only a few times of day where the streets of New York City are practically deserted and this is one of them. There are a few eager joggers and early risers, but the vibe is quite mellow compared to what it will be in the next thirty minutes. As I pull open the door to my building, I look down at my watch and sigh when I see it's only six o'clock in the morning. *How am I going to make it through the day?*

I ride the elevator alone and I can't help but think of how difficult it will be to bite my tongue around Jennifer today. Max, Lia and my legal counsel have all convinced me to play it cool and pretend I don't know anything. I was willing to be defiant, but Laurie's last sentence has been looping in my head. Gabe's team wants to scratch the surface a bit more and verify Laurie's allegations before I put myself in a compromising situation. If there's a link between those monsters and my parents' death, I don't want Maleficent to tip off the owners of BoostaSlimz-X30 Green Tea & Ginger Cleansing Total Body Cleansing System—obviously she knows more than she's willing to let on.

When I push open the door to the office, a wall of silence hits me. The space looks so empty without the usual busyness. In some strange way, I look forward to occupying my thoughts with work.

As I turn the corner on my way to my desk, a voice comes from one of the conference rooms. *Shit, I thought I was going to be alone. I'm not in the mood to make watercooler chitchat this morning with one of my colleagues.* I drop my coffee on a desk nearby and try to make out the voice in the background before deciding if I should go say hello or not. I'm too far away to hear clearly. I decide to tippy-toe closer to find out who else could possibly be at work at such an early hour. When I make out the person's voice, I freeze.

Jennifer.

To say I'm annoyed to find her already at work would be an understatement. My first instinct is to go back down the elevator and find a coffee shop I can work from, but then I remember I need a few important files and a number of back issues to magazines in my cabinet to help me write my plus-size features. With a sigh, I walk back to grab the coffee I left on one of my colleagues' desks and I plunk myself behind my iMac. I shrug my shoulders and resign myself to the fact Jennifer has ruined my plans to have the office all to myself for the next few hours. *If her conversation becomes too distracting, I'll put my headphones on to drown out her annoying voice.* I grab my coffee and take one last big gulp before diving into my work.

As much as I try to focus on writing this article, I can't help but catch a few snippets of my boss' conversation. Suddenly a question she asks breaks my concentration and I find myself listening in more intently.

"Baby, do you know how much I miss you?"

I guess she's talking to her husband Seth. Funny, she never sounds this loving when she's speaks to him usually. She must be buttering him up for something.

I chuckle to myself and get back to my writing.

"Please get me out of here. I'm suffocating."

Huh?

I'm doing my best to focus on my work, but Jennifer's voice is carrying through the empty office and her last statement has me intrigued. *Trouble in paradise? Forget about work. This is way too juicy.* I pretend to type just in case Maleficent walks out of the conference room, but I'm really listening in on her conversation.

"I told you a year ago when you came up with this plan that I hated being far away from you. Every day we're apart is like torture for me."

Okay, she's not talking to her husband. Does she have a lover? Oh, this is only getting better.

"Please, stop worrying. I'm still playing it cool despite the fact I'm dying to see you again soon. As far as everyone here knows, I was in Hong Kong dealing with a sick aunt. No one suspects anything so far—not even my assistant. I made great headway with the product while I was there, honey."

Product? Who is she talking to so early in the morning?

"Of course I can't avoid Candy forever. I'm painfully aware I work with her. I'll have to keep my feelings about her in check until we can sort this mess."

When I hear my name, I hold my breath. *Why is she talking about me like that?* Something about

Jennifer's tone sounds too personal for it to be about work. For some inexplicable reason, I get up from my chair and I tippy-toe until I get as close as possible to the conference room.

"Thank God for small favors. At least I've not had to deal with Candice since her cat died. Yvette, my assistant, was the one who told me about the pesky creature's passing."

So she's known about Leo from the beginning but never brought it up?

"Pity the furball ingested some of the diet pills."

She knows about the pills Leo swallowed? So she does read my blog.

I duck under a desk near the conference room. My gut is screaming at me to keep a low profile and I tuck my body in as best as I can to be as inconspicuous as possible as I listen in on her conversation. *Holy shit.* My heart is beating so fast I feel like I'm going to throw up, but in a moment of lucidity, I fish in my back pocket to find my phone. *There's no way in hell anyone will ever believe this if I don't record it.* I push the Voice Memos icon on my phone and hold it as close as I can without being made out.

"I was able to quickly put two and two together the minute Yvette told me about the news, since I've been pushing our fat plus-size editor to take the BoostaSlimz pills home to test them."

Fat plus-size editor? Bitch.

"Listen, I can't believe they were able to link Marvel West back to our pills so quickly."

Our pills?

"We didn't even have time to set up a contingency plan. And this is particularly annoying since last month was one of our bestselling months. We sold hundreds of millions of dollars' worth of our diet pills online to desperate women looking to get back into their skinny jeans. I was hoping Candice would have completed her editorial by now on our pills to boost sales even further given the prime target of *Sassy* magazine's audience."

Oh my God, there's no remorse in her voice whatsoever. She was willing to let me ingest those pills fully aware they were dangerous.

"I'm pissed off at all these stupid incidents that keep getting in our way. Now the latest news has gone viral and the police will start looking for the bad guys."

What does she mean? Is Jennifer connected to the company behind BoostaSlimz-X30?

"How the hell do you expect me to keep calm? You've been safe in Malaysia since Candice's parents' convenient death."

What?

"You've said this before about Teddy Westerman. Killing him was going to allow us to lie low and surge back a few years later and make a fortune with the formula he deemed unacceptable for human consumption. You might have gotten rid of him, but what good does it do us now? I told you these pills required more testing. Not once have you mentioned these were potentially deadly, honey."

Jesus fucking Christ.

"Had you not pushed me to give Candy those pills we'd still be undercover. I wanted the money as much as you did. If you really wanted to get rid of her before she turned twenty-five, there were more effective ways than to force me to work with her to keep an eye on her and then convince me to trick her into taking those pills."

What does any of this have to do with my next birthday?

"Quintin, you knew all along that if she took enough of those pills you wouldn't have to honor the clause in your corporate structure where Teddy names his only daughter as the beneficiary of his shares, which, may I remind you, represent forty percent of your pharmaceutical company. Let's not forget he also appointed her to sit on the board of directors on his behalf. I told you from day one you were giving him too much, but you refused to listen because you never imagined he'd become a liability."

Quintin? As in Quintin Grayson?

There's only one person I know named Quintin—my dad's former business partner at Bio-Cytrax Cosmeceuticals.

Oh, my God.

Now I get it. The day my grandparents and I went to the lawyer's office for the reading of the will, there was an envelope that read, "For Candice on your twenty-fifth birthday." My grandmother had me place it securely in a safety deposit box along with a few other valuable papers, but it slipped my mind. I haven't opened that box in years. I didn't know what was in that envelope, but I surely never imagined it was this. Suddenly Jennifer raises her voice and brings my attention back to the conversation again.

"Your ass is not on the line like mine is if it gets out I partly own BoostaSlimz, Quintin. No. You're going to listen to me for a change. I want you to get me out of New York. I want you to wire money to my Cayman Island account, get me two first-class plane tickets to Bali, I want a brand-new home and new ID and papers for me and your son."

Wh-what? What does she mean by 'your son?'

"Malcolm is the only good thing in my dreadful life here in New York since you're so far away from me and we can't see each other too often to avoid raising suspicions. I'm not leaving him behind with a man who's not his real father. Once Seth realizes Malcolm isn't his, he'll turn his back on him and our boy will be left to fend for himself. At least in Bali he'll be safe and you can start building a fatherly bond with him."

Jesus, Jennifer's son's father is Quintin and not her husband Seth?

"Don't worry about how I'll break the news to Malcolm about having to leave his so-called dad behind. Let me deal with those details and you worry about the rest. I wish you had taken care of Candy at the same time you took care of her grandmother's attorney who was snooping around well after the case went cold."

Quintin is responsible for the death of our lawyer?

"Had you dealt with her a long time ago, I wouldn't be working at this dreadful job and I wouldn't be stuck here in Manhattan married to a man I can hardly stand. I've always wanted only one thing, Quintin… to be with you."

Holy hell. I've heard enough, I need to get out of here now.

I shove my phone inside my bag in a hurry and I crawl from under the desk. I run to the door and grab the stairs instead of waiting for the elevator. By the time I reach the fourteenth floor, I'm out of breath and sweating after rushing down six floors, but I'm too afraid to stop now. *I can't believe what I've heard. My grandmother never trusted Quintin and now I find out he killed my father to silence him. Is Jennifer also responsible for my parents' death?*

There are millions of questions colliding in my head, but I keep running down the stairs as if my jacket is on fire. I get out of the office building so fast I bump into a few people, who let me know in no uncertain terms how annoyed they are with me. The sidewalk is already bustling with New Yorkers making their way to work and my abrupt arrival doesn't deter any of them.

My handbag got caught in the handle as I was flying out the door. I straighten up and head back towards the entrance of *Sassy* magazine to unhook my bag. Once I get over the humiliation, I hail a cab. *I need to get as far away as possible from Jennifer.*

Getting a cab during morning rush hour in Manhattan is as easy as crossing the Nile River in

Egypt by foot. As soon as I see a free one approaching, someone else jumps in front of me and snatches it from me. After fifteen frustrating minutes, I finally dash towards one before a suited executive standing next to me spots it. Once I'm safely seated at the back of the taxi, I give the cabbie my directions as I dial Gabe's phone to let him know about Jennifer's involvement in this sordid story and to inform him I'm on my way to his office with the recording of the conversation I just overheard. When Gabe lets me know he'll call one of his contacts at NYPD and request for a detective to come to his office to meet me, I know this case is about to get scarier and more twisted than it already is. I immediately call Max, Lia, Lexi and Devin to let them know I may have inadvertently walked in on the confession of the century.

Chapter Ten

Six months later

Max and I are sitting at the back of his chauf-feured Mercedes Benz and we're on our way to meet friends. My boyfriend has gathered Lia, Devin, Lexi, his brother Gabe, Francis, Sheena and Deidra in the private room of the VIP members' den on the forty-first floor of the Bymark hotel for a special gathering. He's also invited his parents and his younger brother Lucas, who's coming with his pregnant wife Keira to join us.

Today is a big day of celebration for all of us, but especially for me. *God, I still can't believe this gorgeous man sitting next to me is mine.* I lose myself in his loving gaze before turning away to admire nightfall in New York as the car whizzes down a main artery.

The past few months have been surreal. After five long and traumatizing years, my parents have finally been vindicated. The last six months have been a journey into the past where I was finally able to discover why my parents had been so brutally murdered. After the verdict came in and it was clear this nightmare was behind me, Max whisked me away to his home in Brazil where we've been staying for the past six weeks until we came back to New York four days ago.

The first few days in Rio were pure agony. I couldn't stop crying from sadness and joy. I was crushed by the weight of the truth and I was also liberated once and for all.

During the trial, Max asked me to move in with him. I was spending most nights at his place anyways because the thought of being at my place without Leo was becoming more and more unbearable, but Max wanted to make it official between us. He insisted on me being close by so he could take care of me during this trying time.

It took me a few weeks to adjust to my new luxurious surroundings and to accept the fact we were at this stage of our relationship. Once I did, Max suggested I rent out my grandmother's apartment to take advantage of the fact it's located in a coveted area of the city. I was lucky enough to find the perfect tenant—a handsome young teacher who moved from Minnesota for a position at NYU. I'm relieved my place is in good hands and I'm grateful someone will occupy the space while I live with the man I love.

Not a day has gone by without me reliving every moment since I walked in on Jennifer's early morning conversation with my parents' killer. It's been looping in my head like a film roll from old Hollywood. I shake my head and close my eyes, fighting off another sudden pang of sadness.

Max must have noticed because he wraps his hands protectively over mine. "Baby, it's over. You have to let it go."

"I know. Sometimes I relive parts of this drama and before I know it, I'm sucked into a vortex of bad memories."

"I understand, but remember this, Jennifer and Quintin will rot behind bars for the rest of their lives for what they've done to you and for Marvel West's death. In many ways we have Damon West to thank. He went after BoostaSlimz-X30 with a vengeance and for once his media tirade has paid off big time because it helped bring so many poor victims to the forefront who had suffered from health issues and the families of those who died after taking the pills. When you combine this with the recording you made at *Sassy* magazine on that fortuitous morning, the damaging evidence Laurie had kept for all these years, the fact she was willing to trust Gabe enough to share it all, your father's revised will in that safety deposit box and Lexi's brilliance in connecting all of the companies that are part of Quintin Grayson's massive conglomerate, this case was cracked wide open and all the ugliness came spewing out."

"Eventually I'll accept the gruesome fact— my former boss was the lover of the monster who slaughtered my parents to keep my dad from revealing the truth behind those deadly pills."

"At least you were able to confront her during the trial about her part in this tragedy. She had a vendetta against you because you were standing in between her and a lot of money."

"I know. It's just when I think of it all, I'm still so angry and I'm still in pain."

"No one can blame you for being angry and you are entitled to release the pain when you're ready, baby, but Gabe's team have done a superb job at catching the bad guys and stripping them of all their money, including the multimillions they made selling poison. You're safe now," Max says, leaning towards me before dropping a kiss on my forehead.

Jennifer was arrested within a few hours of my arrival at Gabe's office and since she could only have one phone call, she ended up calling the only person she could think of—Seth Weingarten, her husband. The police interrogated Jennifer until she coughed up Quintin's exact location in Malaysia. The authorities there apprehended Quintin in the middle of the night and the FBI snatched him to bring him back to America to stand trial.

Jennifer's carelessness played in our favor. She never expected to be caught, which explains why she didn't think twice about calling her murderous lover from the phone in the boardroom.

Within three weeks, the soul-shattering truth came out. Once the authorities had worked with the Malaysian government to safely apprehend Quintin Grayson and all the paperwork had been secured to ensure he couldn't get away on a technicality, the press went wild. It was impossible for Max and I to hide our involvement and I'm so grateful we made the decision long before this frenzy broke to let people around us know we were together—including the execs at *Sassy* magazine. My boyfriend had a meeting with some of the VPs to let them know we had been dating for a while. As much as we dreaded the public's attention, the media were kind to me. They did report about my relationship with Max and they did follow me around for a while, but at least they weren't trying to dig up dirt on us. I guess the sensationalism of my case was enough to keep them busy.

As you can imagine, it didn't take long for news to leak that Jennifer Lau had married Seth under false pretenses and she'd passed off Quintin's son as his. She'd been involved with Quintin for years, but she'd distanced herself when he went into hiding after he had ordered a hit against my parent's life. Obviously they were still able to see each other since it's now official Malcolm isn't Seth's son. The Weingarten clan were devastated by the scandal. Seth immediately pushed for a divorce, wanting to get Jennifer out of his life and save his reputation from the woman who'd had a hand in ruining my life.

I'm completely lost in my thoughts until Max's voice brings me back to reality.

"Are you going to be okay tonight? If you don't feel you're up to it, we can turn the car around and go back home." Max is caressing my arm and looking at me with such loving eyes. I don't think I could have managed the last six months of my life without him by my side.

"I'll be fine. You've gathered all my friends at the Bymark hotel and besides, it's a big day of celebration."

"I know it's still difficult to make peace with it all despite the settlement. Those millions will never bring back your parents or your beloved cat, but at least it's a major vindication and it proves your grandmother Barbara was right all along."

"It's far more than I ever expected. I'm still not quite sure what to do with all this money."

"I can't say I've ever dated a multimillionaire before." He smiles tenderly.

"You're too funny. I'm still the same girl, but my bank account is bulging in a way I never thought possible." I smile back.

It's funny because during the first few months when we were dating, I was always so worried Max and I would get busted for having sex in the Fashion Archive room and risk getting fired, but in the end, I quit my job at *Sassy* magazine a few months into the trial because everything was too much to handle and I couldn't deal with the curious stares at the office. My life was exposed enough, I didn't need to witness people talking about my melodrama at the water cooler.

Gabe had been confident all along I'd be able to get a generous settlement given the irrefutable proof we had against Quintin and the fact authorities acted quickly to freeze his international accounts. The judge awarded me seventeen point three million dol-

lars and he also ordered Quintin to pay for my astronomical legal fees. Gabe had gone all-out on this one
and hired the best investigators and experts in the
business to make sure Quintin didn't get away with
murder twice. Max was more than happy to pay his
bill, but I'm grateful the judge properly punished my
parents' killer. I never imagined I'd have so much
money in my life, but as Max has said, the money will
never bring back my mom, my dad or Leo.

Max leans down and brushes my lips. "We're
here, baby. I'm sure your friends will cheer you up in
no time."

"You're right. I haven't seen them in six
weeks and I'm dying to reconnect with them. Not to
mention I'd love to thank Gabe, Francis and Sheena
again," I say, responding to his passionate kiss. "Let's
get up there. I can wait to hug everyone."

* * *

As we ride to the VIP members' den of the
Bymark hotel, I can't help but flash back to the first
time I made this journey to the forty-first floor with a
man I'd had a bad crush on since he caught my eye
over brunch. Never in a million years could I have
ever imagined nine months later my life would look
like this. I can't help but smile at myself, remember-
ing some of the hot scenes of our first kinky interlude,
and Max notices my mischievous grin.

"What's going on inside your head?" he says,
narrowing his hazel eyes.

"Nothing," I respond, lifting my eyes to the ceiling.

"Your smile suggests otherwise, Candy. Your mood has dramatically changed."

"I was thinking of the first time you brought me up here."

"I see. You mean the first time you took my breath away?"

"Max…"

"You should be used to me gushing all over you by now, baby." Max takes a step closer and embraces me in his strong arms before taking my lips in a hungry kiss.

"I'll never get used to it. Don't ever forget to keep reminding me."

When we reach the top floor of the hotel, I reluctantly extract myself from him.

"Let's go enjoy the party and then I'll whisk you back to my place and spend the rest of the weekend in bed with you."

"I like the way you think." I beam up at him as we walk hand in hand to meet our friends to celebrate the end of a nightmare.

When Max opens the door, I'm greeted by some of my favorite people in the world. We step in ready to start the celebrations when I recognize Andrew, the same manager who took such good care of us the first time I came to the Bymark hotel to meet my cousin Trish. He's standing at the door as if he's been waiting for our arrival all day long.

"Mr. Keller, it's good to see you again. Ms. Westerman, I'm delighted to be working on this floor tonight so I can partake in the celebrations. Like the rest of New York, I've been riveted by your story and I prayed they'd put those monsters in jail forever."

"Thank you, Andrew. I'm so glad it's over."

"It is, and tonight is about new beginnings. Isn't that right, Mr. Keller?"

"Andrew, I've been badgering my sexy girl-friend for weeks now, but I don't think she's quite convinced yet. I hope your words appease her."

We all laugh.

"Let me go back to the kitchen and make sure everything is ready for tonight and I'll let the two of you enjoy your guests." Andrew nods to the right before turning on his heel. As he makes his way to the back of the room, he's already ordering staff to circulate the room with trays of champagne and tempting hors d'oeuvres.

"Let's go greet everyone." Max grabs two glasses and we cheer before joining our friends.

I kiss and hug Devin, Lia, Lexi and Deidra before turning to Gabe. I nearly choke up when I meet his eyes. I haven't seen him in six weeks since he stood in Max's penthouse to announce the judge had ruled in my favor, and there are no words to express the depth of my gratitude. I drop my head against his chest and I hug the man who's helped me close the most horrific chapter in my life.

I quickly run to Sheena and Francis and grab both of them by the waist for a communal hug. When I see Max's mom Jasmina waving at me, I run to her as well and I embrace her so tightly, it's as if I never want to let her go. She's been such an incredible uplifting spirit during these last six months and we've grown so close.

The vibe in the room is so high and I didn't expect to miss all these people so much. After kissing and hugging everyone in the room, I turn my attention to Lia and Lexi. Things have been understandably crazy and the recent trip to Rio has forced my friends and I to keep in touch via text messages and Skype video chats, but nothing compares to seeing them tonight.

"Look at you. You're so tanned." Lexi marvels at my golden skin and her eyes sparkle as she takes me in.

"I know. It's so sunny all the time in Brazil and even with big hats and sunscreen, it's impossible not to come back with a tan."

"Can you believe we're celebrating such a monumental moment?" Lia grabs my face and plants a big kiss on each cheek before wiping off her lipstick. "I mean, you won. You finally brought Goliath to his knees," she says with a tear in her eyes.

"Stop with the crying or else I won't be able to hold it together tonight," I say, running my index fingers under my eyes. "I wore waterproof mascara, but if you continue, it won't do me any good."

"Okay, I'll stop, but honey, I'm so happy for you."

"The vindication, the colossal settlement and getting those monsters behind bars is great, but you living with the man of your dreams is pretty damn phenomenal." Lexi is grinning from ear to ear as her eyes shift from my face to Max's.

"Look at my girls." Devin joins us and all four of us are so emotional from not seeing each other for so long, we embrace each other in a warm bear hug. "Candy, it's over, hun. I told you this before you left New York to spend time with your rich boyfriend in the land of the gods and I'm reminding you now, Jennifer and Quintin will never leave prison alive."

"I know. I feel for their son, though. He's going to be the one paying the price for his parents' sins."

"Oh, yeah. What happened to little Malcolm?"

"Lia, Jennifer's dad may be extremely rich, but his fortune couldn't prevent his daughter from paying for her evil ways. Not only will she rot in jail forever, the authorities appointed her parents Malcolm's guardians. He's now living with them in Hong Kong."

"Jennifer must be devastated, but she brought this on herself."

"Lexi, I feel badly for her in some ways because her son is so young, but you're right. It's her doing and she can't blame anyone else."

"In any case, it's been a royal mess, but it's over, *fini, finito*, done, no more."

"Yeah, Devin, it brings me some level of joy, but it's never going to bring my parents back."

"No, it won't, but you have closure, which you didn't have five years ago." Devin strokes my cheek and I cup his hand in mine. *My God, I love my friends.*

"Max keeps repeating this all the time."

"Did I hear my name?" Max, standing an earshot away, turns around with a huge smile on his face. He was caught up in an animated chat with his brothers, but the second he hears his name he veers his attention to us, dragging Gabe and Lucas to join in on our conversation.

"Devin and you are on the same page, baby."

"You're right. My sexy girlfriend is finally free. Listen, guys, I think it's time for this party to really get started. This hot chick has a bright future in front of her and without the support of amazing people like yourselves, tonight wouldn't be the same." Max wraps his arm around me and kisses me tenderly, earning him a few whistles from our friends.

* * *

The last four hours have been blissful. I can't believe how happy I am right now. I'm sitting next to the man I love with all my heart with New York at my feet and I'm celebrating a joyous day surrounded by my friends. What more can a girl ask for?

Our five-course meal was to die for. Deidra and Max selected a menu fit for royalty. The two appetizers were out of this world and the rest of the meal didn't disappoint one bit. We started with a salad of forest mushrooms served on a bed of Belgian endives, followed by a butter-poached lobster served on melted King Richard leeks. I can't believe they flew these crustacean delights all the way from Nova Scotia, Canada. It must have cost a fortune.

The parade of dishes for the main course was divine. We first started with a *canard à l'orange* glazed with clementine oranges served with wild rice followed by charcoal Kobe grilled steak flown straight from Japan. The duck was amazingly succulent, but nothing prepared me for how the Japanese steak melted in my mouth.

Dessert is a decadent and sinful display of the most tempting sweets I've ever seen in my life. I've only seen dessert tables at weddings, but this spread is honestly heavenly. The champagne is flowing and the atmosphere in the room is mellow. I look around me in awe and I can't help but fight off a pang of emotion. I might have lost my parents at a young age, but I've been blessed enough to have the most incredibly loving people in my life. I don't think I could be happier than I am right now.

Max locks eyes with me and I read something so intense, I have to look away. I brush off the fire I see in his hazel gaze, blaming the endless flow of amber nectar filling our glasses, but he leans in and whispers something in my ear that catches me by surprise.

"We should thank everyone for coming out tonight. What do you think?"

"It's a great idea, honey, but everyone still seems to be having so much fun. Are you tired? Do you want to go home?"

"Not at all. I'm so happy right now for you, for us, and I want these people to know how I feel."

"If you get up now, everyone will think you're putting an end to the festivities," I tease.

"You're right. Maybe it's too early," he says.

"Are you okay? You look very pensive and serious all of a sudden."

"I'm good. I'm excited because it's such a big day," he says, kissing my forehead.

"Of course." His words reassure me and I poke my fork into my plate and bring a piece of decadent chocolate cake to my mouth.

"Why don't I go to the dessert table for a second round? Do you want anything else?"

"No, thank you, baby. This whole meal has been insane. It's so up there in my food-porn world."

"I'm pleased you enjoyed the evening. Tonight was all about you, love."

"This night is perfect, Max," I say leaning into him to kiss him.

"I can make it even better."

"You can't coerce me into following you in the bathroom for a quickie, mister," I whisper in his ear.

"Nah. I had something more long term in mind." Max's gaze is so heavy I hold my breath when he kisses me again.

"What do you mean?"

Instead of answering, he looks in Deidra's direction and nods. His right-hand person clasps her hands together and she instantly lights up like a Christmas tree. I'm still confused by what's happening, but all of a sudden Max rises to his feet and lifts his champagne glass.

"May I have your attention, please?"

I thought he wasn't going to thank everyone for coming yet. What's going on with him?

"As you all know, tonight is a big event for the beautiful woman sitting next to me. There's a reason why I selected this room for the celebration—this is the location where I first fell head over heels for this incredible woman. As she was admiring New York at her feet," he says, pointing to the large window behind me, "I was admiring her in awe."

Huh?

Max's words cause my cheeks to flame up and I bring my hands up to hide my face.

"It's true I had been stalking her column online well before meeting her in person"—he chuckles—"but the day I looked into her eyes on a Sunday during brunch, I couldn't get her out of my mind. I had planned on going back to brunch at the same place the following week, but as luck would have it, I bumped into her on the fourteenth floor of this hotel."

What is he doing? Why does he sound so formal?

"After a few hours of flirting, I decided to bring her up here hoping to seduce her, but I was the one who succumbed to her charms."

"Max…" I bring my hand to his arm, hoping he'll look at me and explain what's going on, but he simply winks at me from the side and continues talking.

"I can't remember when I fell in love with her, but I know one day I woke up next to her divine body and I knew I wanted to wake up like this every single morning."

Oh my God, did he say such intimate things in front of all of our friends?

I look at Deidra hoping she'll shed some light on Max's strange behavior, but she simply smiles at me. I look around the room and everyone seems to be captivated by my boyfriend's speech and I'm unable to make eye contact with anyone.

"She made me the happiest man in the world when she moved in with me a few months ago. It's been an amazing experience, but I was hoping for something more..." Max's words trail off. He places his glass on the table, turns around to face me and drops to one knee in front of me.

"Oh." I inhale when I finally clue in on what's happening. *God, this cannot be real.*

Max fishes inside his pocket and the next thing I know he's flashing a brilliant diamond ring in front of me. I look up at him and widen my eyes, too choked up to speak.

"Baby, your settlement was only part of the reason why all our friends are here tonight. I've invited them all here as witnesses to my undying love for you. They've known for weeks I officially wanted to make you mine. Candice Patricia Westerman, will you marry me?"

"Wh-what? You... I mean... Oh my Lord." Tears roll down my face as I try to find the composure I need to express to this man how much I love him. I take a deep breath in and I smile nervously. "You really are asking me to be your wife?"

"I really am."

"I can't think of anything I want more than to be yours, Max. Yes. Yes. Yes. I'll marry you, my love."

He smiles from ear to ear. *God, I love him so much when he grins mischievously like this.* Max pumps his chest out proud like a peacock and he looks around the room to our friends. The crowd claps and falls silent again. He pulls out the ring from the small red box and grabs my left hand with his.

"I hope you like it."

"Are you kidding me? I love it. It's stunning."

He grins again before sliding the round-cut diamond around my finger and he leans in to touch my lips.

"I love you so much, Candy," he whispers between kisses.

The entire room roars and my friends jump up to their feet and run to me. Max's brothers and his parents are hugging him and congratulating him, while Lia and Lexi are crying with joy, one on each of my shoulders. When I look up, Devin stands in front of me with an ecstatic look upon his face. We lock eyes and he approaches me, kisses me tenderly on the cheek and embraces me in his arms. He hugs me for what seems like an eternity before whispering softly in my ear.

"Big girls can find true love and marry their dashing prince."

"I never imaged I could be this lucky or this utterly happy, Dev."

"I knew you could. You deserve this, Candy."

No, this isn't a dream, it's far better than anything I could have imagined. This is my perfect life surrounded by incredible friends and a man who loves me... just the way I am.

Chapter Eleven

"God, what a perfect night. I can't wait to get you upstairs so I can have you all to myself. I'm warning you now, I intend on keeping you locked up the entire weekend."

"I don't know if I'll be able to keep up, Mr. Keller."

"Mrs. Keller-to-be, I'm sure you'll do just fine."

We both smile before losing ourselves in another passionate kiss.

After a magical night I'm unlikely to ever forget for as long as I live, Max and I are riding the private elevator back to his penthouse and we're all hot and heavy. We haven't been able to keep our hands off each other since we left the Bymark hotel. The ride at the back of the chauffeured car must have been the longest ride ever. Both Max and I had to resort to superhuman willpower to restrain ourselves from ravishing one another at the back of his Benz.

"Max, you've made me the happiest woman in the world today."

"Have I?" he asks flirtatiously.

"You know you have." I gently hit his chest with the palm of my hand.

"I love you and I wanted our friends and family to know how deeply I care for you, baby," he says, embracing me in his strong arms. "Finally we're here and you're officially mine to take whenever I want for the next two days." He grins when we hit the top floor.

When the elevator door opens up onto Max's apartment overlooking Central Park, he pushes me inside, forcing me to walk backwards as our lips are still locked in a blazing kiss. Music rises in the background and I look up to the ceiling at the speakers hovering over our heads.

This is strange. "Did you leave the music on before we left?"

"Nah. I didn't," he responds with a boyish smile.

"But there's music playing now. Wait a minute. I recognize this song." I make out the words to Beyoncé's slow remix of her smash hit *Crazy In Love.* "I swear we turned everything off except for a few lights in the living room before we left," I say, pointing at the ceiling as I take a step back.

"I think the song is fitting, since I've been crazy in love with you since laying eyes on you." He lifts his eyebrows and his lips curl into a smile.

"You keep saying these things." I shake my head, feeling my cheeks flame up. "I can't seem to get used to them."

"You should, because you know very well how I feel about you. And by the way, the music is just the beginning," he says, his fiery gaze threatening to burn through my soul.

"What are you talking about? Max, you look like the cat that got the cream. What are you up to?"

"I want this night to be a night you remember forever," he says, looking past me.

I follow his gaze and turn around. When I look around the living area, I can't believe my eyes. "What have you done?" I gasp.

"I asked the same crew who turned my warehouse in the fashion district into a love shack to do the same to my home for our special evening."

"Max..." I bring my hand to my mouth to hide my shocked expression.

There are white candles everywhere and there must be fifty if not one hundred vases of calla lilies throughout his large home. The music playing is so seductive it only adds to the sultry mood. I take a step forward to smell one of the bouquets of calla lilies when I notice the white petals on the wooden floor. They run from my feet all the way up the rustic stairs. I turn to him with my jaw dropped, unable to speak.

"The white rose petals lead straight up the stairs all the way to our bedroom."

"Our bedroom?" I ask, still unable to believe any of this.

"Yeah, it's been our bedroom since you've moved in here, but I hope you now feel at home."

"You're making it hard not to."

"Good."

"Max, you did all of this for me?"

"I recreated what I had planned out in my hotel suite in Miami. I was never able to declare my love to you in the setting I thought fitting for the woman who stole my heart, but I hope tonight makes up for it nicely."

"Are you kidding me? This is magnificent," I say, running back to him.

"Candy, I want to take you into my arms, climb these stairs, drop your sexy body on the bed and I want to make long amorous love to you. I want to enjoy every curve on your body—slowly, tenderly, passionately."

I gasp, surprised and unprepared for Max's sweet words. "You want to make love to me? So no raunchy sex in front of the window?"

"No. Tonight I want your body to be for my eyes only," he says, claiming my lips again.

"Take me upstairs, you sexy beast."

With a roar, he flings me over his shoulder and climbs the stairs to *our* bedroom. When he kicks open his door, he taps and massages my ass a few times before dropping me down to my feet. I spot a few bouquets of white flowers and when I turn around, I realize the romantic vibe extends all the way up here.

"I couldn't possibly have asked them to stop downstairs." He grins like a guilty child.

"No. Of course not," I respond, biting my lip and shaking my head. "Everything is perfect, Max."

This man is my salvation for all the other bad dates, lovers and boyfriends I've ever had.

Reaching out to him, he slips his hand in mine and to my great surprise he pulls me towards him.

"Hey, I was going to pull you towards me," I lament.

"I couldn't wait to wrap you in my arms again." He holds me so close to him I can hear his heart beating.

"I want you to make love to me, Max."

He looks down at me with loving eyes and reaches out for my cheek. Instead of answering, he turns me around and brushes my hair down the front of my shoulders. He slowly unzips my black cocktail dress and allows it to pool sensually at my feet. I brace myself, expecting him to quickly remove my bra, freeing my breasts from their confinement for his own pleasure, but he takes my breath away by showering the back of my neck with warm kisses. The second his mouth touches my skin, I take a step forward, overpowered by the heat emanating from his lips.

"Ahhh," I let out.

"Where are you going? I've barely gotten started." He reaches out and wraps his arms around my stomach before pulling me back to him. He pivots me to face him again and drinks me up from head to toe. "Hmmm, black on black lace underwear? Damn, you're making it hard for me to take you gently.

When I see your heavy breasts trapped in this daring bra and that sexy garter belt, I want to rip the lingerie off of you and take you like a famished animal."

Before I can answer, Max has already taken a step forward, forcing me to take one back. I feel the edge of the bed behind my legs and the next thing I know, he pushes me against the mattress.

"Remove your bra. I'll take care of your panties and garter belt," he commands, flicking off my high-heeled shoes before pressing the soles of my feet against his muscular chest. I lift my ass off the bed and I wiggle the bra off of me, releasing my engorged breasts. I lock eyes with the love of my life and playfully throw my bra at him. He catches it with one hand before tossing it over his shoulder with an amused look on his face.

"I don't know, but from where I lie, it seems like you're hungry for something rougher than nice and slow."

"You're right," he growls, fisting my lace panties and ripping them apart. Without wasting any time, he pulls down my silk nylons before bending over. He lowers his body near my pussy and I close my eyes, anticipating his tongue against my clit, but I quickly bring my gaze back to him when I realize he's pulling the black lace garter belt down my legs with his teeth.

"Jesus," I pant. "Baby, get out of your clothes. I need you inside me right now," I demand.

"You're such a hungry little vixen." Max drops my legs onto the mattress and he takes a step back to peel off of his clothes. Without wasting a second, he strips out of his tailored black suit, kicks off his expensive Italian shoes and pulls off his pants and boxer briefs in one fluid movement.

My God, I never get tired of seeing him naked like this. I take him in and I stop at his left arm. I admire the intricate ink branded on his arm as if it's the first time I've ever seen his tattoo. Max grins, aware of my lustful inspection. He stands in front of me with his hands locked at his waist and an erection so hard, I blink, surprised by the size of his desire for me.

He takes a step forward and drops to his knees. *Oh, yes, God.* He caresses my thighs before spreading my legs open in front of him. He looks up and our gazes meet before he lowers his head towards my eager pussy and starts blowing hot breaths. I'm so utterly turned on, I yank my body up, arching for him and allowing him to devour me at will.

"Christ." The first long lick causes me to fist the sheets at each side of me.

"You can't deny me the pleasure of watching you come. Please, baby, look at me."

I'm so taken by the moment, I have to force myself to open my eyes to meet his hazel stare.

"Much better," he says approvingly before lowering his head towards my wetness.

"Arghhh," I scream out. Max's tongue laps in and out, around and between every fold and dip of my pussy. His eyes are on me the whole time, capturing my every response to his teasing. Feeling his intense gaze as he gives me so much pleasure makes this moment even more intimate. He moans against me and my eyes roll back into my head, unable to withstand his raunchy cry. His lips pull my clit into his mouth and I yell out his name while I clasp my hands on top of his head as if to beg him to never stop assaulting my pussy the way he is now. "Max." I'm nearly delirious. I'm panting and I'm gyrating my hips against his mouth as I ready myself to come long, deep and hard.

"You like that, don't you?" His eyes are burning mine and I can tell from his sly grin how much he enjoys seeing me this lost in this vortex of ecstasy.

I'm far too turned on to speak. "Ahhh," I moan, when he reaches up and squeezes my nipples with his fingers.

His tongue laps and laps and laps. *Damn, damn, damn.* He masterfully keeps me on the brink of an orgasm and then without any warning, he closes his lips around my clit and squeezes a toe-curling climax out of me.

"Sweet Mother of God," I yell out as the pleasure that's been boiling up inside me erupts into a full-blown volcanic roar. I'm breathing so heavy I fear my heart will jump out of my chest. *This is amazing.*

After a few blissful minutes, I find the strength to open my eyes again and I meet his. Max allows me to savor every ripple of my climactic wave as he places sweet kisses on the insides of my thighs as I stare down at him.

"Baby, I need to be inside you," he declares, getting back up on his feet. I've been so consumed by how outrageously sinful his tongue feels against my throbbing pussy, I forgot all about his erection, but the minute he unfolds his body, I'm faced with the hunger of a man ready to fuck me senseless.

Max grabs me by the ankles and pulls my body towards him until my ass meets the edge of the bed. I feel him right there and I know the slightest movement will allow him to easily plunge into me. But he doesn't move. He stares at me long and hard.

"Candy." My name is a low growl, a warning and a promise all wrapped into one word. "I don't know if I can do this." Max looks so tortured, I panic.

"What's wrong, baby?" *Does he not want me anymore? Is he calling off the wedding?*

"I want to take you with as much untamed fervor as I always have. I don't know if I can do this nice and slow thing."

Oh. My. God. "Baby, don't hold back. Take me as you wish. I'm all yours," I plead before lying back.

He pushes me slightly upwards against the mattress before kneeling on the bed in front of me. He grabs my legs and turns me around so I can face him before spreading my thighs wide. I immediately reach out to grab his cock and bring it to my throbbing pussy. He grabs my hand, forcing his cock to rub against my hardening clit.

Yes, yes, yes.

"Holy hell, this feels so good," I moan.

He slides his other hand down my thigh. My juices coat his hand the second he reaches for my pussy, and when my body trembles, I dig my fingers into his forearms. *How can I already be so wet?*

"Christ," he groans, meeting my gaze. "You're ready for me again."

He moves my hand aside, grabs his hard cock and slides it deep inside me. He grabs my hips to steady my body and rams into me hard and fast. His rhythm is nearly frantic, as if this is our first night together. He's completely unleashed his sexual fury upon me. There's nothing soft or sweet about the way our skin slaps together and my cries are swallowed by his hungry kisses. *His willingness to make love to me has turned carnal, almost feral—just the way I like it.*

"Don't stop," I beg, desperate to lose all reason and to come with so much force I feel I've stepped over the edge.

"I wasn't planning on stopping until I make you scream out my name so loudly the concierge in the lobby runs up here to make sure you're still okay."

Shit.

As if to prove his words, he pounds into me mercilessly until my body caves in, unable to take more. I hit my second orgasmic peak with a guttural moan as I drag my fingernails down his arms. He rides me until he reaches his own climactic wave, slamming into me one more time before withdrawing his cock and placing it on top of my stomach. He comes all over my body as he let out another deep roar. He reaches down and rubs his cum all over my soft stomach before extending his finger towards my mouth. I open without hesitation and lick his fingertips—one by one.

Fuck, he's branded me—again.

Max rolls next to me and we lie in our king-size bed exhausted and utterly satisfied. He's spooning me in his loving arms and I feel so safe right now, like I always do when he holds on to me so possessively.

"I'll never be able to walk tomorrow."

"You won't need to. Remember, I'm keeping you under lock and key all weekend so I can ravage you at will." He chuckles, brushing my hair off my shoulders.

"Yeah, I guess you're right. I'll just stay in bed all weekend with my legs spread open ready for you to take me at a moment's notice."

"Good girl. You'll make a perfect wife." He laughs. Without even having to look at him, I feel something about him change. "I love you with all my heart, Candy," he whispers into my ear.

There are no words to express the depth of the happiness I feel hearing him drop such sweet confessions into my ear.

I've never been loved like this, ever.

The realization of what I share with Max hits me and in this enchanting moment I become aware of how my life is about to change. This is my happy ever after. The one I never thought possible for a big girl like me. Unable to contain the flood of emotions overpowering me, I burst into tears.

"Baby, what's wrong? Did I hurt you? I know I tried to be gentler, but you bring out this force from me."

"No, Max. You didn't hurt me. You've created the perfect day for me. I'm nearly floating on sunshine and I thank my lucky stars I bumped into you at the Bymark hotel. I'm so elated there are no words for me to express how much I love you."

"Honey, don't cry. Today is the first day of many magical days to come. I love you so much and I want to show you every single day of my life."

THE END

* * *

More Saucy BBW Romance

If you loved Curves Envy,
you'll also love *Deliciously British*.

Two Sexy and Strapping Alpha Brits. One Disillusioned Curvy BBW Texan. One Unforgettable Summer Filled With Unspeakable Naughty Pleasures!

This romance is full of mind-blowing passion. Proceed at your own risk... but, it's well worth the hotter-than-hell ride!

Lose yourself in a Sexy BBW Billionaire Romance with a touch of Ménage Romance!

Deliciously British

Available in Paperback

Are You Craving More?

If you liked Candy & Max's story, you'll love my other steamy romance books!

I should warn you, every book I write will definitively leave you very hot and bothered!

Get Your Hands On My Next
Sizzling Romance!

Discover Your Next Read!

www.scarlettavery.com

****

Get Your FREE SECRET Chapters!

Thank you for purchasing this romance!

I'd love for you to lose yourself in more
sultriness, sexiness and steamy passion!

When you sign up today, I'll send you the following
Secret Chapter for Part 4 of this serial:

*You'll want to read about how Max plans on transforming
his warehouse for a romantic evening with Candy!
(This is Max's POV)*

*** <u>PASSWORD FOR</u> Secret Chapter Part 4:
Warehouse-Transformed

Note: the password is case sensitive!

Sign-up TODAY!

www.RomanceBooksRock.com

***If you've already signed-up to my list from previous
books, you can visit the same page to download
the Secret Chapters for this romance***

****

Acknowledgements

Thank you to my family and friends who have been so supportive in helping make my dreams come true.

To my fans and readers, I want to thank you for your emails, messages and testimonials. They mean the world to me. Your encouragement keeps me going every single day. I absolutely loved writing this story and I sincerely hope you enjoyed it.

A huge thank you to my amazing team. My incredible assistant China is kick ass and I consider myself lucky to have found her. My cover designer Ilian is truly talented. I'm always in awe by how well he translates my notes into a visual masterpiece.

Thank you Chrissy Becker for catching the typos the editor and I missed. I'm grateful that you'd be willing to help make my books better.

I also want to say a huge thank you to my Sirens. I love how the sexy readers from my Street Team keep me on my toes. Their feedback has helped shape many of my stories and cover selections.

Last and certainly no least, I want to thank all the bloggers, reviewers and romance Facebook groups who helped me get the word out about this book. Without you, this naughty story would remain lost somewhere on Amazon.

I REALLY LOVE Reviews!

I put my heart and soul in each one of my books and I hope I was able to allow you to escape to a naughty place!

If you enjoyed this book, don't forget to leave a review on Amazon or the site of any other retailer you purchased this book from!

I highly appreciate your reviews, and it only takes a minute to write & post one.

I can't tell you how much this means to me!

You'll find the list of all my books on the following page...just in case you'd like to leave a review for other books of mine you've read but didn't have time to leave a review.
www.scarlettavery.com/i-love-your-reviews/

You can also leave me a review on Goodreads:

www.goodreads.com/scarlettavery

Where Scarlett Hangs Out!

There are four ways for you to find my books:

1. My site – If you want to buy my books online, you'll find them on Amazon. For now, I sell my saucy tales exclusively there. If things change, I'll be sure to let you know. Here's the link to my site to view my entire catalogue of sauciness ➺ http://scarlettavery.com/

2. AMAZON – If you want Amazon to automatically notify you via email with a link every time I push publish, click the yellow tab under my author picture here ➺ http://smarturl.it/ScarlettAveryAmazon

3. BookBub – Is another place for you to check out my entire library of books. Make sure to follow me so BookBub let's you know of my new releases ➺ https://www.bookbub.com/authors/scarlett-avery

4. GOODREADS – Is another place where you can find my books and where you can leave reviews! See it all here ➺ http://smarturl.it/ScarlettOnGoodreads

Where else do I hang out?

1. FACEBOOK Fan Page – This is where you can hang out with me the most! I'm there every single day. Come join the fun ➼
https://www.facebook.com/pg/AuthorScarlettAvery

2. INSTAGRAM - Is my new hangout place. We post original content there every day!
Catch me here ➼
https://www.instagram.com/scarlettaveryauthor

COMPLETE DISCLAIMER

About the Publisher

Absolutely Naughty Publishing is part of a Canadian Corporation.

SexyRomanceNovels@gmail.com

DISCLAIMER

acting on the contents in this book. Every character in this book is over eighteen years of age. The material in this book is for entertainment purposes ONLY.

This book contains sexually explicit scenes and adult language. It may be considered offensive to some readers.

ABOUT THE AUTHOR

Bestselling Amazon Author Scarlett Avery's Book Boyfriends aren't like ANY others you've ever cuddled to before.

These dirty-talking, DOMINEERING, saucy seducers will make you forget all the other ones. Yeah, Scarlett's Alpha Males are that DANGEROUSLY HOT!

Be warned: Her books have been dubbed, "Epic & Mind-Blowing"! This Canadian romance author's books will melt your e-readers and they will leave you on the edge of your seat!

I dare you to discover how SIZZLING they REALLY ARE...

P.S.: Once you start reading Scarlett's books, there's NO going back!

JOIN US: I entertain my sexy readers daily on my Facebook Fan Page. Make sure you join the party: **www.facebook.com/AuthorScarlettAvery**

84330445R00285

Made in the USA
Middletown, DE
18 August 2018